LOVE
—*at Any*—
COST

Books by Julie Lessman

The Daughters of Boston

A Passion Most Pure
A Passion Redeemed
A Passion Denied

Winds of Change

A Hope Undaunted
A Heart Revealed
A Love Surrendered

The Heart of San Francisco

Love at Any Cost

THE HEART OF
SAN FRANCISCO
· 1 ·

LOVE
— *at Any* —
COST

A NOVEL

Julie Lessman

Revell

a division of Baker Publishing Group
Grand Rapids, Michigan

© 2013 by Julie Lessman

Published by Revell
a division of Baker Publishing Group
P.O. Box 6287, Grand Rapids, MI 49516-6287
www.revellbooks.com

Printed in the United States of America

Library of Congress Cataloging-in-Publication Data
Lessman, Julie, 1950–
      Love at any cost : a novel / Julie Lessman.
            pages cm. — (The Heart of San Francisco ; 1)
      ISBN 978-0-8007-2167-1 (pbk.)
            1. Single women—California—San Francisco—Fiction. 2. San Francisco
(Calif.)—History—20th century—Fiction. 3. Love stories. 4. Christian fiction.
I. Title.
PS3612.E8189L65 2013
813'.6—dc23   2012046732

Scripture used in this book, whether quoted or paraphrased by the characters, is taken from the King James Version of the Bible.

The internet addresses, email addresses, and phone numbers in this book are accurate at the time of publication. They are provided as a resource. Baker Publishing Group does not endorse them or vouch for their content or permanence.

13   14   15   16   17   18   19   7   6   5   4   3   2   1

To the Lover of my soul,
Who taught me about "love at any cost"
two thousand years ago on a hill outside of Jerusalem.
I will love You and worship You
all the days of my life.

But lay up for yourselves treasures in heaven, where neither moth nor rust doth corrupt, and where thieves do not break through nor steal: For where your treasure is, there will your heart be also.

—Matthew 6:20–21

1

Sweet thunderation—deliver me from pretty men! Twenty-two-year-old Cassidy McClare peered up beneath the wide feathered brim of her black velvetta hat—legs, luggage, and magazine scattered on the dirty platform of Oakland Pier train station.

"Miss, I'm so sorry—"

You certainly are. Hair askew, she blew a curl from her eyes along with a broken feather dangling over the rim of the "fashionable" hat Mama begged her to wear. Reining in her temper, she forced a smile at a man in a stylish straw boater who'd just swept her off her feet—*literally.*

A whistle shrieked and the Overland Limited belched a cloud of steam into the air, the smell of smoke and coal wrinkling her nose. Apparently the "gentleman"—and she used the term loosely—hadn't seen her, too busy rushing to wave goodbye to the girl he'd just put on the train. With a deafening screech, the train groaned on its rails, chugging away while people moseyed and milled on the platform, gaping at a girl sprawled on her backside in a House of Worth tailor-made suit. A curious sight,

9

indeed . . . not to mention embarrassing. Even for a non-prissy ranch girl from Humble, Texas.

The heat of summer asphalt warmed her bottom while the man's gaze warmed her face, his frank perusal sending off warning bells she'd heard before. And, unfortunately, ignored. She issued a silent grunt. *But never again.* Struggling to rise, her lips went flat, not unlike the hatbox her mother had foisted on her, which she'd just crushed on her fall from grace. *Fooled by a pretty boy once, shame on him. Fooled by a pretty boy twice, shame on me.*

"Are you okay?" Nudging the boater up, he held out a blunt hand attached to a muscled arm that strained beneath a crisp, white pinstripe shirt, its casually rolled sleeves in stark contrast to a meticulous four-in-hand tie and a high starched collar. He could have walked off the pages of *Men's Wear Magazine*, easily six foot one with a boyish smile that lent a roguish air Cassie recognized all too well. A thick curl of dark brown hair that was almost black toppled over his forehead, obviously a stray from the slicked-back style of the day. Hazel eyes the color of coffee with cream assessed her with a crimp of concern wedged between thick, dark brows, reminding her so much of Mark, she cringed.

Make that cold, bitter coffee.

Hand still extended, he eased into a smile that at one time would have generated as much heat as the platform beneath her body, a gleam of white in a chiseled face that sported a California tan. "I beg your pardon, miss, but I never even saw you." A sparkle warmed his gaze as it slowly trailed down the upturned brim of her hat, past renegade curls from her upswept hair to her white silk shirtwaist, hesitating long enough to prompt a blush in her cheeks. "Which is pretty hard to believe," he mumbled, almost to himself. His bold look continued to roam her gored navy skirt only to halt with several blinks at the peek of her forbidden cowboy boots—the ones she'd put on *after* Mama and Daddy left the station. A grin inched across his face and his eyes slowly trailed back up as naturally as his dimples deepened with the lift of his smile. Heat suffused her cheeks, as much from the obscene number of petticoats Mother had insisted she wear as the Romeo's frank perusal. *Flattery will get you nowhere, mister.* Her lips took a slant. Though it'd certainly gotten Mark's ring on her finger. She issued a silent grunt. *A history lesson unto itself,* she thought, the smell of horse manure from buggies lining the terminal oddly comforting.

And appropriate.

Lips clamped, she ignored both the Romeo and the disparaging glance of a passerby and tugged on her trumpet-shaped skirt to hide her socially unacceptable footwear. Oh, how she wished she could have worn her "shocking" jeans from the ranch instead of the fashionable suit Mama requested. Huffing out an unladylike sigh, she accepted the Romeo's proffered hand, feeling like she'd been hit by a train, and not the one on the tracks. His massive palm dominated hers, and she popped up with all the grace with which she'd toppled over her luggage in the first place: *none.*

He stooped to retrieve her magazine, using it to slap the dirt from her skirt as if shooing flies from the rump of a horse, and she waved him away, mortified that a stranger was swatting at her backside. "Please, I'm fine, truly. No harm done, I assure you."

"No, I insist . . ." Paying her no mind, he collected her blue handbag and dented hatbox after righting her Oshkosh suitcases, cherished gifts from her father when she'd gone to Europe with her cousins three summers past. *Before* the oil wells ran dry, ending life as she'd known it.

Shaking his head, he handed her the purse and magazine, then dangled the sorry hatbox in the air, sucking air through clenched teeth. "Gee, I'm sorry," he said, giving her an endearing little-boy grin she'd lay odds had gotten him off the hook more times than not. "But I think this box may have seen better days."

As have I. Cassie winced at this brazen man whose casual air, rugged good looks, and wind-tousled hair reminded her way too much of the man who'd broken her heart. But . . . better days were ahead . . . she hoped. She and her cousin, Alli, just graduated with teaching degrees, and Aunt Cait didn't know it yet, but Mark's rejection had sent Cassie northwest for that very reason. Not just for the summer this time, but to join forces with Aunt Cait and Alli in their dreams of a school for poor and disadvantaged girls on the Barbary Coast. For Cassie, San Francisco was not only her chance to put the pain and humiliation of Humble behind, but it ensured she could focus on a teaching career instead of a man. Her lips kinked. Doting on lots of children instead of just one. And girls to boot, because if there was one thing she'd learned in Humble, Texas, it was that boys—little or big—were nothing but trouble.

Squaring her shoulders, she took the box from his hand with as much dignity as possible after picking herself up off the ground. "Thank you, it's no problem, really." She offered a polite smile, then turned to go, tripping over her luggage till he steadied her with a clasp of her arm.

"Wait!" At her startled look, he slipped both hands in his pockets with a sheepish grin, glancing up beneath the longest lashes she'd ever seen on a man. "I'd like to make it up to you, see you home, buy you lunch, whatever." His eyes sparkled with humor. "After all," he said, tone husky, "girls have fallen for me before, but never quite this hard."

"I b-beg your p-pardon . . . ," she sputtered, heat scorching her face. She leaned in, her Texas Irish going head-to-head with his California dimples. Her pride bucked as much as that prize filly Daddy had to auction off with most of his herd. "*Stampeded* is more like it," she said, painfully aware this was *just* the type of man for whom she tended to "fall." A fact that only steamed her temper more, giving the high-pressure steam locomotive nothing on her. She gesticulated with a shaky hand, making her fluster all the more obvious, but she flat-out didn't care. Anger hogtied all Christian kindness, vibrating her words with more fury than warranted. "M-manhandled by some . . . some . . . Casanova chasing a train to say goodbye to a woman." She reloaded with a deep breath, then gave it to him with both barrels, unleashing her fury at Mark and every man just like him. "And then, great day in the morning, you have the nerve to . . . to . . . ogle *me* while the tracks are still warm?" Boots wobbling, she nodded at the train with a fold of her arms. "I suspect your *sweetheart* would have a few choice words to say about that!"

The dimples took on a life of their own. "First of all, miss," he said with a half-lidded smile, obviously enjoying the scold, "if you'd been manhandled by me, trust me—you'd know it. Secondly, my 'sweetheart' would say nothing because I don't have one, which," he said with a mock grimace, "suddenly doesn't seem like such a bad thing. And thirdly . . . ," he hiked a thumb toward the departing train, heating her cheeks with a wink, "that was my cousin."

"Horse apples!" The whites of her eyes expanded while her cheeks flamed red hot, which, given the flush of heat beneath her blue suit, might be considered warmly patriotic. Sweet chorus of angels, did he think she just fell off the turnip truck? She'd *seen* him—watched him swallow the girl up in those ridiculously muscular arms, heft her up like a sack of grain while he twirled her high in the air. Cassie fumed, feeling her blood pressure rise. *Talk about manhandling!* And now he wanted to take *her* to lunch? Her chin snapped up. "And I'm the Queen of England," she hissed, suddenly wondering why she was berating some poor dope whose only sin had been to accidentally mow her down and look good doing it.

Giving a slow whistle, he stepped back with two hands in the air. "Look, miss . . . uh, I mean, *your majesty* . . . I didn't mean any harm—either by knocking you down or my offer to make it up to you." He gave her a quick salute. "I think it's best if I just take my leave, but before I do . . ." The dimples returned in force as he nodded his head behind her. "You might want to brush off your posterior really well, because I think you may have a burr in your saddle." Giving her a wink, he strode away, hands in his pockets and a whistle on his lips.

Cassie stared while what was left of her anger seeped out of her gaping mouth. Sweet soul-saving mercy—Mama would tan her hide but good had she seen how Cassie just acted. Never had she been so rude in her entire life. She slumped and put a hand to her eyes. "God forgive me," she whispered. "What in the world is wrong with me?"

But she knew the answer before the words even left her tongue. The pretty boy was right. She had a burr in her saddle, a pebble in her boot, an ache in her heart. Heaving a weary sigh, she brushed the back of her suit, wishing more than anything she could tell Pretty Boy she was sorry for lashing out. That it wasn't him personally, just men like him.

Men like Mark.

Inhaling deeply, Cassie blasted out her frustration along with the acrid fumes of oil and grease. Retrieving her pocket watch, she checked the time, fingers grazing the smooth, cool casing of the men's gold timepiece Nana had given her, a cherished keepsake of a great-grandmother Daddy said she reminded him of. Nana McClare had been as unconventional as a woman could be in an era that focused on a pretty face instead of a keen mind. And like Cassie, Daddy reminded, a woman as solid, dependable, and unfrilly as the watch in Cassie's hand. "Always remember," Nana would say, "life is an adventure and every day a fresh start . . . especially with God by your side."

"Oh, Nana, I hope so," she whispered, praying for a summer to help her forget. Forget the ridicule of young boys because she was different. Forget the high-society matrons who'd thumbed their noses at her from little on. Forget the whispers of their daughters when the new bachelor in town courted Cassie instead of them. Her chest squeezed, having little to do with the corset as tears stung her eyes. Then forget when that same bachelor cast her aside like everyone else had.

Shaking off the hurt, she put a hand to her forehead, shielding her face from the glare as she scanned for a sign of her cousins or their driver. Her lips quirked as she arched a brow at the sky. "I prayed *I* would forget, Lord, not them." She shook her head and smiled, and in the shrill wail of a faraway train, faith suddenly whooshed through her like a prairie breeze, so strong and powerful she felt it clear down to the tips of her pointed boots. She breathed in deeply, noticing the scent of San Francisco for the first time since she debarked, its crisp bay air, salty sea spray, and faint smell of fish. It smelled like change and she closed her eyes, thrilling at the tangy breeze that feathered her face. "Oh, Lord, let it be so," she whispered, a smile curving her lips. "Let me forget the past and start anew." A gentle wind tickled her hair, and her smile bloomed into a grin because somehow she knew, as sure as the dimples on Pretty Boy's face.

She would.

Jamie MacKenna dialed the Blue Moon Bar & Grill and leaned against the glass wall of the mahogany phone booth inside Oakland Pier station, feeling as stripped of his pride as the booth was stripped of its polish—weathered, splintered, and as tired as he. Eyes closed, he waited for his boss to answer the phone, wondering what in blazes he'd done to earn the royal shellacking from the Queen Mother. A corner of his mouth hooked at the memory of the pretty little rich girl who'd fallen hard, but not over him, apparently—a situation he seldom encountered, if at all.

He pinched the bridge of his nose as the phone continued to ring, properly humbled by the woman's distaste for him. At twenty-five and newly graduated from Stanford Law, he was used to a warmer reception from women—a lot warmer, as a matter of fact—and although the petite blond was pretty in a cute and clumsy kind of way, she certainly didn't compare to some of the women who vied for his attention. A slow exhale breezed over his lips. Although never had he seen more unusual eyes—the color of his favorite green agate marble as a boy—like pale green jade, hypnotic, mesmerizing, fringed with honeyed lashes as thick as her Texas drawl. He frowned, aware he was still thinking of her, which meant the little spitfire had wreaked havoc on his emotions, a reaction that both annoyed and appealed. He flapped the front of his Oxford shirt in an attempt to cool off, giving the testy little princess credit for one thing: she sure knew how to spike a man's pulse.

She was obviously one of those nose-in-the-air rich girls with a vendetta against men, smacking of wealth and privilege in her expensive suit and top-of-the-line luggage. He shook his head. Although a socialite in cowboy boots was a first. He exhaled loudly, grateful he'd never have to see her again. Rejection had a way of piquing his interest, enticing him to do what his friends Blake and Bram claimed he did all too well—charm a jury, win a lost cause, lift an underdog so high, he'd think he could fly. "I swear, Mac, you could coax a jury into acquitting Jack the Ripper," his best friend Bram Hughes always said, and Jamie had to admit it seemed to be true. Whether it was his innate desire to please, the warm smile he'd inherited from his mother, or the strong angular jaw from an alcoholic father now dead and gone, he wasn't sure, but people—especially women and juries—seemed to like him.

"Blue Moon."

His boss's voice jolted him back. "Hey, Duff—is my mother still there?"

"Sure, Mac, hold on."

Jamie loosened his tie, throat so parched, he wished he had one of Duffy's fountain Dr Peppers, the only drink he ever touched whenever he was in a bar. He waited while the sound of ragtime filtered through the phone with a familiarity that felt far more like home than the ramshackle flat he'd once shared with his family in the same neighborhood. Back then, they'd lived in a sleazy cow-yard of the Barbary Coast—a brothel with an apartment building above—until Jamie went to work on the docks at the age of twelve after his father drank himself to death. Desperate to get his mother and sister out of the slums, he worked additional jobs, supplementing his mother's meager seamstress income and a stipend from his aunt. Pride swelled when they finally moved out of the red-light district and into a boardinghouse in a respectable neighborhood several blocks away.

It'd been a struggle excelling at his studies—first in college and then in law school—while tending bar two nights a week, weekends at the Oly Club and Saturday mornings keeping books at the Blue Moon. Yet somehow he'd managed to win more mock cases than anyone in his class, a fact that made his mother proud. A pride hard-earned by the sweat of his brow and that of his mother, who now also worked as a cook at the Blue Moon.

He heard the crackle of the receiver as somebody picked up. "Jamie?"

"Hi, Mom—I just put Sara on the train to Tulsa." He glanced at his watch. "The schedule says she'll arrive by Monday at two, so can you let Aunt Sophie know when you call?"

He heard his mother's sigh of relief. "Yes, of course." She hesitated. "It's been a long time since your sister enjoyed herself like she did with your cousin here." Her voice wavered enough for Jamie to notice. "Thank you for switching your shift at the Oly to take Sara to the station. You're a good brother, Jamie, and I hope your boss will understand."

A good brother? Jamie's gut clenched. *Hardly. Then Jess wouldn't be crippled.* He forced a casual tone. "Mr. Burke gives me free rein, remember?" He paused, head bowed and eyes focused on a cigarette butt on the floor. "How's she feeling today?" he asked, hoping against hope she would say what he wanted to hear.

She took too long to answer, and he winced at the cheerful voice she always resorted to when she didn't want him to worry. "Tired, but that's to be expected with Sara's visit."

"And the pain?" He closed his eyes, dreading his mother's answer.

Longer pause. "We had to use the last of the laudanum," she whispered.

He put a hand to his eyes. "I'll stop by Doc Morrissey's on my way home." Sucking in a deep breath, he shifted his focus. "Did you bother to eat today?"

"Yes, son, before I came in to work. Toast and tea, then Duffy's dumplings later," she said quickly, as if desperate to put his mind at ease. A hint of a tease seeped in as she switched roles to become the mother. "And you?"

He managed a smile. "Like a horse—leftover meat loaf from yesterday's blue plate special, which, by the way, was some of your best. Duffy says if I keep it up, he'll dock my pay."

The lilt of her laughter thickened his throat. "Well, you better get back for your shift or he's liable to follow through." She hesitated. "I love you, Jamie," she whispered, and the rasp of those gentle words nearly sparked forbidden moisture in his eyes. "No mother could have a better son, nor Jess a better brother."

"Love you too, Mom." He gouged at a pain in his temple, wishing more than anything Jess were well and he could put them both in a house on Nob Hill. His eyes flickered closed. *Where they belong.* "I'll bring you and Jess dinner when I get off."

She laughed. "No, don't spend the mon—"

"It's Thursday, fried chicken special at the Corner Bar, Jess's favorite, so don't argue."

"You've gotten very pushy now that you're a lawyer." Her voice shimmered with pride.

"Let's hope," he said, teeth gleaming in the glass of the windowed booth. "We both know I won't get that house on Nob Hill with my looks."

"Oh, I don't know," she teased, and it felt good to laugh with his mother.

"Love ya, Mom. See you at seven." He hung up the receiver and smiled, almost oblivious to the hum and buzz of the station as his words circled in his brain. *"Won't get that house on Nob Hill with my looks."* He peered into the glass, noting the flicker of a muscle in the hollow of his cheek. His lips clamped into a hard line that carried the faint bent of a smile.

Wanna bet?

2

"Sorry we were late, Cass, but Market Street was a zoo." Allison McClare plopped on the lavender canopied bed in the spacious guestroom where Cassie would stay for the summer, obviously unconcerned about wrinkling her full-length chiffon dress. She lay on her side, elbow cocked and head in her hands. "It was awful—a horse and buggy reared when a Benz truck tried to outrun a cable car. Hadley braked so hard, I almost ended up in his lap in the front seat of the Packard." Her lips took a twist. "Which wouldn't have been the first time since the poor dear is near deaf and can barely hear shouts or horns, not to mention he forgot his glasses—*again*."

Cassie grinned. "How is sweet Hadley? Rosie still picking on him?"

Her cousin chuckled. "Of course, although not as much as she picks on Uncle Logan, for pity's sake." She shook her head. "Goodness, maybe it's just men Rosie can't abide because she sure rides Uncle Logan without mercy. But dear Hadley?" There was a smile in her tone, laced with affection. "The sweet man's only sin, apparently, was being Uncle Logan's butler growing up, yet he takes Rosie in stride, as usual. I feel so sorry for him because Mother had to rig this thunderous gong in the kitchen when the doorbell rings, which annoys Rosie to no end." She sighed. "Unfortunately, Hadley's vision isn't much better, so Mother sent him to the optician to get glasses as thick as soda pop bottles." She giggled. "Makes his eyes look three times their size and rather like the sweetest owl. Of course, he misplaces them a lot, which drives Rosie absolutely crazy when they work in the kitchen. But he's such a dear, nobody minds if he can't see or hear or runs late." She paused, grating her lip with an impish smile. "But then . . . it rather sounds like this is one time 'late' may have been a good thing . . ."

An armful of dresses in hand, Cassie slid her cousin a wry look on her way to the wardrobe, lips swerving off-center. "Absolutely. A potent reminder of just *why* I left Texas."

"Mmm . . . just how potent are we talking?" Mischief tipped the edges of Alli's rose-colored lips while green eyes twinkled, the exact color of her delicate jade earrings, another gift from Nana. Soft strays of ebony curls from her upswept Gibson Girl hairstyle framed her face, a perfect complement to cream-colored skin. A summer breeze fluttered both her curls and her sheer, ruffled sleeves while sunlight blazed through French doors overlooking a garden where pink rosebushes wreathed an Aphrodite fountain.

Hefting the clothes with a grunt, Cassie hung them in the wardrobe with a roll of her eyes, determined that Alli understood loud and clear men were *not* on her list of sights to see. *Especially pretty men.* "Too potent for his own good, and ours, I can tell you that. A pretty-boy yahoo with dark, curly hair, chiseled jaw, hypnotic eyes, and more 'mussels' than San Francisco Bay." Cassie shivered. "Sweet Texas tea, it's enough to drive me into a convent."

Alli chuckled and rolled over, head on a plush eyelet pillow. "Probably not—I'm pretty sure they don't allow boots, lassos, or spurs."

"Or blue jeans and a Stetson," Cassie said with a scowl. She fingered a coiled rope in the bottom of her suitcase, rubbing the smooth hemp between forefinger and thumb. A smile tugged at the sudden thought of "Pretty Boy" all trussed up like a steer. Closing her eyes, she imagined breathing in the sweet smell of hemp and home, and instantly tranquility flooded. Quirky certainly, and maybe even a little bit odd, but nothing calmed Cassie like the feel of a lasso in her hand. Since her father had taught her to rope a fencepost at the age of four, she'd been a little girl who snuggled with a lariat at night rather than a blanket or bear, preferring tying knots and rope tricks to baby dolls and tea parties. The edge of her mouth crooked. And it had certainly come in handy once or twice with boys who had taunted her as well. Her smile went flat. Too bad Mark had gotten under her skin before she could hog-tie him and send him packing.

Alli jolted up, nose in a scrunch. "Wait—*please* tell me you did not bring that nasty old rope with you all the way from Texas. For mercy's sake, Cass, heaven knows where it's been!"

Cassie's eyes narrowed as she hugged the lariat to her chest, chin high. "You're lucky I didn't bring my Winchester, Allison 'Priss' McClare, and this top-grade piece of hemp has been with me since I was a tot, I'll have you know—in my bed at night and on my hip at the ranch."

Allison's smile tipped. "Yes, I know, Annie Oakley—you slept in my bed many a summer, remember? But good gracious, Cass, I'd rather my cousin not smell like a horse."

Grazing the rope to her cheek, Cassie drew in a deep breath filled with the smell of horse and hay and *home*. She blinked, desperate to dispel the moisture beneath her lids, but it was no use. The fight leaked from her voice as a tear leaked from her eye, stealing her trademark spunk. "It calms me, Al," she said quietly, fingering the twine. "Makes me feel safe and in control."

Sympathy radiated from Alli's eyes. "Something you didn't feel with Mark, I guess?"

"No," she whispered, chest constricting at the memory of Mark asking for his ring back, robbing her of her future as well as her heart.

"Well, you can't convert," Alli teased, obviously trying to lighten Cassie's mood. "No convent would take a nun who smells like a horse and has a lariat on her hip instead of a rosary."

Cassie's smile rebounded, as dry as her tone. "Wish I'd had the rope on my hip at the train station, I can tell you that," she muttered. "Would've lassoed Pretty Boy and tied him up nice and neat with a pretty, little bow." She fumbled with the buttons of her infernal high-necked shirtwaist. "And at least hiding away in a convent is better than being a sitting duck for some fortune-hunting man." She heaved a weighty sigh before slipping the blouse off and sailing it toward a purple velvet settee. "Or maybe I should say 'sitting pigeon' given these ridiculous pigeon blouses we're forced to wear. I'd like to wring Charles Gibson's neck for turning us all into air-deprived Gibson Girls." She huffed. "*Along* with that pretty-boy polecat at the station. No doubt he's another louse like Mark Chancellor, and obviously not very bright."

"You don't know that," Alli said with a grin.

"Oh, yes I do." Cassie issued a grunt. "Expecting me to swoon over a two-timer like him? Humph! Face it, Al—I've always been good with numbers, and trust me—I had his the minute he asked me to lunch. Like Daddy says, the boy's plumb weak north of the ears." She flopped down on the bed, and before she could rein them in, more tears glossed in her eyes. "Botheration, Al, why do men have to be such rats?"

Alli shifted to face her. "They're not all rats," she said softly, giving Cassie's arm a gentle squeeze. "Blake's not too bad for a brother, you know, and he's got a couple of dreamy friends that are really nice. And then there's Uncle Logan . . ." She paused, a wrinkle wedging her nose. "Although I suppose he's not the best example since he is still single and a bit of a rogue." She puffed out a sigh. "But even so, he is pretty wonderful, so not all men are rats like Mark."

Cassie loosened the buttons of her voile skirt, a wry tilt to her lips. "Maybe not, but a Texas-size rat like Mark has a way of curbing a girl's interest in any man."

"Mercy's sake, I hope not." Alli sat straight up. "I've got an itch for adventure this summer, Cass, and I need you to be focused and engaged."

Cassie arched a brow.

"Whoops. Sorry," Alli said, offering a feeble grin. "Poor choice of words."

A wispy sigh drifted from Cassie's lips. "Well, I'll go where you want me to go, Al, but don't expect me to turn on the Texas charm for any of the Romeos you have in mind." She shimmied off both her skirt and several layers of petticoats, pitching them on top of the blouse. "The idea of flirting with a man right now is as blasted uncomfortable as these ridiculous female trappings." She scooted around, her back to Alli. "Here—untie this silly S-curve corset Mother made me wear, will you? Sweet suffering saints, why do women put up with these things?"

Alli's low chuckle blew warm against Cassie's neck. "To turn heads, Cass," she said in a conspiratorial whisper, "and trust me, with this gorgeous flaxen hair of yours, your dainty figure, and those mesmerizing green eyes, you are going to turn aplenty." She wrinkled her nose. "That is, if I can manage to hide the boots."

"Don't you dare touch my boots!" Stays loosened, Cassie immediately gulped in a deep draw of air before pumping it out again. "Besides, the only male head I want to turn right now is Mark Chancellor's." Her smile was devious. "Preferably with a slap of my dainty hand."

Alli's laughter filled the spacious bedroom with a musical sound, warming Cassie inside as much as the hazy shafts of sunlight that streamed through the French doors. Her cousin gave her a playful squeeze of her neck. "Well, trust me—we are going to do everything in our power to see you have a wonderful summer and forget all about Mark Chancellor."

"Who?" Cassie said with a tight hug. "I barely remember the sorry excuse for a man."

"Good!" Alli bounced up. "Because your total lapse of memory begins at dinner tonight."

"What?" Cassie jolted up. "Wait—it's just family tonight, right?"

Alli spun around without answering, hurrying to rifle through her cousin's dresses until she found one of the fussy evening gowns Cassie's mama had forced her to pack. "Here we go," she said with a bright smile, holding up a sea-foam green taffeta Mama swore matched the pale green of her eyes. "Mother thought it might be fun to dress up for your first night, so this is perfect." She gnawed on her lip. "Of course you'll have to wear the swanbill corset . . ."

"Perfect-for-what?" Cassie enunciated carefully, quite certain she didn't really want to know. "Or maybe I should say for 'whom,' because I refuse to truss up like a show horse."

"Come on, Cass," Alli said with a pout. "You're my best friend and I've missed you. It's your first night in San Francisco in forever, and we just want it to be special. Is that a crime?"

Cassie drew in a calming breath and released it in a show of humility. "Okay, okay . . . I'll wear the stupid dress and straitjacket corset, only *please*—tell me it's only family tonight."

"Absolutely," Alli said with a flourish, laying the whispery pale-green dress on the bed. She stood up straight with a gleam in her eye, hands clasped behind her back. "After all, Bram is a fourth cousin, and Jamie spends so much time here, he's practically family anyway."

The blood leeched from Cassie's face, no doubt tingeing her skin the same seasick green as the dress. *Oh, good—a perfect match.* She opened her mouth to speak, but her words were a rusty rasp like Daddy's cowhands the morning after a night in town. "J-Jamie? Bram?"

Alli all but preened, the same mischief in her face as when she used to dare Cassie to join her on forbidden adventures. "Oh, you remember Bram—you met him briefly the summer we went to Europe. He and Jamie are Blake's best friends. Trust me, you're going to love them."

"Trust you?" Cassie croaked, eyes narrowing considerably. "You were the one who saddled me with Theodore Swaller at your eighteenth birthday party, if you recall."

"Oh, boo, that's right." Alli scrunched her nose, then quickly dismissed the incident with a wave of her hand. "Well, don't worry, Jamie and Bram are both taller than you, neither has lazy eye, and you know," she said with a finger to her chin, "I don't think there's a single pimple between the two." She squinted in thought. "At least I don't think so . . ."

Cassie hurled an eyelet pillow at her cousin. "So help me, Allison Erin McClare, if either of these two clowns have any notion of sparking me, I will hold you personally responsible."

"You have nothing to worry about." Alli snatched the pillow

midair. "Bram's a sweetheart and a perfect gentleman." Her smile turned wayward. "And Jamie's just plain perfect."

A hoarse groan dragged from Cassie's lips. "Please tell me he's not one of those womanizing scoundrels I just escaped in Texas."

Alli tilted her head. "Well, there is a bit of the rogue in the boy, no question about that, but you have nothing to worry about, I assure you. He and Patricia Hamilton have been very cozy lately, and she'll be here tonight. I hope you don't mind, but my best friend Lydia Hamilton is sweet on Blake, so I invited her as well as her sister Patricia." Her nose bunched. "Not all that crazy about Trish as she tends to monopolize Jamie, but Senator Hamilton has this crazy rule—you invite Liddy, you invite her sister. So you see—you should be able to relax and make new friends without fear of anyone 'sparking' you." Alli bobbled the pillow with a smirk before aiming it back. "That is . . . if you still know how after keeping company with horses and pigs."

"Leave Mark out of this," Cassie said with an evil grin. Alli's pillow pelted the side of her head and she giggled, memories of pillow fights and slumber parties thickening the walls of her throat. Her cousins McClare were the only family she'd ever really known except for Mama and Daddy, and goodness, Alli, Meg, and Maddie were far more like sisters. Ostracized by the snooty Humble elite for her eccentric ways, Cassie had lived for summers in San Francisco or trips to Europe, precious moments with family that always made her feel like she'd come home.

Home. Tears stung her eyes and she blinked them away. *The perfect place to heal.*

"Wait—are you crying?" All jest faded from Alli's face as she hurried to where Cassie sat on the bed. Sidling in, she tucked her head to Cassie's, an arm cradling her back. "Gosh, I'm sorry about Theodore, but I was just jealous 'cause Peter Rutherford liked you better than me."

Cassie's smile swerved. "I had sore feet and a sick stomach for days, not to mention a head cold after Norman Godfrey cornered me in the billiard room."

"Oops. But I apologized, remember?" Alli said with a sincere dip of brows.

"Only after Peter Rutherford invited you to visit his parents' Napa vineyard."

"Oh, double boo, that's right." She grated her lip, then glanced up with a conciliatory smile. "But actually, Cass, I did you a favor. Peter gave me a personal tour of the wine cellar, and trust me, it left a sour taste in my mouth that had nothing to do with the grapes."

Cassie's jaw dropped. "You never told me that!"

Alli bumped her shoulder with a sheepish smile. "Couldn't—I was too embarrassed."

"Well, serves you right, you little brat." Cassie pinched her waist. "But so help me, Al, if either of these two clowns corner me in the billiard room tonight, I'll be showing you 'sour.'"

Allison lunged away, giggles bouncing off the walls as she sashayed to the door. She turned in a dramatic pose, hand on the knob. "Or thank me," she said with a dance of her brows. "Because trust me—these two make Mark Chancellor look like the rump of your prize filly."

A deep-down chuckle rolled from Cassie's lips, the first real laugh she'd had in way too long. Alli winked and closed the door, leaving Cassie with an image of Mark she could live with.

That of a horse's behind.

3

Studying herself in the mirror, Cassie sighed. Or tried to—the confounded corset wasn't making it easy. She tugged up on the filmy off-shoulder sleeves of the taffeta gown and wished it didn't expose so much of her pale skin. Especially given the hint of tan on her face from working outdoors on the ranch, dusting her nose and cheeks with too many freckles to count. But it couldn't be helped, she supposed, especially since Alli had piled her hair loosely on her head in a full chignon that accentuated the long curve of her neck. Another sigh attempted escape. At least Alli's face powder worked wonders in toning Cassie's freckles and tan. She had to admit the wispy flaxen curls feathering her head and throat lent an ethereal air that made her feel graceful and beautiful for the first time since Mark had broken their engagement. From that night, Cassie refused to pretty up for anyone, wearing nothing but jeans and buckskin skirts except for the tailored suits and skirts she was forced to wear to church. But as her mother had so painfully pointed out, her cousins' Nob Hill home in the big city was not some cattle ranch in East Texas, and the comfort of leather and denim would no longer suffice.

"Just forget about Mark and enjoy being a girl again," Virginia

McClare had begged, ever worried that her only daughter would end up an embittered tomboy. Cassie smoothed shaky hands down a full bodice to her tightly cinched waist, palms gliding over slim hips that spilled into a trumpet-shaped gown. Enjoy herself? In a corset? Her full lips twitched. *May as well be a noose.* She peeked at the clock on the vanity, then blew out a gust of air that fluttered the delicate tendrils at the side of her face. "Thunderation, I'm late!" she muttered to the Gibson Girl in the mirror. "Sweet mother of pearl, why did I take a nap?"

"Because you were exhausted from days on a train?"

Cassie spun around and grinned, the sight of her younger cousin Meg swelling her heart. "Meg!" She shot forward to give her a hug that made her giggle. "Let me look at you!" Cassie said, studying the shy and plump sixteen-year-old who'd always excelled in academics rather than social graces. A redhead like her mother, Meg had more of a pale strawberry blonde shade that washed out fair skin infused with freckles. A wide grin offered glints of gold in wire braces the dentist assured would work magic on Meg's crooked smile. From early on, Allison had been the beauty and Meg the gentle wallflower who preferred to fade into the shadows where she could adore her older sister and cousin from afar. Cassie's throat ached at the awful pranks and teasing Meg endured in school—just like Cassie—and she hugged her again. "You're getting to be a lady, Miss Megan McClare, and soon to be a beauty like your sister."

Megan ducked her head in a shy manner, a twinkle dancing in eyes more vibrant green than Cassie had ever seen, even behind gold wire-rimmed glasses. "Aw, Cass, you know I'll never be pretty like Alli and you, but that's okay—lawyers don't have to be pretty, just smart."

Tugging on a waist-long lock of her hair, Cassie pursed her

lips in a parental manner. "There's nothing wrong with being both smart and pretty, young lady, now is there?"

"I guess not," Meg said with half-giggle, half-sigh, "but let's not hold our breath, okay?" She fingered the sheer sleeve of Cassie's dress with a look of awe. "You've grown up, too, Cass—you're a vision in that dress." Her smile went flat. "Which proves quite neatly that Mark Chancellor is an idiot."

"That seems to be the general consensus," Cassie said with a crooked smile. She tucked a hand to her cousin's waist. "Are Aunt Cait and Alli downstairs?"

"They are, and Mother's dying to see you since you were napping when we came home, but Uncle Logan waylaid her in the foyer, so she sent me up to fetch you instead."

"Waylaid her?" Cassie grinned as the two made their way down the plush carpeted hall toward the curved staircase, arm in arm. "So Uncle Logan's still smitten, is he?"

Meg giggled, skittering the gleaming mahogany steps that swept down the far side of the foyer. Color-rich oil paintings graced cream satin-style papered walls, descending along with rose-carpeted steps. "More than ever, but whenever Alli or I mention Uncle Logan's obvious affection for her, she simply says he's her brother-in-law and friend and nothing more. Claims Daddy was the love of her life and she's found contentment as a widow." Meg peeked at Cassie beneath thick lashes, a glimmer of sympathy in her eyes. "But you know Uncle Logan—he never gives up. Comes for dinner once a week and Mother lets him because she thinks we need a male influence in our lives." All but hopping from the last step, Meg whirled around with a sparkle of tease. "Although I'm not sure Mother thinks Uncle Logan is the proper influence to have."

Cassie chuckled. "Proper influence, no, but a doting uncle who loves his family?" She tweaked Meg's waist. "He's certainly got Aunt Cait there."

Her smile softened when she entered the parlour, and for Cassie, it was a step back in time. A summer breeze drifted through a tall bay window, carrying a distinct whiff of eucalyptus from Aunt Cait's garden and the crisp scent of the sea. For a brief moment, Cassie paused to savor the pungent smell of lemon oil on cherry-wood furniture buffed to a gleam and the familiar fragrance of Aunt Cait's perfume—a calming mix of lavender with a tease of spicy clove. Floor-to-ceiling sheers fluttered against windows onto Powell Street where the clang of the trolley and the whir of the cables could be heard. True to her name, the family parrot, Miss Behave, would emit the occasional squawk or insult, tutored, no doubt, by Blake or Uncle Logan. The sights, the smells, the sounds of family flooded Cassie's senses with wonderful memories of piano sing-alongs, Uncle Logan's candlelight ghost stories, and games of hide-and-seek in a narrow three-story mansion on Nob Hill.

"Cassie!" Her five-year-old cousin Maddie hopped off Uncle Logan's lap in front of the hearth where he and Aunt Cait play-fully squabbled over cribbage. "I missed you!" she said, bound-ing forward, auburn curls springing while her giggles sprang off satin-striped walls of champagne-colored wallpaper.

"Awk, awk, Cassie's a brat, Cassie's a brat." Miss B.'s greeting, tutored by Blake long ago, coaxed a grin that took her back to better times. With an unladylike grunt that belied the dignity of her dress, she hefted the little girl in her arms, and the sweet smell of talcum powder and Pear's soap tickled her nose. "Ohhhh, I missed you, too, Madeline McClare," she said in a gravelly voice that made her cousin giggle. "Especially games of Marco Polo at Sutro Baths!"

"Cassie . . ." Aunt Cait rose in one graceful movement, eyes glimmering with moisture, and Cassie's throat thickened at the sight of the woman who came nearly as close to a mother as Cassie's own. She hurried over, face aglow with affection for her only niece, and Cassie marveled at the natural beauty of Caitlyn McClare. At the age of forty-three, her aunt could almost pass for Alli's older sister. Deep auburn hair piled loosely atop her head like Cassie's own displayed not a hint of gray, its soft and lustrous curls a perfect frame for a classic oval face with luminous aquamarine eyes. Full lips tilted into a welcome smile while a delicate blush accentuated the creamy skin of a woman who was aging well. Her lavender gauzy dress caressed her graceful five-foot-eight frame like a whisper, almost lending a floating effect as she glided into her niece's arms. "Congratulations on your graduation—your parents must be so proud." Her full lips pursed in a mock scowl. "But two summers in a row is entirely too long to stay away, young lady, so I demand you come every summer henceforth, do you hear?"

Cassie laughed, and the sound buoyed her with a swell of joy that even the corset couldn't restrict. "I agree, Aunt Cait, and you have my word that all future summers will be spent in San Francisco." She offered a sheepish grin as she shifted Maddie in her arms, pressing a kiss to her little cousin's cheek. "And longer, if it's not any trouble . . ."

"Oh, pshaw! As if my favorite niece could be any trouble—"

"Your *only* niece, Mrs. McClare." Uncle Logan strolled forward with a rogue of a smile, distinguished in his white bow tie and black dinner jacket. He scooped both Cassie and Maddie in his arms at the same time, the lovely smell of lime shaving soap and a trace of wood spice from his occasional Turkish cigarette swooping her back to her childhood. At forty-five, he was a wealthy bachelor about town that many a society matron attempted to corral for their daughters, but to no avail. A lawyer who dabbled in politics, Logan McClare was a man who afforded himself the company of many women rather than just one, although Cassie suspected that would change at the mere consent of Aunt Cait. He set her back on her feet with that easy, fluid grin that wreaked havoc with the female pulse and cocked a dark brow that matched sable hair with a hint of silver. "But let's not be hasty. Perhaps we should consider a few things before you agree. For instance, I don't have to let you win at arm wrestling anymore, do I?"

Maddie giggled and hooked her uncle's neck, scrambling from Cassie's arms into his.

"Absolutely not!" Aunt Cait chuckled, looping Cassie's waist to steal her away. "No more of your hooligan games, Logan Mc-Clare—these girls are sophisticated young women now."

"Well, Cass is anyway." Blake McClare tweaked Alli's neck on his way to give Cassie a hug. A younger version of his uncle, Blake had the same clear gray eyes as Logan, bottomless pools of tease for those they loved, which could easily ice into anger if given just cause. And, like his uncle, a cleft in his chin that always darkened with beard by the end of the day. From there on, he was his mother's son, deep auburn hair and a slight build, his height a head short of his uncle's towering six two. He held Cassie at arm's length and whistled. "Gosh, squirt, if this is how they grow 'em in Texas, you should have brought a friend."

"Ahem." With a pointed clear of her throat, Alli shot a warning glance at Blake before tugging the Hamilton sisters forward. She hooked an arm to the waist of a petite woman with a curly upsweep of chestnut hair and sparkling brown eyes. "Cass, this is my best friend, Lydia Hamilton . . ." Her smile dimmed. "And . . . of course . . . her sister, Patricia."

Cassie blinked wide when Liddy overpowered her with a hug as warm as the girl's smile while her sister—a tall, dark-haired beauty—stood behind, as cool as her ice-blue dress.

"Enough with the hugs—I want news from Texas." Aunt Cait said in her ear, quickly steering her to a carved cherrywood couch while the others returned to their game of whist. "So . . . how are your parents?"

Cassie's smile stiffened as she perched on the edge of the cream brocade sofa, but she quickly deflected it with a bright span of eyes. "Oh, just fine, Aunt Cait—Daddy's run into a few dry holes, but he's hoping that will change soon."

"A few dry holes?" Logan said with a scrunch of brows. He set Maddie down, and she promptly bolted to where the others played cards. After shedding his jacket, Uncle Logan reached for his cribbage chair and swung it around, dropping his coat over the back. He straddled the chair and rested starched white sleeves on the back, studying Cassie with concern in his eyes. "How many?"

Cassie peeked up, a touch of warmth in her cheeks. Daddy had warned her not to say anything about their dire financial state to his brother, but Cassie was too worried to hide the quiver in her voice. Not when a Texas fever wiped out most of their cattle herd last year and the ranch was in jeopardy of auction. "Four," she whispered, battling the prospect of tears.

"Four?" Shock was evident in his voice. "But Quinn said it was just a minor setback—"

A reedy breath floated from Cassie's lips. A minor setback, indeed, one that bled their savings dry. "Yes, well, Daddy is still hoping to turn it around, Uncle Logan . . ."

He scowled, and the dark cleft in his formidable chin suddenly loomed ominous. "I told him he should have stuck with cattle ranching instead of drilling for oil. Blast it, Cass, if he needed help, he should have called me. What kind of idiot is he?"

Aunt Cait patted his arm with a patient smile. "A McClare idiot, Logan. He's your brother, remember?" She lifted her chin enough to send him a message. "It's Cassie's first night in San Francisco. Don't you think this conversation can wait?"

He eyed Cait with a gum of his lips before taking Cassie's hands in his. "Sorry, Cass, I didn't mean to spoil your arrival dinner—I'm just concerned."

She nodded, lowering her voice. "I shouldn't have said anything, Uncle Logan, because Daddy asked me not to, so you have to promise you won't breathe a word to anyone—not Daddy, not my cousins, no one." Her frantic gaze flitted from her uncle to her aunt, calming somewhat at the look of tender concern in their eyes. "But Aunt Cait, I just couldn't *not* tell you because we need you to join us in prayer. Daddy, Mama, and I really do have faith it will all work out, but we could sure use the prayers of someone with a strong faith like you."

"With four dry wells, it's going to take more than—" He stopped, lips compressing at the jut of Aunt Cait's brow. "Sorry, Cait, but it's true."

Her aunt's eyes softened, a trace of sadness in their depths. "For you, Logan, perhaps, but not for Quinn and Virginia, and not for Cassie or me. Faith in God can move mountains."

One corner of Logan's mouth edged up. "Is that so?" The gray eyes glinted with a dare. "Well, let's see if it can 'move' you into the winner's column, Cait, because when it comes to faith, you're going to need a mountain to win at cribbage tonight."

A serene smile settled on her aunt's features as she laid a hand on Cassie's arm. "As tempting as it may be to pit my faith against your vanity, Logan, I much prefer to chat with my niece." She glanced up at the gold-plated clock on the mantel before offering him a calm smile. "But cheer up. As soon as Bram and Jamie arrive, you can go head-to-head with them."

His slow grin was a perfect match for the gleam of challenge in his eyes. "But I'd rather go head-to-head with you, Cait," he whispered, giving Cassie a wink.

A pretty shade of rose dusted her aunt's cheeks. "You're incorrigible, Logan McClare, and I have a mind to never play cribbage with you again."

He laughed, the sound bold and confident as he returned the chair to the game table. "But you will, Cait, and we both know it." Giving her a disarming grin, he reached for a neatly folded copy of *The San Francisco Examiner* from the coffee table and ambled toward the cordovan easy chair he claimed as his own. "Since I have a few moments before the other gentlemen arrive, I'll let you ladies chat while I peruse my stocks."

"The divil, you say!" Mrs. Rosie O'Brien stood at the door, her brogue as thick as her disdain. Aunt Cait's notorious housekeeper and nanny scowled. "The only pa-rusin' you'll be doing, Mister 'Beware', is in that dining room for a welcome supper for your niece."

"Rosie!" Cassie jumped up, giggling at the intentional slaughter of her uncle's name which marked a humorous enmity that went back as far as she could remember. Dressed in her gray uniform with a calf-length white apron, Rosie often appeared as starched as her lace cuffs and collar, but behind that gruff exterior lay a heart as big as San Francisco Bay. "I've missed you!" she said, embracing the slip of a woman who had been Aunt Cait's nanny from little on.

"Awk, Rosie's the boss, Rosie's the boss!" Miss B. quipped, and everyone chuckled.

At sixty-five, Rosie was still a handsome woman in spite of her bristly nature. Dark hair heavily sifted with silver and pulled back in a tight chignon emphasized steel-blue eyes that whittled Uncle Logan down to size even when her words could not. With a petite frame that was tiny and trim, Mrs. O'Brien wielded power in the McClare household that far exceeded both height and rank, a fact evidenced by the family's so-ugly-he's-cute bull-dog, Logan Junior. Despite Logan's objections, Rosie had won when she'd suggested naming the pet for the uncle who'd given it, citing the "creature's propensity to intestinal odors" as com-monality enough.

"Aw, but it's grand to have you back with us, Cassidy Mc-Clare," Rosie said with a grin, patting a veined hand to Cassie's cheek. Blue eyes in a squint, she peered at Uncle Logan who stood stock still, newspaper still dangling from his hand. "Sure, and it's high time we feed this scrawny, little thing from the cow ranch, wouldn't you say?"

Lips gone flat, Logan glanced first at his watch and then at Aunt Cait, obviously ignoring Rosie to the best of his ability. "We should wait for Bram and Jamie, don't you think, Cait?"

"I suppose . . . ," Caitlyn said with a concerned glance in Rosie's direction.

"Oh, aye, that's a grand idea," the housekeeper said with a grunt, the mulish press of her lips matching Logan's to a T. "Bar the starving lass from her welcome dinner, why don'cha?"

"Now, Rosie," Aunt Cait said softly, "dinner'll keep for a mo-ment or two, won't it?"

Rosie's chin angled high. "Sure, if it's cowhide you be wantin' to serve. Fixed a rump roast, I did—" She spared a sliver of a smile in Logan's direction. "In *his* honor." Her gaze swiveled back to Aunt Cait with a spike of a dark brow. "Any longer and may as well serve the poor lass the sole of my shoe, but then I suppose cow leather will make her feel right at home."

Aunt Cait sighed, gaze flicking from Rosie to Logan and back. Her lips twitched at the obvious clamp of his jaw. "All right then, Rosie—we'll be right in."

The elderly housekeeper shot Logan a smug smile on her way to the door.

Logan tossed the newspaper on the table and snatched his dinner jacket off the back of the chair, slipping it on with a growl. "Blast it, Cait, why do you let the help push you around?"

"Rosie is not just the 'help,' and well you know it. For goodness' sake, the woman's been an anchor in my life since I was born. Besides," she said with a half smile, "she pushes you around, not me." She rose. "And heaven knows I'd be lost without her."

Logan extended his arms with a grunt, adjusting his sleeves for comfort. "Then it's high time you 'found' yourself, Caitlyn—it *is* your house, after all, and you should have the final say when dinner is served. I can tell you one thing, if it were my house—"

"But it's not, now is it?" Aunt Cait said softly, standing her ground with a lift of her chin as always when Uncle Logan pushed too hard.

His jaw began to grind, a symptom with which Cassie was all too familiar when her outspoken uncle attempted to restrain his tongue, and she couldn't help but bite back a grin. Poor Uncle Logan—a powerhouse attorney used to getting his own way— except with Aunt Cait.

"Blast it, Cait, she doesn't like me." He tunneled a hand through perfectly groomed hair, bludgeoning until several strands toppled askew.

"Of course she likes you," Aunt Cait said in a soothing tone.

"No, she doesn't," Alli called from across the room, studying her cards. She glanced up, her face the picture of innocence. "She says Uncle Logan's a pain in the posterior." She gave him a wink. "Of course, the term she actually used may have been 'rump'..."

"Awk, pain in the rump, pain in the rump..."

"See?" Logan stabbed a finger in Alli's direction, his voice reduced to a hiss. "She's even turned the blasted parrot against me and my nieces and nephew as well." He scowled. "First you, the parrot, then my own flesh and blood."

Aunt Cait stepped toward him and adjusted his tie. "Don't be silly, Logan, nobody's against you..."

"We all love you, Uncle Logan, don't we, Cass?" Alli called, taking a trick in whist.

Cassie's smile was angelic. "Absolutely. Who else would have taught us poker?"

"Good gracious—you taught them *poker*?" Aunt Cait took a step back, hand to her chest.

A loud whistle pierced the air. "Awk, ante up, ante up..."

"Traitor." Uncle Logan glowered at Cassie, the semblance of a smile tugging his lips.

"And don't forget the shell game and darts and spoon on the nose..." Alli bobbed her head in cadence while shuffling the cards.

"Awk! Whoop-whoop—eye on the shell, eye on the shell..." Logan winced.

Tugging on a ruffle of her mother's dress, Maddie glanced up. "I love Uncle Logan too," she said with childlike wonder. "He taught me how to make money by pitching pennies."

"And ghost stories that kept me up at night," Meg said with a giggle.

Aunt Cait folded her arms. "Gambling? Horror stories? You are nothing more than a juvenile delinquent, Logan McClare. It's a wonder these children turned out at all."

He offered her his arm with a boyish smile. "That would be your influence, Cait. But their spirit of fun and adventure?" He waggled a brow. "I'm afraid that's pure Logan McClare."

Lips in a slant, Aunt Cait ignored him to cup a hand to Cassie's waist, taking Maddie's hand in the other. "Yes, well, 'afraid' is the operative word." She ushered them to the door. "Goodness, and you wonder why Rosie picks on you—"

Logan paused, jaw slack and fingers stilled while buttoning his coat. "There—you just admitted it! The woman doesn't like me and I have no earthly idea why."

Aunt Cait turned at the door, looking for all her somber stance as if she were fighting a twitch of a smile. "I suggest we get a move on, Logan, and not dally over the obvious." With a squeeze of her niece's waist, she turned to lead the way to the dining room, her voice laced with tease. "I don't advocate gambling, of course," she whispered, head tucked to Cassie's, "but I'll bet before Rosie's done with your uncle—" eyes twinkling, her aunt glanced over her shoulder before giving Cassie a wink—"his rump will be more charred than the roast."

4

*J*amie glanced at his watch and picked up his pace, loping the final blocks to the Blue Moon where he'd told Bram to pick him up instead of the boardinghouse. *But, dash it, now I'm late!* He huffed out a sigh and began to sprint, hoping to make better time. Yes, they'd be late for dinner at the McClares', but then his mother was worth it.

"Do you have time to take these clothes to Julie and Millie?" she'd asked, hesitation in her tone that belied the excitement in her eyes over clothes she'd sewn for their old neighbors.

"You bet," he'd said without the slightest reluctance, adjusting the tie of his tuxedo in the mirror before turning to deposit a kiss to her cheek, grateful for any task he could do for his mother. Still, it always felt strange returning to the seedy cow-yard they'd lived in until his father had died, especially dressed to the nines for a welcome dinner on Nob Hill. Even so, few things gave his mother more joy than sewing clothes for the lost women and children who lived in the brothel on the first floor, many of whom had become her good friends. And his.

"Whoo-ee, Jamie MacKenna," Julie said as she'd eyed him in the secondhand tuxedo Bram had passed down. Butting a hip to the door, she gave him a lonely smile in a faded kimono, red hair trailing one shoulder while faded bruises mottled her neckline. "Well, aren't we dressed to kill! You sure you wanna have supper with some prissy girls on Snob Hill instead of me?"

Dressed to kill. By thunder, he hoped so. Dressed to kill all memories of a wretched past in the bowels of the Barbary Coast, not only for his family, but for women like Julie Graves. He issued a low grunt. An appropriate name for a poor soul buried alive in the deep, deep "grave" of the Barbary Coast. All the more reason for Jamie to court wealth and political influence while he courted senators' daughters in a game where the end justified the means. Robin Hood of the Barbary Coast—taking from the rich to give to the poor.

"Regrettably, yes," he said with a forced grin, heart wrenching over the dark smudges under her eyes that made her look fifty instead of twenty-nine. He handed her his mother's package containing clothes for her, Millie, and Millie's little girl Bess. "Although I'm quite certain an evening spent with you would be far more interesting, Miss Graves," he said with a dip of his head, top hat to his chest, "I'm afraid I'm obliged to keep my commitment tonight."

"A commitment, huh?" she said with a tease of a smile that somehow came off sad. "Sounds a bit stuffy to me."

He smiled. "Commitments usually are, Julie—at least on Nob Hill." *But necessary if one hopes to help innocent young girls like you used to be.* A nerve flickered in his cheek. *And* his mother—once a homeless fifteen-year-old forced to work in a depraved dance hall to even survive. He studied Julie while she tore into the tissue-wrapped package like a little girl at Christmas, tired eyes suddenly aglow, and an ache stabbed in his chest. She and the other ladies of the evening had shared a commonality with Jamie's family that went well beyond the roof over their heads. They were misfits all, shackled to the Barbary Coast, and Jamie swore that someday, somehow, he would work to change that for as many young women as he could. To set women like Julie and Millie free from the bondage of poverty and degradation that left a slime over the Coast as vile as the sewage that slithered its streets. Just like he'd set his mother and sister free, first by moving them to a boardinghouse in a poor but decent neighborhood awhile back, and then someday soon, God willing, to a home on Nob Hill.

God willing? His jaw tightened at the mental slip of tongue. It wasn't God who worked three jobs while going to school, no matter what his mother and sister thought, and it wasn't God who would sacrifice love for money in a marriage of convenience. No, it was Jamie MacKenna who "willed" that things would change for those he loved. But first, he needed the wealth to buy his own boardinghouse and then the political stature to fight prostitution and dance halls, an evil blight that ate away at women's lives like cancer. Young girls like his mother, Millie, and Julie—with no place to go, forced into slavery of their bodies. His gut cramped as he stared at the hope-ravaged soul before him because he knew his dreams would come far too late for someone like her. Grazing a gentle hand to her cheek, he offered a melancholy smile. "Get sleep tonight, Julie—alone. You need the rest."

Her lips tipped in a sad curve. "That I do, Jamie MacKenna, that I do."

The blare of a horn jerked him back to the present as he jogged down Montgomery Street. He slowed his gait to catch his breath, only to have it hitch again when a brand-new Flint roadster almost collided with a horse and buggy. Curses defiled the air along with the stench of raw sewage and gasoline fumes, and for the thousandth time, he realized just how lucky he was that he and his family no longer lived in the Barbary Coast.

"What took you so long?" Bram called from the front seat of his brand-new cherry-red Stanley Steamer, a graduation gift from his parents. Clouds of steam billowed from beneath the parked vehicle as it hissed and rumbled at the curb.

Jamie hopped into the front and released a weighty sigh, finally able to relax against the plush leather upholstery. The knots in his stomach unraveled as he angled his top hat back. "Mom asked me to deliver clothes to some old neighbors." His smile, like his words, held an apology. "Sorry I'm late—Alli will have our heads."

Bram's chuckle sounded above the chug of the car. "Only because that's all that'll be left after Rosie gets through chewing on us." He maneuvered the tiller to ease out into traffic, glancing both behind and ahead. "Next time let me know when your mother has a delivery, and I'll pick you up early and drive you there."

"No, thanks, buddy, the Blue Moon's just fine."

Bram shook his head, passing a buckboard and horse. "You're crazy, Mac, you know that? So you were born in the Coast, so what? It's not like you're a part of the slums anymore."

Oh, but I am, Jamie thought with a tight smile, *it's a permanent stain on my soul.* "Sorry, Bram, but that's part of my life I don't want anyone to see." He looked away, unwilling to give an inch, even to the best friend who saved his life on a daily basis. His "imaginary" life, that is, with fashionable hand-me-downs and ready loans that Bram insisted Jamie need never pay back. But he always did, of course, even if it meant tending bar most of the night at the Blue Moon before eight hours of classes the next day. Jamie expelled a noisy sigh lost in the chug of Bram's car. Nope, no one knew from whence he hailed, nor would they. *Ever.* Especially Bram and Blake, the two most important people in his life other than his family.

He'd met them at the Olympic Club, a prestigious gentlemen's club where Jamie worked since college. The fates had smiled on him through Logan McClare, a board member of the Oly Club who thought Jamie had "gumption" to work three jobs and still tackle higher education. So he introduced him to his two nephews, and the three men had been inseparable in law school, where Jamie had been the recipient of a merit scholarship to assist "needy and worthy students." His jaw twitched. He was certainly that—a Barbary Coast street rat in dire need of rich buddies to give him a leg up. The edge of his mouth crooked in a smile. But in the end, they'd given him far more than that.

The Three Musketeers, they called themselves—quickly becoming the two closest friends Jamie ever had. His lips veered to the side. The only friends he'd ever had, if truth be told. Fourth cousins twice removed, Bram "Padre" Hughes, Jamie's best friend, could have easily been a minister, and Blake "Rake" McClare was a rogue who took after his uncle Logan in his endless pursuit of women. Two friends as different as night and day, while Jamie shored up the middle—moral enough to steer clear of Blake's reckless pursuits of the flesh, but rogue enough that his morality had little to do with Bram's God. His jaw compressed. And poor enough to appreciate the opportunities they afforded him in his relentless pursuit to marry well.

The very thought caused his pulse to race. "So, know anything about this Texas cousin?"

"Cassie?" Bram smiled and turned the tiller to steer past a horse and buggy that was making a left turn, missing a cable car by mere yards. "Not real well, although we met once briefly a few summers ago. Seemed like a sweetheart, though. More like a sister to Alli, Meg, and Maddie than a cousin. Pretty, bright, no-nonsense—you know, real down-to-earth for an oil heiress.

Her father is Logan's brother Quinn, the maverick McClare cattle rancher turned oil man. Made a small fortune in Texas oil the last few years and looks to make more. Could be wealthier than Logan before all's said and done, if you can imagine that."

Jamie whistled. "An oil heiress, eh? And pretty to boot? Be still my heart."

Bram grinned, the wind whipping wheat-colored hair against his top hat. He shot Jamie a sideways glance. "I thought you had your sights set on the senator's daughter?"

"I do," Jamie said with a grin that matched Bram's, "but let's not rush things, Padre. Haven't decided to officially court her just yet. Besides, throw in a wealthy heiress from one of the top political families in the state?" He shook his head. "Not sure I can pass that up."

"What happened to no mixing business with family, counselor?" Bram said, reminding Jamie of his caveat to pursue social contacts of the McClares and not the McClares themselves.

Hiking a shoe to the stainless railing of the carriage seat in front of the dash, Jamie flashed a grin, dark curls buffeted by the breeze till one tumbled over his eye. "The fine print being the McClares of San Francisco, buddy boy, not an heiress from the windswept prairies of Texas. And, yes, the McClares' mansion has been like a second home with all the time I've spent there with Blake and you. Heaven knows Alli and Meg are certainly more like sisters, which is why I've been forced to focus on their wealthy friends instead. But . . . new McClare blood, part of a family that could help my career and my bankbook?" He wiggled his brows. "I just may have to work on my Texas drawl."

Bram shook his head, easing past a peddler on a bicycle. "You're something else, MacKenna, you know that? One of the nicest guys I know, hard-working, smart, give the shirt off your back—"

He smiled. "That is, if it didn't belong to me first. Yet under that heart of gold is a fortune hunter with the glint of gold in his eyes. Doesn't make a lot of sense, you know?"

"Sure it does." Jamie grinned. And why not? His dreams were worth it—from his hopes to provide a surgery that could heal his sister someday, to his drive to be the youngest senator from the state of California and effect change in the Barbary Coast. He gave Bram a wink. "May as well fall in love with a rich girl as a poor one."

"So you say," Bram said with a shift of gears, "but it's been my experience that life doesn't always comply. You fall in love with whom God chooses, Mac, and sometimes a fortune doesn't come along with it."

Jamie propped hands to the back of his neck, absently staring down Market Street with a stiff smile. "See, Bram, that's where you make your mistake—leaving everything up to some deity who may or may not exist. Well, not me. I've gotten this far on my own ingenuity, so I see no reason to depend on some fairy tale for the most important thing in my life—" his smile veered into a scowl—"marrying well so I can take care of my family because God hasn't had the time."

Bram peered out of the corner of his eye, a frown pinching his face despite a melancholy smile. "God has both the time and inclination, Jamie. He's the Savior you see every week on that cross at church, remember? The One who laid down his life for you and your family?"

Jamie exhaled his frustration, triggered as always when "Padre Hughes" wandered into the realm of God, something he was prone to do. "Sorry, Bram, but the only 'savior' I see is yours truly, laying his life down to deliver his family from injustices your Savior allowed."

Bram's car crested a hill, and Jamie averted his gaze, his anger suddenly surging like the whitecaps out on the bay. Injustices, indeed, like a drunk for a father who not only beat and berated them until he took his last breath, but robbed them of a life that should have been theirs. Bitterness burned in Jamie's gut like acid. Brian MacKenna, one of the pampered Nob Hill elite, whose sins of the flesh included siring an illegitimate son with a dance-hall girl. A man disowned by his holier-than-thou father—Jamie's grandfather—a pillar of the church and a true "man of God." Jamie issued a silent grunt. A grandfather now as defunct as his son's inheritance, no qualms about turning his back on both his son and his seed.

Shaking off his dour mood, Jamie cuffed Bram's shoulder in an effort to restore his good humor. "Besides, Padre, I have you to put in a good word for me, if God even exists, so I'll just focus on the socialites I'm lucky to meet through you and Blake while you say your prayers." Jamie winked. "Just make sure they include a senator's daughter for your very poor friend—or an oil heiress from Texas."

Leaning back, he closed his eyes, his adrenaline suddenly pumping as much from the thought of marrying a McClare as the exhilaration of sea air in his face. He could almost smell the shrimp boats on the breeze, hear the whistles of the Alaska Packer fleet shipping out on its yearly sojourns to the Bering Sea, and almost taste the succulent king salmon brimming in their holds come August. A distant horn signaled the departure of the square-rigger *Star of Alaska*, the fastest windjammer in the fleet, and Jamie's pride suddenly swelled like the waves crashing the serrated shoreline of The Embarcadero. Despite being born an illegitimate child in the sewers of Barbary Coast, he adored San Francisco.

The clock tower chimed the half hour as they passed the Ferry Building, the busiest passenger terminal in the world second only to London's, a source of civic pride to the city . . . and to Jamie. With its 660-foot-long sky-lit two-story concourse, steel-arched trusses, and Tennessee marble walls, it ushered in as many as 50 million passengers a year. Jamie drew in a deep breath scented with the tang of the bay and the distinct smell of burning wood from cable car brakes, and poor or not, he was grateful he'd been born here. He heard the blare of a distant horn from the *Eureka*, a side-wheel paddle steamboat with the distinction of being the largest auto and passenger ferry in the world, and pride expanded in his chest. Someday he would leave his mark on this town, making political history in Frisco.

His lips curved into a satisfied smile. Step one had been a law degree, and step two was marrying well. As far as Jamie was concerned, a Texas heiress might be just the ticket—especially one who was "pretty, bright, and no-nonsense." He paused. *No-nonsense?* His eyes popped open as the Stanley Steamer rattled and strained to climb Nob Hill to the McClares', the smell of gasoline converting water into steam pungent in the air. He squinted over at Bram. "No-nonsense, huh? What the blazes is that supposed to mean?"

The Stanley slowed to a crawl, inching along the curb in front of the McClares' three-story pale-yellow Victorian. Bram pressed the foot brake and hookup-pedal button to ease the car to a stop. Twisting the valve off, he gave Jamie a wry smile. "It means Cassie doesn't put on airs or act like people who do. She's as natural and down to earth as cow patties in a field and you, my friend, won't be able to con her, so I suggest you focus on Patricia instead."

Gaze narrow, Jamie cocked his head, challenge lifting the corners of his mouth. "Is that a dare, because if it is, I'm game." He swung down from the seat, landing on his feet with a thump.

Bram chuckled and hopped out of the car, adjusting his dinner jacket and combing his hair before replacing his top hat. "Nope, more of a warning, Mac. Alli said Cass just got hurt by some pretty-boy fortune hunter that soured her pretty badly on men." He strolled around the car to where Jamie stood and patted him on the cheek. "That's you to a T, MacKenna, so I'd say you don't stand a chance." He adjusted the cuffs of his sleeve with a crooked grin. "And who said life wasn't fair?" He flicked a curl on Jamie's forehead. "I'd comb your hair if I were you, Mac—the Greek god has locks tumbling about his well-sculpted face." His eyes narrowed to a squint as he tilted Jamie's cheek. "And blood? What the blazes did you do, get in a street brawl?"

Jamie scowled. "Yeah, with a dull razor." He rubbed his jaw, wincing at its soreness. "I'll have to duck in the privy to wash it off." A slow grin eased its way across his face. "Although from the sound of this Texas McClare, it sounds like she might cotton to the rough-and-tumble street type who's not afraid of drawing a little blood."

Bram laughed. "Not as long as it's yours."

Jamie stared, mouth agape in a half smile. "You don't think I can do it, do you?"

Bram fussed with his tie, then tapped on his hat, the grin still in place. "Nope. The woman will eat you for breakfast and spit you out, buddy boy, and don't say I didn't warn you." He winked. "She's from Texas, remember? She can spot a coyote a mile away." He handed Jamie his comb. "Here—comb your hair or even Patricia won't give you the time of day."

A grunt rolled from Jamie's lips. "Humph. That one would not only give me the time of day, pal, but the family gold heirloom timepiece along with it." He snatched the comb and gave it a pass through his hair. "Not to mention her father likes me since

I worked with him on that fundraiser for Stanford Law last year."
Jamie grinned. "You might say the Senator and I have gotten
closer than even his daughter and me."

"That close, huh?" Bram pocketed his comb, baiting him with
a smile.

Jamie straightened his tie. "What can I say? He likes my gumption, so when it comes to courting his daughter, I assure you, the
man will give me the time of day, month, and year."

"Well, I'd take it then, Mac, because the senator's daughter is
smitten, and your odds of marrying well are a lot better with her
than a McClare."

Jamie's grin was almost predatory. "Wanna bet? Care to put
your money where your mouth is, Bram old boy?"

Bram studied him, head cocked and wheels obviously turning
in his head. A smile that was nothing but trouble slid across his
face as easily as his money would slide into Jamie's pocket once
he won the bet. "You know, I believe I'd like to see you get the
thrashing you deserve, MacKenna, because you're becoming a
little too big for your britches." He jagged a brow and grinned.
"Or mine, I should say. Because despite your fame and fortune
as a boxing prodigy tutored by Gentleman Jim Corbett himself,
I do believe this little filly will knock you out cold." He extended
a hand with a gleam of white teeth that triggered a fresh rush of
adrenaline in Jamie's veins. "You're on, Mac—turn Cassie Mc-
Clare's head, and I'll pay for every Dr Pepper you guzzle when
we're out, for the rest of the year."

"You mostly do anyway since I beat you at pool every week,
but at least I won't feel obligated to pay you back." Jamie paused,
assessing Bram through narrow eyes. "And not that it matters
since the possibility is completely remote, but what do you get
if you win?"

Slinging an arm to Jamie's shoulder, Bram ushered him up the brick steps of the McClares' painted lady. Typical for clustered Nob Hill residences, its compact but graceful columned verandas and lavish bay window seemed to welcome them "home." "Something money can't buy, old buddy." His laughter echoed in the marble portico as he lifted the brass knocker on the arched burlwood door. The confidence in his tone was nothing short of smug. "Pure satisfaction at seeing Jamie MacKenna turned away by a girl."

5

can't tell you how proud I am of both you and Alli," Aunt Cait said, buttering a roll while laughter drifted from the other end of the table where Alli and Blake amused the others. Candles glowed and silverware tinkled in the rectangular dining room in which Cassie had shared many a family meal. Pastel pink, cream, and green floral wallpaper lent a coziness that belied the spacious size of the room and its high-domed ceiling resplendent with a crystal chandelier. A cherrywood chair rail circled mid-wall, a handsome match for a polished wood floor that smelled of lemon oil and shined as much as the silver on the table.

"For young women to acquire a teaching degree in today's world is impressive," Aunt Cait continued. Lacy sheers fluttered behind her from a bank of tall windows, infusing the room with the smell of the sea and Aunt Cait's honeysuckle vines, both scenting the air with memories of Cassie's childhood. Her aunt's smile turned melancholy as her gaze trailed into a soft stare. "I had hoped to teach after I married, but Blake came along so quickly, I never got the chance." Her sigh was resolute, followed by a definite twinkle in her eye. "But that will all change when Alli and I open our Hand of Hope School next year."

Cassie's heart fluttered at the prospect of being part of Aunt

Cait's dream to reach out to underprivileged girls. "Oh, I am *so* excited about your school, Aunt Cait," Cassie gushed, "and you will make a wonderful teacher! One of the reasons I loved spending summers here was all the fun things you taught us to do—playing the piano, embroidery, history, and the arts. I do believe my mother was almost jealous of all the adventures we had, seeing the sights of San Francisco."

Her aunt's eyes twinkled. "Yes, we do have some wonderful memories, and this summer I plan to make plenty more." She blew on her spoonful of steaming chowder, her smile suddenly dimming. "Your mother wrote me about Mark, Cassie, and my heart grieves for you."

The soup pooled in Cassie's mouth, burning as much as the mention of Mark's name. She gulped the chowder down and bit back a wince, unwilling for her aunt to see the devastation he'd caused. "Thanks, Aunt Cait, it's an awful period in my life I'm hoping to put behind me, and there's no better place to do so than here with you and my cousins."

Her gaze flitted to where Uncle Logan entertained the others before she blew on her chowder, hoping to cool the sting of its heat as thoroughly as she hoped to cool her anger over Mark. And she needed to. Badly. She didn't like herself very much lately—no fun, no sparkle, and nerves as tight as the noose she hankered to cinch around every pretty boy's neck. She wrinkled her nose. No question her heart had become as hard and shriveled as the jerky Mama made at Christmas, and she was pretty sure God was disappointed too. *Pray for them which despitefully use you* . . . The chowder on her spoon rippled as she blew, the Scripture she'd read this morning stirring her guilt along with it. A sigh swelled in her chest. Well, she certainly hadn't done much of that for Mark, she supposed, something that would have to change. *I promise, Lord, I'll try to do better.* She paused to test her soup, nose in a scrunch. After all, everybody needed prayer, even a skunk. Taking a taste, she glanced up with a tentative smile. "As a matter of fact, Aunt Cait . . . how would you feel about me teaching at your school?"

The spoon in her aunt's hand clinked to the bowl as she stared, turquoise eyes welling with moisture. She reached to swallow Cassie in a tight hug. "Oh, darling, nothing would give me more pleasure than having you here. You've always been like one of my own, Cassie, you know that." She pulled away. "But how do your parents feel about that—you moving away?"

Cassie's appetite suddenly cooled along with the soup. "Actually, they don't know yet," she whispered, gaze fixed on the half-finished bowl of clam chowder. She blinked to clear moisture from her eyes before lifting her gaze. "But they realize how painful Mark's betrayal has been, so they'll understand. I thought maybe, if you didn't mind, I'd see if I could retain a teaching position here until your school is open, then teach with you and Alli for a year or so, till I feel ready to return to the ranch."

Aunt Cait squeezed her hand. "Whatever you need, darling—you know we love you."

Cassie nodded and quickly spooned more chowder to deflect her tears, but it was as if the soup had been tainted by the sour taste of Mark's rejection, a rejection compounded by years of being spurned by Humble's elite. Till Mark, she'd never let her guard down or opened her heart so completely, and the hurt was still so raw, Cassie wondered if a year or two would even suffice. Other than family and friends at the reservation or on the ranch, he'd been her only friend in Humble, the only boy who not only accepted her for who she was, but actually seemed to love her for it. With him, she could be the down-to-earth, steer-busting tomboy rather than a silk and lace debutante, and the freedom had caused her to fall hopelessly in love.

Her throat contracted, trapping the liquid until she thought she might choke. She'd been fine pretending she didn't care until she'd seen Aunt Cait, and then all the warmth and love that spilled from this woman suddenly flushed out the pain inside, along with renegade tears she couldn't control. Napkin to her mouth, she quickly rose, grateful Uncle Logan had captured the others' attention with a colorful tale. She swabbed the cloth to her face with a shaky smile. "Goodness, please excuse me, Aunt Cait, I believe I have something in my eye . . ."

Like heartbreak. She battled a heave as she slipped out behind her aunt to hurry down the hall to the bathroom. Closing the door, she collapsed against the vanity with a broken sob. "Oh, Lord, please get me through this without any more tears. I'm so tired of weeping." A sigh shuddered from her lips as she dabbed her eyes with wadded toilet paper, finally blowing her nose. She blinked in the mirror, almost smiling at the pitiful sight she presented—eyes rimmed red and face all blotchy. Sucking in a deep swallow of air, she blasted it out again, shoulders in a slump. "Just how much water are you going to shed over this low-down skunk, Cassidy McClare?" she whispered.

With another heavy exhale, she turned on the faucet and cupped water to her face, enjoying the cold sting on her skin. "Till I drown my sorrows, I suppose," she muttered, wishing she could drown that skunk instead. She patted her face dry with the hand towel monogrammed with a gold *M*, guilt welling now instead of her tears. "I'm sorry, Lord. Mark's not a skunk, exactly—just a man who chose his father's money over me." Her eyelids fluttered closed as she gripped the edge of the sink. "And a man who truly doesn't know you the way that he should. Please, Lord, help me to forgive him and help him be the man you want him to be." Her eyes flipped open. "And the man I want him to be too . . ." Her lips quirked. "Gone—forever."

Refolding the hand towel, she carefully replaced it over the brass hook that hung on the wall, then squared her shoulders to scowl in the mirror. "Straighten up, Cassie McClare, you're not one of those silly-frilly socialites who swoon over a man with a bat of her eyes, so you have no business blubbering over one either. You're a Texas McClare and tough as cowhide, so get on with your life doing something that matters—helping Aunt Cait and Alli teach young girls to survive in the world—with or without a man." She adjusted her skirt with a firm lift of her chin, mouth in a wry bent. "And preferably without—both a corset *and* a man."

Head high, she opened the door and plowed straight into a rock wall, caught off-guard when she ricocheted off a crisp white shirt that smelled of soap and starch and a hint of spice.

Wobbling on her heels, she emitted a high-pitched squeak as she lost her balance, arms flailing until a hand gripped her firmly at the waist. "Pardon me, I—" Hazel eyes blinked wide, the shock on the man's face equal to hers until a slow, easy grin finally stole it away. "Well, I'll be," he whispered, "so *you're* the Texas McClare?"

She shoved him away and slapped at the back of her waist, as if his touch had scorched her dress like it scorched her body. "Great balls of fire, you are just not happy unless you are mowing me down, are you, Mister . . . ?"

He grinned and offered a bow, annoying her further with a blaze of white teeth that made him more handsome than she remembered. "Jamie MacKenna at your service, Miss McClare." He had the audacity to relax a palm to the wall, stance casual as he grinned, caging her in. "And, yes, it would appear I have a knack for bowling you over—Cassie, is it?"

She groaned and put a hand to her eyes, the sudden urge to throttle Allison itching her fingers. Venting with a noisy exhale, she peered up, pulse stuttering at his close proximity. "Miss Mc-Clare to you," she said with a fold of arms, "and didn't your mother teach you to knock?"

The dimples flashed. "Actually, my fist was poised to do so, but you barreled out like a Texas tornado before knuckles could even tap wood." He actually winked. "Either that, or I missed the day my mama taught that lesson, along with the one not to mow pretty girls down."

"Apparently." She attempted to pass without success and arched a brow. "Do you mind?"

He snapped to attention, offering his arm. "Not at all, Miss McClare. May I escort you?"

"No thank you." She swept past with a regal lift of her chin, her smile as stiff as her tone. "Alli tells me you and Miss Hamilton have been quite cozy lately, so I doubt she'd approve."

His chuckle followed her. "Just for the record, ma'am, 'cozy' is not 'committed.'"

"Obviously," Cassie said as she entered the dining room, "at least in your case."

"Jamie!" Maddie sprang from her chair like a tiddlywink, shooting into his arms with a giggle when hoisted high in the air. "Rosie said she was gonna string you up for being late."

"One can only hope," Cassie muttered as she slid into her seat.

"She did, did she?" He planted a kiss on Maddie's cheek and set her back in her chair before his gaze lighted on Aunt Cait. "Sorry we're late, Mrs. McClare," he said, tone contrite despite a twinkle in his eyes, "but if Rosie's on the warpath, it's all Bram's fault." He glanced around the table, eyes finally lighting on Patricia with a smile. "Hello, everyone ... Patricia ..."

Bram grunted, rising to extend both a bright smile and his hand across the table to Cassie. "Like anyone's going to believe *that*, MacKenna." He gave her a wink as he shook her hand. "Welcome back to San Francisco, Cassie. Last time I saw you, you were barely nineteen and on your way to Europe. It's good to see you again."

"Likewise, Bram," Cassie said with a warm smile. "And congratulations on the law degree and the job in Uncle Logan's firm. You'll learn a lot from that man."

"A little too much, I'm afraid," Aunt Cait said with a wry smile, squeezing Pretty Boy's hand when he leaned to buss her cheek. "Cassie, this is Jamie MacKenna, Blake's good friend, but more like second sons, really, both he and Bram. Jamie will be working for Logan too, along with Bram and Blake, so he's practically family."

Pretty Boy offered a handshake, and Cassie swore his pearly whites twinkled along with those blasted hazel eyes. "Which means we're practically related," he said with a wink.

She tilted her head, smile as wooden as the palm she extended his way. "Another 'cousin,' no doubt," she said sweetly, placing her hand into his. On contact, his large fingers seemed to consume hers, and her skin tingled like she'd been zapped with one of Daddy's newfangled electric cattle prods. Heat shimmered from her nails straight up her arm and neck, bleeding into her face with enough fire to cook Rosie's roast.

Those clear hazel eyes glimmered with humor while he raked her head to toe, making the sting of the cattle prod cool by comparison. "Your majesty," he whispered with a slight bow, voice husky and brimming with tease. "From the lovely lay of your dress, I assume all burrs have been appropriately removed from your saddle?"

You betcha, and now lodged in my throat . . . She tried to reclaim her hand, as stunned and lightheaded as when she'd been thrown from Daddy's prize filly for the very first time.

"Your majesty?" Aunt Cait said with a frown, gaze flitting from Cassie's blazing face to the pretty boy's annoying smirk. "You two know each other?"

"Not exactly 'know,'" he said.

He had a death grip on her hand and a lock on her eyes. The deepest dimples she ever saw flashed with a half-lidded smile that heated her temper along with her cheeks.

His smile worked its way into a grin. "Ran into her at the train station where I apparently swept her off her feet."

Cassie sprung up as if bucked by a rodeo bronc, yanking her hand away. "Mowed me down is more like it," she blurted. Leaning in, her taffeta bodice quivered with every ragged heave. "And the only burr in my saddle today, Mr. MacKenna, was you."

Eyes bugging wide, Alli jumped up, suddenly all ears. "Wait—*this* is the 'pretty-boy yahoo' you told me about, the one who ran you down at the train station?"

"Yahoo?" Jamie said, brows bunched in a frown.

Bram grinned. "Cheer up, Mac. After all, she did say you were 'pretty.'" He shook his napkin free with a chuckle and placed it in his lap. "Although that's a far cry from free Dr Peppers in a bar."

Blake leaned in at the other end of the table, his grin as broad as Bram's. "No kidding, MacKenna? You bowled Cassie over?"

"Bulldozed is more like it," Cassie said with a fold of her arms.

Jamie shrugged and shot Blake a sheepish grin, kneading the back of his neck. "Afraid so, and I'm sorry to say she fell pretty hard." His gaze settled on Cassie with a dangerous smile that seemed all too familiar. He leaned in with a whisper, his tease sultry and low. "But then they usually do."

She stabbed a finger at him, shooting a hard gaze at Blake over her shoulder. "*This* is your friend? This . . . this . . . womanizer?"

Bram chuckled. "I thought you said she didn't know you, Mac?"

"Cassie darling," Aunt Cait said with concern in her eyes, "I don't know what Jamie did to anger you so, but I assure you he is not a womanizer."

"No?" Cassie spun around, almost grateful for the corset so she couldn't blow. "Explain that to the girlfriend he put on the train before he asked *me* out to lunch."

"Girlfriend?" Blake's lips inched into a half smile. "You holding out on us, MacKenna?"

"Yes, girlfriend," Cassie snapped, grateful she could expose this Lothario for the scoundrel that he was. "Completely manhandled her in broad daylight before putting her on the train, and the tracks were still warm when he turned his attention to me."

"It-was-my-cousin," Jamie enunciated slowly, the smirk on his face fading enough for his irritation to show. "And of course the tracks were still warm—a 450-plus-ton locomotive just rolled by on a hot summer day."

"Your cousin—ha! Likely story. Kissing cousins, no doubt."

"Uh, Cass . . ." Alli chewed on the edge of her smile. "It *was* Jamie's cousin—he brought Sara by a number of times." She shot Jamie a sympathetic smile. "So she's on her way home to Tulsa?"

"Yeah," Jamie said with a tight smile. His eyes shifted to Cassie, gaze narrowing considerably. "A little 'manhandled,' maybe, but none the worse for the wear."

Cassie could have had Texas heatstroke—no difference—her cheeks were on fire and her pride was in flames. She stuttered, her apology wedged in her throat. "I, um . . . well, I'm, uh . . ."

"Sorry?" Jamie offered with a patient lift of brows.

Her lips went flat. "Yeah, that."

He held out his hand again, a tease hovering on his lips. "So am I—truce?"

"We can always draw up a contract if you don't trust him, Cass," Uncle Logan said with a grin.

Cassie forced a smile and shook Jamie's hand. "That's okay, Uncle Logan. With four lawyers in the room and a gal who can hog-tie a steer in fifteen seconds, I'll take my chances."

A slow smile inched across Jamie's face. "I certainly hope so," he whispered.

"I suppose you expect to be fed despite waltzing in late?" Rosie barreled through the kitchen door with a soup tureen while Hadley followed seconds later with a bowl of green beans. She did a double take, leering at the butler. "I said '*greens*,' Mr. Hadley." The whisper she ground out could've been heard down on the wharf. "Not '*beans*.' Those are for the next course."

An eyelash never flicked on the weathered face of the tall, silver-haired butler who had served the McClares for years. Forever at odds with Mrs. O'Brien—or at least she with him—the English-born manservant possessed a dignity far keener than either his sight or hearing, tipping Cassie's lips into a faint smile. With his usual grace and unruffled air, he calmly offered a slight bow to the crotchety housekeeper, an almost imperceptible curve on wide lips that never uttered a crass word or complaint. "Beg pardon, Mrs. O'Brien," he said with a crisp English accent, promptly toting the bowl of green beans back to the kitchen.

With a roll of eyes, Rosie doled out chowder while Jamie hooked an arm to her waist, giving her a kiss on the head. "Sorry we're late, but it was Bram's fault," he whispered loudly in Rosie's ear. "Heaven knows I wouldn't be late for one of your meals, Mrs. O., if my life depended on it. Everybody knows you're the best cook in the Bay area, and good gravy, I'd propose tomorrow if I thought you'd accept." He winked. "Or maybe I should say, 'great chowder.'"

Flatter-fop. Cassie gave him a thin smile, annoyed that Rosie's cheeks sported a soft blush as she playfully swatted him away before ladling soup into his bowl. "Oh, go on with you, Jamie MacKenna," she said with a scowl that was more of smile. "Sure, and you're loaded with more blarney than the sacred stone itself." She turned to Bram, eyes narrowed in tease. "And you—it'd serve you right to eat in the kitchen for being late."

"B-but . . . it wasn't my fault, Mrs. O.—"

"No 'buts,' Abraham Hughes," she said with a stern look that couldn't hide the twinkle in her eyes, "except in this chair." She ladled his soup while Hadley returned with a hefty tray of individual salads, which he quickly dispensed.

"You always did like him better than me," Bram said with a grin, squeezing Rosie's waist.

"That's because I'm a 'pretty boy,'" Jamie said with a smirk. "Just ask Cassie."

"You forgot 'yahoo.'" Bram dove into the chowder with gusto.

Jamie reached for the rolls, addressing Cassie with a wounded tone offset by laughter in his eyes. "Surely you didn't mean that, did you, Your Highness?"

"Oh, she meant it, all right," Alli said, popping a leaf of salad in her mouth. She swallowed and grinned, leaning forward to wink at Jamie at the other end of the table. "And it's up to you to change her mind, Jamie old boy, so good luck with that."

"Maybe I won't need luck," he said softly, smiling at Cassie from across the table.

Her cheeks warmed as his eyes fused to hers.

Slowly sipping his chowder, he studied her, his perfectly chiseled jaw shifting with every chew of the clams, then swallowed and took a sip of his water, eyeing her over the rim. "I have a talent for changing people's minds, you know."

And I have a talent for falling for skunks, but never again . . . Cassie stabbed at her salad a little too forcefully, meeting Pretty Boy's eyes in silent challenge. The heat of his gaze could have wilted the lettuce, but she had enough hurt in her heart to ice it right back up again. She assessed the serious intent of his eyes, the quiet confidence in the faint slope of his smile, the relaxed posture of broad shoulders in a man who expected to get his own way. At one time his sculpted good looks and quiet resolve would have melted all resistance, but not anymore. She speared a lettuce leaf and smiled, her manner as cool as her heart. Change her mind?

Not on your life, bucko.

6

Nose in the air, Alli turned a page in a pretend book with great drama, and Jamie's lips tipped in a smile. Alli had just acquired her teaching degree from San Francisco Normal School, but she missed her calling as far as he was concerned. *Look out, Sarah Bernhardt.*

"A book, a book!" Maddie shouted, bouncing up and down on Uncle Logan's knee with no little force, thrilled that she was allowed to participate in the grown-ups' game of charades.

Nodding furiously, Alli tapped her nose, then tugged on her ear. With a quick swipe, she leaned to tousle Blake's hair, mussing it till it poked up in several places.

"Hey, no fair using the opposition for your advantage," he groused, swatting her away.

"Mess up . . . dishevel . . . wrinkle . . ." Liddy fired guesses without mercy, perched on the edge of the sofa like a spring-propelled toy, ready to launch.

"Tousle, muss, rumple . . . ," Patricia called out, not to be outdone.

Alli jabbed at her nose and pulled on her ear before slapping three fingers on her arm.

"Third syllable!" Maddie announced with glee.

Alli stroked one arm as if touching silk.

Almost gritting her teeth, Liddy clenched her fingers. "Feel . . . touch . . . skin . . ."

"R-rumpelstiltskin!" Meg bounded up from the chair with a squeal.

Alli cheered while moans circled the room from the opposition, and Jamie glanced at his watch, noting that Cassie had slipped out to the powder room a while ago. Amidst all the clamor of gloating and boos, Hadley arrived as if on cue, bearing trays of apple tarts with coffee and tea.

Jamie leaned toward Bram, keeping his voice low. "Cover for me, will you? Cassie's been gone awhile, so I'm going to round her up for dessert."

"Sure you are," Bram said with grin. "You mean dessert for yourself."

With a slap of his friend's back, Jamie offered an off-center smile. "As fond as I am of apple tarts, buddy boy, Texas tart sounds pretty good right about now. Wish me luck."

"You're gonna need it, my friend. Don't say I didn't warn you."

Laughing, Jamie ducked into the foyer, grateful for the commotion that allowed him to sneak out without notice. He poked his head in the study, kitchen, and conservatory before passing the empty bathroom on his way up the stairs. A smile slid across his lips at a shaft of light peeking beneath the burlwood door of Liam McClare's prized billiard room where Jamie, Bram, and Blake spent much of their free time. He shook his head, his interest piqued now more than ever. Most women had no interest in billiards or spending time in such a masculine room. But then Cassie McClare, he was quickly discovering, was not most women.

Without a sound, he eased the knob and pushed the door ajar, his smile blooming into a grin. Cue skillfully aimed, she bent low over the table, affording Jamie a generous view. The crisp, clean sound of ivory striking ivory rang in the air followed by the softer ricochet of balls spinning into pockets. The lady was clearly no amateur, evident by her near-perfect stance—not too close to the table, left foot forward, right foot behind and body twisted for a clean stroke. The staccato crack of the balls held a magical rhythm—like the girl herself—as if cue, ball, and woman were a single entity, weaving a spell.

Lost in her game, she was oblivious when he quietly entered the room and closed the door, watching as she methodically chalked her stick after every shot before circling the table with all the ease of a pool-hall hustler. His jaw dropped when she executed a three-ball shot he'd only seen one other time in a bar down on the wharf. A low whistle escaped before he could stop it. "Holy cow, remind me not to play you for money."

Whirling around, she almost lost her balance, knuckles white on the cue and face leeched pale. "Thunderation, what is it with you and not knocking?" she rasped, bodice quivering with every breath.

"And interfere with that mesmerizing display of skill and prowess?" He slipped hands in his pockets and strolled in, his gait as casual as his smile. "The likes of which I've seldom seen in a man, much less a woman?" He perched on the edge of the table. "Not on your life, Miss McClare. Where'd you learn to play like that, anyway?" he asked, his fascination with this unconventional girl growing by the moment.

"Uncle Logan and my father," she said with a heft of her chin, his compliment dusting her cheeks with a pretty shade of rose that actually accentuated her freckles.

Jamie shook his head with a fold of arms. "Oh, no you didn't, at least not Logan. I've played many a game with him, and I have never seen a shot like that out of him or Blake."

The blush deepened. "Uncle Logan says I'm a natural," she said defensively.

He studied her through a squint, in total agreement that she was, indeed, a natural. Heart-shaped face, luminous green eyes a man could drown in, and hair the same soft pale yellow of the angel wing cactus that bloomed in Jess's window. Her creamy skin glowed with just enough freckles to give her that clean, wholesome air of the outdoors. After dinner, Logan had prompted her to sing while Alli played the piano, and never had Jamie been mesmerized by a voice so clear and true. He was certain the woman couldn't be from a cattle ranch in Texas, but from heaven instead. She possessed an almost angelic quality, and his eyes drank her in, following a shimmering stray from the pretty upsweep that framed her head like a halo. The silky curl traced the curve of her bodice, and he had a sudden urge to see her hair down, spilling as free as he suspected Cassie McClare liked to be, untethered by convention or fashion.

He rose and sauntered over to retrieve a cue, then casually twirled it in his hands, his eyes connecting with hers. He smiled that little-boy smile that had gotten him farther than any college degree. "He says the same about me, you know—in billiards, boxing, and the law."

She folded her arms, her smile as flat as the effect of his, apparently. "And women?"

He grinned, eyes never straying as he chalked his cue. "Sometimes. Up for a game?"

"With you?" She arched a brow. "No, thank you, I don't play games with men like you."

Ouch. She was obviously a woman who was honest and forthright, what you see is what you get, and so help him, what he saw, he definitely wanted. But . . . she didn't want him. *Yet.* He softened his approach. "Come on, Cassie, one game of eight ball isn't going to kill you, and then you'll have the chance to give me the thrashing I so richly deserve."

She hung her head and huffed out a sigh, finally meeting his gaze with a candid one of her own. "Mr. MacKenna—"

"Jamie—please."

"Jamie, then . . . ," she began slowly, as if attempting to ease the blow of what she was about to say. Sympathy radiated from those remarkable green eyes that reminded him so much of a pure mountain stream—unspoiled, refreshing. *And* icy enough to tingle the skin. Long lashes flickered as if begging him to understand. "Look, no offense, but you just broke my heart."

He blinked. "Pardon me?"

"Oh, not you exactly," she said, dismissing him with a wave of her hand, "but a man just like you—you know, handsome, smart, the kind that melts a woman with a smile?"

A ridge popped at the bridge of his nose. "Uh, thank you—I guess?"

She looked up then, head tilted in much the same way a mother might soothe a child, expression kind and tone parental. "Look, I'm sure you're a very nice person, Jamie MacKenna, and we may even forge a friendship before summer is through, but you need to understand something right now if that friendship is ever going to see the light of day." She took his hand in hers, patting it as if he were five years old, and in all of his twenty-five years, never had a woman given him a more patronizing smile. "You have zero chance . . ." She held up a hand, index finger and thumb circled to create an *O*, then enunciated slowly as if he were one of the livestock back on her ranch. "Zee-ro chance of *ever* turning my head because I have no interest in you or any man right now, especially a pretty boy." She gave him a patient smile edged with just enough pity to get on his nerves. "I'm sorry to be so blunt, but I see no point in hemming and hawing around a pesky hornet when I can just stomp on it before it stings."

His jaw sagged. "Hornet?" He'd been called a lot of things, but somehow, out of the pursed lips of this Texas beauty, this stung his pride more than the blasted hornet. A nerve pulsed in his cheek as he replaced his cue in the rack, his smile cool. "Is that so? And what makes you think I have any interest in turning your head?"

She folded her arms again and hiked one beautiful brow, daring him to deny it.

And, oh, how he wanted to. His jaw began to grind. But he couldn't because it would be a bald-faced lie, and they both knew it. He exhaled and pinched the bridge of his nose, finally huffing out a sigh. "Okay, you're right, Miss McClare—I was trying to turn your head. But I'm not stupid—I can see you obviously have no interest in me whatsoever."

"None," she confirmed, brows arched high in agreement.

He nodded, head bowed as he kneaded the back of his neck. "Which means, of course, there's no attraction whatsoever . . ."

"Oh, perish the thought." Her body shivered in apparent revulsion. "Not in a million years . . ."

He cocked his head, a trace of hurt in his tone. "Nothing—not even a glimmer?"

She shook her head, face scrunched as if she tasted something bad. "Good gracious, no."

He exhaled loudly. "All righty, then," he said with a stiff smile, his pride effectively trampled. Rubbing his temple, he supposed there was only one thing left to do. He extended his palm with a conciliatory smile. "Well, I'm glad we got that out of the way. So . . . friends?"

She stared at his hand as if it were a rattler about to strike, then shifted her gaze to his, lids narrowing the slightest bit. Absently scraping her lip, she tentatively placed her hand in his.

His fingers closed around hers and he smiled. *Ah, sweet vindication . . .*

In a sharp catch of her breath, he jerked her to him so hard, the cue in her hand literally spiraled across the plush burgundy carpet. Thudding against his chest, she emitted a soft, little grunt, and her outraged protest was lost in his mouth, the sweet taste of her lips shocking him even more than he had shocked her. She tried to squirm away, but he cupped her neck with a firm but gentle hold, deepening the kiss.

A grunt broke from his mouth when her foot nearly broke his ankle. "I'll tell you what, Miss McClare," he said through clenched teeth as pain seared his leg, "I'll give you feisty . . ."

"You . . . haven't . . . *seen* . . . feisty," she rasped, flailing in his arms. With another sharp jolt of pain, she cocked a very unladylike knee into his left thigh, stealing his wind while her words hissed in his face. "Oh . . . why . . . didn't . . . I wear . . . my boots . . . ?"

Because it's my lucky day? Jamie thought with a grimace, determined to prove the lady a liar, at least on the score of attraction. Body and mind steeled to win, he jerked her flush and kissed her hard while she pummeled his shoulders in a flurry of fists. All at once, her scent disarmed him—a hint of lilacs and soap and the barest trace of peppermint, and he stifled a groan while he explored the shape of her mouth, the silk of her skin, the soft flesh of her ear.

Relief flooded when her thrashing slowed and her body listed against his with a weak moan. He gentled his mouth, softly nuzzling before finally pulling away. Satisfaction inched into a smile when she swayed on her feet, eyes closed and open mouth as limp as her body. "Nope, not in a million years," he said, his breathing as shallow as hers. He planted a kiss to her nose.

Roused from her stupor, her eyes popped open in shock and she suddenly lunged, fury sputtering as she hauled back a fist, clearly hoping to dislocate his jaw. With all the grace and speed of his Oly Club boxing title, he skillfully ducked, chuckling when her tight-knuckled punch bludgeoned the air. Hands in his pockets, he made his way to the door, delivering a gloat of grin over his shoulder. "Well, I guess you have a deal, then, Cassie McClare—friends it is."

She spun around, eyes flashing. "You are nothing but a yellow-bellied snake of a womanizer, Jamie MacKenna, and if you ever lay a finger on me again, I'll hog-tie you so fast—"

He laughed, hand on the knob. "Come on, Your Highness, I did us both a favor—now that we know there's no attraction, we can be friends, right?"

"When polecats fly," she screamed, and he grinned, shutting the door with a wink.

Something hard crashed against the wood and he winced. "Yes, ma'am," he whispered to himself on his way down the hall. "Definitely the makings of a beautiful friendship."

7

Sweet thunderation! Where's a cattle prod when you need one?
Cassie sagged against the pool table, heart racing as if she'd just bulldogged a Texas steer. She put a shaky hand to her chest, certain the corset would pop given the heaving of her lungs. Closing her eyes, she attempted to rein in her temper, but the image of Jamie MacKenna kissing her senseless rose up so strong, she wanted to spit. With a tiny little shiver that felt *way* too warm, she flailed a hand to her mouth in an effort to sanitize her lips, sputtering as if the taste of him made her nauseous.

Roiling, puking, sick-to-her-stomach nauseous. And heaven help her, it did—but for all the wrong reasons. She put her head in her hands, wishing she could just retch, purging herself of any thought of that low and despicable kiss from that low and despicable man. The dominance of his arms, the warmth of his breath in her ear, the possessive touch of his hands. Instead of vomit, a low groan rose in her throat at the memory of the taste of his mouth—a mouth that had tamed her on the spot, stealing her thunder with a strike of lightning instead. Great balls of fire, even his scent seemed to linger—a hint of clove and spice from Bay Rum shaving soap and the trace of a Hershey bar snatched from the candy bowl in the parlour. She shivered again, the warm

Alli nibbled the edge of her smile. "I'm not saying Jamie can't *seem* like a womanizer—"

"Seem?" One of Cassie's brows shot up a full inch.

"Oh, all right—yes, Jamie can be a bit of a womanizer, just like Uncle Logan and Blake I suppose, but I promise, underneath that roguish veneer, he's really a pretty decent guy."

"A womanizer? Decent?" Cassie folded her arms in a huff. "I'll tell you what he is—he's a snake charmer, Alli, a man who charms every woman in sight, including you, apparently."

With a heft of her chin, Alli shot right back. "I'll have you know, Cassidy McClare, that that's not just my opinion, it's my brother's and Bram's too."

"Well, of course it is!" Cassie rolled her eyes. "They're men—they stick together."

Alli shook her head, lips pursed. "Maybe, but not when their sisters are at stake."

"What do you mean?" Cassie said, gaze suspicious.

"I mean that originally Blake hoped Jamie and I would hit it off because he hated Tom with a passion, and Blake would have never wanted that if Jamie were a true womanizer."

"So you say." Cassie flopped back in the chair, convinced that Jamie MacKenna was nothing more than a scalawag magician who had obviously cast a spell on Alli as well.

"No, I didn't say it—Blake said it." Alli sighed. "Told me flat-out I should show Tom the door and consider Jamie instead. Said Jamie's one of the most decent guys he's ever met other than Bram and a hard worker who'll go far in life. He worked three jobs to put himself through school, supports his mother and sister, and he's a champion boxer, who devotes what free time he has to teaching young boys on the street how to defend themselves."

Cassie's lip curled. "How 'bout the women he kisses—does he teach them too?"

"Oh, Cassie, stop! Jamie may be amorous, yes, but Blake says he's moral to a fault."

"To a fault?" Cassie's voice cracked as it climbed several octaves. She let loose with an undignified grunt. "Well, the 'fault' part I believe," she said, wondering how on earth any man could be considered "moral" when he practically seduced a woman within hours of meeting her.

"Yes, 'moral,'" Alli defended. "According to Blake, he seldom drinks even though he works part-time as a bartender on the Barbary Coast."

"A Barbary bartender who doesn't tip the bottle?" Cassie grunted again. "Ha!"

"It's true. Blake says Jamie only drinks Dr Pepper when they go out, so you see? His morals are above reproach."

"Oh, you mean like tonight?" Cassie said, tone sticky-sweet.

Alli giggled. "No, not like tonight with mere kisses . . ." She leaned in to whisper in Cassie's ear, the subject matter tinting her cheeks with a pretty blush.

Cassie's eyes rounded at Alli's secret, her cousin's blush obviously catching because Cassie's face burned so much, she thought she might peel. "Good grief, Allison McClare, how in the world would you be privy to information like that?"

Alli peeked at the door, lowering her voice to a near-whisper. "Because Blake told me. Apparently Jamie's mother was a dance-hall girl on the Barbary Coast who fell in love with Jamie's father at the age of fifteen, and the rat refused to marry her until after Jamie was born."

"Oh, no," Cassie said in a hush. Her heart turned over. "Jamie's illegitimate?"

"Shhh . . ." Alli shot another glance at the door. "Blake says Jamie doesn't want anyone to know but him and Bram. Apparently he's terribly ashamed of it, which is why he's worked so hard to get a law degree and make something of himself. Not only that, but Jamie's father was an alcoholic who died when Jamie was twelve, so now you know why Blake says Jamie's moral to a fault—the man refuses to overdrink or . . . ," she lowered her voice, "well, you know, with any woman before he puts a wedding band on her hand."

"Goodness," Cassie whispered, her anger seeping out. The memory of Jamie's brazen kiss haunted, and her body instantly tensed. She stood to smooth her dress. "Sorry, Al, I don't care how moral or upstanding the man is underneath his sheep's clothing, that one kiss told me he's as big a wolf as Mark and just as selfish, thinking only of himself." She started for the door.

Puffing out a sigh, Alli rose. "Yes, he's human, Cass—and, yes, I'm sure he thinks of himself." She paused. "But not before his mother and crippled sister."

Cassie turned, blood leeching from her face. "He has a crippled sister?"

Alli nodded, joining her at the door. "Run over by a horse and buggy when she was two and Jamie blames himself. Told Blake if he had only stayed with Jess like his mother had asked instead of playing with friends when the toddler had napped, she'd be normal today and painfree." Alli shook her head, sympathy lacing her tone. "For pity's sake, he was only a kid, Cass, and that kind of guilt is a heavy load for anyone to carry, much less a little boy." She released a heavy sigh. "Jess is pretty housebound now because of a limp that bothers her if she's on her feet too much, so she and Jamie's mother seldom go out, even though Mother has invited them here for dinner and holidays repeatedly over the years. I've only met them both two or three times—once at Jamie's graduation and then twice at Jamie's church, but Jess is a real beauty and the apple of Jamie's eye. I'll tell you what, Cass, it broke my heart when I saw her limp because she seems almost deformed, each step slow and feeble. I can't help but think that's part of the reason she stays away, because she's embarrassed and doesn't want to distress her brother. Whatever the situation, Blake says guilt is eating Jamie alive."

"Oh, that's awful . . . ," Cassie whispered.

A weary sigh parted from Alli's lips. "I know, but apparently Jamie's researched a new surgery that can repair Jess's damaged hip and alleviate her discomfort. Unfortunately, it's very expensive and has a ridiculous wait list, so Jamie's written dozens of letters to the Cooper Medical School, begging them to consider Jess for one of their few pro bono surgeries. Meanwhile he's saving up for the surgery himself despite Blake, Bram, and Uncle Logan all offering to help. Claims it was his negligence that crippled his sister, and it will be his hard work and sacrifice that frees her." Her eyes misted with tears. "His mother and sister are everything to him, Cass, and my heart breaks for him because they are poorer than poor, barely eking by in a boardinghouse close to the Coast."

"Oh, Alli, I . . . well, I didn't know . . ."

Alli slipped a hand to Cassie's waist. "So you see, Cuz, underneath that handsome, carefree façade, Jamie MacKenna really is a pretty wonderful guy." She gave her a little squeeze. "I wish you'd give him a chance because believe me—I wouldn't steer you wrong."

A smile trembled on Cassie's lips. "I know, Al, but I'm just not ready . . ."

Alli ducked, giving Cassie an impish smile. "He doesn't exactly repulse you, does he?"

Blood gorged Cassie's cheeks. She swallowed hard. "Not exactly."

Laughing, Alli pinched her, easing some of the tension in Cassie's chest. "I thought as much. For all your protest and flashing eyes, I sensed a spark between you two."

Cassie sniffed. "Yeah, well the next 'spark' may be the flash of gunpowder if he lays another hand on me anytime soon."

Alli grinned. "Just tell him you only want to be friends. Then when you get to know him and see what a great guy he is, you won't mind when he steals your heart."

As Alli opened the door, Cassie released a noisy sigh, then sucked in a bolstering swallow of air. She slid her cousin a grim smile. "Yes, well, when it comes to my heart, Cuz, it's not the stealing I have a problem with." The smile angled into a quirk. "It's the 'breaking' part I mind."

8

"Oh, Liam—sometimes I miss you so much it aches . . ." Closing her eyes, Caitlyn McClare leaned against the stone wall of her study veranda, face lifted to capture the sweet scent of a gentle wind from the bay as it fluttered the loose tendrils of her hair. The late summer night settled over the city like a mist, filling her senses with the haunt of the sea and the music of crickets and tree frogs. Somewhere the faraway shriek of train whistles and the groan of fog horns blended with the clang of trolley bells and music of steam pianos floating up from dance halls on the Barbary Coast.

Releasing a fragile sigh, Caitlyn opened her eyes to the sprinkle of lights throughout the Coast and Fisherman's Wharf. Mirrored in the inky waters, they shimmered and danced beside a mango ribbon of moonlight that striped San Francisco Bay. Moisture pricked in her eyes, and the lights blurred into a million hazy stars, whisking her decades away to the night on the wharf when Liam proposed.

The stepdaughter of one of the richest men in San Francisco, she'd been swept off her feet at barely seventeen by a handsome college boy named Logan McClare. Accepting his proposal of marriage with stars in her eyes, she enjoyed a close friendship with his older brother as well, never realizing the true depth of Liam's feelings. When Logan betrayed her with another woman, Caitlyn was crushed. The more spiritual and grounded of the two brothers, Liam had seen her through one of the most painful times of her life. Although Logan had begged forgiveness, she'd broken the engagement nonetheless, fearful she'd never be able to trust him again. Wild and worldly, Logan was nothing like Liam, the brother who offered something Logan could not—trust, a deep faith in God, and a friendship so true, it had mended her heart. In a whirlwind courtship, Liam proposed, a man of like mind and like faith, who promised to love, honor, and cherish her all the days of his life. A tear trailed her cheek. And he did.

Their marriage had been a comfortable one. Not tempestuous and passionate like her feelings for Logan, but gentle and sweet and a balm to her soul . . . and never had Caitlyn missed him more. Over a year and a half had passed since an aneurism stole him away, snuffing the light from her eyes as surely as it snuffed the breath from Liam's body. Only through the grace of God and the love of her children had she survived, finally coming to a place where she could embrace life again. *And* pursue a passion she'd shared with her husband—to purge their beloved city of the title of "the wickedest town in the USA," compliments of the Barbary Coast.

Hands firm on the marble balustrade, she stared off into the distance toward the sea and the seedy section of town, heart aching for the poor and misguided souls who called the Barbary Coast home. Before Liam died he was a key member on the Vigilance Committee to help eradicate blocks of opium dives, slave dens, brothels, parlourhouses, dance halls, barrooms, and concert saloons that tainted the city, an effort attempted twice before in the 1800s by the Vigilantes. Some called it Sodom and

Gomorrah, and although Caitlyn seldom stepped foot in the Coast, she knew it to be true from the stories Liam had told her. A lawyer like his brother Logan, Liam had been a driving force in the ongoing efforts to dismantle the Nymphia, a three-story brothel that fostered nudity, peep shows, and prostitution. Liam had been instrumental in the first police raid a year after it opened, spearheading legal battles to close the 150-cubicle bordello that had become a festering sore in an already downtrodden city.

Caitlyn swiped at her cheek, now slick with tears over the plight of so many. Tragic men, hopeless women, and innocent children who would not remain that way for long on the streets of the Coast. Children like Jamie MacKenna, one of the few who'd scratched and struggled to rise above the degradation with a dream for something better. Her heart warmed at the thought of her son's best friend, who had no idea that Blake's parents knew from whence he hailed. But the moment Logan had met him at the Olympic Club and introduced him to Liam, Jamie MacKenna had become a beacon of hope to both Liam and her, a shining example of what prayer and action could do to set people free from the death hold of the Barbary Coast.

"Oh, Liam, Jamie would make you so proud," Caitlyn whispered, the sea breeze cooling the tears on her face. "And God willing, I will too." Her thoughts returned to the decision she'd made after months of prayer, the words of her good friend, Walter Henry, echoing in her brain.

"Caitlyn, we need you on the committee, pure and simple," he'd insisted, one silver brow arched high. "We need your dignity, your grace, your passion for Liam's work. Please—don't let Liam's dream die. Pick up the baton, Cait, and run! With your husband's memory, his influence, and your faith, we can win and offer hope to thousands of poor souls who have no hope at all."

"Oh, Walter, I know nothing of politics and legalities—what can I possibly offer?"

He bent to kiss her hand, his fervor stirring the fervor in her soul. "Cait, we have all the knowledge and expertise we need ad nauseam. The one thing we lack is heart, and I know of none purer than yours, my dear. Mark my words—with you on this board, *nothing* can stop us."

Caitlyn stared into the summer night, her heart fluttering in her chest like the wind through her hair. *No . . . nothing except Logan McClare.*

Her eyes drifted closed at the thought of the one man who scared her more than any other. Liam's lawyer brother had battled the committee on every front, thwarting their efforts to clean up the Coast, and Cait had no desire to contend with him as well. Till now, Logan had always been courteous and respectful since her marriage to Liam, keeping his distance, and for that she was grateful. He'd been a godsend during Liam's funeral, despite being as catatonic as she, revealing a mourning for his brother she hadn't expected. Although he was known as a deadly opponent in the courtroom and on the political scene, Logan's one weak spot was clearly his family, and even when Liam was alive, her brother-in-law was a frequent visitor to their home, forging close relationships with each of her children.

Caitlyn relinquished a weighty sigh. *And, apparently, hoping for that with their mother as well.* Oh, he laid low for a while following Liam's death, certainly, providing friendship and counsel, but lately, something had changed. Suddenly Logan McClare, the man about town, became Uncle Logan, the man about her house more than she was comfortable with. Over the years, Logan had a standing invitation for Sunday dinners, to see his nieces and nephew, of course. But in the last six months, his visits had escalated until the girls were begging her to let him come to dinner three times a week, and Caitlyn could feel the tension of that request in the roiling of her stomach. Yes, her children needed their uncle, the only mature male influence in their lives. Cait's mouth crooked. That is, if one considered Logan McClare "mature," something with which she wasn't inclined to agree. She was increasingly concerned about his influence on her son, who thought Uncle Logan could do no wrong. In fact, Blake's cavalier attitude toward women reminded her so much of the Logan she almost married, that Cait had had more than one talk with Blake from college on, praying he would heed her concern. For decency's sake, Logan had no roots whatsoever except his love for her children, appearing in the society pages on the arm of a different woman every night of the week. Except, of course, the nights he was with her and her children. Suddenly he transformed from a free-wheeling bachelor to the consummate uncle, showering her children—and her—with undivided attention and love.

A tremor skittered through her that had nothing to do with the cool sea air. No, her brother-in-law scared the living daylights out of her. Despite almost twenty-six years in a companionable marriage with his brother and children who filled her days and nights with joy, she could feel it. Logan McClare was worming his way in—into her family and into her heart, and the very thought stole the breath from her lungs. He had a magnetism that called to her, commanded her to love him, and it took everything within to fight the pull he wielded. And the closer he got to her children, the closer he came to her, setting her on edge whenever he entered the room.

She braced her hands on the stone balustrade and scanned the heavens with frantic eyes. "Please—I cannot fall in love with Logan McClare. He's godless and ruthless and I can't trust him with my heart. Strengthen me, please, gird me with your grace and help me to withstand the onslaught of his charm, because, Lord, I am so very afraid . . . afraid to love him." The cool of the night shivered through her as more tears slipped from her eyes, and with a final quivery sigh, she slowly bowed her head, painful heaves rising in her throat. "Because the truth is," she whispered, the very words quaking her soul, "I fear I've never stopped . . ."

"Aunt Cait?" Cassie peeked out the French door of the darkened study, the frail sound of her aunt's weeping freezing the blood in her veins. "Is something wrong?

"Oh!" Aunt Cait spun around, swiping the tears from her face. "Nothing, dear, truly—just a little melancholy, that's all, thinking of your Uncle Liam. What are you still doing up?"

"Couldn't sleep." Cassie joined her aunt on the veranda. "I hoped some warm milk might help." She tightened the sash of her robe and looped an arm to her aunt's waist, sharing her mourning over a man who'd been so dear to them both. She tucked her head to her aunt's. "I miss him, too," she whispered, "but after the loss of Mark in my life—a man I loved for only a short time—I can only imagine the grief you must still bear after a lifetime of joy."

She felt rather than saw the lift of Aunt Cait's smile, and Cassie closed her eyes, allowing the soothing caress of the hand on her back to fill her with the comfort of home. Soft-spoken and sure, Aunt Cait possessed a magic like few others, able to lift a heart or calm a soul better than most, and that magic did not fail now. Peace settled on Cassie's mind like the hand caressing her back, Aunt Cait's tranquil tone and touch easing the tension of her body.

"It *was* a lifetime of joy," she whispered, her voice as soft and faraway as the lights flickering on the bay. "And I know deep down, Cassie, that God spared you with Mark Chancellor so he can bring a man who will cherish you like my Liam cherished me. A man like that is rare enough, but a man like that who loves God is a priceless treasure, and I hope you never settle for less." She searched Cassie's eyes. "Was Mark a man of faith?"

Cassie grunted, the sound harsh against the still of the night. "Faith in himself, yes, but in God?" She shook her head, bitterness bleeding into her words. "Oh, he attended church, prayed at meals, and said all the right things, but when we were alone?" Her laugh was grim. "Faith was the farthest thing from his mind." Her body shimmied from a chill, and Aunt Cait pulled her close. Cassie bowed her head, her next words tinged with shame. "So much that my own faith suffered as well. I was so in love with the man that I found myself allowing liberties I shouldn't have."

"Liberties?" Aunt Cait whispered, the barest hint of alarm in her tone.

"Oh, nothing immoral—I know better than that, but that didn't stop Mark from trying." She leaned on her aunt's shoulder, eyes trailing into a faraway stare. "But we'd cuddle and kiss on the porch longer than we should have because I was so crazy for him, I could barely say no." Her lip quirked. "And trust me, I said 'no' a lot because Mark was always pushing for more. I kept telling myself it was all right since we'd be married soon, but now I know it wasn't. Every kiss, every sweet nothing bonded my soul to his, making it so hard to forget him." Her eyes fluttered closed. "I pray I never get that close to a man again without a gold band on my hand."

"Good girl." Aunt Cait kissed her hair. "And the right man will wait, Cassie, not push for you to compromise your convictions."

"I hope so," she whispered.

"I *know* so." Aunt Cait's voice was gentle but firm. "Before your Uncle Liam, I was engaged to a handsome rogue much like yours, and I was just as moonstruck as you, finding it difficult to keep the young man in line." Her aunt's sigh feathered warm against Cassie's cheek, filling her senses with the wonderful scent of Pear's soap and lavender. "Fortunately, I broke the engagement, and when your Uncle Liam courted me, he was a perfect gentleman with a faith as deep as mine, so he treated me with respect, putting my wishes before his own."

"That's what I want, Aunt Cait, and I have no intention of settling for less."

"I'm glad, darling, because I promise you—there's no better way to guard your heart from heartbreak and the wrong man in your life than to follow God's precepts." She swept a stray strand from Cassie's face. "This is going to be a good summer, Cass. I feel it in my bones."

Cassie gave her a tight hug. "Thanks, Aunt Cait—I think so too." She cinched her robe a bit more snugly, then stifled a yawn. "Goodness, I may not need that milk after all."

"Good night, darling." Aunt Cait gave her shoulders a final squeeze. "Sweet dreams and may the angels keep the bad ones away."

"You, too, Aunt Cait." Cassie kissed her aunt's cheek and stole into the study, heaving a weary sigh when her aunt turned to stare out at the bay, head bowed as if something still weighed on her mind. *A common condition tonight*, she thought with a wrench of her heart, aching for her aunt as well as herself. Uttering a silent prayer for them both, Cassie mounted the steps, hoping that, indeed, the angels would keep the bad dreams away. Her lips tipped up while her gaze did the same. "And, Lord—if they can do the same for Mark Chancellor? So much the better . . ."

9

"C an't sleep?"

Cassie glanced up to see Uncle Logan striding down the second-story hallway, obviously from the billiard room where male laughter could be heard amid the crack of ivory. Her ears honed in on Jamie's voice, and much to her annoyance, her stomach did a little flip. Her smile lapsed into a scowl. "Nope. Counted sheep, steers, horses, pigs, and armadillos, but all I've got to show for it is an imaginary zoo, albeit odorless, thank heavens."

Swallowing her in an embrace, he kissed her head and tipped it up with a sympathetic smile, the scent of lime soap mingling with tobacco and a hint of port. He'd shed his coat and tie, shirtsleeves rolled to reveal muscled arms with dark hair while the black bristle on his jaw lent a pirate air. "You're a McClare, Cass—restlessness runs in our blood." He shot a quick glance down the stairs and lowered his voice. "Don't tell your aunt, but did you try warm milk with honey and bourbon? One of Nana's tricks that works for me every time."

The memory of her eighty-two-year-old great-grandmother warmed Cassie's heart like the bourbon would warm her throat, no doubt. Nana had been as unorthodox as Uncle Logan in her own shocking way, and a source of utter joy to Cassie and her cousins. She grinned. "Only one of many tricks as I recall," Cassie said, her smile melancholy. "But no, I haven't, although I was actually on my way down to get some warm milk," her smile tipped, "*without* the bourbon, when I noticed Aunt Cait on the veranda. We chatted and now I'm ready to turn in."

Her uncle's gaze darted downstairs, brows in a scrunch. "Cait's still up? I thought she only had five or ten minutes of paperwork before heading to bed."

"Me too," Cassie said, "but she probably just wanted to enjoy the night air." She nodded down the hall. "You're calling it quits? Sounds like the party's just getting started."

He glanced behind him and grinned. "It is. We have a very volatile billiards tournament going on, and I'm in charge of reinforcements." He leaned close. "But, if you can't sleep, I'd pay good money to see you take Jamie down a peg or two. The man's downright cocky since he's fleeced both Blake and me, and now he has poor Bram in his sights."

A full-fledged grin eased across her lips. "Believe me, Uncle Logan, there's nothing I'd rather do than de-peg Mr. MacKenna, but I'm not dressed for pretty-boy humiliation."

Chuckling, Logan tweaked a loose curl on her shoulder. "You oughta take it easy on the man, Cass. Other than his propensity to cockiness at boxing or pool, he's not so bad."

"So I've heard," she said with an off-center smile. "And I hope to make him even better with a hefty dose of humility." She kissed his cheek. "Good night, Uncle Logan. See you soon?"

He tapped her nose. "If your aunt doesn't change the locks first. G'night, Cass." Logan watched her ascend to the third level, his heart swelling with pride as if she were his own daughter. She certainly could have been—she was a McClare through and through—gutsy, determined, smart, and no-nonsense, a combination he admired. His thoughts veered to Caitlyn as he descended the steps. *Not unlike Cait*, he mused, all the more deadly wrapped in a gentle and graceful package. His pulse sped up as he approached the open French doors where moonlight spilled in along with the salty scent of the sea and Cait's pillar roses from the garden below.

She was nothing but a silhouette in the dim glow of a quarter moon, casually reclined on her wrought-iron settee. Still as a statue, she sat back, head resting and arms folded, seemingly entranced by the glimmer of the bay. Pale moonlight made her glow like the purest of alabaster, caressing her skin like he longed to do. *You were such a fool,* he berated himself for the thousandth time, first for cheating on her and then for ever letting her go. But he'd been too young and too stupid to realize no other woman could even come close to the rare gift he'd once held in his arms, nuzzled with his lips, treasured in his heart. A bitter lesson learned far too late, stealing his joy far too long. His jaw ground to rock. *But not anymore.* No, Liam may have had the privilege of loving her for almost twenty-six years, and rightfully so. But now it was his turn, and he would *not* lose her a second time. He unrolled the sleeves of his shirt and rebuttoned the cuffs, watching her with the same fierce determination that served him as one of the city's most respected lawyers. She *would* be his someday, he vowed. His mouth crooked. *Once I win her back, that is* . . . He sucked in a deep breath and opened the door. "Cait?"

She jerked so fast, she actually rattled the settee, a clear indication his presence rattled her as well. He couldn't help the smile that twitched on his lips, her wide eyes and parted lips evidence that he was making headway. He obviously made her nervous, a new development that hadn't been evident before—not during her marriage to his brother nor after his death. But in the last six months? Oh, yeah, Caitlyn McClare was on her guard and that could only mean one thing. His smile eased into a grin. She was scared to death of her feelings. He closed the screen door behind him. "What are you doing out here in the dark?"

She cleared her throat and lifted her chin in that defensive way she had when he got too bossy ... *or* too close. "Oh, more paperwork than anticipated, but I just finished and I'm afraid the sea breeze lured me out." She rose, obviously intending to make a clean getaway, feigning a yawn that was hardly convincing. "Goodness, it's late and I'm exhausted. I best head up."

He stayed her arm with a hand as she tried to pass and didn't miss the slight catch of her breath. "Cait, can we talk?" His palm slid to her wrist, gently kneading. "Please?"

Tendons in that deliciously creamy neck tightened when she swallowed, body tense as she stepped back. Nervously buffing her arms, she gave a little shrug before offering a wavering smile. "It can't wait? I'm so tired right now, my mind is pure mush."

He grinned, tugging her over to the settee with a coax in his tone. "Actually 'mush' is right where I need you, Mrs. McClare, since I have favors to ask. Between your mush and my legal skills of persuasion, I just may win this case."

He eased her down on the settee, then sat beside her, biting back a smile when she scooted over. Body stiff, she faced him, arms crossed at her waist. "All right, Logan. What is it?"

Tamping down his humor, he shifted to speak, his pose relaxed despite jitters in his stomach. He draped an arm over the settee and studied her, his manner sober. "Cait, it's no secret that you and your children are the most important things in my life ..."

She shot to her feet. "Logan, I'm sorry, really, but I'm very tired ..."

"What I have to say won't take long, I promise." Skilled in the art of wooing a jury, he infused a touch of humility in his tone. "Surely you can spare a few moments?"

He attempted to draw her back and she shook her head. "All right," she said, arms clutched as if it were the dead of winter while she eased to the wall. "But I prefer to stand."

"That's fine," he said quietly, sinking back into the settee. He was silent for several seconds as he watched her, her body rigid against the balustrade. Moonlight eclipsed her like a halo, and the shadows in her face could not obscure the wariness in her eyes. Drawn to her as always, he fought hard to stop himself from jumping up and pulling her into his arms, telling her how much he wanted her, needed her. But she would bolt faster than a fawn in a forest afire, and that was the last thing he wanted. Exhaling softly, he massaged the bridge of his nose, his voice edged with fatigue. "Cait," he began again, tone as calm and controlled as if he were addressing a difficult client. "Family means everything to me, and now that Cassie is here for the summer, I'd very much like to be able to come over more than once a week."

She blinked, jaw distended enough for him to notice. "That's it? That's the favor—to come over more often while Cassie is here?"

Her chest slowly expanded and released as she visibly relaxed, and he clamped his lips to thwart the smile that itched. *Good grief, did she think I was going to propose?* No lawyer worth his salt would offer a proposition like that without perfect timing and emotional groundwork being laid. And everyone knew, from Nob Hill to the Barbary Coast, that Logan McClare was worth his salt and then some.

He perched on the edge, hands loosely clasped. "Well, the first one, anyway."

"Oh." A muscle quivered in her throat. "What else?"

He huffed out a sigh and peered up, head cocked to assess her with a frank gaze. "I want to do things with the kids this summer—bring them to my Napa estate for a picnic, take 'em to Sutro Baths for the day, dinner and dancing at The Palace Hotel and then to the Cliff House. You know, things like the Buffalo Bill Wild West Show the first week in August?" Pausing, he sat up straight with brows bunched. "Wait—will Cassie still be here then?"

A smile softened her lips as she nodded, giving him one of those sweet looks that melted his heart—the kind she gave Blake and the boys whenever they did something she thought was adorable. His heart swelled with love, this time forcing a dip in his own throat.

She leaned back to the wall, arms resting on either side. That remarkable lavender dress swished as her hip shifted to bear her weight on one leg while the other relaxed, knee bent to butt a delicate slipper to the bottom of the wall. A rose-scented breeze played with tendrils of her hair, fluttering it against the curve of a neck he craved to caress with his mouth. He could sense rather than see the sparkle in those gentle aquamarine eyes, eyes that could make a man sell his soul for the sake of love. He sucked in a deep swallow of air.

Like me.

Her voice was soft with just a hint of her Bostonian accent that slipped out whenever she was at ease. "Quinn and Virginia don't know it yet, but Cassie hopes to teach in San Francisco for a year or two." Her smile turned melancholy. "A fresh start to put the past behind."

He studied her in silence before slowly rising to his feet, closing the distance to stand beside her. Hip to the wall, he casually traced the smooth edge of the marble balustrade with his palm.

"Yes, a fresh start," he said, following the motion of his hand until the tips of his fingers brushed hers. He peered up beneath lidded eyes when she quickly pulled away, arms barricaded to her waist in emotional defense. "Which brings me to my last favor, Cait," he whispered, voice huskier than intended. "It's been almost two years—don't you think you could use a fresh start too?"

"No . . . ," she whispered, shaking her head hard. "It feels like yesterday that Liam . . ." Her words broke on a heave as tears shimmered in the moonlight. "I'm just not ready . . ."

"Aw, Cait . . ." Before she could stop him, he cocooned her in his arms, his own grief over the past becoming one with her own. She attempted to pull away, body unyielding as her muffled sobs quivered against his chest, but he tightened his hold, gentle but firm while he stroked her hair. "I can't stand to see you in pain," he said, his voice hoarse, "so let it all out. Go ahead and thrash and cry and rail against the gods for the loss of someone you loved, but don't let it eat you alive." He bent his head to hers, the sound of her weeping slicing him open, exposing a love for her so deep and so raw, it shocked him to the core. Her body wracking against his, she allowed him to lead her to the settee where she wept in his arms. When her quivers subsided, he handed her a handkerchief, smiling when she sniffed and blew her nose like a little girl. "Feel better?" he whispered, thumb grazing the edge of her jaw.

She nodded and sniffed again, eyes glazed with sorrow as they trailed to the bay, lost in a faraway stare. "I miss him, Logan . . . so much."

"Me, too, Cait," he said quietly. *More than you know.* Missed forgiving his brother before it was too late . . . and missed the closeness they'd once shared so very long ago.

Before the woman in his arms had torn them apart . . .

His mind in a fog that surely matched Cait's, he absently feathered the curls at the nape of her neck, his thoughts as melancholy as hers. She didn't seem to notice, so lost in her soulful reverie was she, sagging against his chest with a wispy sigh. "S-sometimes," she whispered, voice thick with remorse, "I still get angry at him, as if he had any say in leaving . . ."

He drew in a deep breath, barely aware as he gently kneaded the back of her neck. "I know, I wrestle with that too." He exhaled. "Among other things . . ."

With a catch of her breath, she pulled quickly away. "Oh, Logan, I'm so sorry—I shouldn't be burdening you like this."

He angled a brow. "Do you feel better?"

She paused before a faint smile tipped the edge of her mouth. "You know, I believe I do."

He gave her hand a light squeeze. "Well, then, that's what friends are for." Gaze fused to hers, he skimmed her knuckles with the pad of his thumb, wanting more than anything to pull her into his arms and whisper his love in her ear. But if he learned anything in law school, it was that timing was key, and Caitlyn McClare was too important, too special—too critical to his happiness—to risk botching it like before. And so he caressed her face with his eyes instead, stroking her cheek, tracing her lips in his mind, loving her vicariously through his thoughts. Until she finally belonged to him. And it was coming. Oh, yes, it was coming . . .

Patting her hand, he rose and pulled her with him, nudging her to the door. "You look beat, Cait, better get some sleep."

He opened the screen, and she hurried through, turning halfway when he clicked it behind her. "You're not coming in?" she asked, perfectly sculpted brows inched up in surprise.

"Nope." Nodding toward the second story, he reached in his jacket for a cigarette from a gold monogrammed case, giving her a little-boy grin. "I know you don't like me to smoke in the house, and I don't indulge all that much anymore, but I need a break. Especially after getting my clock cleaned in pool by one of your boys. But don't worry, I'll lock up when I'm done."

She studied him with a soft look that held traces of affection, surprise, and wonder. "Thank you," she whispered. Her head tilted, and in the moonlight, she looked like that same innocent girl he'd fallen in love with. His throat suddenly ached. Truth be told, she still was, and the pull she wielded was so powerful, he felt his rib cage constrict. Her tender smile did funny things to his gut. "And I'm not worried," she whispered, her next words packing a wallop. "Because I trust you, Logan. Good night."

"G'night, Cait." Snapping the case open and shut, he put a cigarette in his mouth before lighting it with a shaky hand, figuring he'd need the whole blasted thing to calm him back down. He took a sharp inhale and blew it out, the weight and meaning of her words abundantly clear, at least to him if not to her. Elbows on the balustrade, he stared out at the shimmering bay, the tip of his cigarette glowing red in the night. Trusting him once had been her biggest mistake. He slowly exhaled, his thoughts drifting like the curls of smoke that rose in the sky. He'd make good and sure trusting him twice wouldn't be her second.

10

A low whistle slipped from Jamie's lips. "Holy thunder, Abraham, would you look at those gams!" He swallowed hard, his tongue as dry as the mountains of sand dredged out by Sutro Baths on the far side of the shore.

San Francisco's premiere indoor swimming facility was abuzz with people enjoying seven seawater and freshwater pools beneath a four-story glazed roof of 100,000 panes of stained glass. Sunlight dappled the people and water below with rainbow colors while children splashed and played with parents and friends. The pools fairly shimmered with activity like a sea of minnows, from bathers milling on the platforms to swimmers flying high on toboggan slides, swings, flying rings, and trampolines. The crash of the surf on the rocky shore outside filtered in between the laughter and shrieks of children of all ages, each and every one thrilling to Adolph Sutro's man-made wonder. The largest and most magnificent bathhouse in the world, San Francisco's top summer attraction lured people far and wide, a veritable Atlantis where ten thousand bathers could experience a love affair with the sea all at one time.

A love affair, indeed, Jamie thought with a race of his pulse, but not with the sea. Despite the buzz and hum of this water wonderland, his gaze was fused solely on Cassidy McClare, the breath in his lungs heaving to a stop the moment she stepped from the ladies' locker. Even in Sutro Baths' standard black woolen rental bathing suits, she was a vision, sporting a thigh-high hem striped with white that showcased the most beautiful legs he'd ever seen. He sucked in a sharp breath and shook his head. *Heavenly days, I'm in love!*

"Hey, you ogling my cousin, MacKenna?" Blake said in a tease, palming seawater into Jamie's face as he, Bram, and Jamie sat on the side of the pool. Feet dangling in the water, the three men fared better than most in Sutro's standard issue of black men's one-piece rental suits, revealing broad shoulders and hard-muscled bodies honed to intimidation at the Oly Club gym.

A low chuckle rumbled from Bram's throat. "Oh, he's doing more than ogling." He brushed a fly from his shoulder. "Trust me, Mac has designs on Cass for ogling and more."

Jamie flicked a handful of water at Bram, a hint of annoyance in his tone. "What are you talking about, Hughes, Cassie and I are just friends."

"Sure you are," Bram said with a grin. "I've never seen you this far gone over a 'friend' before, and since it's Blake's cousin, I figure he has a right to know."

"Know what?" Blake gave Jamie the eye. "You smitten with our Texas girl, Mac?"

Sliding Bram a thin gaze, Jamie cuffed the back of his neck as he shot Blake a sheepish look. "You could say that, or in Texas vernacular, you might say I'm hog-tied in love."

Blake grinned and slapped Jamie's back. "Well, I have no problem with you being in the family. May as well be, as much as you eat us out of house and home."

Jamie gritted his teeth, gaze roving to where Cassie and her cousins were making their way over. "Just one problem, Blake. When it comes to men, she's as skittish as a newborn colt. It's taken weeks for her to even talk to me, and the only way I could get her to be civil was to tell her I just wanted to be friends."

"Which is nothing but a brazen lie," Bram said with a chuckle. He thumped the side of Jamie's head. "How's it feel, MacKenna, not to have a woman swoon at your feet?"

Jamie slapped his hand away, flashing some teeth. "More like you mortals, I guess. I'll tell you what, though, it sure helps me to understand you a lot better, Hughes."

"Well, you must be making some headway." Blake squinted at Cassie out of the corner of his eye as she chatted with Alli. "Seems she's been a lot less crusty with you lately."

"Yeah, she has," Jamie said with a soft smile. "Which means just a few more weeks of friendship, and then I make my move."

Blake skewed him with a look. "Your *move*? With *my* cousin?"

Jamie grinned. "Purely legitimate, McClare—nothing more than a kiss to convince her we've moved beyond friends. I'm not stupid enough to pull anything funny with a girl like her, trust me. Good grief, the woman would rope and brand me if I got fresh, which I have to admit—" he offered a crooked grin—"would be well worth the risk."

Maddie skipped forward, an auburn pigtail bouncing off the wide straps of her black skirted swimsuit. "Alli says we're going to play Marco Polo," she said with a clap.

"You bet we are," Alli said. "Any takers?" She propped her hands on the hips of her full-skirted black rental bathing suit.

"The sooner we get in the water, the better," Cassie said, tugging at the cinched waist of her suit, emphasizing a shapely body that left Jamie tongue-tied. "These things are itchy."

I know the feeling, Jamie thought with a garbled clear of his throat. The "itch" to know Cassidy McClare better was driving him *crazy*. Hopping to his feet, he leisurely stretched arms overhead, bending side to side to loosen up for the game. "Let's do it, then—I'll be Marco."

Bram jumped up. "I guess we know who's going lose *this* game," he muttered, his grin annoying Jamie to no end. He ambled over to tug on Meg's saffron-colored braid before latching a brotherly arm over her shoulders. "Stick with me, Bug, and I'll keep the bad shark away."

Meg giggled, cheeks tinged pinker than sunburn. With an adolescent crush that was obvious to everyone but Bram, it was a toss-up as to which glowed more—her eyes or her face.

"Come on, squirt, you're with me." Blake scooped Maddie up with a nuzzle to her neck that produced a joyous squeal. "Hold your nose, kiddo, we're going in . . ." The squealing ended with a loud splash when Blake jumped into the waist-high pool with his little sister, prompting a peal of giggles when she popped back up in his arms.

"Last one in the water is the backside of a baboon!" Cassie leapt into the pool as gracelessly as possible, legs flailing and wisps of gold trailing from a happily haphazard chignon. A smile eased across Jamie's lips, and he followed suit, making a beeline to where Cassie was splashing with Bram and Blake. "Oh, here's the baboon now," she teased, turning on him with a slap of water before darting behind Bram for protection.

His approach slow and methodical, Jamie supplied a challenging smile. "I wouldn't be hanging your hat on him, Sugar Pie," he said in the lazy Texas drawl he'd perfected to get under her skin. "Because when I'm through with you, Cowgirl, that pretty face is gonna make a baboon's backside look plum pale." He lunged around Bram, but the little brat was slicker than a minnow's ear, hurtling away to hide behind Blake and Maddie, who promptly cheered her on.

"Come on, City Boy, no stalling." Cassie gave a sassy sway of hips. "*Or* cheating."

"I beg your pardon," he said with a hand to his chest. "I don't *have* to cheat."

"Except at tennis," Blake said with a chuckle.

"Only because it doesn't take any brains, McClare." Jamie swooped a swell of water in Blake's direction, causing Maddie to squeal and kick on his shoulders.

"No, just brawn, which you're short on too." Bram grinned, bracing Meg's shoulders.

"I got all the brawn I need in my fists," Jamie said with a cocky smile, "which, may I remind you, won you and Big Mouth over there many a bet at the Oly Club."

"Uh, excuse me, 'Marco,'" Alli said with a superior lift of her brow, "for someone calling others a 'big mouth,' you're sure jawing a lot. Can we get started before I shrivel into a prune?"

"Too late." Blake tugged on her sagging suit, which was too big for her petite frame.

"Okay, everybody, you best scatter." Jamie closed his eyes and waded through the water with a confident air. "Because even blind, I'm dangerous—Marco!"

"Polo!" Shouts split the air, and Jamie grinned, honing in on a sassy feminine voice to his right. He sloshed on with one goal in mind: to get his hands on Cassidy McClare. "Marco!"

"Polo!" Voices rang out, along with chuckles and the wild swish of water, none of which could throw him off track from the throaty giggle of a sea nymph with a Texas drawl.

Easing forward, he could almost feel her nearby, his senses alert to the gentle lapping of water from someone attempting to back away. "Marco!"

"Polo . . ."

He grinned. Her feeble response signaled a stealthy attempt at escape. Victory coursed through his veins as he shouted, his cry that of a warrior in battle. "Marco!"

There was no giggly response this time, only a squeal and a thrash of water when she lunged away, but his swim skills had been finely tuned at the Oly Club, where he'd swum many a lap in the water-polo pool. He dove with eyes wide, those beautiful legs floundering in a futile attempt to flee. For several pulse-pounding seconds she wrestled wildly in a blur, and he would have grinned if he could have done so without taking in seawater. He looped her at the waist and shot straight up in a gush of foamy water, his grin breaking free. Unwilling to let go, he held her longer than necessary, her body flush to his while she spit and swiped at her eyes. Mouth to her ear, he couldn't resist. "A baboon's backside has nothing on you right now, Cowgirl."

"So help me," she sputtered, elbowing him till he released her with a grunt. She spun around to kick him in the shins, but the water slowed the impact, so she finished him off with a knee to his left thigh.

"Ouch," he said with a groan. He massaged his leg with a grimace that wasn't all pretend. "What is it with you and that bony knee of yours? You can't pick a different thigh to gouge? This one's still blue from the last time."

"Good!" She gave him a playful shove. "Serves you right, Mac-Kenna. You are just not happy unless you're manhandling somebody, are you, you overgrown bully?"

He offered a lopsided grin as soppy as the itchy woolen bathing suit matted to his water-slick chest. "Nope, I'm a 'man,' and heaven knows I do like to 'handle,' so I'd say you're it, Cowgirl." His drawl managed to coax a semblance of a smile from those wet, pouty lips.

"Hey, MacKenna!" Alli said, hands on hips. "It's water tag, Pretty Boy, not wrestling at the Oly." She winked at Cassie. "Bet you wish you had that mangy lasso right about now, don't you?"

Cassie pushed a wet strand of hair out of her face. "You have no idea." Lips pursed, she zoned in on Blake, water lust in her eyes. "You're next, McClare."

"Hey, why me? I've got an innocent child on my shoulders." Blake took several steps back, hands gripped tight to Maddie's stubby legs. "Tell her, Maddie."

The little imp actually wiggled in delight, little hands pasted across her brother's eyes. "Ooooo—get him, Cass—it'll be fun!"

Jamie grinned. "If you can tell which one's the little girl."

Cassie laughed, green eyes as thin as pine needles. "You're next, MacKenna, if I can't get Blake, so don't get too comfortable."

Don't I wish. Jamie gave her a smug smile, but his heart was pounding harder than the surf outside the Baths. He slogged over to Bram and Meg, leaning close to Bram's ear. "Marco Polo is now officially one of my favorite games," he whispered.

"Prone to contact sports, are you?" Bram cupped his hands to his mouth, responding to Cassie. "Polo!"

Jamie lowered his voice so Meg couldn't hear. "You bet. It's all I have till I can court the woman right and proper."

"Give it time, Mac," Bram said, backing away from Meg for privacy. "The girl's battle worn and gun-shy, so you'll have to take it real slow."

"Tell that to my heart." Jamie's smile took a twist. "Polo!" He muffled his voice, eyes never straying from Cassie. "The woman's everything I want, Bram—smart, sassy, beautiful, funny—and the icing on the cake? A McClare. A family so wealthy and politically connected, we'll all be living on Nob Hill as one big, happy family before the little MacKennas arrive." He released a slow, wavering breath. "The truth? I couldn't have dreamed anyone better suited for me—Polo!"

Bram studied him with a wary eye. "Cassie is a catch, Mac, no doubt about that, but don't rush into anything, please. Give her time to see if it's what she wants too."

"Oh, she'll want it all right," he muttered, jaw steeled. "You know me, Padre—when I make up my mind to go after something, it's as good as done."

Bram paused, his eyes suddenly serious as Cassie lunged for Blake. "I know, but for all her cowhide exterior, Cassie's heart is too vulnerable right now for you to rush her just because it's what you want. And you may think she's the woman for you, but you need to be fair to Cassie and give her time to make the decision for herself."

"I don't have time," Jamie said, his tone suddenly hard. He thought of his sister, her crippled hip denying her the life she was meant to live, and had no inclination to wait. Cassie McClare was not only his ticket to true love, but she was his sister's chance at an operation and *his* chance to make political and financial strides. "Sorry, Bram—but I know in my gut she's the woman I need." He watched as she scooped Maddie up in her arms, the two of them giggling and drenched to the bone. Setting her little cousin down, she commenced to somersaults while his heart did the same. *And the woman I want?* She shot from the water like a sea nymph, water sluicing down the most fascinating woman he'd ever known, wet or dry. Jamie's Adam's apple dipped in his throat. *Oh, yeah . . .*

Sweet Texas tea, I could get used to this! Breathing in the scent of the sea, Cassie stretched on the sundeck with a lazy smile, soaking in the afternoon sun that radiated through the panes of glass overhead. She lay there with eyes closed, feeling the vibration of people running and walking on the wood decking, hearing the rustle of potted palms lining the railing beside her. Loud splashes of water were punctuated with shrieks of children and the laughter of a group of girls sunbathing a few feet away. The smell of seawater on damp wood merged with the pungent smell of wet wool from thousands of waterlogged bathing suits. It reminded her of wet dog, and homesickness struck at the thought of her golden retriever, Gus. From there, her mind veered to Mama and Daddy, causing her to miss them so much, she vowed to write a letter after dinner.

Out of nowhere, the smell of popcorn taunted and she sniffed a deep breath, causing her stomach to rumble. *Oh, crumb! I should have gone to the concession stand with everyone else.*

Something flicked off her face, and she swatted, guessing it to be a fly. It landed in her hair, and she batted several times, hoping to shoo it away. It tickled the hollow of her throat and she scowled with a slap at her neck. "Thunderation, go bother somebody else, you little pest!"

"Can't. Nobody's as fun to torment."

Jolting up, Cassie shaded her eyes, squinting up at a "pest" who was anything but "little" as he towered over her with a devilish smile. A piece of popcorn hit her square on the nose, bouncing off before she realized what it was. Her mouth tipped. "If you value your life, MacKenna, you best start aiming for my mouth—I'm starved."

A kernel ricocheted off her teeth, and his husky chuckle made her mouth go dry, as much from the look in his eye as from the popcorn. "It helps if you open it for something other than lame threats, Miss McClare."

Her eyes narrowed. "Let me get my lariat, Mr. MacKenna, and I'll show you lame." Her jaws extended wide, and popcorn pelted the back of her throat. She grinned, mouth watering around the salty morsel. "Mmm . . . not bad for a pretty boy."

He gave her a mischievous grin. "You should see my other skills."

She wished the heat in her face was sunburn, but she knew better. And apparently so did he because he chuckled before dropping to sit beside her, muscled legs tented as he handed her the popcorn. "Better be careful, Cass, your face is getting red."

She snatched the bag, miffed when more blood scorched her cheeks. "Thank you," she muttered, rattled by his close proximity. She averted her eyes from thickly sculpted arms to hard-muscled legs, painfully aware her "sunburn" was getting worse by the moment. "Where are the others?" she asked, anxious to divert attention. Spending time with Jamie MacKenna as friends in a group was one thing. Lying beside him alone on a sparsely populated sundeck in bathing suits was something else altogether. Suddenly Cassie was painfully aware of her bare legs and tucked them to her side, wishing the others would return soon.

"Blake was hungry, so he talked everyone into snacks." He grabbed the towel draped over his shoulder and bunched it into a pillow, then lay down with hands to the back of his neck, biceps bulging and legs crossed at the ankles. "I decided to take pity on you with popcorn." His tone held a tease. "Seemed like the gentlemanly thing to do for a friend."

A friend, yes. She chanced a peek at narrow hips, a washboard stomach, and broad shoulders that stirred a dizzy swirl in her middle, none of which had to do with the bobbing of the deck. *A dangerous proposition, indeed,* she thought with a shaky exhale. Oh, he'd apologized for his outrageous behavior in the billiard room that night, over and over to be exact, but the damage was done. Almost as if the low-down varmint had branded her brain on purpose, the memory of his kiss so powerful, she'd go weak at the mere thought. Her lips went flat. And the way they were pasted together when they'd vaulted from the water after Marco Polo? Great balls of fire, her legs were so limp, she would have sunk like an anchor if he hadn't held her up, making friendship with this man a risky venture for sure.

Eyes closed, he thrust his formidable chin in an apparent effort to capture the rays of the sun, giving her the courage to study him unaware. He was, undeniably, the most handsome man she'd ever seen, even more so than Mark, and that was saying something. Thick, dark lashes entirely too long for a male rested against a perfectly sculpted face that even at this early hour hinted at the shadow of a dark beard. Damp curls feathered in the breeze, giving him a reckless air only enhanced by full, wide lips edged with the barest of smiles. No, he was entirely too beautiful to be trustworthy and too masculine to be above suspicion—something she'd learned the hard way, and she wasn't about to make that mistake again. She breathed in deeply, willing herself to be calm despite the flutters in her stomach. Friendship with Jamie MacKenna may be a risky venture, but it was far better than the alternative, and she had little choice since he was Blake's best friend.

He chose that moment to open his eyes, and blood gorged her cheeks when he caught her staring. Clearing her throat, she quickly scooted against a potted palm in front of the railing, tucking her legs beneath the skirt of her suit. Bag in her lap, she placed several kernels in her mouth, striving for nonchalance. "So . . . you met Blake and Bram in law school or college?"

Shifting to his side, he propped his head on his elbow to peer up beneath those ridiculous lashes. "Neither—met 'em at the Oly Club where I worked during college. It's their influence—with your Uncles Logan and Liam—that helped me get a foot into Stanford where the three of us attended law school. You might say I owe Blake and Bram my life—they're not only the best friends I've ever had, they're the only ones."

He opened his mouth wide to indicate he wanted popcorn, looking so much like a baby bird waiting for a worm that Cassie grinned as she aimed. He snapped the popcorn midair before gulping it down with a smile. "Mmm . . . good at billiards, poker, and target-throwing." His smile veered wayward. "You good at everything you do, Cowgirl?"

She scrunched her nose. "Mostly, if you exclude men." She squinted and took aim at his mouth again, anxious to steer the conversation away from herself. "The only friends you've ever had?" she inquired in jest. "What, too busy wooing girlfriends to make time for the male variety?"

He captured the kernel with a firm click of perfectly white teeth. "Nope, too busy studying and working three jobs to make any friends—male or female." He held out a cupped palm, and she poured popcorn in, a piece of which he promptly tossed in the air and caught with his mouth. "You know, that's the third time you've accused me of having a girlfriend, Cass, but the truth is I've only dated a handful of women because I simply haven't had time before now."

She stopped mid-chew. "Now, why do I find that so hard to believe?"

Another kernel popped in the air, and he caught it with ease. "I don't know—maybe because you've got me pegged as nothing more than a pretty-boy womanizer?"

A piece of popcorn lodged in her throat, and she began to

hack, prompting him to jump to his knees and tap her on the back. "You okay?"

She waved him away, quite sure her "sunburn" bordered on heatstroke. Sucking in a deep breath, she peeked up with a guilty smile.

He laughed, the sound warm and intimate despite the other sunbathers scattered across the deck. Sprawling on his side again, he gave her a boyish grin that made her stomach somersault like the kids in the pool. "That's okay—I had you pegged as a spoiled princess with a burr in your saddle, so we're even. And," he said with a zag of his brow, "both of us apparently wrong." He tossed another piece of popcorn, chomping it with a firm clamp of his jaw. "Besides, what else were you supposed to think when I so brazenly sealed our friendship with a kiss?"

"Exactly," she said, attempting to swallow the lump in her throat. "Besides, Alli says you have a penchant for senators' daughters, Miss Hamilton, in particular, and you *are* very attractive, so I just assumed . . ."

"Assumed?" He targeted her with a kernel, which promptly bounced off the tip of her nose. "If I did that in a court of law, Miss McClare, I'd never win." He grabbed the piece and downed it before extending a palm. "So . . . shall we start over?"

She studied his hand, cheeks heating at the memory of when he'd offered it the last time.

His grin softened into a smile. "No tricks this time, Cass, you have my word."

Her gaze met his, and her heart did a little swoop at the connection that sparked. Swallowing hard, she gave him her hand, heart stuttering when his palm swallowed it whole, giving her a gentle squeeze before letting go. "Friends," he whispered, hazel eyes fused to hers.

She nodded slowly and brushed loose hair from her eyes, shaky fingers tingling from his touch. "Goodness, it's hard to believe someone like you has never had a girlfriend or anyone you've cared for. It just seems like you're so . . . ," she gulped, "experienced."

"Nope, just a quick study." Lying back, he cocked his hands behind his neck. "Other than a few girls here and there, till now, all of my attention has been devoted to two women—my mother and my sister." He closed his eyes, smile dimming. "They mean everything to me," he whispered, voice hoarse. He cleared his throat, apparently striving for casual once again. "So, between family, school, and jobs, you'll be happy to know I haven't had a lot of time to womanize."

She paused, her heart aching as she chewed on the edge of her lip. "Alli told me your sister is crippled," she whispered. "I'm so sorry, Jamie."

His eyes remained closed, but a muscle jerked in his cheek. "Yeah, she is, but not for long, I hope. I'm working on getting her help, a newfangled operation I've read about."

"Goodness, I'll certainly be praying about that."

He glanced up, eyes narrowing, but not from the sun. "Don't waste your breath, Cass, for all the good it will do." At her look of shock, he vented with a noisy sigh, then rubbed the bridge of his nose. "Sorry, but I don't put a lot of stock in prayer. It's kind of hard to believe in a God who hasn't lifted a finger for us all of our lives and then cripples my sister too."

Cassie's eyes splayed wide. "You don't believe in God?" she whispered, stunned that a man who appeared to have everything was missing the only thing that really mattered.

His jaw stiffened. "Not much, and even if I did, I'm not sure I'd like him a whole lot."

She gasped, suddenly aware she needn't have worried about their friendship being a risk. There was no way she'd allow herself to fall in love with a man who didn't share her faith.

He turned back on his side, elbow cocked and mouth tipped in a conciliatory smile. "You don't have to look so scandalized. My mother and sister are advocates, even if I'm not. They're always praying about everything, and I even take them to church every week like a model son. But when it comes to Jess's surgery and providing for my family?" He shook his head, lips pursed. "I just prefer to fend for myself, that's all." He looked up, the edge disappearing from his tone as he gave her a faint smile. "Life's obstacles are daunting, and we all have to overcome in our own way." His eyes softened. "But then, you should know all about that," he whispered, voice as tender as the look in his eyes. He paused. "What happened in Texas, Cass?"

The breath hitched in her lungs at his gentle probe, catching her off-guard. Normally she was a vault with everyone but Alli and Aunt Cait, preferring to keep her secrets to herself. But there was something about his serious and vulnerable manner that completely disarmed her, as if he connected with her pain despite his teasing swagger. He reached for her hand, giving it a gentle press, and somehow she saw her own grief reflected in his eyes. "Forgive me, please," he said quietly. "You don't have to answer that—I tend to get pushy at times."

She shook her head, managing a tremulous smile. "No . . . no, for some reason I . . . feel like talking about it, Jamie, which is odd because I'm usually very private."

He squeezed her hand and released it, their eyes locked as he waited for her to continue.

Inhaling deeply, she swung her legs around and folded her arms on tented knees, gaze fixed on the sky and voice as far away as the glittering panes overhead. "You see, I've always been considered a little . . . odd."

"Odd?"

She rested her chin on her arms, wondering why she felt compelled to allow Jamie MacKenna a glimpse into her world. Maybe because he'd given her a glimpse into his, no matter how brief or bitter. Or maybe she just really needed a friend right now. Whatever the reason, somehow deep inside Cassie felt as if she could trust him to accept her for who she was, and that felt better than anything had felt in a long, long time. Her lips curved in a bare smile. "I don't know if you've noticed, Mr. MacKenna, but I don't exactly fill the bill for high society. Back home, I prefer blue jeans to dresses, ranching to socializing, and horses to men. Which, to the upper echelon of Humble, Texas, is completely unforgivable."

He grinned. "Horses to men? Tarnation, I never stood a chance, did I?"

She shook her head and laughed. "Nope, especially not after Mark."

"Ah . . . Mark," he said with a squint. "The crux of the problem, I take it."

She closed her eyes, and instantly her smile faded. "Yes, Mark . . . ," she whispered, her voice tapering low. Fighting a prick of tears, she continued, her thoughts traveling back to Humble. "He was quite the catch, you know, son of a wealthy sawmill owner from Houston who'd just moved to Humble to open a sawmill." Her lips quirked. "*And* find a wife. Since the oil boom, Humble has quite an upscale society, you see. So you can imagine how the society pages painted it when the handsome Mr. Chancellor chose to court the reclusive tomboy of Mr. Quinn McClare instead of socialites who vied for his attention."

She stretched out and leaned back to study the sky through the crystal-like panes. "From little on, I never quite fit in high society because Mama taught at the Indian reservation before she married Daddy and after, and so I spent a lot of time there, and Humble elite didn't cotton to that. They made fun of me because my friends were Indians and not the daughters of wealthy landowners or oilmen. It got so bad Mama yanked me from an exclusive girls' school in town to teach me at the reservation school instead. Of course it didn't help that I refused to attend debutante balls or society teas. That gave rise to more gossip and rude names, which I have to admit hurt at first." Her chin jutted up. "But they weren't my friends, so I pretended it didn't matter, opting to spend time with the people I cared about most—my best friends, Morning Dove and White Deer. To me 'coming out' meant fishing outside with Daddy at the river or riding Domino—my polka-dot mare—in the hills with Red or Merle, Daddy's loyal hands." She glanced at Jamie out of the corner of her eye, mouth skewed in a wry smile. "Certainly not prissing up for some fancy ball, trussing up in a corset to catch a man's eye."

He smiled that slow, languid smile with which she was rapidly becoming familiar, his scan of her legs warming both her cheeks and her belly. "Trust me, Cass, you don't need a corset to catch a man's eye."

With a self-concious tug of her lip, she tucked her legs back under her skirt. "Well, thank you, but it's a Gibson-Girl world, which is why I said no when Mark asked me out."

"You did?"

"Yep. It was bad enough being rejected by Humble's upper-crust—I didn't feel like giving some man a potshot at me too." Her pulse slowed to a painful thud as her eyes trailed into a hard stare. "But Mark was . . . ," her throat convulsed with a hard swallow, the memory of his affection shrinking her ribs, "so . . . kind and attentive and indifferent to whether society approved of me or not, and I . . . ," emotion jammed in her throat, "couldn't help myself—I fell in love."

"Cass, I'm sorry . . . ," Jamie said softly.

"Me too," she whispered with a swab of her eyes. "The day Mark proposed was the happiest day of my life, making me feel normal for the first time ever."

"What happened?" His voice was quiet.

A cold chill shivered despite the warmth of the sun. She closed her eyes, remembering with painful clarity the day Mark broke the engagement. *"I love you, Cass,"* he'd whispered, repentance heavy in his tone, *"but I can't afford to lose everything and start over."*

Translation: I love my father's money more than I love you.

How ironic . . . right after Daddy's wells went dry . . .

"Cass?"

Her eyes jolted open. "What?"

He rested his hand over hers, grazing it with his thumb. "What happened?" he repeated.

She forced a smile as stiff as her jaw. "Oh, nothing much. His daddy just threatened to disown him if he married me, that's all. Said I was too different and Mark deserved better." A knot jerked in her throat. "So he . . . broke the engagement. A week before the wedding."

"Aw, Cass . . ." He rose to his knees to bundle her in his arms, stroking her back with a warm, firm touch. "He was a moron who didn't deserve you," he whispered, tucking his head to hers. He kissed the top of her hair and jumped to his feet. "Hey, what do you say I pretend I'm Mark, and you try and drown me?"

She tilted her head. "You'd let me do that?"

He tugged her up and to the water. "Sure, that's what friends do, isn't it?" he said with a lazy grin, absently kneading the skin of her palm.

His touch unleashed a shiver of heat that forced a lump to her throat. *Maybe*, she thought with a gulp, slipping her hand from his to race him to the water. But she was dead certain there was something friends did *not* do . . . at least, not with a friend like him.

They don't fall in love.

11

Jamie's rib cage constricted at the sunken shadows under his sister's eyes, evidence of a bout of flu that had weakened and left her bedridden all week. Prone to illness since she was a little girl, Jamie wondered how much of her frail constitution could be attributed to the hip injury that prevented her from being a normal young woman. Running with other children or even simple walks in the park had resulted in so much pain the next day that Jess remained homebound except for Sundays when she'd limp across the street to St. Mary's for church, refusing Jamie's assistance like she did when she climbed Mrs. Tucker's boardinghouse steps.

"For pity's sake, James MacKenna," she'd say, "I'm a sixteen-year-old woman with two perfectly good legs even if my hip doesn't comply. I refuse to be coddled and carried wherever I go." And then she'd stubbornly navigate the steps one at a time, wincing and resting after each until she'd turn and glow at the top like she'd just scaled Mount McKinley.

Of course she was always sore after, some days the pain worse than others depending on the weather. Jamie glanced out the window of the bedroom his mother and she shared, stomach cramping at the rivulets of water that slithered the glass. No doubt the dark smudges under his sister's eyes were as much from the rain that always exacerbated her condition as from the flu, and for the thousandth time, Jamie silently cursed a God that refused to heal a young woman who worshiped him with all of her heart.

Stifling a yawn, Jess leaned against her pillow, pale cheeks framed by lustrous black curls spilling over her nightgown while she studied the chessboard with ochre eyes so like his own.

Jamie glanced at the clock on her nightstand. He needed to leave to deliver Mom's package to Millie if he was to meet Bram at the Blue Moon in time for Logan's birthday dinner at The Palace Hotel. He sighed. "Sorry, Peanut, but I need to go, and you need to rest." Tugging one of her silky curls, he rose and carefully moved the chessboard to the bureau before pushing his chair against the wall. "You'll need all the rest you can get if you have any hope of whipping me in chess tomorrow," he said, straightening his tuxedo jacket with a firm tug and a wink.

"If?" She gave him an imp of a smile before she flinched, pain strangling her features when she attempted to shift in the bed, barely a bump under the cover. Her smile appeared strained. "Law degree or no, Jammy," she said, teasing with the nickname she'd given him when she was two, "I think we both know who's going to win."

"You think so, huh?" He assessed her with a lift of brows. "Only if you don't fall asleep like you did last night." He bent to deposit a kiss to her cheek. "Get some rest, kiddo—love you."

"Love you too, Jammy." She yawned, eyelids weighting closed, pale face that of an angel's except for the telltale fatigue that indicated a particularly grueling day. He retrieved his top hat from the dresser and headed for the door, turning at the sound of her voice. "Oh, and by the way," she called, eyes popping open to reveal a hint of a twinkle, "you look awfully handsome tonight. Who's the lucky girl—Patricia?"

"Nope. Miss Hamilton will not be in attendance."

Jess slid farther beneath the thin cover with another yawn, clasping her hands on top. "Oh, too bad. You look awfully gorgeous tonight and you smell good too." She tilted her head with a sweet smile. "Will there be any other ladies who've caught your eye?"

He grinned. "A Texas cousin, but she's gun-shy 'cause some pretty boy broke her heart." He shook his head. "Unfortunately, she thinks I'm 'pretty,' too, and just wants to be friends."

Her grin matched his. "You are pretty, even if somewhat lacking in chess."

His eyes narrowed in tease as he brandished a finger. "That remains to be seen, you little brat, so I suggest you catch up on your sleep because you're gonna need it." He blew her a kiss as his smile sobered. "I love you, Jess," he said, voice hoarse.

Snatching his kiss, she placed it on her heart before blowing her own. "Me, too, Jammy."

His throat ached while he closed her door, head bowed and hand limp on the knob. She'd looked so tired tonight, worn, barely touching the chicken he'd brought from Duffy's—her favorite, no less. Six at night and she was already in bed. The very idea slumped his shoulders.

He made his way downstairs, pots banging in the kitchen where Mrs. Tucker prepared dinner for her boarders. He found his mother in the deserted parlour, sewing on the worn floral sofa of the Victorian-styled room where the gloom of the day peeked through burgundy tasseled curtains. She glanced up, dark circles beneath her eyes that matched those of her daughter, and his throat convulsed. At forty-two, she was still a beautiful woman, but the strain and stress of caring for Jess and working shifts at the Blue Moon were taking their toll, aging her more than Jamie liked. Jess had a particularly taxing week, which always meant his mother did too, and he was worried about her health as much as his sister's. He released a quiet sigh. *And* her state of mind. With Jess in more pain lately, his mother didn't get out as often as before, and Jamie could see the result in a mild malaise that invaded the parlour.

"You look very handsome, son," his mother said, laying aside the sewing she took in to help meet the bills. Lines chiseling her brow, she rose and walked to where he stood as if privy to the whisperings of the demons that forever haunted his mind. She slipped her arms to his waist in a loving embrace, and with a catch of his throat, Jamie swallowed her up in a silent groan, eyes closed as he rested his head against hers. Her scent comforted him—the sweet fragrance of the lavender oil she rubbed into Jess's joint mingling with the pungent smell of ginger tea from her cup on the coffee table, faithfully brewed to reduce the inflammation of her daughter's hip. Too thin and too frail to suit her son, Jean MacKenna was a slip of a thing at five foot four to his six foot one, and yet she never failed to infuse him with a mother's strength as if he were still a little boy. Her voice—as gentle and soothing as the hand now massaging his back—had a melodic lilt that was almost spiritual, calming the angst in his gut. "Things will get better for Jess," she whispered. "God will see us through, you'll see."

Both his hold and his eyes squeezed tighter and he almost wished he could beseech God like his mother and sister did, begging him to deliver Jess from this life-crippling condition. Localized osteoarthritis, the doctor called it, resulting from trauma. "Expect pain with all normal movement," Doc Morrissey had warned, "as well as limited range of motion and swelling of the joint." All symptoms that worsened with time despite endless prayers of his mother and sister.

And his.

Patting his back, his mother returned to the sofa to resume her sewing with a proud, if tired, smile. "You're a handsome man, James MacKenna, especially the way you look tonight." She inclined her head, a hint of a sparkle lighting hazel eyes so like his own. "I suppose a certain senator's daughter will be at the McClare birthday party as well?"

"Not tonight," Jamie said with a zag of a smile, striding over to set his top hat on the mantel before adjusting his tie in the distorted mirror above.

"I see. So when do you plan to officially court her, this beauty who's stolen your heart?"

He glanced over his shoulder. "She's only stolen my eye, Mom, not my heart. But rest assured—the moment I decide on *the* girl, you and Jess'll be the first to know."

He turned to assess the hand-me-down dinner jacket Bram had insisted on giving him, claiming ill fit or general dislike, and as always, gratitude swelled for a best friend who was more like a brother. Exquisitely cut from the finest wool, the jacket emphasized Jamie's broad shoulders before tapering to a slim waist where the tails cut at an angle. The straight-standing three-inch collar and white bow tie accentuated the firm cut of his clean-shaven jaw, and thanks to his friend Siu Ling at the Chinese laundry, Bram's old white shirt was immaculate and crisp, its pearl buttons the fashion of the day. His critical gaze traveled from normally unruly ebony curls slicked back, past hazel eyes Alli had declared "deadly," to hard-chiseled cheekbones steeled with determination, confirming he was a man of class and distinction. His full lips quirked. An image obviously more distorted than the mirror.

Swiping his top hat from the mantel—another hand-off from Bram—he turned and paused, shooting a quick glance out the window where a touch of sun was finally peeking through. "It looks like the rain stopped, Mom, and the sun's trying to come out. Why not take a quick walk to the corner to say hello to Mrs. Lowe? Jess is probably asleep."

She shook her head, shoulders sagging with the motion. "Not up to it tonight, Jamie. I'll be fine, though. I have a lot of hemming to do, so you go and have a good time, you hear?" She nodded to a small paper-wrapped package on a table by the door. "Are you sure you don't mind delivering my sewing to Millie? I don't want you to be late."

"Nope, it's practically on my way." He tucked the parcel under his arm and strode over to give her a kiss goodbye. "Good night, Mom. Love you—don't wait up." He shot her a wink and slipped out the door, checking his watch as he hurried to the next block to catch the trolley. He didn't have time to walk to the Coast as usual, especially since the cable car traveled just a few streets over from the old cow-yard where they'd once lived.

As always, a malaise settled as he walked the final seamy block, the music of steam pianos and gramophones blasting from dance hall after dance hall where half-clad women called out lewd invitations from windows above. Names like The Living Flea, Dead Man's Alley, and Murder Point, so-called pleasure palaces that reeked of alcohol and stale perfume and the pungent scent of opium. As usual, the street was littered with trash and people, some passed out, some fighting, and some too drunk to care.

The sound of a baby crying reminded him the Barbary Coast was no place for infants or children. Nor Jean MacKenna and her family. But, it was all his mother had been able to afford back then, her meager dance-hall salary finally giving way to seamstress work to supplement his father's sporadic paychecks ... if he hadn't drunk them away first. When Brian MacKenna died, Jamie wanted to quit school altogether to work fulltime, but his mother refused.

"I don't want you to end up poor like me," she'd whisper whenever he'd tried to argue. "I want you to make me proud, Jamie—get an education and make something of yourself." She'd hug him then, tears brimming, and it was all he could do to deflect moisture of his own. So he'd stayed in school and studied hard while his mother squirreled away every spare penny for his education. The very thought caused tears to sting in his nose. She'd sacrificed her life for him and Jess, so he gladly sacrificed his for them—his childhood, his friendships, his sleep. He gave his all to school and work, determined to make a better life for the woman who'd devoted hers to them.

Obscenities drifted from an open window as he mounted cracked steps, anxious to deliver his mother's package and get out. He opened a scarred wood door that was defiled, he was certain, by everything from booze and vomit to urine and blood, eternally grateful he and his family escaped the polluted sewers of the Barbary Coast.

He entered the foul-smelling brothel on the first floor and was instantly met by shouts and sniffles. Heart squeezing, he bent down to a quivering lump of curls hunched on the first step of a staircase that once led to his family's flat. "Bessie, what's wrong?" Ignoring the tyke's filthy dress and matted hair, Jamie scooped her up, scanning from pudgy bare feet and scuffed knees to a threadbare romper with numerous patched holes. The grimy face of a four-year-old cherub peeked up with fat tears in her eyes, and he placed a kiss on her cheek. "Are you hurt?"

The little waif shook her head and flung chubby arms around

his neck, painful, little heaves racking his heart as well as his body. "M-mama . . . ," she choked out, pointing a shaky finger toward her mother's flat, "bad man . . ."

Something thudded hard against the wall, and a woman's muffled scream iced the blood in Jamie's veins. Temper tightly coiled, he kissed Bessie's head and pounded on the opposite door, face grim when Julie peeked out.

"Julie, can you keep Bessie for a moment and take this package for Millie?" He handed the little girl and parcel off, nodding toward Millie's door. "Millie has a problem."

Julie's gaze widened, flicking to Millie's door and back. "Sure, Jamie," she said, pressing a kiss to Bessie's cheek. "Come on, sweetie—I've a biscuit for you, all right?"

With short, little heaves, Bessie nodded and clung to Julie while Jamie moved toward Millie's door.

"Cecil—you don't owe me a dime—just leave, please!" The sound of Millie's voice was tinged with terror.

Flexing his fingers, Jamie pressed a palm to the cracked door and eased it open. "Millie? You okay?"

Swear words defiled the tiny flat along with whiskey and sweat. A grizzled drunk singed him with a glare, the smell of urine and body odor roiling Jamie's stomach. "It's none of your bloomin' business, you cheeky sod. You can have her when I'm done."

Jamie ignored him, gaze shifting to Millie huddled in a corner, tears streaking her face and blood on her cheek. A nerve twittered his jaw. "Answer me, Millie, did he hit you?" His teeth clenched so tight, he thought they might crack. *Like Cecil's face when I'm done.*

"Jamie, no, he'll hurt you!" Millie scrambled to her feet, her cheek just beginning to bruise.

Cecil grinned, revealing rotted teeth as putrid as the rest of him. "That's right, bloke, better run afore I mess your prissy outfit along with your prissy face."

"Or try." Calmly removing his top hat, Jamie hooked it on a peg by the door and carefully hung his jacket as well. Without a word, he slowly rolled up the sleeves of his shirt, his gaze dispassionate. A cold smile skimmed his lips at the memory of weekends at the Oly Club, where Gentleman Jim Corbett often schooled him in the art of boxing.

"Why, you blasted upstart . . ." Cecil lumbered forward with fists raised, and the sting of Jamie's well-aimed punch slammed the man's jaw to the side before he crumpled to the wooden floor in a heap, out cold and blood trailing his lip.

With a rock-steady hold that belied the angst in his gut, Jamie dragged him to the door and tossed him in the hall to a round of applause from several scantily clad women. "Jamie, you're our hero," Julie shouted, Bessie wide-eyed in her arms.

He grinned. "Wouldn't take much if this is the riffraff you're comparing me to, Julie." He unrolled the sleeves of his shirt and prodded Cecil with the toe of his black oxford shoe, prompting a low groan. "Cecil, I suggest you take your business elsewhere from now on, because if these ladies tell me you've been around, I'll be obliged to break your arm along with your jaw—is that clear?"

Cecil didn't answer, and Jamie jerked the scruff of his neck, his tone composed even if his nerves were not. "I said, is that clear?" A garbled grunt escaped Cecil's bloody mouth, and Jamie released him, head dropping with a thud on the filthy floor. "Good, because these ladies are my friends. Now, I'm going to wash your blood off my hands, get my hat and coat, and if you're still here when I get back, I'm going to finish you off, understood?"

Lumbering to his feet, Cecil stumbled out with a glazed look while Jamie cleaned up in Millie's water basin, then returned to the hall, hat in hand and coat over his arm.

"Oh, Jamie, you're a lifesaver, ye are," Millie said with a quivering smile. "And Julie is right—you're our hero." She reached up to kiss him on his cheek before her eyes went wide. "Aw, the dirty bum has gone and bloodied your shirt."

"You got another fancy doings tonight, Jamie Boy?" Julie said with a wink, auburn curls dangling over one bare shoulder of a faded dressing gown. "Because ye look good enough to eat, Mr. MacKenna, make no mistake."

Jamie glanced at the blood on the sleeve of his shirt. "As long as I keep my coat on, that is." He tapped the top hat on his head and slipped into his jacket. "And yes, Julie—I have a dinner at The Palace."

A blonde from the next flat sighed, her stained kimono heaving with regret as she peeked out her door. "I'll tell you what, mister, in that fancy suit, you're every woman's dream."

Julie winked. "Hope you reel in a rich one, Jamie, 'cause nobody deserves it more."

Extending first one arm and then the other, he buttoned his cuffs with an easy smile. "I'll do my level best, ladies, so wish me luck."

"You won't be needing any luck, James MacKenna, and I'll bet me mother's eyeteeth on that." Millie repositioned his top hat with an affectionate smile. "Thanks again, Jamie, and if there's aught I can do to repay ye, ye just let me know, you hear?" Her smile was radiant for a woman with a black-and-blue face. "Now, you go and have a grand time."

He bent to kiss her good cheek. "You might want to love up on Bess a while, Mil, she was shaking pretty hard." He tweaked her chin. "Mom sent clothes and books too. Julie has them, okay?"

The light in Millie's eyes dimmed while her gaze drifted to where Julie was playing snuggle monster with Bessie, giggles ringing out with every kiss. "Och, I'd give anything to get her out of this place," she whispered.

Jamie swallowed hard, not sure what to say. He kneaded her shoulder. For him and his mother and sister, freedom was a reality, but to Millie and the others who called Barbary Coast their home—with no money, no education, no skills—hope was as empty as their pockets. He placed a coin into her hands, giving her a squeeze. "Put this in a safe place for Bess, and promise you'll add to it every week, no matter how small. Someday soon there will be enough to buy a new dress and shoes so you can look for decent work, where you and Bess won't be in danger." He bent to connect his gaze with hers. "Promise me, Millie."

She nodded, the motion dislodging a tear from her eye, and then she lunged into his arms to hug him so fiercely, the muscles constricted in his throat. "You're a rare find, Jamie MacKenna. I pray God showers you with all the blessings you so richly deserve, including a wealthy wife and a fancy house on Nob Hill."

He laughed, and the sound echoed in the dingy hall spidered with cracks. "I'm not sure how many 'blessings' I deserve, Mil," he said with a wink at her and the ladies, "but the rich wife and fancy house on Nob Hill?" Ambling to the front door, he tossed a rogue's grin over his shoulder. "I'm hoping it's only a matter of time."

12

Chin in hand, Caitlyn swayed to the music of The Palace Hotel orchestra, feet tapping a waltz beneath the crisp linen tablecloth aglow with candles. The scent of gardenias drifted from exquisite blossoms gracing the table where they'd enjoyed Logan's birthday dinner. Closing her eyes, she almost felt seventeen again, a starry-eyed girl whirling in the arms of Logan McClare, the most handsome man in the ballroom of the brand-new Palace Hotel. Even now, the powerful scent of his lime shaving soap merged with the tang of lemon oil from the lustrous oak dance floor, conjuring a memory so strong, her heart swooped in her chest. Her eyelids lifted to see Logan spin Maddie on the dance floor, her daughter's shin-length taffeta dress ballooning while auburn curls fluttered in the breeze. He gobble-kissed Maddie's neck, and Caitlyn's smile faded. *She might have been his daughter instead of his niece ...*

"Goodness, you belong on that dance floor, Aunt Cait." Cassie slipped into a chair next to her, back from the ladies' room. "I could see your toe twitching from across the room."

Caitlyn glanced up, lips easing into a languid smile. "I'll get my chance, Cass. Both Jamie and Bram promised me a dance, so I'm just biding my time."

Cassie leaned close, mischief in her tone. "You mean Uncle Logan hasn't asked yet? The way he's been ogling you, I just assumed you'd be the first name on his dance card."

"Cassidy Margaret McClare!" Caitlyn grabbed her napkin and promptly fanned herself. "Good heavens, your Uncle Logan is my brother-in-law, young lady, and nothing more."

Cassie's chuckle floated in the air. "Maybe nothing more to you, Aunt Cait, but I've only been here a little over a month, and already I can see Uncle Logan is smitten, just like Alli says."

"Alli said that?" Alarm crept into Cait's tone while heat crept up her cheeks.

Her niece's grin tipped in tease. "And not just Alli—Meg and Blake joke about it too."

"Good heavenly days," Caitlyn whispered, bolting her water down. "Well, it's simply not tr—" She froze midsyllable, the memory of that night on the veranda halting her air. His tenderness, his comfort over her missing Liam, his unsettling words. *It's been almost two years, Cait—don't you think you could use a fresh start too?* It was the first time she'd seen desire so blatant in his eyes, and it had scared her as much as hearing her children had noticed it too. Yes, he'd been more attentive to them all in the last six months, dropping in more than ever before. And heaven knows he could be an outrageous flirt with any woman including her, lavishing attention on any female around, which is all she'd assumed it to be. But now she suspected her uneasiness in his presence wasn't just the unwanted feelings he awakened in her . . . Her hands shook as she gulped an unladylike swig of water. *But am I doing the same to him?*

"Simply not true?" Cassie repeated softly with a duck of her head, sympathy edging her smile. She touched her aunt's arm. "Really, Aunt Cait, would it be such a horrible thing if it were?

132

Uncle Logan is one of the most eligible bachelors in the city—attractive, fun, and crazy about you and your children. Call me a dreamer, but it seems like a match made in heaven."

"No, not in heaven." Cait's whisper was no more than a rasp as her gaze followed Logan dancing with her daughter, eyes closed while he snuggled her close. "Oh, that it were . . ."

"What do you mean?"

Caitlyn looked up, startled that she'd spoken out loud. She stared at her niece, heart thumping, then blinked, her words cleaving to the roof of her mouth. She'd never intended to discuss her past with anyone, and certainly not with her own children, determined they need never know their father was not her first love. But the silence threatened to choke her, and her longing to confide in someone who would understand was growing greater every day. She assessed the deep ridges of concern in her niece's face and suddenly realized Cassie may well be that perfect someone, a woman badly bruised by a man with no faith in God. *And* a woman who just may need to hear what Caitlyn had to say.

Body quivering as much as the water in her glass, Caitlyn quickly downed it before leaning close, hand to her niece's arm. "Cassie, I've never shared this with anyone—not my children, my friends, no one. But somehow I feel compelled to confide in you. Not just because I'm tired of carrying this burden alone, but because I believe it's something you need to hear." She brushed a strand of hair from her niece's face, eyes warm with affection and concern. "But first, you must promise this will be our secret and you will not tell anyone else." Her gaze flicked to the dance floor where Jamie danced with Alli, and Bram with Meg. "Especially your cousins."

Cassie nodded, her unusual pale-green eyes as wide and clear as a mossy mountain pool.

Filling her lungs with a heavy dose of air, Caitlyn slowly released it again, squaring her shoulders. "Remember the handsome rogue I was engaged to before your Uncle Liam?"

Cassie's head bobbed in slow motion, her breathing suddenly suspended.

A lump dipped in Caitlyn's throat while her gaze darted to where Logan was trading partners with Bram. "Well, you see . . . it was your Uncle Logan."

A gasp popped from Cassie's lips, the mountain pool swelling to lake proportions.

Cait couldn't help but smile, her niece's reaction tilting her lips. "Yes, I'm afraid so."

A waiter appeared with a sterling pitcher in hand, replenishing Cait's water glass. "Oh, bless you," she said, awarding him a warm smile. She took a quick drink and set it back down, fingers absently grazing the cool moisture of the crystal goblet. "In fact, it was in this very room where Logan proposed to me almost twenty-seven years ago." A frail sigh drifted from her lips as she leaned back in the chair, eyes straying to where he danced with her second daughter. "He was quite the catch in those days, you know, a rogue about town, much as he is now. But we fell so desperately in love and I was so naïve, that I just naturally assumed his wild ways were over."

Her eyes trailed into a vacant stare, the awful memory still able to constrict the muscles of her throat. "A painful assumption that forced me to grow up quite quickly, I'm afraid. Right after we became engaged, I discovered Logan was having an affair with another woman. An 'innocent final fling,' I believe he called it when he begged my forgiveness, but the damage was done. I realized I could never trust him again, not just because of his many indiscretions that I subsequently learned about, but because I knew deep in my soul he was not a man of God." Her lips bent in a sad smile. "Something I had conveniently closed my eyes to because I was so much in love."

Her eyelids slowly lifted. "I have no doubt, Cassie, that God spared you from a less-than-fulfilling marriage with Mark. I believe he spared me from the same through the incredible friendship—and eventual deep love—of your Uncle Liam." She patted Cassie's hand. "As much as I care for your Uncle Logan—and I do—it grieves me to say when it comes to other women and God, he hasn't changed all that much. And if I've learned anything from my dear, sweet husband, it's that I will never—*ever*—settle for another relationship without God in the center." She gently cupped Cassie's cheek, the intensity in her voice bleeding from her very soul. "I love you, darling, and I'm asking you to promise the same. Promise you'll save your heart for God's best, a man who loves God as much as you do. Because therein lies a love like no other."

Moisture glimmered in her niece's eyes. "I promise, Aunt Cait—you have my word."

"Mama, Mama—Uncle Logan said we can have an overnight in Napa if you say yes!" Maddie flew into her arms totally breathless, cheeks as flushed as Cait's, no doubt, as Logan followed behind with a smile that quivered her stomach. "He says he wants all of us to come for Fourth of July—Bram and Jamie too!"

"Is that so?" Cait notched a brow, her demeanor calm even if her pulse wasn't. She bundled Maddie on her lap. "And just exactly why must it be overnight?"

"A three-day weekend, Mrs. McClare," Logan said easily, the twinkle in his eye doing nothing for her peace of mind. He offered a slight bow before seating Meg in her chair. "The Fourth is on a Friday this year, so I thought it'd be fun to make a weekend of it, especially since I'll be tied up for the next month and won't be able to see as much of the kids. But, by the Fourth, I'll be at your complete and utter disposal to celebrate with my family."

Her lips sloped into a dry smile. "Mmm—utter disposal." She tilted her head. "Now, if that only meant 'disposal' of your plan to fill my children's summer with nothing but frivolity."

"Ah, but not just your *children's* summer, Cait," he whispered, bending to give Cassie a squeeze while he smiled at Caitlyn, his shuttered gaze toasting her cheeks.

"Please, Mama? It'll be fun." Maddie whirled on her lap, stubby arms clinging to her mother's neck. "Meg and I want to go, and so will Alli."

"So will Alli what?" Allison asked, out of breath as she plopped in her chair.

"Spend the Fourth of July at my estate in Napa," Logan interjected. "A family event, and Jamie, Bram, Liddy, and Patricia are invited too."

A gleam lit Alli's eyes. "Oooo . . . is your handsome neighbor home for the summer?"

Logan gave her a wink. "He is, and asking when my nieces are coming to visit."

Pleasure glowed in Alli's cheeks. "Then count me in." She wiggled her brows at Cassie. "Just wait till you see Mr. Roger Luepke, Cass—he's beautiful!"

"I'll have you know, Al, the term 'beautiful' does not apply to any man worth his salt," Blake said, returning from a dance with a girl from the next table.

"Sure it does," Alli said with a tussle of Jamie's hair. "Just look at Pretty Boy here."

"Hey, hands off." Jamie batted at her. "These blasted curls are hard enough to restrain."

"Like the man, no doubt," Cassie quipped, sending a ruddy flush up Jamie's neck.

His lips stole into a little-boy smile. "I'll have you know restraint is my middle name, Miss McClare," he said with a fake Texas drawl, "unless needlessly provoked."

"So . . . ," Logan interrupted, scanning the table before honing in on Cait. "Everybody game? Dinner on the patio followed by fireworks Friday night, a swim picnic by the lake Saturday afternoon, dinner and games into the wee hours of the morning?"

"Yes!" Maddie bounced on Caitlyn's lap, her excitement echoed by everyone at the table.

Except me. Caitlyn drew in a tight breath, quite certain spending the weekend at Logan's would not be a good thing, at least not for her. Her mind scrambled for an excuse. "I'm so sorry, Logan, but we can't miss church on Sunday."

"You won't," he said calmly. The edge of his mouth twitched at the groans that rounded the table, not the least of which was from Maddie who rattled Caitlyn's arm with panic in her eyes. A deadly smile curved on his lips, once capable of reducing her insides to mush. She absently pressed a hand to her stomach as he continued. "You remember Harold Hough, don't you?"

Heat steamed Cait's cheeks at the mention of Logan's friend from college, the best man in their wedding before she'd broken the engagement. Mercifully, Logan didn't wait for her answer. "Well, old Harry's been Father Harry at a church in Napa for the last ten years now, so he'll be staying over as well." He took the chair next to Cait, giving her elbow a light tweak. "So we'll all attend his church in the valley Sunday morning."

She blinked, eyes suddenly spanning wide at his words. *Logan McClare? In church?* Her voice came out as a croak as she pulled Maddie close on her lap. "All?"

"I'm not the heathen you think I am, Cait," he said quietly, his words warm and laced with tease. "Harry's been working on me a long time, you know."

A muscle dipped in her throat. *No . . . I didn't.*

He tickled Maddie's stomach, the effect unleashing a shiver through Cait when his fingers grazed hers in the process. "Come on, Cait, everybody's on board but you." He tugged Maddie from her arms, settling her into his lap with a kiss while his gaze fused to Caitlyn's. A gleam of a dare lit gray eyes that sparkled like the sterling silver spoon her daughter aimed at his half-eaten dessert. "Besides, what if the Vigilance Committee actually coerces you into joining their ranks?" he teased, his cavalier tone making it clear he didn't think she would. "Your family time will be cut short, so it's best to make memories while you can, especially while Cassie is here." He gave her a playful wink that likely painted her face the color of the strawberry garnish Maddie now spooned in her mouth. "Who knows? This could be your golden opportunity to coax me to side with you at the next Board of Supervisors meeting."

Her pulse slowed, knowing full well that as one of the most influential members of the San Francisco Board of Supervisors, he could be a valuable ally in her efforts to clean up the Coast. Since Liam's death, Walter and the other members of the Vigilance Committee had begged her to use her influence with Logan, but she had turned them down. She certainly held no sway over a man who had a vested interest in keeping the Coast alive. A lump thickened in her throat. *Until now, apparently.* Assessing the challenge in a gaze that boldly held her own, she paused, not a woman prone to coaxing, and yet . . . the stakes had never been higher. *Nor the risks*, she reminded herself with a queasy feeling. Especially since Logan had no idea she'd already accepted the position. She drew in a fortifying breath and released it slowly. "All right, you're on. Allow me to share Walter's plan and take us to church, and we have a deal."

Maddie sprang from Logan's lap with a loud squeal, rounding the table to tell the others the good news. Logan chuckled, his husky tone for her ears alone. "Why, Caitlyn McClare, you little siren, you—who would have thought?"

Lunging for her water, she wished she could cool her cheeks with it instead. *Or douse a smirk on a handsome rogue's face.* She closed her eyes to shut him out, throat convulsing as she glugged, glass bottom up.

"Mama, Mama, I'm so excited!" Cheeks flushed, Maddie skipped to her side, perching on tiny toes to plant a kiss to her cheek. "We get to sleep at Uncle Logan's—isn't that great?"

Great? Caitlyn blinked. For the Board, maybe. She promptly upended her glass before Logan smiled and emptied his water into hers. But for her? Ice slivered down her throat after she bolted it down again.

Most definitely not.

13

"Tell me, Sugar Pie, don't they dance in Texas?" Jamie said, seating Meg in her chair.

Eyes in squint, Cassie glanced up, the wrinkle in her nose making him smile. "Yes, we dance in Texas, City Boy, so next time they play a two-step, you just let me know, okay?"

Hooking a palm under her arm, he lifted her to her feet. "Oh no you don't, Cowgirl, you're in the big city now and your boots are at home, so come be civilized with me." She attempted to sit back down, but he held on tight, eyes scanning head to toe in natural reflex while his skin warmed at the sight of a girl in folds of pale-blue satin. He swallowed hard, her off-the-shoulder dress trimmed with delicate garlands of chiffon and tiny pink rosebuds that dipped low enough at the neckline to cause a lump in Jamie's throat. Wisps of gold loose from her graceful chignon fluttered over creamy shoulders with a hint of soft freckles, grazing her skin like he *so* longed to do. Even her scent of lilac water and Pear's soap seemed to tease, making the dinner jacket he wore entirely too warm.

Sucking in a quiet breath, he notched a brow. "You've been perched all night like a prairie dog on a dirt pile, Cassidy McClare, and lest you forget what happens when a pretty boy is needlessly provoked, I suggest we mosey out to the floor."

"Jamie, please . . . ," she groaned, yanking as if battling in a tug-of-war before finally plopping back down. "You're supposed to be my friend—please don't make me."

Alli nudged from behind. "Oh, come on, Cass—it'll be fun." She laughed, pinching Cassie's waist to prod her off the chair. "Jamie's a good dancer, so he won't embarrass you."

A deep flush swarmed Cassie's cheeks, making her peaches-and-cream complexion look more like strawberry punch. "It's not Jamie I'm worried about," she rasped, heels digging in with a hard slant when Jamie pulled her to her feet once more.

Jaw slack, he released his hold, and she plopped back in her chair with a soft thump. "You can't dance?" he said, mouth agape. "Well, I'll be—never seen a girl who can't dance."

The green eyes narrowed, thin as a blade of grass. "You've never seen a girl hog-tie a skunk either, but keep it up and you may get your chance."

"Come on, Cass, we all took lessons in Paris, remember? You know how to dance." Alli ducked to give her a smile, her thumb absently caressing the satin material of Cassie's pale-blue dress at the very spot where it clung to her thigh, causing a knot the size of Cassie's clenched fists to bob in Jamie's throat.

"That was over three years ago, Al, and I wasn't any good then, either."

"But surely you danced a lot with what's-his-name in Humboldt?" Jamie waved a hand in the air, unwilling to taint his tongue with Mark Chancellor's name.

The lushest, pinkest lips Jamie had ever seen—or tasted—quirked into a dry smile. "No, as a matter of fact, I did not, and it's Humble," she stressed in a clipped tone, "which is exactly what you'll be if you force me to go out on that floor."

He laughed and hauled her back up. "Trust me, it'll be fun. I'll teach you how to dance."

"Trust you?" She attempted to quietly twist and tug on the way to the floor, the heels of her ballerina slippers sliding while she hissed in his ear. "You are nothing but a bully, Jamie MacKenna, and I'm rethinking this friendship, I can tell you that."

He pulled her into his arms with a decadent smile. "Rethinking the friendship, eh?" He pressed close to the side of her head, his words hot in her ear. "Uh-oh . . . you falling for me, Miss McClare?"

"Bite your tongue." She seared him with a nasty look that broadened his grin.

He lifted her right hand in his and braced her shoulder blade with his other. "What if I'd rather nibble on something else?" he teased, chuckling when her cheeks bloomed bright pink. She tried to jerk away and he resisted, palm skimming to her waist to lock her close. His thumb suddenly feathered satin against skin, and his Adam's apple jogged in his throat. "Merciful Providence, Cass," he whispered, his voice little more than a rasp, "you're not wearing a corset?" Shock laced his tone, both at her lack of undergarments and the humiliation of just blurting the question out, unleashing a rash of fire up his neck.

She gasped, those full, pink lips agape while her face fused to scarlet. "That is none of your business, Mr. MacKenna," she snapped. Her tone was as pointed as the thumbnail she gouged into his arm in an attempt to break free.

He clasped both of her hands. "Okay, okay, Cass, I'm sorry, really. Truce?" His gaze and tone softened even if his grip didn't. "Please?"

She glared while her body finally relaxed. "Just because we're friends does not give you the right to make inappropriate comments, is that clear? Sweet thunderation, you're lucky my hands were restrained, or I would have dislocated your jaw."

Tone repentant, he offered a sheepish smile, massaging his jaw as if she had whopped him good. "*Very* lucky, indeed, Miss McClare, and you have my word it won't happen again."

She expelled a weighty sigh that shimmered the satin of her bodice, then made a quick scan of the floor where couples whirled to a waltz. "Well, let's get this buggy across the river, MacKenna, because heaven knows people won't be staring any more than they already are."

"Yes, ma'am." He quickly tempered his smile and resumed position with her right hand in his left while he cupped a palm to her back, elbow out. "Now rest your left hand on my arm and just follow my lead. It's basically a box pattern to a count of three—one step backward, one step to the side, feet together." With his brief demonstration, she timidly glided along, a mere wisp of a woman floating in his arms while he counted out the pace. "One-two-three, one-two-three . . ." He paused and smiled. "See? Not hard. Ready?"

A faint smile emerged through the pout. "Does it matter?"

He grinned. "Nope." With a firm clasp of her hand, he guided her through the steps, his pulse picking up when she moved easily to his flow, as natural and fluid in his arms as if she belonged there all along. *And you do, Cassidy McClare, whether you know it or not.*

When the music ended, she looked up, green eyes glowing. "So, how'd I do?"

"Like you've been dancing all of your life, Sugar Pie." A grin tipped the corners of his mouth. "Congratulations, Cowgirl . . . you just graduated from the two-step to the three-step."

Her husky chuckle warmed his heart, and he laughed out loud when her feet did a little jig. "Oooo-oooo, can we do it again?"

"You bet." *And again and again and again . . .* "And this time I'll even teach you how to hold a conversation instead of counting out loud."

She teased her lip—and his heart—at the same time. "Goodness, you may regret this, MacKenna, because now I'll be dragging *you* to the floor."

One can certainly hope. "Naw, this is fun," he said, drawing her close as the orchestra began to play, more than content to hold her in his arms for the rest of the night. He'd danced with many a woman before, but none attracted him like Cassidy McClare. Delicate fingers clasped his, not unlike a child's hand in that of an adult, eliciting a protective urge he'd never experienced with a woman before. At six foot one, he towered over her by at least a foot, a slip of a thing adrift in pale-blue satin while wisps of corn silk fluttered her neck. The wide eyes and hint of freckles gave her a dainty, almost fragile air that made him feel more like a man than all the boxing matches, street fights, or innocent flirtations he'd shared in the past. She was absolutely, unequivocally everything he'd ever wanted in a woman. Palm warm against her back, he spun her around, pulse accelerating when her head lazed back with eyes closed, unleashing a throaty giggle that vibrated his skin. His gaze traced from the curve of her neck to the hollow of her throat, and his breathing thickened at the thought of his lips doing the same. He exhaled slowly, desperate to project the air of casual confidence he'd honed to an art in a society in which he longed to rise to the top. *Easy does it, MacKenna,* he warned, smiling as he whirled her in his arms. "See? I told you you could trust me."

"I'm afraid it's going to take more than a spin on the floor, Pretty Boy," she said with a sassy smile. She tilted her head with an adorably eager look just as the song ended. "Again?"

He laughed. "If you don't make me carry you off the floor when I wear you out."

"Oh, as if you could," she said, smirk firmly in place.

Grinning, he drew her close when the orchestra began to play "In the Good Old Summer Time," and Jamie couldn't help but think how appropriate it was for this summer of all summers. Newly graduated, a promising career at Logan's prestigious law firm, and maybe even marry a McClare. He grinned, sweeping Cassie wide to watch the soft tendrils of her hair flutter in the breeze. Once again she'd closed her eyes, and the song just naturally parted from his lips, his baritone rich if slightly off-key. "In the good old summertime, in the good old summertime . . ."

Her lashes lifted in a slow sweep, and those green eyes held him spellbound while the lyrics slowed and softened on his tongue, his melody capturing her as much as her eyes had captured him. He continued his song, the lyrics fading to a whisper. "You hold her hand and she holds yours, and that's a very good sign . . ." His gaze flicked to her lips and back while his voice grew husky and hoarse. "So, what do you think, Cassidy McClare . . . is it?"

"Is what?" she whispered, gaze bonded to his as if hypnotized.

"A good sign?"

"Is what a good sign?" she repeated softly, a hint of that same starry-eyed look he'd seen when he'd kissed her in the billiard room. His heart swelled with pride and more than a little hope. *She's falling for you, MacKenna—almost as hard as you, so don't mess this up . . .*

A smile glided across his lips as he allowed his gaze to drop to her mouth and back. "You know—me holding your hand, and you holding mine," he whispered, "like the song says."

Her full lips parted as a lump shifted in that long, beautiful throat, and he was pretty sure the heat in her cheeks was catching when it hiked his body temperature by several degrees.

"No, Ma, you can't make me—she's ugly!"

Jamie glanced up, lyrics and song forgotten at the sight of a tall, gangly boy shrugging off his mother's hand. He bolted from the table where a scarlet-faced girl hunched in apparent shame, eyes downcast as she knotted nervous hands in her lap. The woman, as red-faced as the young girl, appeared to be apologizing to the girl's mother who hovered next to her daughter. Jamie's gut clenched when he realized the young girl was crying, and his heart turned over at the cruelty of the young man. No more than sixteen, the girl's nondescript brown hair was styled in the loose upsweep of the day, but her features were plain and marred by acne. Her red satin bodice heaved as she wept, causing her chubby body to quiver like the tomato aspic he'd had for dinner. The injustice of it stung deep, calcifying Jamie's jaw. Years of slurs and taunts echoed in his brain—*gutter trash, street arab, slum rat*—causing his fingers to itch for just one shot at the little punk who'd rejected her. He thought of both Jess and Meg and all the ridicule they'd endured at the hands of hooligans just like this kid—Jess because she was crippled, Meg because she was plump—and it took everything in him not to hunt him down and throttle him good. He expelled a blast of air. "Why can't people just leave each other alone?" he muttered.

"What's wrong?" Cassie asked, her brows pinched as she attempted to follow his gaze.

"Cass," he said quietly, eyes glued to the girl, "would you mind terribly if I took you back to the table—there's something I need to do."

"Well, no, I suppose not," she said slowly, glancing over her shoulder at the table at which he'd been staring. Her eyes flared wide. "Wait—is that young woman crying?"

"Yes, she is . . . ," he said quietly, firmly leading Cass from the floor.

"So, how'd she do?" Alli asked, smile fading when she saw Jamie's granite jaw. Ignoring her, he seated Cassie with a gentle squeeze of her shoulder. "The next dance is mine, Miss McClare," he said before disappearing through the crowd. Approaching the girl's table, he could hear her quiet heaves and the soothing whispers of her mother while a man Jamie assumed to be her father stood close, gently kneading her shoulder.

Jamie offered a short bow. "Excuse me, Miss—but may I have this dance?"

Three heads shot up, eyes agape. No one spoke, and Jamie's heart softened at the girl's soggy lashes and mottled cheeks. He extended his hand, the smile on his lips as gentle as his tone. "If you'd rather not, I understand, but it would enhance my evening if you did."

She blinked, blue eyes glazed with tears and cheeks dotted with circles of dusty rose that grew as he awaited her answer. Something strong squeezed in his chest, and in that moment, Jamie knew nothing could enrich his evening more, short of time with Cassie.

"Janet, the young man is asking to dance," the woman whispered.

The older gentleman rose and offered his hand in a shake. "Dr. Winterberger, young man, and this is my wife, Delpha, and our daughter Janet. And you are . . . ?"

"James MacKenna, sir," Jamie said, reciprocating with a solid grasp of his hand.

"I say there," the doctor said with a squint, "did I see you seated with Logan McClare?"

"Yes, sir—Mr. McClare is my mentor and employer as well as a good friend."

He studied Jamie with a keen eye. "McClare, Rupert and Byington is my law firm, son. I've never had dealings with Logan, of course, but Thomas Rupert and I go way back."

"Is that right?" Jamie grinned, facial muscles easing more from the shy smile on the girl's face than the legal connection with her father. "I have great admiration for Mr. Rupert—he interviewed me for the position, of course, along with Mr. McClare and Mr. Byington."

The doctor nodded. "Well, it appears they made a wise choice, given the courtesy of your manner." He turned to his daughter. "Janet—this young man has had the courtesy to ask for a dance—I suggest you comply."

"Yes, Papa," she said with a chew of her lip, peeking up at Jamie beneath heavy lashes.

"Shall we?" Jamie offered his arm, and the young woman tentatively placed her hand over his, following his lead as he ushered her to the floor. On their way, they passed the young man who'd made her cry, his sullen look glazing into shock at the sight of Janet on Jamie's arm.

"You look very pretty tonight, Miss Winterberger," Jamie said, loud enough for the hooligan to hear, and the kid actually froze to the spot, jaw distended while he stared.

"Thank you," she whispered, and her glow of innocence brought a smile to Jamie's lips. Taking her hand in his, he noted the lift of her chin and the squaring of her shoulders despite her gentle manner and timid hold, making Janet Winterberger very pretty, indeed.

At least, to him.

14

"Who's Jamie dancing with?" Alli peeked through the throng of dancers, green eyes in a squint. "I don't think I've ever seen her before, and we come to The Palace fairly often."

"I'm not sure," Cassie said, hand splayed to her chest to slow the chaotic beat of her heart. "But I think she was crying."

"Crying?" Alli blinked, dark brows sloped in question. "Whatever for?"

A sigh floated from Cassie's lips as she watched Jamie chatting and whirling the girl to a waltz, his heart-melting grin skipping Cassie's pulse. "I don't know," she said, biting her thumbnail, "but I think he asked that sweet young woman to dance to make her feel better."

"Yep, that sounds like Jamie," Alli said with a chuckle. "Most men with his looks tend to be rather self-absorbed, but that boy is definitely one of a kind." She turned back to Cassie and swatted at her with a playful scold. "Hey, stop that! Chewing on your nails is a bad habit."

Cassie spit out a sliver. *So is Jamie MacKenna, but I can't seem to stop that either . . .*

"I thought you quit biting your nails." Alli snatched a fork to poke at her dessert.

149

Pthu! Another splinter sailed through the air while Cassie continued with the other thumb, eyes trained on the "bad habit" who was laughing with the girl on the floor. "Started again . . . after Mark," she muttered with another spit.

"Well, stop it, you goose!" Alli grabbed Cassie's hand, her laughter belying the concern in her eyes. "What's with you tonight? Did Jamie do something to upset you?"

"Yeah," she mumbled, "he asked a shy, little wallflower to dance."

The whites of Alli's eyes expanded as comprehension dawned. "Wait a minute," she said with a slow smile, "you're falling for him, aren't you?" She grinned. "After that long-winded spiel you gave me about not trusting a hair on that pretty boy's head?"

"Oh, hush," Cassie whispered, her gaze darting around the table to see if anyone else had heard. She exhaled slowly, relieved the others were engrossed in one of her uncle's stories. Turning back, she seared her cousin with a narrow gaze. "Over my dead body."

"You mean dead 'pride,' don't you?"

Alli's wink unleashed heat in Cassie's cheeks that stung almost as much as her blasted pride. She clamped her cousin's arm, fingers tightening to a pinch. "Look, Al, this is not funny. I'm shaking in my boots here, and I left 'em at home, for pity's sake! I have *no* time for this."

"Sure you do," Alli said with a massage of Cassie's shoulders. She ducked to smile into her cousin's eyes. "Every girl has time for a really great guy who could make her happy."

"No!" Cassie's tone came out too sharply, tears smarting despite her best efforts.

"Hey," Alli said, eyes tender. "You're really scared, aren't you?"

Cassie shot to her feet, body trembling. "Feel like some air?" she whispered.

"Sure." Alli rose and took Cassie's hand, smiling at Caitlyn when she glanced their way. "Mother, Cassie and I will be out on the veranda." Giving Cassie's palm a squeeze, she led her toward a bank of floor-to-ceiling windows at the far end of the ballroom. Each was draped in rich, claret velvet, a striking contrast to warm honeyed wood walls that rose to an exquisite vaulted ceiling. Austrian crystal chandeliers sparkled like diamonds overhead as she ushered Cassie through a beveled glass door onto a veranda where the smell of sea breeze mingled with that of the city below. Steering her to a private stone bench at the far end, she pressed her to sit and then sat beside her. "Okay, what's going on, Cass?" she said quietly.

The night was warm, but Cassie tucked her arms tightly to her waist as if she were chilled. "I can't fall in love with him, Al," she whispered, eyes lagging into a cold stare. "I'm too raw. Mark wounded me, and I'm just not ready for this."

Alli sighed, the sound swallowed up by the gentle trickling of the fountain nearby. "He's not Mark, Cass, he's one of the good guys—"

Cassie spun to face her, her breathing shallow. "I know, but he's not for me."

"But how will you know till you try? The guy's smitten. For heaven's sake, he lights up every time you walk in a room. He's a great guy and we all love him—what more do you need?"

Her lips tipped into a sad smile. "More, I'm afraid." She peered up beneath weighted lids. "He has no faith, Al."

Alli blinked. "What do you mean he has no faith? He goes to church every Sunday."

A sigh withered on Cassie's lips. "Yes, he does, but he doesn't believe."

Silence prevailed as Alli stared in obvious disbelief, the faint sound of the orchestra harmonizing with the splash of the fountain and the hum of the city below. "That's ridiculous. How can someone not believe in God, especially when he has a God-fearing family?"

Cassie rubbed her temple, grimacing at the headache that suddenly appeared. "I think he's angry inside—over his sister's illness and the life they've been forced to live, I don't know." She drew in a heavy breath scented with the fragrance of potted tea roses that dotted the veranda wall. "All I do know is I won't give my heart to a man again till I know he's given his to God. Because I don't just want to share a bed, a family, and a life, Al—I want to share a faith as well."

"Oh, goodness, Cass, I didn't know," Alli whispered, shoulders slumped. "That makes me sad because I love Jamie." She clutched Cassie's hand. "I'm so sorry."

"I know, me too." Cassie exhaled slowly. "Especially after seeing him reach out to that girl like he did." She sucked in a calming breath as thoughts of Jamie MacKenna triggered her pulse. "I've been picked on and ostracized my whole life in Humble, so nobody knows better than you, Al, just how much Jamie's actions with that girl meant to me, someone with a soft heart for the downtrodden." She sighed. "There's a powerful lot of good in a man like that."

"Yes, there is," Alli agreed. She hesitated. "What are you going to do?"

Cassie gave a little shrug that sagged her shoulders. "Keep him at arm's length as a friend, I guess." She offered Alli a melancholy smile. "And pray."

"I'll join you," Alli said with a tender smile. "Even Jamie Mac-Kenna can't win against prayer." She patted Cassie's arm and lumbered to her feet, brushing the wrinkles from her dress. "Ready to go back in?"

"Not just yet." Cassie stood and gave her a hug, then nodded skyward with a wry twist of a smile. "I think I'd like to have a few words with You-Know-Who first."

Alli laughed. "Always a good plan, as Mother says."

"Yes, it is," Cassie said with a chuckle, "and trust me—I plan to give him an earful." With a final hug, Cassie strolled to a shadowed corner of the veranda to lean on the marble balustrade, peering at the city while the breeze from the bay feathered her hair. From stories high overhead, the autos and horse-driven carriages looked like miniature toys, bustling about to the bleat of distant car horns and the muted clang of the trolley. Buffing her arms, she lifted her gaze to the inky sky, glittering with stars that winked and waited for her to beseech their Maker.

"God, it's me, and I need your help. You see, Jamie MacKenna and I have become very good friends, but I have to admit—my heart is leaning towards more." She closed her eyes, the next words chilling her skin. "But he doesn't believe in you, Lord, and I know you don't want me unevenly yoked, so I guess you'll either have to take these annoying feelings away or . . . ," she peeked up with one eye, "hog-tie him till he cries uncle, 'cause heaven knows he needs you." Eyelids lifting, she squinted up at the sky. "Oh, and he tells me his mother and sister have been talking to you for a long time, so I'm pretty sure you'd want to answer their prayers too, and this is the perfect opportunity." She paused, the tease fading from her tone. "But whatever you decide—friends or more—*please* get ahold of his heart, because when the cows come home at the end of the day, he really is a pretty wonderful guy." With a final soggy sniff, she swiped at her eyes, a trace of a smile shading her lips. "That is, for a pretty boy."

"So . . . two questions, Cait," Logan said. "One—why did you finally agree to dance with me after declining all night and two—why did you agree to Napa?" He spun her in his arms, the orchestra's rendition of Jere Mahoney's "For Old Time's Sake" haunting him as much as he hoped it haunted her. His heart thudded as he studied her in the soft glow of the chandeliers overhead. The flawless porcelain skin, the eyes the color of jade, and that lustrous auburn hair piled high with enough loose strays to tease an alabaster neck, leaving no doubt that his attraction to her had never waned. Oh, he'd buried it deep when she'd married his brother, certainly, allowing him to survive the loss of her in his heart and in his bed, but somehow it surfaced with a vengeance in the last year, and that alone told him that the timing was right.

She'd been chattering nonstop while they danced, so out of character for a woman as content with silence as conversing with family and friends, and he couldn't help the faint smile that shadowed his lips. She was obviously nervous—the song, the dancing, the memories—all too close to home for them both, and her unease reminded him of the girl he'd proposed to years ago in this very ballroom. She'd been shy and sweet and oh, so tempting, but innocent to a fault. A "fault" that resulted in utter shock when he'd dallied with another. He exhaled slowly, his regret hidden behind an easy smile. *Just one more chance, Cait—for old time's sake?*

She stared at him now on the heels of his questions, the chatter suddenly nowhere in sight, and he was fascinated by the flare of her pupils, the shift of her throat, those full lips so ripe for tasting now parted in shallow breaths. He awaited her response while heavily fringed eyelids flickered in thought, and he realized her pull on him was stronger now than the night he'd slipped the ring on her finger. He hadn't been just smitten with her then, no, he'd been besotted, but a man whose desire for her, regrettably, was far outweighed by youthful lust.

"Why did I finally agree to dance with you?" she repeated, her voice as wispy as the gauzy pale-yellow bodice that rose and fell with every breath she took. Her chin lifted enough for him to know she was steeling herself for battle, promptly broadening the smile on his lips. A good sign—at least she was battling something. Her feelings for him, perhaps? Or his for her?

"Yes, why now?" he said, with a shuttered smile. He slowed his steps as the music ended, but held firm lest she bolt away. "After cruelly turning me away all night."

Color toasted her cheeks, and the chin rose higher. "I danced with you because you asked, Logan McClare, and I didn't prior because I was engaged in stimulating conversations." She stepped back a fraction of an inch despite his lock on her waist.

The strains of "Absence Makes the Heart Grow Fonder" filtered through the ballroom, and Logan found himself hoping that the song was prophetic for Cait. Heaven knows it was for him. He grinned. "Come on, Cait, you're not a woman prone to untruths. Why don't you just admit the only reason you said yes is because it's my birthday and you felt guilty?"

A pretty shade of rose burnished her cheeks and he laughed. She was so easy to read . . . *and* rile. He swept her in a wide arc, savoring the way wisps of her auburn tresses fluttered in the breeze. "Besides, Mrs. McClare," he said softly, "I can be stimulating too." The rogue in him took over as his gaze flitted to her lips and back, his voice a husky whisper. "Or don't you remember?"

Color swamped her throat and cheeks, nearly swallowing her whole, and he laughed out loud, firming his grip when she tried to pull away. "Come on, Cait, I'm sorry, but you're just so easy to bait." His smile ebbed into a tender look. "You always were, as I recall."

Shooting a nervous glance at their table, she fixed him with a stern gaze, gold flecks of fire in those startling green eyes. "*Please* keep your voice down." Her nostrils flared slightly as she drew in a calming breath, chin engaged once again. "And I'd appreciate it if you would not refer to our past to anyone, including me." Her tone softened. "We are friends, Logan, please keep that in mind. I am not one of your many women to be toyed with, I am your sister-in-law. I ask that you treat me with the respect due your brother's wife."

He gave her a veiled look. "You mean my brother's widow," he said quietly.

Her jaw set. "Either way, you are my brother-in-law, and it's uncomfortable when your comments or actions are overly familiar."

Grip firm, his eyes and voice softened. "You forget, Cait," he whispered, his humor no longer a mask for his feelings, "I *am* overly familiar with you whether you like it or not. I know your habits, your expressions, every nuance of your face. I know you take Earl Gray with sugar in the morning and Chamomile without at night. I know you have a habit of jutting your chin when backed into corner and that you tend toward melancholy when fatigued. You pick at your nails when you're nervous and you twirl your hair when in thought, and despite your love for the classics," he said in a rush, exhaling slowly, "you have a secret fondness for dime novels." His voice trailed to a whisper. "Especially on rainy days."

She stared, lips parted, as if poised for her lungs to start breathing again.

Her hand felt small and warm in his and with a shift of his throat, he gently circled her palm with his thumb. "We have *history*, Cait," he said softly.

Tears glimmered as she carefully slipped her hand from his, the grief in her face a mirror of his own. "Yes, we do. But that's no basis for a future." Slowly, gently, she cupped a palm to his cheek. "I need a friend, Logan, nothing more." The bridge of her nose puckered as she studied him intently. "Can you be that for me—please?" The orchestra began to play, and she took his hand. "Can we celebrate your birthday as family members who respect and support each other?" She peered up, a gentle woman with a gentle request. "And friends—good friends?"

He paused, unable to breathe for the ache in his chest. Bracing his palm to her shoulder, he lifted her hand to begin the dance, a dance of will and heart that he was determined to win. He smiled, his manner as kind as hers. "Sure, Cait, friends." With casual grace, he whirled her to the music, her body suddenly relaxed and fluid and calm.

For now.

15

"Is Cass in there?" Jamie squinted at the ladies' room door Allison had just exited with a group of society matrons, their brows in a scrunch.

Alli perched a hand to the waist of her pale-green dress where ruffles swept to her hip. She tossed her head back, midnight-black curls shimmering beneath a crystal chandelier as she blew wisps of bangs from her eyes. "Why? You planning on going in?" she asked, a mischievous gleam in piercing green eyes much darker than Cassie's.

Jamie's lip swerved. "No, but she owes me a dance, and I plan to collect."

"Mmm . . . only a dance?" Tongue in cheek, Alli folded her arms to stare him down.

His collar suddenly felt on fire, and he scowled. "What, does she tell you everything?" he groused, absently gouging the back of his neck.

"Uh-huh, which means I have her ear all the time while you, my good friend," she said with a pat of his cheek, "only had her lips—once."

Okay, now his entire dinner jacket was aflame. Hands sweating, he pried a finger inside his collar to release some of the heat. "Aw, come on, Al—have a heart."

Alli laughed and swallowed him in a tight hug. "You are *so* adorable when you're embarrassed, you know that? Just like a little boy caught misbehaving." She stepped back, bracing his arms while the smile softened on her lips. "You like her a lot, don't you?"

Jamie plunged his hands in his pockets, feeling every bit of that little boy she'd just accused him of. "Yeah, I do." He inclined his head, coaxing with a boyish smile. "So . . . you gonna help me steal her heart or not?"

A delicate sigh escaped Alli's lips as she patted his arms and let go. "I'd like nothing better, Mac, but there's only so much I can do." She glanced up, sympathy radiating from her eyes. "She has reservations, Jamie, and they're good ones. You need to talk to her."

The sweat beneath his collar glazed to ice. "What do you mean 'reservations'? Like her lack of trust because of that louse in Texas?"

"Yes, but it's more than that." She cupped a hand to his cheek, her voice soft. "Just talk to her, before you get hurt. I care about you too much to see you pursue something you can't have, especially a relationship with no future."

Jamie caught her hand and held on, his eyes issuing a challenge. "Oh, we have a future all right, Allison, you mark my words on that, whether your cousin wants to admit it or not."

Alli assessed him through pensive eyes. "I'd like to believe that, Jamie, I really would. But you have to be prepared to let it go if Cassie says no."

"She won't," he said with a shift of his tie, his confidence as shaky as his fingers as they tugged at the cuffs of his coat. "Where is she—do you know?"

"On the veranda, I think. Left her there not ten minutes ago."

He bent to press a kiss to Alli's forehead. "Thanks, Al—wish me luck."

"I'd rather you ask me to pray, Jamie," she whispered, "and so would Cassie."

He eyed her over his shoulder, lips in a clamp. "Sure—whatever works." Annoyance prickled as he made his way to the door, quite sure it would be his efforts and not God's that would turn Cassie McClare's head. Drawing in a steady breath, he reached for the brass knob of the veranda door. A welcome wash of briny air cooled the sweat on his brow as he stepped outside, blinking to adjust to the darkness where a smattering of couples nuzzled here and there. He scanned the marble veranda, gaze searching the stone wall till he spotted her at the far end, tucked away in the shadows. She stood, face to the sky and palms on the balustrade while a breeze fluttered her hair. His throat went dry, and he realized he was already way in over his head. *I care about you too much, Jamie, to see you pursue something you can't have.* His jaw molded tight. *Oh, I'll have her, all right,* he vowed. *Whatever it takes . . .*

He approached silently from behind, the chords of "Hello, Central, Give Me Heaven" floating in the air with the scent of lilacs from Cassie's perfume, and Jamie was almost tempted to pray, so close was "heaven" within his grasp. With a silent exhale, he moved to the wall to stand beside her, casually leaning over the balcony with arms folded and eyes lifted to the sky. "Wishing on a star, Miss McClare?" he said softly, turning to study her in the moonlight.

She smiled, her satin dress shimmering from either a breeze off the bay or a contented sigh. "Something like that." She peeked up. "That was really nice what you did tonight, Jamie."

He deflected with an awkward grin. "Naw, 'nice' would be boxing the ears of that little hooligan who made that sweet little girl cry." His humor faded as his gaze returned to the sea, a tic pulsing in his jaw. "Nothing makes me angrier than that—people picking on people, belittling them, ostracizing them, thinking they're better when they're not." He sucked in a sharp breath, suddenly aware of his harsh tone. "Sorry, Cass, but few things grate on me more than that."

"Sounds like painful experience," she said quietly, gaze fixed on her hand as she picked at her nails.

He glanced at the nubby beds of her long, slender fingers and smiled. Holy thunder, he even liked that about her, the fact that she wasn't like every other woman who polished their carefully manicured nails with tinted powders and creams. No, Cassie was as natural and unconventional as the gentle spray of freckles that dusted her nose and shoulders, telling Jamie loud and clear that her beauty was not just skin deep. It was honest and real and true all the way to the bone. He straightened to face her, hip cocked to the wall. "You could say that, I suppose, but I prefer to focus on the pleasurable experiences, such as teaching a cowgirl to dance." With a slow reach, he tucked a loose strand of hair behind her ear, lingering several seconds too long. "I seem to remember you owe me a dance, Miss McClare."

Her pert little chin angled high. "Is that so?" She nodded toward the ballroom. "Then I suggest we remedy that."

She turned toward the door and he caught her hand, drawing her into his arms for a waltz. "My thoughts exactly," he whispered in her ear, twirling her before she could object.

"Jamie!" Her voice was a raspy scold. "What are you doing?"

"Teaching you to dance, Sugar Pie, and judging from your progress, I'm pretty good."

He caught her off-guard with a wide spin, holding her closer than he had inside, and she giggled, body gliding with his as

161

naturally as breathing. "Oh, I have to admit, this *is* fun," she said with a heady sigh. She paused, thick lashes edging up. "But . . . were you holding me this close inside?"

He grinned and whirled her in several broad sweeps in a row, hoping she was at least a fraction as dizzy as his heart. "Absolutely," he lied, unable to resist the slide of his hand to her waist when the music came to an end. He bent close, exercising every sliver of willpower he possessed to keep from suckling the lobe of her ear. "Dizzy?"

Dizzy? Cassie closed her eyes, lips parted in shallow breaths. Reeling might be a better word, not unlike the time she'd been bucked by that filly in the county-fair rodeo. Her head spun faster than their palomino weather vane during a Texas thunderstorm, and now her pulse was pumping faster than their oil rigs used to do. Chest heaving, she opened her eyes to Jamie's half-lidded gaze lingering on her lips, and her stomach looped while her hands began to sweat. She tried to back away, but the press of his palms lured her close.

"Jamie, no . . . ," she wanted to say, but her body stifled the words, weighting her eyes shut as his mouth hovered close enough she could almost taste the crème brulee he had for dessert.

"So help me, Cass," he whispered, "this doesn't feel like friendship anymore . . ."

Her gasp met the caress of his lips, gentle and yet possessive as they nuzzled her mouth, swaying with restrained passion until he relented with a low groan, fingers sifting into the wisps of hair at the nape of her neck. He cupped her head to deepen his kiss, and her hand fisted his shirt, clinging tighter than she had to that filly's neck on the ride of her life. *Bloomin' saints*, she thought, as woozy as if she'd just bolted some wine, *make that the second ride of my life . . .*

Jamie jerked away, chest heaving and a glaze in his eyes—or maybe it was just her—tenderly framing her face with massive palms while his thumbs feathered her mouth. "I'm falling for you, Cass," he whispered, the shock of his words icing her skin. Gone was the self-assured womanizer and in his place, a little boy with a hint of puppy-dog eyes, the slightest bit of trepidation in his tone. "I love being your friend, truly . . ." The white bow tie and tall winged collar shifted with his Adam's apple while his voice faded to a whisper. "But I want more."

"More?" She was too much in a fog to stop her eyes from fluttering closed when he bent to graze her lips with an achingly gentle kiss.

"Yes," he breathed in her ear, the effect akin to a Texas heat wave. "I want to court you."

The fog lifted as quickly as her eyelids, which shot up faster than a renegade bronc with a loose saddle of burrs. *Merciful Providence—as in marriage?*

"Promise you'll save your heart for God's best, Cass—a man who loves God as much as you do . . ." Aunt Cait's words haunted her mind while Jamie's haunted her heart. She felt the wild thump of his pulse beneath her fingers still embedded in his shirt, and with a harsh catch of her breath, they sprang flat against his rock-hard chest, palms thrusting him back. "J-jamie, no . . . I'm sorry, but I can't . . ."

Something steeled in his jaw when those hazel eyes locked with hers, penetrating her heart as easily as his kiss had done. "Yes, you can, Cass, because you're falling for me too . . ."

"No, Jamie, I'm no—" The words died in her throat when his mouth took hers with a fury, unleashing waves of heat that rolled through her body as he delved deeper, chest heaving against hers when he finally pulled away. With a heated gaze, he slowly traced from the quiver of her jaw to the hollow of her throat, grazing her skin with the pad of his thumb. "Your pulse says different, Cass," he said quietly, the shocking truth leaving her limp in his arms.

Her eyes drifted closed, palms splayed to his chest. "That may be, Jamie, but we can't . . ."

"Why?" It was little more than a hiss, the first flicker of temper she'd ever seen in the gallant Jamie MacKenna, matching the sudden tension of his hold. "Because of that snake-bellied ex-fiancé who taught you not to trust any man?"

She eased from his grip, distancing herself with a wobbly step back. "Yes, because of Mark," she said, buffing her arms. "And because I've learned I can't trust just any man. Trust is key with me, Jamie, and it's the only foundation I'll settle for in the marriage I hope to have."

The breath caught in her throat as he gripped her again, the plea in his tone matching the urgency in his eyes. "You can trust me, Cass—I've tried to prove that this last month as a friend, but friendship isn't enough anymore. And I'm not just 'any man'— I'm the one who loves you and needs you and wants to make you his wife."

Slipping from his grasp, she eased away, her heart cramping at the look of hurt in his eyes. "I care about you, Jamie, way more than I should, and you're a good man, you are. But I need more than a good man." She paused, almost hesitant to say what was in her heart for the pain it would cause. "I need a good man who needs God as much as he needs me."

His jaw dropped a full inch while a nerve pulsed in his temple. "That's what this is about? Because I told you I don't believe in God?" He wheeled around, slashing shaky fingers through his hair, the mutter of garbled words stinging the air. Pivoting halfway, he glared, hands slung low on his hips. "Let me get this straight, because I want to be sure I understand. You're falling in love with me and I'm in love with you and I'm already practically one of the family . . . but you're stomping on my heart because I don't believe in God?"

She clutched her arms to her waist. "That sounds so harsh when you put it that way . . ."

He hiked a brow. "Oh, it is, Miss McClare, it is." He gouged the back of his neck, finally facing her head on. "So, where does that leave us, then? You want me to convert, is that it?"

She shook her head, heart sinking. "No, Jamie," she whispered, "not for me—for you."

His laugh was bitter. "I've done just fine up until now, Cowgirl. I don't need him."

A frail breath drifted from her lips. "No," she said quietly, "but I do." She rubbed her arms while she avoided his gaze. "And so does the man I hope to trust with my heart someday." The cool sea air shivered through her. "It's chilly—we better go in."

He halted her with a touch of his hand, a tinge of anger to his tone. "So, where are we, then, Cass? Two friends who want more but can't because God stands in the way?"

"No, just two friends." Her smile was sad. "Unless you don't even want that."

His mouth clamped tight. "No, I can handle it, Miss McClare. How 'bout you?"

She forced a smile, chin high. "If I can trust you to keep your hands to yourself."

"After that lecture on trust?" Jamie hooked her elbow to steer her toward the door, lips flat and tone even worse. "To borrow a phrase that is spot on, Miss McClare—'perish the thought.'"

"You *told* him?" Alli paused in front of Cassie's vanity table, fingers paralyzed on black ringlets atop her head as her eyes flared wide in shock. Perched on the vanity bench in corset and chemise, she stared at Cassie in the mirror. "That you wouldn't court him? Sweet heavenly days," she muttered, stabbing several hairpins in with a vengeance before whirling around. Long, black curls spiraled over the satin ribbon straps tied at her shoulders. "Was he hurt?"

Cassie sighed, the lasso in her hands failing to bring its usual comfort as she lay on her bed in a funk, long hair spilling over the pillow. "Devastated . . . before he got angry, that is," she whispered, remembering the vulnerable look in his eyes when he'd told her he wanted "more" than friendship. She lovingly fingered the twisted hemp, its beloved smell of home unable to penetrate the gloom in her heart. "Said he was falling for me and wanted more."

Alli abandoned her toilette to hurry over to where Cassie lay, easing down beside her. "Oh, Cass, that breaks my heart."

"Mine too," Cassie said with a mournful sigh. "I really care about him, Al, and I'd give anything if it could be different. But I promised myself and Aunt Cait that the man I'd marry would have a strong faith in God, and you and I both know that's not Jamie."

Alli blinked, her affection for Jamie evident in the glaze of moisture in her eyes. "Well, you don't know," she said quietly, "maybe it could be . . . someday."

Cassie shivered, Alli's tears prompting her own. "I can't risk that, Al, falling in love with a man who may never have faith in God."

Alli kneaded her shoulder. "But you're already halfway there, Cass, so maybe Jamie's worth the risk? Maybe he just needs time to come around, to show him an image of God that could woo his soul like you've wooed his heart."

Fear coiled in her stomach like the lasso in her hands, and shaking her head, Cassie hurled a husk-stuffed leather cow with more force than intended, the one Daddy made for her to practice roping. Lips clamped, she rose up to swing the lariat in a circle overhead, launching it at the cow. "Sorry, Al—I'm still a little too raw from Mark to be a sitting duck for another man right now, even one I'm halfway in love with." The lasso neatly cinched around the toy's neck, and Cassie jerked with a snap, landing the fat, little cow back on her bed.

Alli nabbed it, lips in a slant. "Somehow, I don't see *you* as the 'sitting duck,'" she said, bobbling the cow in her hand. "More like Jamie as a hapless steer about to be roped when you save him from himself."

Snatching it from her cousin's hand, Cassie lobbed it across the room with a grunt. "Yeah, and who's gonna save me when the steer becomes a bull who tramples my heart?"

Her cousin paused. "Oh, I don't know . . . God?"

Cassie peered from the corner of her eye. "You sound more like your mother every day."

Alli tipped her head, offering a teasing smile. "And that's a good thing, right?"

"Yes," Cassie relented, venting with a noisy sigh. "Except Aunt Cait made me promise to save my heart for a man who loves God."

"So, save it," Alli said, "with a friendship that shows Jamie what he's missing—both with you and with God."

Cassie grunted in the grand fashion of one of Daddy's cowhands. "Easier said than done." She whirled the lariat in the air and chucked it at the cow, hooking its neck. "The man can put a lip-lock on me faster than I can rope a steer, and when he does, I'm the one who ends up hog-tied." She wrenched it back to her lap, staring at its button eyes with a melancholy smile. "Just like he did on The Palace veranda."

Alli spun to face her, jaw dangling like the rope in Cassie's hands. "Merciful Providence, Cassidy McClare, he kissed you again and you didn't tell me?" She snatched the poor cow and flung it away. "That was days ago, and we swore to tell each other everything!"

Sneaking a peek, Cassie tugged at her lip. "I know, and I'm sorry, but I was ashamed."

"Because of one measly kiss?"

Cassie sucked air through a clenched smile, heat crawling her face. "Actually, it was three, and trust me, they were anything but 'measly.'" She gulped, the memory warming her skin as well as her cheeks. "I swear, Al, the man melts me into a puddle right on the floor."

"*Well* . . . don't-let-him," Alli said with a firm jack of her chin, enunciating each syllable. She leaned in, eyes sparking like jagged emeralds. "That's what got you into trouble with Mark, if you recall. Succumbing to his kisses till your heart was too far gone, and frankly, you and Jamie are too important to me for you to botch this up, Cass, so toughen up!"

Cassie's grin wobbled. "I don't remember you being so all-fired 'tough' with Tom Alt."

A blush bloodied Alli's cheeks as she folded her arms. "Yes, and that's exactly how I know. Mother warned me to keep a clear head, that a man's kisses can weaken a girl's resolve, but did I listen? No! And I was crushed when I found out he was a fraud after we'd announced our engagement, just like you when Mark broke it off before the wedding."

"I know." A sigh quivered from Cassie's lips.

"Look, Cass, when it comes to falling in love, neither of us have done too well, but together we can be strong." She stuck out her hand. "Let's make a pact right now that we'll keep each other accountable—with prayer and *no* secrets—so neither of us are charmed into heartbreak anymore, okay? You? By not letting Jamie MacKenna get within an inch of your lips till he turns over a new leaf, a man with faith in God courting you good and proper."

"And you?" Cassie asked with a teasing grin.

Alli's lips veered into a crooked smile. "The same with Roger Luepke—if and when I should be lucky enough to see the man in Napa."

"Deal!" Cassie grinned, feeling as if a weight had been lifted from her shoulders. Adrenaline began to flow as she considered the very thing to divert their attention from two pretty boys who threatened to steal their hearts. She shimmied against the headboard with a contented sigh, hugging the lariat to her chest. "Oh, Al, I can hardly wait to teach at Aunt Cait's Hand of Hope School—to rechannel our energies into something more productive and worthwhile than just mooning over men. Has she said anything more about the building she's hoping to buy?"

The mention of her mother's dream was all it took to spark Alli's eyes as she shifted to sit cross-legged on Cassie's bed. "No, just that it's an old abandoned house on the edge of the Barbary Coast, but Mother says she submitted a petition to the Board of Supervisors docket for next month, so maybe soon. I haven't seen it, but I do know it was condemned by the fire marshal, which is why she needs board approval. Of course, it needs a lot of work, but Mother claims it's the perfect size and location and within easy access for so many young girls." Alli released a wispy sigh. "We've already selected a curriculum and spoken to a number of teachers who are just as excited as we are. And Mother's friend Walter from the Vigilance Committee says the Board's sure to jump at the chance to rectify the blight of that old house."

Cassie stared at the ceiling, her thoughts far beyond Jamie

MacKenna. "Honestly, Al, I think I could be happy as a spinster for the rest of my days just teaching young women the importance of education and fending for themselves." Her throat thickened at the thought of Mark's rejection. "After what Mark did, I never want to be dependent on a man's love again as if it and it alone is responsible for any happiness I might have. No, siree—I have a mind and I hope to use it to empower young women to make choices in life other than just being subject to a man's attention." She grasped Alli's hand, a fervor in her tone that swelled inside until she thought she might burst. "Oh, Al, just think! To continue the work of women like Susan B. Anthony and Julia Ward Howe, pioneers in the women's suffrage movement. To help pave the way for a world where women are free to be all that God intends us to be. Goodness, you and I have an opportunity to be a part of that, and what better place than the Barbary Coast where thousands of women are still enslaved in brothels and dance halls?"

"I know!" Alli said, tone breathless. "And we also get to use our talents in the process—you with math and singing, and me with English and drama." She plopped back on her pillow and stretched out on the bed, ankles crossed and bare feet twitching. "Goodness, I don't think I've been this excited in a long, long while."

A low chuckle rumbled from Cassie's chest. "At least not since you saw Roger Luepke," she said with a tweak of Alli's shoulder.

Alli grinned. "You may be right . . ." She suddenly paused, head cocked. "Wait—do you hear something?"

Cassie listened, a pucker crinkling above her nose. "Sounds like somebody whimpering." Holding her breath, she inclined her ear, then jumped up to peek in the hall, heart slamming at the sound of muffled weeping behind Meg's door. "Al," she whispered, "I think Meg's crying."

Alli jumped up to follow Cassie. "Meg?" Cassie said with a light tap on her cousin's door, "are you all right?"

The crying stopped, and Cassie knocked again. "Meg, can we come in? Please?"

At Meg's nasal response, Cassie opened the door . "Oh, honey," she said, making a beeline to where Meg lay on the bed, curled in a ball.

Alli rushed to sit beside her sister, gently stroking her hair. "Meggie, what's wrong?"

Loose strands from Meg's reddish-blonde chignon fell across her face as she wept, her typically creamy complexion now blotchy and red. She looked up with shaky heave, white linen skirt rumpled and green eyes rimmed raw behind gold wire-rims. "D-devin C-caldwell m-made f-fun of m-me at Amanda Rice's b-birthday p-party . . ." Her voice lapsed into a sob.

Alli hugged her tightly, eyes on fire as she peered up at Cassie. "Oh, so help me, Cass, Devin Caldwell is one brat I'd love to see you string up with your lasso. That twerp has been tormenting Meg since the first grade."

A hiccup popped from Meg's mouth as she blew her nose. "Unfortunately, he's not a 'twerp' anymore, which is the whole problem. He's always been the smartest and most popular boy at St. Patrick's, but a real runt who made fun of me because I always beat him in the spelling bees between St. Vincent's and St. Patrick's." She sniffed. "Now he's as tall as Blake and just as handsome and picks on me all the more whenever our schools have joint events."

"Maybe he likes you," Cassie said, crouching to tuck Meg's hair behind her ear with a gentle smile. "Sometimes boys will pick on a girl when they're smitten."

A tiny grunt erupted from Meg's throat that almost made

Cassie smile except for the sudden glaze of tears. She shook her head, strawberry tresses quivering with the motion. "No, Devin's always been mean to me, so he's not smitten, not with the awful things he says."

"Like what, honey?" Cassie plunked down beside her to cup Meg's hands in her own.

Meg sat up, tearstains dotting her glasses. "He calls me tubby and four eyes and wallflower among other things, but usually to my face, not in front of a whole crowd like he did today . . ." Her voice started to bubble again.

"Oh, Meg . . ." Alli embraced her while Cassie caressed her arm. "Then he's nothing but a pompous, arrogant toad, and if you want, Cass and I can go rough him up—she brought her lasso, you know."

Meg's heave tumbled into a giggle, easing some of the ache in Cassie's chest over anyone picking on her sweet cousin. Removing her glasses, Meg dabbed at her eyes with a handkerchief. "Believe me, there's nothing I'd like more than to see Devin Caldwell trussed up with Cassie's rope, sporting a black eye, but the truth's more painful than his awful insults."

"And what's that, sweetie?" Cassie asked, brushing hair from Meg's eyes.

Meg drew in a shaky breath and released it again, a cumbersome sigh sagging the shoulders of her pretty ruffled, capped blouse. "I like him. Always have from that first spelling bee in the first grade."

"Oh, good grief, Meggie, whatever for?" Alli said in a huff. "The boy's a worm."

"Yes, why?" Cassie said, shocked that Meg could be drawn to such a pickle-brained pest.

Meg blew on her glasses and wiped them clean, her full cheeks circled with pink. "I don't know, he's funny, smart, and very quick-witted, all things I admire." She chewed on her lip before sliding a sheepish glance first at Cass, then at Alli. "Of course it doesn't hurt he has gorgeous blue eyes with a bit of the devil in them and enough muscles to make a girl swoon."

"Humph," Alli said, "sounds like a cocky buffoon to me, and if there's anything Cass and I've learned in our dealings with men, it's to stay far away from knotheads like him."

Meg sighed, twirling a loose strand of hair around her finger. "No problem there—Devin Caldwell doesn't even know I exist except when he takes a notion to harass me."

A grunt rolled from Cassie's lips. "Alli's right, honey, you want to avoid pretty-boy polecats like him." Her smile took a slant. "They're nothing but trouble, trust me."

Meg tilted her head, offering Cassie a weak smile. "But you and Jamie are the best of friends now, Cass, and I heard you call him a pretty-boy polecat once."

"Humph—he still is, sweetie, but I'm a glutton for punishment, apparently." Cassie exhaled loudly, her breath fluttering more strays from Meg's disheveled chignon.

Meg followed suit, venting with a wispy release of air. "Mama says the best way to deal with someone like Devin Caldwell is to heap burning coals on his head like the Bible says."

"Oooo, branding—I like that." Cassie shot Alli a wink. "And cow patties are good too."

Alli chuckled, and Meg actually grinned. "I agree, but Mama claims heaping coals means returning good to someone instead of bad like they do to you. She says in ancient times, women carried hot coals on their head to light their own home fires and keep their houses warm, so heaping hot coals on someone's head meant blessing them instead of returning evil. Which is *so* hard to do with Devin." A twinkle of mischief lit her green eyes as her teeth tugged at the edge of her smile. "And I do try, believe me, but I have to admit I also work really hard to beat him at all the scholastic competitions between our two schools, and that makes him so mad!" Her giggle was soft. "Don't tell Mama, but it feels wonderful and so very liberating!"

"Good girl!" Alli gave her sister an affectionate squeeze. "It's nice to know that as sweet and shy as you are, Megan McClare, there's still a bit of the dickens lurking inside."

"I'll say," Cassie said with a grin. "Because you're going to need it in the future when you catch the eyes of pretty boys like Devin Caldwell who want to court you." Cassie's lip veered left. "That and a cattle prod." She blasted out a heavy sigh. "Much as it goes against my grain, I suppose Aunt Cait is right, which means we probably should handle Devin Caldwell the same way I handled Jamie MacKenna."

Alli leaned forward with a mischievous grin. "What, swoon at his feet?"

Cassie stared her down, eyes narrowed in warning. "So help me, Allison McClare, you are going to get your comeuppance in Napa, you mark my words." She squeezed Meg's hand. "Nope, we probably need to pray for the knothead because God knows he needs it."

"Don't they all?" Alli grinned, taking her sister's other hand in hers.

"Oh, yes," Cassie said with a firm jut of her chin, "but unfortunately . . ." She deposited a kiss to Meg's cheek before her lips zagged into a droll smile. "Not near as much as us."

Jamie rammed the receiver on the hook so hard, it actually quivered for several seconds, bobbling the candlestick phone.

Crumpling the letter from Cooper Medical, he blasted out a thunderous sigh and slumped over his polished wood desk, with his head in his hands, barely noticing when the balled-up letter slipped from his grasp. An unusually oppressive heat shimmered in from the third-story window of McClare, Rupert and Byington, bringing with it the smells and sounds of rush hour on Market Street in the summer. The pungent odor of horses and manure collided with the smell of gasoline and burnt-wood from the cable-car brakes while horns, whistles, and trolley bells jockeyed for prominence on a street that was a cobblestone zoo.

Dear Mr. MacKenna, we regret to inform you . . . Jamie hissed out a colorful word that crackled the air. "Dash it all, another blasted roadblock," he muttered, yanking hard at the stiff, tubular collar of his white shirt, wishing he could rip off the silk tie that nearly choked him to death. He kneaded the bridge of his nose, wondering how in blazes he was going to convince Cooper Medical to consider a hip cheilotomy for his sister as part of their charitable surgery allotment. Dr. John Benjamin Murphy of Mercy Hospital in Chicago had already done the hard part, devising this blessedly simple procedure to alleviate pain in damaged hip joints, and now the rest was up to him. Jess had long ago accepted the dull ache that was a daily part of her life, resorting to laudanum when the weather was poor or she walked too much, but Jamie could not. Her limp seemed to grow worse every day, and the guilt burrowed in his stomach like a splinter beneath pus-infected skin, throbbing until he thought he'd go mad.

Dread crawled up his windpipe. *What if I can't help her? What if she has to live in pain the rest of her life?* He shoved away from the desk to sink back in his chair, eyes pinched to shut out the thought. *No!* He couldn't fail her, *wouldn't!* If Cooper Medical refused his request each month, he'd just ask Duffy for more night hours to supplement his salary at the firm while working Sundays at the Oly along with Saturday afternoons. He'd hoped once graduated and working for Logan, he could pare back on his night and weekend jobs, saving for Jess's operation from his attorney's salary at an easy pace, possibly in the next two years. And if he married well? Well, then, even sooner. But over the last six months, his sister's pain seemed to intensify, just as Dr. Morrissey had predicted, and Jamie found his patience wearing thin. He was no longer willing to wait to alleviate his sister's suffering, and if he had to work night and day seven days a week, he vowed to get the funds. His jaw tightened. Whatever it took . . .

Even turning to God to marry a McClare?

The thought stilled the turmoil in his gut. *Yes.* Even turning to God to marry a McClare. Taut muscles slowly relaxed at the decision he'd made in the week since Cassie had turned him away at Logan's party. He needed an operation for his sister and a decent home for his family, in a boardinghouse *he* owned where he could help women like Millie and Julie. He couldn't do that on a new counselor's salary, no matter how generous Logan had been. True, his family no longer lived in the slums of the Barbary Coast, but he wanted more than two rooms in a boardinghouse mere streets away from that seedy part of town. Yes, it was clean and safe and out of the sewers, but it was not near enough for the woman who'd given him her all.

"You know, it's just a guess, but I'm pretty sure Logan would rather you slept at home."

Jamie jerked in the chair, the sight of Bram cocked against the door bringing a scowl to his face. His eyes flicked to the mantel clock at the front of his desk before searing Bram with a thin gaze. "It's long past quitting time, Hughes, for your information.

Besides, you call *this* using your time wisely—harassing exhausted counselors?"

Chuckling, Bram strolled into Jamie's office and plopped into one of two cordovan leather chairs, fingers tapping on the arms of the seat. His smile inched uphill. "Yeah? Well, try eight hours of depositions with a cigar-smoking thug, a deaf ninety-year-old, and a mother of hyperactive twins under the age of three." He massaged his temples with the span of forefinger and thumb. "Trust me, my prized globe wasn't the only thing spinning today—I have a doozy of a headache. Don't suppose you have any aspirin powder left that the doctor prescribed?"

"You kidding?" Jamie scrounged in his drawer for the tin of aspirin powder he kept for days like this. "Here, a pinch is all you need," he said, tossing it to his best friend while shoving his half cup of cold coffee across the desk. He grabbed his Phillips' Milk of Magnesia as well and uncapped the bottle. "Don't know what I guzzle more—the aspirin or the milk of magnesia."

He tipped it straight up, throat muscles glugging while Bram gave a low whistle. "Take it easy, Mac—that's not ten-year-old scotch, you know."

Jamie replaced the lid with a scrunch of his nose. "You're telling me." He dropped the bottle into the bottom drawer before slamming it closed with his shoe.

Bram's eyes flicked from the crumpled paper to his friend's face. "Another rejection?"

"Yep." Jamie expended another weary breath and sank back in his chair. "Their caseload is full and there's nothing they can do." He snatched the letter and sailed it into the waste can. "The deuce it is," he growled, resting his head on the back of his chair. He closed his eyes. "It's full all right—with Nob Hill favors."

"So . . . why don't you call in your own?"

"What?" Jamie peered at Bram through leaden lids. "The only medicine man I'm on favorable terms with is Dr Pepper, and I doubt that'll get me too far with the bigwigs on the Cooper Medical Board." His lips pursed in thought. "Although come to think of it, I did meet a Dr. Winterberger at The Palace a few weeks ago."

"Who says it has to be a doctor?" Bram stretched in his chair, hands propped to his neck.

One eyelid peeled up. "Last time I looked the Cooper Medical Board were all physicians."

"Yeah, but the funding committee is not."

Bram's words oozed through Jamie's tired brain like warm milk of magnesia, coating his nerves as well as his stomach. With a sharp catch of his breath, he shot up, jaw sagging into a smile. "You are a genius, Hughes, you know that? Why the devil didn't I think of that? Who do we know on the funding committee?"

Bram's lips veered sideways. "It's not who we know, Mac, it's who Logan knows."

Jamie's heart commenced to a slow thud. "Who?" he said, his voice hushed with hope.

A grin split Bram's handsome face. "Andrew Turner—the committee's president."

Jamie gaped, a slow smile curving the corners of his mouth. "The D.A.? No kidding?"

"No kidding—fraternity brother. Want me to talk to Logan for you?"

"No, it needs to come from me, Bram, but thanks." Jamie rubbed the scruff of his jaw, his thoughts back on his sister.

"So, you ready?" Bram lumbered to his feet, tugging on the sleeves of his gray sack suit.

Jamie's gaze flicked up. "For what?"

"Dinner at the McClares' . . ." He paused, one sandy brow cocked high. "You know . . . the pre-Napa dinner? To discuss all the details?"

Jamie groaned, thoughts of his sister eclipsing everything else. "That's tonight?"

"Yes, but I can extend your regrets." Bram buttoned his jacket, eyeing him with concern.

Jamie huffed out a sigh. "No, I'll be there—not for dinner, of course, because I promised Jess chicken from The Corner Bar, but after." He rose to his feet. "Will you let them know?"

"Sure." Bram pushed in his chair and ambled toward the door, delivering a knowing smile over his shoulder. "Them? Or her?"

A chuckle rumbled in Jamie's throat as he cranked at his tie some more, loosening it to cool the sweat ringing his collar. He rounded his desk. "Them. I'll take care of her."

"So far, it looks like you'll be buying your own Dr Peppers for the rest of the year, Mac." Bram flashed some teeth. "The wager was 'love' as I recall, not friendship, so I'm not sure how you're going to pull that rabbit out of your hat."

A smug smile slid across Jamie's lips as he followed his friend into the reception area. "It's called the old MacKenna magic, old buddy, so I suggest you keep your pockets full." He opened the outer door, allowing Bram to go first. "Because first it's friendship where I woo . . ." He slapped him on the back and shot him a wide grin. "Then it's lovestruck and I do."

16

S o, it's settled." Logan tossed his napkin on the plate and stretched in his chair to study Caitlyn at the other end of the table while Rosie collected dishes practically licked clean. He clamped a hand to the plate that held his third helping of dessert so Rosie wouldn't steal it away. "Hadley will drive you and the girls to Napa the afternoon of the 3rd, and the boys and I'll follow after work." He glanced up at Rosie as she passed and took a stab at a conciliatory smile. "That trifle put The Palace to shame, Rosie—you're a great cook."

"The best," Bram said with a wink at the housekeeper who promptly gave him a crooked grin. Logan stifled a grunt, sliding Bram a narrow look. *Says the man who walks on water.*

The housekeeper's gaze slid to Logan, and her smile withered. "A little too great, apparently," she mumbled, reminding him that nothing he could say or do would ever change Rosie's opinion of the "flea-infested skunk" who'd broken her little girl's heart. "May as well pop a tent outside much as you come to dinner," she groused in a gravelly tone reserved just for him. The titter of laughter around the table steamed the back of his neck. His lips compressed as he locked eyes with Cait, hoping

180

that just once, she'd keep her piranha in line. *As if anyone could,* he thought with a flash of irritation, noting the near-smile on Cait's face.

"Tent? When there's a perfectly good doghouse in the backyard?" Cait said sweetly, brows arched over jade eyes that sparkled like emeralds. "Inscribed with his name, no less?"

Reaching to scrub the bulldog who lay at her feet, Alli winked. "Goodness, with that scowl on your face, Uncle Logan, it's hard to tell you and Logan Junior apart."

"Humph . . . the dog smells way better," Rosie said, muttering loud enough for all to hear.

Logan glared. *Says the hound permanently clamped to my hind quarter.* Jaw grinding with every giggle around the table, he cocked his head to sear Caitlyn with a gaze so heated, the woman should be sporting a sunburn. *"Cait?"* he said, tone clipped and brow angled, clear indication he was waiting for her to put an end to Rosie's blatant humiliation.

"Dinner was wonderful as usual, Rosie," Caitlyn said, lips twitching as if she were fighting a smile. She glanced at the sideboard, starting to rise. "Any coffee left?"

Rosie had it poured in Cait's cup before the woman could clear her chair. "Anybody else?" the housekeeper asked, conveniently ignoring Logan's lifted cup as she scanned the table.

"Nope, we have a whist tournament waiting in the parlour," Blake said, tugging Cassie from her seat. "Come on, Cuz, it's you, me, and Maddie against the less fortunate."

"In your dreams," Alli said to her brother, prodding Bram to his feet. "Meg is a genius, Bram was champ of his fraternity, and I'm just plain smarter than you." She patted his shoulder. "Before we're through with you, you'll be sharing that doghouse with Uncle Logan."

"Hey . . ." Logan skewered her with a glare, prompting Alli to plant a kiss on his cheek.

"Don't worry, Uncle Logan," Meg said with a hug. "I love you even if Rosie doesn't."

"Me too," Maddie said, giggling when Logan tickled her waist.

The chatter and chuckles faded as the card players quickly exited and Rosie stole away to the kitchen, leaving nothing but the tinkling of Cait's spoon while she stirred the cream in her coffee. Exhaling a heavy blast of air, Logan rose and moved to the sideboard to refill his cup to the brim. Black and bitter—like his mood was prone to be.

"I'm sorry—I didn't realize you wanted any," Cait said in a gentle tone.

He returned to his seat and took a sip, his gaze ominous over the rim of his cup. "For the love of decency, Cait—must you encourage her? God knows I'm more than well aware the woman despises me without adding indigestion to my meal."

"I'm sorry, Logan," she said with a slope of brows, "but it's just that you're so easy to bait." A playful sparkle in her eye told him she was parroting his comment the night they'd danced at The Palace. She gave him a little-girl smile that warmed his body more than the coffee, a hint of tease flirting on her lips. "Especially when you're in a mood."

"A *mood*?" He snatched his fork from the table to stab at the trifle. "What the deuce is wrong with my mood?"

Cait's smile was patient. "Well, nothing, I suppose, except that you're grinding your jaw with a cream dessert that doesn't require chewing, your tie is askew like you've been wrestling with the devil, and your hair—" her gaze flicked to his head and back, a hint of apology in those deadly green eyes—"looks like you've gouged at it more times than the trifle."

His gaze narrowed as he jabbed another bite in his mouth, a definite edge to his jest. "So I'm not fond of Rosie 'trifling' with me, Cait—is that a crime?"

"No, no it's not . . . ," she said with a faint smile that slowly ebbed into concern. "But I'm not fond of seeing a dear friend so out of sorts, either." She leaned forward to rest her chin on clasped hands, eyes probing his. "What's bothering you, Logan? I hate to see you like this."

Then marry me, Cait.

He unleashed a disgruntled sigh. "I lost a case today." He tossed his fork down and massaged his temple, appetite suddenly gone. "That doesn't happen very often," he said quietly.

"An important one?"

"They're all important, Cait. I'm the head of the firm—I'm not supposed to lose."

"You can't win all the time, Logan." Her voice was gentle.

He glanced up and met her eyes with a pointed look that spoke his mind, if not his words. "*Nobody* knows that better than me," he said, his gaze locked with hers as he poured himself more wine. He bolted a third of the glass with a hard swallow, the implication of his words coloring her cheeks.

She quickly took a sip of coffee. "Heavens, everyone knows you're the best lawyer in the city, but you're a human being, for goodness sake—you simply cannot win every case."

"But I should have won this one." Releasing a heavy breath, he absently toyed with the stem of his glass, eyes lapsing into a stare as glazed as the scarlet liquid that coated the bowl. "My client was guilty, and I knew it, and I let it affect my case." He downed another healthy swig. "A good lawyer doesn't do that."

"No," she whispered, her respect carrying from across the table. "Just an honest one."

He kneaded the bridge of his nose. "It's not about honesty, it's about integrity. A good lawyer does his job to the best of his ability, no matter personal feelings. I failed at that today."

"Everyone fails sometime, Logan, even you. You need to allow yourself some mistakes."

He peered up, pinning her with a hooded gaze. "You didn't," he said quietly.

Her cheeks burned so scarlet, he could almost feel the heat. Hadley saved her with a gruff clear of his throat. "Mrs. McClare— there's a gentleman to see you, a Mr. Andrew Turner."

"What the devil does he want?" Logan's tone was close to a snarl, fairly commonplace where Turner was concerned, his name akin to the foulest swear word in Logan's well-heeled vocabulary. He seized his sterling silver fork and commenced to bludgeoning the remains of the trifle. "Send him away," he snapped.

Caitlyn rose like a royalty, head back and shoulders square, ignoring Logan to award Hadley with a kind smile. "Thank you, Hadley. Will you please show him to the study for me?"

Hadley gave a short bow with a click of heels. "Very good, miss. Scones with that tea?"

A twitch of a smile diffused Logan's anger somewhat when Hadley misheard Cait's request. But the confounded woman would never let on about the butler's poor hearing to save her soul, her heart too soft to tread on anyone's feelings. His twitch turned to a scowl.

Except mine.

"Yes, Hadley," she said, volume bumped up. "Tea and scones in the study would be lovely, thank you." Her smile could have warmed a dead man's soul, but the moment the butler left, she frosted Logan with a look. "The last time I checked, Mr. McClare,

I was mistress of my own home, so I'll thank you to allow me to conduct my own affairs."

"Not with that weasel, Cait, you can't trust him."

She paused while pushing in her chair, one brow notched in unspoken question.

He shot to his feet, slamming the fork onto the plate. "Okay, all right—you couldn't trust me at one time, either, but for the love of decency, haven't I proven myself? With the kids, with your legal affairs, with you?" He jabbed a finger toward the door. "Blast it, Cait, Turner is the slimiest D.A. we've had in years, and I flat-out don't trust him, and neither should you."

A harsh gasp parted from her lips. "He is no such thing! Andrew is a God-fearing man who shares my interest in cleaning up the Coast." The hard line of her jaw softened as she approached, stopping to distance herself a good two feet. "I appreciate your concern, Logan, truly, but I'm a grown woman who can take care of herself."

A grown woman, oh, yes . . . Logan scanned her head to toe, barely aware of the habit he'd long since cultivated with the woman before him. His gaze returned to her face where a blush was in bloom. A begrudging smile tipped his mouth. "I'm well aware, Cait, but Turner's a snake." He honed in with a fold of his arms. "What exactly is his business with you?"

A lump shifted in her creamy throat before her chin elevated in the way it always did when battling his intimidation. A ridge creased in his brow. *Or maybe her guilt?*

"And exactly what business is that of yours?" she asked, the full lips suddenly thin.

He moved forward and nearly smiled. Instead of a dainty step back as was her custom, the chin jutted higher and the shoulders straightened. *A tightly strung bow taking sharp aim* . . .

Hands balled at his sides, the competitor in him swelled. He peered down, dwarfing her with his height. "You're my business, Cait—the welfare of this family at Liam's bequest."

Her lips parted in a shallow breath, shock evident on her face. "You mean Liam—"

"*Yes* . . . he did," he said in a tone that brooked no argument. He latched firm hands to her arms, voice gentling along with his touch. "Liam loved you, Cait, and he asked me to watch out for you . . . to protect you. And the simple truth is, I do not trust Turner." He released her then, a slow exhale as he attempted to mollify his tone. "I repeat—what business do you have with that slime?"

She took her customary step back. "Really, Logan, there's no need for slander or melodrama or calling the man out. He's simply here to discuss—" Her eyes peeked up beneath a fringe of heavy lashes, the grate of her lip all but shouting her guilt. "The Vigilance Committee."

"The Vigilance Committee?" His brows dipped thunderously low. "To badger you into a token board position you have no intention of accepting?"

"No . . . ," she said quietly, retreating yet another step back. "To discuss the presidency to which I have already agreed."

His jaw fell while his temper rose. "You've accepted? Without consulting me?"

"You are *not* my guardian, Mr. McClare, no matter what Liam may have said, and I will make—and disclose—my own decisions in my own time, is that clear?"

Blood warmed his face. "Even if they're reckless?"

A shot of color bruised her cheeks while her eyes glittered like jagged glass. "Don't you dare preach to me about 'reckless,'" she breathed, chest heaving while she singed him with a look that silenced the rage on his tongue. Lips pressed tight, her inhale quivered with anger before she released it again, a flicker in her jaw clear evidence of her attempt to restrain her temper. "This-discussion-is-over," she said in a clipped tone seldom used, confirming he'd overstepped his bounds—*again*. Her voice was terse. "Good night, Logan."

He watched her hurry from the room, his eyes following her graceful form as she glided into the study, careful to close the door. "No, not over, Cait," he whispered, truly annoyed at how the woman had an infernal gift for making him crazy. "Not by a long shot."

Jerking his tie loose, he strode toward the sound of laughter that did little to ease his sullen mood. Caitlyn McClare had no business presiding on an all-male board, especially one with the potential to drive an even bigger wedge between Logan and her. Cursing under his breath, he stormed into the parlour and peeled off his jacket, hurling it on the love seat. With a tic in his temple that belonged only to Caitlyn McClare, he rolled his sleeves and yanked a chair to the table, ignoring the gaping stares. "The deuce with whist," he said, sweeping the table with his arm. He shuffled the cards into a ragged, little pile. "We're playing poker, so ante up."

"But Mama doesn't like us to play poker," Maddie said, tone innocent and blue eyes as wide as Caitlyn's would be if she were to walk in the room.

"Awk, awk, ante up, ante up . . ."

Logan shuffled and dealt the cards, sailing them hard to each player with a clamp of his jaw. Reaching into his pocket, he tossed a fistful of change onto the table along with a thick wad of bills. He slipped Maddie a wink before flashing a menacing smile. "Good."

17

"You know, there's just something intrinsically wrong with a sweet, innocent girl winning at poker." Jamie held the door as Cassie floated into the billiard room, the scent of lilacs lingering like she, unfortunately, lingered in his mind. He was glad Logan left when Caitlyn broke up the poker game, taking Bram and Blake along while everyone else opted for bed, giving Jamie a rare chance to be alone with Cassie. His lips crooked. Although it'd cost him a half-night's wage at the Blue Moon to bribe Blake to forgo "chaperoning," a task his mother—and Cassie—had expected. Not to mention Blake's ribbing that Cassie would hang him out to dry—both in pool and in courtship. His eyes followed the jaunty sway of her hips as if she wore her ranch issue of scandalously curved blue jeans rather than a pink chiffon dress, and his mouth went dry at the thought. He quickly cleared his throat. "Playing poker—much less winning—is not something one expects of a lady, Miss McClare. Even if she is a cowgirl from lower East Texas."

Her chuckle floated behind, as soft and billowy as the pink chiffon. "What can I say? Father wanted a boy, so he settled for a tomboy to which he could impart his skills." She peeked back, nibbling her lip in that adorable way she had when she felt sorry for him.

Like now.

Her sympathetic smile suddenly tilted just short of sassy. "Now that I've fleeced you at cards, are you sure you want to do this?" The scalloped hem of her dress wisped across the carpet as she made a beeline for the billiard table with the same unwavering assurance with which he entered the boxing ring at the Oly. She commenced to setting up the table with a rack of the balls, humor lacing her tone. "I can't help but worry about your male pride, you know, losing to a woman—*again*. Like Daddy always says, 'There's a time in a man's life when he just needs to cowboy up and ride into the sunset.'"

Ride away? Not a chance, Cowgirl. Jamie closed the door, and the click seemed to drain the blood—and the sass—from her cheeks. "B-Blake is joining us, isn't he?" she said in a rush, a hint of a wobble in the luscious line of her throat. "We should leave the door open till he comes."

He offered a gentle smile to allay her fears. "I'm afraid Bram and Blake bowed out, Cass, something about joining Logan for a nightcap on the Coast, and with the billiard room so close to Mrs. McClare's bedroom, we should really keep the door closed." Hoping to deflect the anxious look in her eyes, he tossed a cocky grin. "And I wouldn't worry about my pride, if I were you," he said with a swagger that matched his stride across the room. "I guarantee you'll be too busy worrying about your own." He handed her a cue before chalking his. "Hate to burst your bubble, Cowgirl, but I was hustling in pool halls while you were still riding your pony."

"Were you now?" A squirm of her smile told him she wasn't impressed. She replaced the cue he'd given her and took another. "Sorry, I prefer the mushroom tip." With a focused squint, she carefully applied a slight edge of chalk around the cue's perimeter rather than grinding it as most novices did, then clunked the cue stick on the floor several times. "A hustler, eh?"

"Yeah," he said with a hike of his jaw, his faint smile issuing a challenge. "Not to mention Oly Club billiards champ two years in a row."

"My, my, a title as well." She tilted her head, green eyes sparkling with humor. "And are you the pretty-boy champ too?"

"That settles it." He stripped off his jacket and tossed it over a wing chair with a perilous grin. "I'm going to put you in your place, Miss McClare, right where you belong."

She gave him a wide-eyed stare, lashes aflutter. "In the trophy case?"

No, in my arms. "I'll even forgo the coin toss and let you have the break."

"Mmm . . . chivalrous *and* brave." She leaned over the end of the table with an open-hand bridge, breaking the balls with a loud crack, her crisp and powerful precision turning his tongue to cotton. She winked. "But," she said with that same annoying sympathy, "not very bright. Because you see, when I put you in *your* place, Mr. MacKenna, it'll feel like Alcatraz."

His jaw dropped when five balls spun off into pockets so fast, his eyes glazed over. "How d-did you do that?" he rasped, awe overriding any loss of pride. "I've never seen that before . . ."

"Merciful Providence, me either . . . ," she said in apparent surprise. Arms folded, she rested a finger to her chin. "I've never been able to pocket more than four balls on a break before, and goodness—all of them solid!" Her gaze flicked to the abundance of striped balls still littering the table, brows ascending in contrition before she offered a sunny smile. "Guess that makes me solids. Oh my stars, but this is fun!"

"Yeah, fun," Jamie said with a grunt, feeling the sting of male pride now that the shock had worn off. "How in blazes did you learn to do that?"

"Well . . . ," she said with a pretty toss of her head, "when I wasn't riding my 'pony,' I was playing pool with Daddy, who in the absence of a son, taught his daughter everything he knew about the three 'P's'—poker, pool, and pinochle." Hand braced to the table, she bent low with cue in hand and eye on the ball. "Apparently he was somewhat of a pool shark before he met Mama, and gracious, don't even get me started on pinochle." She squinted. "Six ball, far right."

Another loud crack sent her last two solids swishing into the far pocket.

"I don't believe it," Jamie whispered, mouth slack as he circled the table, unable to fathom what he'd just witnessed with his own eyes. "Holy thunder—the last time I saw a shot like that was when Johnny Kling played at the Oly."

Cassie scrunched her nose. "Kling. The Cubs ball player who plays pool in off season?"

"Yeah . . ." Jamie's mouth hung open so far, she could have shot a few balls in there too. He blinked, his love for this woman growing by leaps and shots. And his awe? Deeper than the solids in those blasted pockets. "Sweet thunderation," he muttered under his breath, "marry me now . . ."

"Pardon me?"

"Nothing." He cleared his throat and nodded toward the table. "I think you need to put me out of my misery, Miss McClare."

The lip grate was back. "Oh, right . . . sorry. Side left pocket." With an expert aim that was almost a caress, she promptly plunged the eight ball—and Jamie's pride—into the dark recesses of gloom with another perfect shot. In a slow pivot, she faced him once again, one dainty hand cupping her stick while she nibbled her thumbnail with the other. The apology in her eyes was as thick as the chalk on his cue. "Sorry, Jamie, I had no right to take advantage of you."

He grimaced. That stung. *Don't worry, Miss McClare, I plan to return the favor . . .* Threading fingers through the hair at the back of his head, he huffed out a sigh and laid his cue on the table before offering his hand with a stiff smile. "Stellar game, Cowgirl. You should be proud—I'd say I've been properly tarred and feathered, not to mention hog-tied."

"Forgive me?" She shook his hand, the green eyes soft and somehow vulnerable.

Strolling around the table, he emptied the pockets and set up once again, rolling the balls until the cluster was nice and tight. Like his jaw. "Sure. On one condition."

The mossy-colored eyes narrowed imperceptibly. "And what might that be?"

His smile eased into a grin as he led her to the far end of the table. "Teach me," he said with as much humility as he could muster. "I want to learn how to break like that."

"Pardon me?" Her tauntingly kissable lower lip sagged a full inch.

He jagged a brow. "What? You think I'm too proud to admit I can't play as well as you? Well, I'm not. I know a professional when I see one." Hands braced to her shoulders, he prodded her into position, then sat on the corner of the table and folded his arms. "If I'm ever going to challenge you—" he dipped his head to peer at her sharply—"and we both know I am—we're going to level the playing field first."

"You want *me*? To teach *you*?" Her jaw remained in a stupor.

He dared her with a shuttered gaze. "Unless you're scared . . ."

That snapped her mouth shut. "Scared? Of a street hustler I could beat with my eyes closed?" Her tongue rolled to the side of her mouth with a grin, the tip peeking out as she hunkered over the table with cue firmly in hand. "Not likely, Pretty Boy. Observe and learn . . ."

With a gentle coax, she slid the stick back and forth, eyes squinting at the colorful triangle. An explosion of cracks erupted, and balls went flying into at least three pockets in a series of clunks, prompting a low whistle from Jamie's lips. "I'll tell you what, Miss McClare, you sure wield a mean cue." He hopped up to rack the balls, then hovered close beside her when she bent over the table.

A little squeak escaped as she jerked up. "What are you doing?" she said with a gasp, cue and hand splayed to her chest. She arched away, as if to distance herself.

He grinned and nudged her back in place. "I've observed and now I'm going to learn." Her body stiffened, luring another grin to his lips. "What can I say? I'm a hands-on kinda guy."

"Oh, no you don't . . ." She tried to dart away.

He clamped her arm. "Come on, Cass, we're friends, and I need to be side by side so I can sense your rhythm, get the positioning right when you make that break." A smile inched across his face as he slowly released her. "Unless, of course," he said, tone careful, "you really *are* scared . . ."

Her jaw gaped like the hole she was about to put in his pride. *Scared?* Of wiping an annoying smirk off a pretty boy's face? Not a chance. Hypnotic hazel eyes studied her with a lidded gaze, and she battled a telltale gulp. However . . . scared silly his close proximity might ignite feelings she'd tried so hard to ignore? *Oh, you bet.* She fought a shiver that threatened her spine. Since the night on The Palace veranda, she'd been on her guard, keeping him and their friendship at arm's length. But . . . it hadn't been easy. And she had a suspicion he knew it.

He grinned, and those impossibly deep dimples translated into deep, *deep* trouble. "You *are* scared, aren't you?" he said with a husky tease that triggered both her temper and her pulse.

"Only of trampling your tender feelings, bucko, but if you're not worried, neither am I." She spun around and leveled her cue, forcing herself to concentrate. "Let the trampling begin."

His chuckle was dangerously low in her ear when he leaned close, crowding her space and stealing her air. "Just talk me through it," he whispered, the warmth of his breath all but caressing her neck as he stood closer than a shadow.

A knot the size of a cue ball ducked in her throat. "You're just a horse hair too close for friends, MacKenna, you know that? I can barely move for your smothering."

"Come on, Cass . . ." His thumb lightly grazed her hand over the cue. "No closer than playing Marco Polo or dancing at The Palace, right? And we did both of those as friends."

Her eyelids wavered closed. *Friends—right.* Hand to the rail, she bent low to squint at the rack, focusing hard on The 1 ball. She sucked in a deep breath. "You w-want to k-keep your grip relaxed and body motion to a minimum," she stuttered, allowing the air in her lungs to slowly seep out along with her jitters. Gaze locked on the ball, her concentration returned to the game, infusing her with the clarity she needed. "Most people make the mistake of raising their body when they straighten their arm, then dropping their elbow, two motions that counteract each other." She raised up to trace the angle with her eye, then resumed position. "Straightening the arm engages the shoulder muscles for more speed, yes, but on the break, accuracy is more important than a little extra power." Gliding the cue through her fingers in five

fluid strokes, she aimed dead center. Adrenaline coursed when
the balls erupted, easily pocketing four of the fifteen. "Oh, drat,
only four this time." Rising, she turned and squared her shoulders,
unable to prevent a smirk from slipping into her smile. "So . . .
learn anything, Pretty Boy?"

"Yeah . . . ," he said, his whisper little more than a rasp. He
skimmed her arms with his palms, throat convulsing as his gaze
strayed to her lips. "I'm in love with a pool hustler . . ."

Her stomach swooped when he lowered his head. "Whoa . . .
back off, City Boy!" Cue stick in hand, she slapped it and two
hands to his chest, effectively halting his approach. "We agreed
to be friends, MacKenna, so get that starry-eyed look off your
face right now."

He ducked away from the cue with a scowl. "*You* agreed to be
friends, Cass, not me," he groused, "and putting my eye out will
serve no purpose whatsoever."

"Oh, I don't know." She prodded him back with the stick,
smudging his white shirt with blue chalk. "It might just get that
lecherous look out of your eye."

Palms raised in self-defense, he softened his stance. "Okay,
okay—point taken, Miss McClare." He brushed the chalk from
his shirt. "Have a heart, will you, Cass? I'm just looking to learn
some trick shots, not get gouged to death."

"Trick shots, my eye—trick moves is more like it."

"Okay, I'm sorry," he said with a heavy blast of air. "Just teach
me the shot, okay?"

"No." She hoisted her chin. "You lost that privilege when you
stepped over the line."

He rolled his shirtsleeves with an endearing smile that tripped
her heart. *And most women's, no doubt.* "Come on, Cass, once more,
please? As a friend? Just teach me the shot?"

She folded her arms, cue safely tucked within. "On one condi- tion," she said, tone curt.

"Anything." The dimples almost twinkled.

She narrowed her eyes. "You keep your hands to yourself, Jamie MacKenna, or so help me, you'll be tweezing splinters from this cue instead of brushing off chalk. Is that understood?"

Ambling over to rack the balls once again, he actually had the nerve to salute her, his smile ramping up to adorable. "Yes, ma'am—hands to myself. Got it."

She fought the twitch of a smile with a loud huff and shrugged several times to loosen her shoulders before hunching over the table to take aim once again. He returned to hover mode and she tried to ignore him, squinting hard to mentally gauge the shot. The stick slid through her fingers as if they were greased. *Nice and easy, Daddy always said, like a pig slipping through slop.* On the final pull, she felt the wisp of something warm on her neck, and she squealed, stick and balls flying when she realized it was Jamie's lips. She whirled around, the heart in her throat effectively sealing both her air and her voice.

He winced, giving her a mischievous grin. "Uh, rather not learn that move if you don't mind, Cass—not exactly the one I'm looking for."

"Oh, really? Well, how 'bout this one, MacKenna?" she said with a purse of her lips, kneeing his left thigh so hard, his grin twisted into a groan.

"Hey, that hurt!" he said, his chuckle threaded with pain. "And from now on, this left thigh is officially off limits, Miss McClare."

"So is my neck, you . . . you . . . wolf!" She swiped at where he'd kissed her, ignoring the shiver that raced at the thought of his lips on her skin. Hands trembling, she folded her arms, indignant he was making this difficult. "I told you to keep your hands to yourself—"

"Ah-hah!" he said with an annoying wag of his finger. "Yes, but nothing was said about lips, Miss McClare, and as a lawyer, I'm obliged to follow the letter of the law, so no hands were involved, I assure you." Playful eyes roved the length of her before braising her cheeks with a wink. "Although it wasn't easy, Cowgirl, I can tell you that."

She stomped her foot, noting with satisfaction that he took a quick step back. "Friends do not nibble on friends' necks, Jamie MacKenna, and if you persist in this, we will *not* be friends."

He laughed and loosened his tie, hazel eyes a glimmer as he moved in close. "My thoughts exactly," he said softly, skimming gentle hands down her arms to effectively cage her in. His smile faded to serious, and the desire in his eyes warmed in her belly. "I already told you, Cass, I don't want to be your friend," he whispered. "I want more."

"Jamie—"

"No, listen to me, please—just for a moment?" His voice pulsed with an intensity that halted her while his fingers tunneled into her hair to cradle her head. "I'm falling in love with you, Cassie, and there's no amount of pretending that can change that. I want to court you, so teach me," he whispered, grazing her cheeks with his thumbs, "not just pool shots, but about faith. Let me see God through your eyes, feel him through your love." A nerve flickered in the firm line of a jaw that sported just a hint of dark shadow, and his eyes seemed to possess her, so gentle and yet so strong. He bent to brush her brow with his lips and her eyes drifted closed, the very sensation heating her skin. "Because I want you, Cass, and everything you have to offer."

Time stood still as he caressed each eyelid with his mouth,

weakening her will as much as her knees. *Oh, Jamie . . .* Her eyes jerked open for a brief moment when his lips found hers, only to flutter closed again when he nuzzled with a tenderness that all but melted her in his arms. Stomach quivering, she opened her eyes to the man who was stealing her heart despite her best efforts. *Oh, Lord . . .*

"Give me a chance, Cass," he said quietly, his very touch a kiss as the warmth of his fingers feathered her face. "Teach me to need him like you do." His gaze dropped to her lips for a shiver of a second before returning to her eyes. "And if he answers the prayer I'm praying right now, you have my word—I will believe . . ."

She swallowed the trepidation coating her throat, his words on The Palace veranda haunting her mind. *"I've done just fine up until now, Cowgirl. I don't need him."*

Oh, Lord, but he does! A wispy sigh wavered from her lips as she cupped a hand to his face, the touch of his emerging beard pricking her palm as much as his eyes pricked her soul. *Help me, God—is this what you want me to do?* She studied the perfectly sculpted face of a man too handsome to be trusted, the bristled jaw of a rogue used to getting his own way, and knew it was a risk to fall in love with Jamie MacKenna. But then it was too late, she suspected, because she was already halfway there, shifting the danger of risk from that of her own heart to the loss of his soul. Drawing in a fortifying breath she gave him a tremulous smile, knowing there could be only one way she could give her consent. "All right, Jamie," she whispered.

His trademark grin curved on his lips. "You'll give me a chance? To court you?"

"Partially." She drew in a shaky breath. "I'll consider court-ship if you can oblige by the rules of friendship first, sort of a pre-courtship trial, if you will. But . . . the terms will be mine."

His slow exhale feathered her face. "Name 'em, Cass—whatever you say." A boyish smile broke free as he leaned in to attempt a kiss.

He grunted when she halted his approach with palms flat to his chest. "Term number one, Mr. MacKenna—no kissing."

The blood leeched from his face. "What?"

She bit back a smile. "And let me be clear since you've been known to bend the rules." She stepped beyond his reach and crossed her arms, her resolve as focused as if she were playing a high-stakes match. "That means no kissing of any kind—not on my lips, my ears, or my neck—is that clear?"

"B-but—"

"Term number two," she continued, ignoring the gape of his mouth. "This friendship will remain a friendship until I deem it to be more, at which point, I will agree to courtship. Which means, Mr. MacKenna, until then, you will keep your hands to yourself, is that understood?"

"That is not my idea of a courtship," he said with a gum of his lips.

"Nonetheless, it's the only courtship you're being offered—take it or leave it."

She heard the distinct grinding of a jaw as he glared. "You're being ridiculous, Cass. So I can't hug you or hold your hand or show any affection?"

Arms folded, she assessed him through cautious eyes, a finger to her cheek while the others rested at her lips, contemplating the ramifications of allowing Jamie MacKenna any liberties at all. She blew out a noisy sigh. "Oh, all right . . . hugs and hand-holding only, but if you so much as step over the—"

"What else?" he snapped, obviously no patience for threats.

Squirming beneath his dagger stare, she turned to make her

way to the loveseat, where she perched on the edge, her hands folded. "What service do you attend?"

"Pardon me?" The deep ridge above his nose told her she was pressing her luck.

"With your family—what church service do you attend, and what time?"

He stared, with a sag of his jaw, hand parked on one hip. "St. Mary's, nine o'clock, why?"

She clamped her lip to stave off a smile. "Wonderful! We attend St. Patrick's at eleven, so that should be perfect."

"For—what?" he bit out, the tic in his cheek keeping time with the one in his eye.

"Why, to join us, of course, after you take your mother and sister home."

She could almost hear his jaw drop. "Wait a minute—you expect me to go to church *twice* every Sunday?"

She nodded. "It's term number three. As a show of faith, of course."

"You can't be serious."

"Completely," she said with a tilt of her head. "The question is, Jamie—are you?"

He huffed out a sigh and turned away, gouging the back of his neck. She watched his broad shoulders rise and fall before he put a hand to his head to knead at his temple. "Yes," he whispered, the sound almost a hiss.

"Good, then we'll meet you in the vestibule." She paused, chewing at the edge of her lip. "And then there's only one more thing—"

He spun around. "Blue blazes, there's more?"

She gave him a sweet smile. "Term number four. In addition to the times that you're normally here, I'd like to see you another night a week on the day of your choice."

He exhaled, the tension in his face visibly relaxed. "Finally, something I can enjoy."

"Oh, you will—*Pilgrim's Progress* is a wonderful read! Can't wait to discuss it."

The tic was back in his jaw. "You're not making this easy, Cass."

She sucked in a deep draw of air and rose, approaching him with a sober look in her eyes. "No, Jamie, I'm not, because trusting you or any man is not easy for *me*. You're asking me to trust you with my heart, but first I have to learn to trust you mean what you say, that courting me is not just some frivolous whim to win over one of the few females who probably ever turned you away." Holding his gaze with her own, she gently squeezed his hand. "I need to know that your desire to win me is greater than your desire to have me, and that I can trust you to do what I ask. Because, Jamie . . ." She placed a gentle palm to his jaw, allowing the love she felt to glow in her eyes. "I have to be sure . . . ," her voice faded to soft, "that if we become one as man and wife, we'll also be one in our faith."

A knot shifted in his throat and he gave a stiff nod, turning his head to kiss her palm. He tugged her close, resting his head against hers. "I want you, Cass, so I have no choice." He pulled away, lips veering into a wry smile. "But I'm going to tell you right now it won't be easy." His gaze flicked to her lips and back with a hard swallow. "Because I want to kiss you so badly, it hurts." He stepped back with a hard exhale, turning to retrieve his coat from the chair. He slipped it on with an off-kilter smile that seemed as flat as his mood. "Which is why I'm going home. Good night."

She blinked, suddenly bereft at the thought of him walking out the door. She took a step forward, a hopeful lilt to her voice as she picked at her nails. "You're leaving already? But don't you want to learn that trick shot on how to break?"

Hand on the knob, he delivered a grim smile over his shoulder. "Sorry, Cass, but I've already learned enough for tonight." He gave her the same salute he'd given earlier, only this one lacked the humor of before. His smile took a hard slant. "*Especially* how to break."

18

"What are you doing here?" Bram asked when Jamie slid on the barstool next to his.

Ignoring him, Jamie signaled Duffy for a drink, then shook his head when the bartender ambled forward with a Dr Pepper in hand. "Not tonight, Duff—I need the hard stuff." *And bad*, if the spasm in his cheek was any indication. He mumbled his thanks while Duffy poured him a whiskey, grateful the house was jumping tonight. He needed the familiar distraction of the cozy gambling hall that had become a second home since Duffy'd hired him years ago. All of it—the raucous laughter of crowded gambling tables, the snappy sounds of a ragtime band, the comforting smell of Duffy's pot roast mingling with that of bourbon and beer and the intoxicating scent of perfume. And women. Oh, yeah—lots and lots of pretty women to dance with, flirt with, and take your mind off whatever you wanted to forget, and he certainly needed to. He slammed the shot of whiskey to the back of his throat. Forget that his heart had just been hog-tied by a Texas beauty who intended to keep him on a short rope.

"Uh-oh . . . whiskey instead of soda pop?" Bram drew air through clenched teeth, shaking his head. "Don't tell me an in-nocent cowgirl fleeced Oly's billiard champ two years running?"

"You have no idea," Jamie said with a grunt. He slapped the empty glass on the bar and shoved it toward his boss, enjoying the burn that crawled all the way to his belly. "Another."

"Hey, slow down, Mac, or you'll drink your paycheck afore you earn it," the owner said with a chuckle. He poured more whiskey with a wink. "'Course, you can always earn your keep on this side of the bar in that fancy suit, making the ladies thirsty."

Jamie bolted his drink and grabbed the bottle with a scowl. "Leave it, Duff, and then leave me alone, will ya? It's my night off, so I'll spend it the way I want."

"Apparently not," Bram said with a worried smile, his gaze drilling into Jamie's temple. "Don't tell me the indomitable Jamie MacKenna struck out with a girl?"

"I should be so lucky," he muttered, staring at the glass in his hands. Huffing a sigh, he waited for the whiskey to calm his nerves. "So, where's Logan and Blake?"

"Logan had one drink and went back to his Palace penthouse, which is good because his mood wasn't much better than yours." Bram nodded at the roulette wheel across the room where Blake was flirting with the girl manning the table. "The 'Rake' has been working on Duffy's new dealer since we got here." He took a swig of his ginger ale, a grin tipping his lips. "Swears he's in love."

"Again?" Jamie poured more whiskey down his throat, the biting taste finally glazing his mood as well as his mind. "Hang it all, I wish I could fall in and out of love that easily." *Unbeholden to a woman.* He stared at the amber liquid in his glass, willing it to numb his brain to the fact that he was no longer in control with Cassidy McClare. Oh, no, she was calling the shots, and he hated that his hands were tied as thoroughly as those blasted steers she lassoed and broke, all trussed up until they couldn't move.

Just like him.

Bram cuffed his shoulder. "No, you don't, Mac. Blake has Logan's blood in his veins, so he's not looking to settle down for a good long while, but you? You're looking for that one woman who can turn your head, your heart, and your fortune, remember?"

"Yeah, I remember," he said, taking another drink. "Although tonight I'm looking to forget." He closed his eyes to knead the headache searing his temple—the one branded in the flesh by Cassidy McClare. He'd been in control of his own life since the age of twelve, holding the reins, making his own decisions, in charge of his own destiny—until now. He upended his glass.

"So, what happened, Mac?" Bram asked quietly. "I haven't seen you touch the hard stuff since Jess got really sick two years ago."

Jamie slammed his glass on the bar. "Cassie said I could court her." He gouged the bridge of his nose. "If you can call it that."

The concern in Bram's eyes creased into a smile. "That's great, Mac."

"Yeah, you'd think so, wouldn't you? Only it doesn't feel so great right about now." Hunched over his whiskey in a near stupor, Jamie twiddled the glass in his hands.

"Well, well . . ." Blake strolled up and glanced at his watch, giving Jamie an "I told you so" grin. "He thumped his fist on the bar to get Duffy's attention, indicating a need for another glass. "Looks like a McClare has redeemed our pride at last." He grabbed the shot glass Duffy slid his way and poured himself a drink, hoisting it in the air. "Because you guzzling the hard stuff can only mean one thing, Mac—ol' Cousin Cass has put you in your place in more ways than one."

Sliding Blake a sour smile, Jamie snatched the bottle back to tip more solace. "Not completely," he said with a grimace. "Although she did clobber me at pool just like you said."

Hip to the bar, Blake studied Jamie with an annoying grin, eyes twinkling like the whiskey in his glass. "And your harebrained notion to court her?"

Jamie knocked back another shot. "Let's just say she got her licks in before she said yes."

Blake stood up straight, surprise curling his lips. "No kidding? Sweet little Cassie, my brokenhearted cousin who'd just as soon shoot a man as look at him? *She* said yes?" He slapped Jamie on the back. "Well, good for you, Mac—Cass is just the girl to keep you in line."

"No joke," he groused, no patience for Blake's banter. "And trust me, it's a tight rope."

"And why's that?" Bram asked, shifting on the leather stool to face Jamie head-on, his glass as empty as Jamie's enthusiasm for a courtship where his hands were tied behind his back.

Exhaling, Jamie gouged his temple. "There are Texas-sized conditions to this courtship, I'm afraid, and every last one of them carries the jolt of being bucked by a longhorn steer."

"Yeah? Like what?" Blake asked, emptying his drink in one long swallow.

Jamie's chuckle was a half grunt. "Like a trial friendship on her terms where I attend church twice on Sundays, a weekly study on some book called *Pilgrim's* something or other, and the biggest burr in my backside?" He slashed fingers through Brilliantine hair that riled curls till they stood up on end. "I can't touch or kiss the woman except for hugs or holding her hand."

Blake let fly with a low whistle. "Jamie MacKenna—hog-tied by a girl. Never thought I'd see the day." He grinned. "Well, good for Cass, but I don't think you can do it."

"Oh, I'll do it, all right," Jamie said. "I just don't have to like it."

"I'm not worried about the physical part," Bram said. "Blake and I both know you can do that. You're a rock when it comes to willpower, Mac, in the ring or with women."

Blake raised his glass in a salute. "I'll drink to that."

Bram propped an elbow on the bar, studying his best friend through a squint. "It's the spiritual aspect that concerns me. I thought your goose was cooked when you told Cass you didn't believe in God, and now suddenly you do?"

"Nope," Jamie said with a swig of whiskey, "but she doesn't have to know that." He turned to give Bram a stale grin. "Besides, you're going to help me."

"Me?" Bram's brows pinched low. "How?"

"Of the three of us, you're the devout one here, Hughes, so I figured you could just fill me in on some of that religious mumbo jumbo since your uncle was a priest and all."

"Uh-oh . . ." Blake banged his glass on the bar and slapped Jamie on the back. "That's my cue to visit the roulette table." He winked at Bram. "Definitely not drunk enough for any of your sermonizing tonight, Padre. Good luck, Mac," he said with a grin over his shoulder. "The McClare women tend to be on the spiritual side, so if I were you, I'd drink up now."

Blake left, leaving Bram's mouth in a sag. "Do I really sermonize?" he asked, tone hurt.

Jamie grinned. "Only to guys like Blake who see a limit of one beer as a sermon." He vented with a sigh, his humor depleting along with his sobriety. "So, you gonna help me or not?"

Bram studied him with concern. "You can't fake faith in God, Jamie," he said quietly.

"Sure you can." Resolved hardened his gaze. "Cassie is the woman I want to marry, so I'm not about to let God stand in the way." He angled a brow. "She wants a man with faith?" He tossed the last of his whiskey down his throat. "I'll give her a man with faith."

"Yeah, but the thing is, Mac," Bram said slowly, gaze as sharp as the guilt that prickled Jamie's gut, "you actually *won't* be giving her that, and I'm not sure that's fair to Cassie. Even so, Cassie's as down-home and bottom line as you get, so she's going to see right through you."

"Not if you're a good teacher." Jamie peered up beneath leaden lids, grateful for the strong and stable influence of a friend like Bram—a man with a quiet faith that didn't judge Jamie or anyone, for that matter. In the seven years they'd been friends, Jamie had come to respect Bram and the unruffled morality that governed his life. Unlike Blake—and Jamie at the moment—he wasn't prone to overindulgence with women or whiskey. Ginger ale and an easy, open manner were his hallmarks. Gratitude swelled in Jamie's chest. And an honest and true relationship that felt more like blood than friendship. A grin tipped his mouth. "Besides," he said with a slap of Bram's back, "If God's a friend of yours, Hughes, he's a friend of mine."

Bram shook his head, waving Jamie off when he offered a drink from his bottle. "Oh, you can put your money on that, Mac. The sad thing is he always has been—you just haven't seen it for that monumental grudge slowing you down."

"A grudge? Slowing me down?" Jamie poured another whiskey and held it aloft in a toast. "There's not a lady or boxer in San Francisco that would agree with that, my friend."

Bram slipped a couple of bills from his wallet and rose with a patient smile. "Maybe not, MacKenna, but that devil of a headache you're gonna have come morning?" He tossed payment for the bottle onto the bar. "Trust me, it doesn't get any slower than lying flat on your face."

"Oh, I just love fireworks." Cassie's bare toes wiggled beneath her white eyelet dress, hands propped behind her head next to Alli on a blanket sprawled on Uncle Logan's lush Napa lawn. Her uncle's laughter drifted from his house at the top of the hill where he sat with Aunt Cait and Father Harry on a curved stone terrace overlooking miles of neighboring vineyards. Bougainvillea spilled from pots on a rock wall, lending splashes of pink that matched the color of the sky bleeding on the horizon. Cassie breathed in the flinty smell of sulphur and gunpowder from the firecrackers shot off after dinner while dusk settled on the valley with an ethereal glow.

"Me too," Allie said, fireflies flitting over Uncle Logan's terraced backyard dotted with blankets and people. Smoke hung in the air like an acrid perfume mingling with the fragrance of rose bushes heavy with bloom, embedding the scent of Napa into Cassie's brain.

Cassie's sigh was one of contentment as she watched Jamie set up the fireworks display with Bram and Roger Luepke. "Fireworks and Napa have to be two of my favorite things."

Alli snuck a sideways glance to where Liddy chatted with Blake while her sister Patricia sat on a blanket a few feet away with Maddie and Meg. "While we're on the subject of fireworks and favorite things," she whispered, turning back to Cassie with a dance of brows, "how's the pre-courtship trial going?"

A glow as pink as the sunset sky warmed Cassie's cheeks. "No fireworks yet, except the ones in his eyes," she said with a sheepish smile. "And in my heart."

Alli shifted to give her a tight hug. "Oh, Cass, I couldn't be happier! I swear when you two are together, the air's as charged as Fourth of July." She tossed another glance over her shoulder at Patricia, whose gaze bore into Jamie. "Of course, with sparks like that, I hope somebody doesn't get burned. Patricia's eyes shoot fire every time she looks your way. She's pretty head over heels, and Liddy says she's not been happy Jamie seems smitten with you."

"We don't know for sure Jamie's smitten," Cassie said slowly, desperate to remain cautious in a situation that involved her heart.

"Come on, Cass, the man goes to church twice a week and is reading books he has no desire to read. Trust me, Jamie MacKenna wouldn't do that for any woman unless he wanted something pretty badly." Alli paused, assessing Cassie through curious eyes. "And speaking of wanting something badly, how's the spiritual training going?"

Cassie's smile faded like the light of dusk while she watched Jamie carry a crate of fireworks to the back of the lawn, muscular arms bulging from the weight. "Okay, I think. He seems to be picking things up quickly, but I worry his heart's not in it for the right reasons." Her stomach did a little flip when he winked on his way back up the hill, and a sweet shiver traveled her body despite the hesitation in her tone. "Do you think I'm doing the right thing, Al?" she asked quietly. "You know, using our relationship to coerce him into seeking God?"

"Look at it this way, Cass—if you open his eyes to God, you just saved yourself years of heartbreak by falling in love with the man God has for you. And if he's not?" She squeezed Cassie's hand. "Then you may just save his soul. Either way, you've won. And so has Jamie."

"I guess we have, haven't we?" Cassie said softly. She breathed in a deep swallow of air, her excitement returning. "I'll tell you what, Al, when Jamie MacKenna stole my wind at the train station that day, I had no earthly idea he'd also steal my heart. But every moment I spend with him, I fall a little more in love." She chewed on the edge of her lip, her smile tremulous at best. "But it's downright scary falling for another pretty boy."

Alli's laughter joined the chatter and giggles from the other blankets, drifting in the air along with the sharp smell of summer and smoke. "Amen to that. My heart's been broken twice now by gorgeous guys, so you'd think I'd learn my lesson. But no, here I am once again, heart thumping over the handsome apprentice of Uncle Logan's neighbor."

Cassie peeked at Roger, concerned over Alli's growing affection for a man as pretty as Jamie. "Well, on the outside, he seems nice enough, and Uncle Logan certainly seems to like him."

"It's not the 'outside' I'm worried about." She scrunched her nose as she watched the men work. "Seems I have a knack for attracting rats and charlatans, first with Peter Rutherford in high school, then Tom Alt two years ago." She shivered. "Pretty boys, both, who deceived me into believing they were something they're not." Her sigh was wispy. "One a rake, the other a fraud."

"Yes, but keep in mind you have Uncle Logan around more now, a watchdog ready to expose any man unworthy of his niece. He'd never allow Roger even close if he didn't approve."

"I suppose . . . Oh, look!" She skittered into a sitting position, bare arms wrapped around the knees of her white day gown. Shiny toes buffed with Graf's Hyglo nail polish paste poked out, twitching with excitement. "They're gonna start!"

Adrenaline coursed as Cassie jumped up to sit cross-legged, grateful no corset restricted her today. And a mighty good thing, too, she thought with a roll of her pulse when Jamie caught her eye with a smile, expanding her chest way too much with a quivery sigh. A thought struck, and her smile suddenly dimmed. "Al . . . ," she began slowly, "you don't think Jamie would be like Mark, do you?" The question choked, shrinking her throat. "You know, a f-fortune hunter?"

Ridges puckered in her cousin's brow as she squinted at the man in question, taking way too long for Cassie's comfort. She glanced over at Cassie, eyes pensive. "I won't lie, Cass—I think he used to be, before you. I remember him joking once with Blake about he may as well fall in love with a rich woman as a poor one, and I do know he's only shown interest in girls from wealthy political families. But . . . ," she cocked her head to give Cass a pixie smile, "I've never seen him look at any of them like he looks at you, and Liddy says he hasn't taken Patricia out in over a month, and they were practically courting." Alli's smile slid into a smirk. "Which means he's falling for you instead, and she's as rich as Midas and a senator's daughter to boot."

"Maybe he thinks I'm rich too," she whispered. "After all, nobody knows about Daddy's dry wells except you, Uncle Logan, and Aunt Cait."

Alli gripped her arms to give her a little shake. "Cass—he's not after you because he thinks you're rich. He's smitten, and anybody can see that. Trust me, he may have bowled you over at that train station, but it was definitely Jamie who took the fall."

Cassie's heart pounded, as loud as the boom accompanying a spider streak of golds and scarlets. She paused. "Well, then, you don't think . . . he's pursuing me because I'm a challenge, do you?" She bit at the side of her lip as she peered up at Alli. "You know, the only woman who's spurned his advances? Hard to get, then once the chase is over, he'll be bored?"

"Aw, Cass . . ." Alli tucked a stray curl behind Cassie's ear. "I know Mark wounded you and believe me, nobody knows more than me how skittish that makes a girl about falling in love. But Jamie cares for you deeply, and he's trying hard to show that."

"I know," Cassie whispered, chewing on a sliver of nail. "I just don't think I could go through that again, you know?" She spit.

Alli stroked her hair. "I know. A heart is a fragile thing, especially in the hands of rats like Mark. But you and I have been praying about your relationship with Jamie ever since you gave him the ultimatum, so I say take a deep breath, trust God, and enjoy the fireworks."

Cassie nodded, eyes straying to where Jamie stood across the lawn in the dark, his boyish grin tingling her skin in the soft glow of a torch. Trust God? Yes, definitely the safe and right thing to do. But enjoy the fireworks? Cassie gulped. Maybe . . . if the loud boom of her heart didn't scare her to death first . . .

19

"One o'clock, two o'clock . . ."

Tease, taunts, and laughter filled the night as cousins and friends scattered to the far reaches of Uncle Logan's estate, scurrying to hide while Liddy was "it" in a game of midnight.

Jamie squinted through the dark in the direction Cassie had taken, pulse racing at the thought of sharing a hiding space with Cassie McClare. His jaw compressed. *Preferably, one nice and tight.* He'd spent the last three weeks doing things her way, trying to woo her with church and book studies, which only succeeded in luring him deeper in love with a woman who wouldn't admit she was in love with him too. Well, tonight he would woo her *his* way, hopefully to convince her she needed to say yes. Yes, to the courtship and yes to becoming his wife. Chin firm, he made his way to the hiding place Blake told him about, bent on turning her head—and her heart—in his direction once and for all.

"Eight o'clock, nine o'clock . . ."

He ducked behind a massive rhododendron into her secret crevice, a narrow corridor created by a deep sunporch on the south side of Logan's estate. Lips easing into a grin, he inched several feet back to where Cassie hid in the shadows with her back to the brick wall.

Even in the dark, he saw the whites of her eyes go round. "What are you doing here?" she whispered, shooing him away. "This is my hiding place, MacKenna—go!"

"Ten o'clock, eleven o'clock, midnight!" Liddy called.

Jamie chuckled. "Too late," he whispered, sandwiching himself behind her with his back to the wall. He looped an arm to her waist, tightening his hold to quiet her when a flicker of lamplight indicated someone just passed. Heady scents rose to taunt him—lilac water and Pear's soap mingling with the loamy scent of moss that never saw the light of day—delicious perfumes all, tingling his skin. His smile tipped at the soft absence of a corset that allowed him to feel the tension in her body along with the race of her pulse, evident in the rapid rise and fall of her chest.

Footsteps faded away, and she tried to whirl around, luring a grin to his lips when she got stuck halfway. "Jamie MacKenna," she hissed in the dark, "what in tarnation are you doing?"

Nudging her back around, he hooked her from behind once again, grazing her ear with a low chuckle. "This is my hiding place, Cowgirl. Can I help it if you stole it first?"

"Yours?!" she whispered loudly, her voice a near-squeak. "This has been my hiding place since I was knee-high to a grape, you pickle-brained polecat."

"I know," he said with a grin in his voice. "Blake told me."

She grunted and wrestled to get free. "Let-me-go! Have you forgotten our agreement?"

"No, ma'am." He firmed his grip, careful to brush his nose to the soft flesh of her lobe before he breathed warm in her ear. "No kisses are involved, Miss McClare," he said softly, taking her hand in his. His thumb teased the inside of her palm. "Hugs and hands only, I believe the fine print said." His fingers skimmed to her wrist, eyes closed to lose himself in the silky touch of her skin, the chaotic sprint of a pulse racing along with his own.

Her shuddery breaths filled the darkened space between them, matched by his own jagged breathing as he buried his face in her hair. "Cass," he whispered, unable to stop the heat that shimmered his skin. "I'm in love with you . . ."

"Jamie . . . please . . ." Her voice was a shaky rasp that seemed to beg him not to stop, and he had no choice but to succumb, tracing her ear with his cheek, the warmth of his breath caressing her temple. The softest of sounds parted from her lips, and with a surge of his pulse, he grazed the nape of her neck, skin against skin, nuzzling with his nose to drink in her scent.

"Jamie, no," she whispered, but never had a "no" sounded more like a "yes." She jerked to face him, lips parted in irregular breaths. "Jamie . . ."

His chest labored as he stared, blood pounding in his ears when her gaze flicked to his mouth. "Cass," he said, his voice husky and harsh, "I'm in love with you and I want to kiss you, but I can't unless you say it's okay." He swallowed hard, his Adam's apple aching when it ducked in his throat. "Is that what you want too?"

Uneven air quivered from her lower lip as her eyes locked with his, a breathless woman in the crosshairs of decision. She finally nodded, her eyes consenting with nary a blink.

The breath he'd been holding rushed out in a groan, and he lowered his mouth to hers, the sweet taste of her causing his head and stomach to swim. "So help me, Cass, I've never wanted any woman like I want you." He kissed her again, delving deeper until her moan met with his.

"MacKenna!" Blake's whispered chuckle caused Cassie to gasp. "I'm sure Cass is tired of fending you off, so I suggest you come out separately so nobody's the wiser."

Swallowing a low groan, Jamie trailed his fingers down the smooth line of her jaw. "You're not mad, are you?" he whispered.

"A little." There was the barest trace of trepidation in her tone.

"But you forgive me?" he asked, gently kneading her neck.

Her nod was as shaky as the sigh that quivered from her lips.

He kissed her forehead, closing his eyes to fuse her scent into his brain. "Good."

"But this means another talk, you know," she said, voice quivering.

His lips curved in a grin. "I was hoping it would . . . one where you agree to let me court you true and proper."

"MacKenna!" Blake's voice held a note of impatience.

"Coming!" Stroking her face one last time, his voice carried a plea. "My faith is growing because of you, Cass, and I want to court you now, not later—please. I apologize for trapping you, but I needed a little arm-twisting to help you see the light." He deposited a final kiss to her nose. "I love you, Cass."

"Get a move on, will ya, Mac?" Blake prodded. "The natives are getting restless."

Jamie edged his way against the brick wall, quietly easing from the dark, narrow space.

"Took you long enough, Casanova." Blake's chuckle was a clear indication he thought Jamie had struck out. He cuffed his shoulder with a wide grin. "How many times does my cousin have to slap you upside the head before you understand 'no'?" His laughter rang in the night air as they rounded the corner to where the others awaited the next game. "I'll tell you what, mister. I saved your hide tonight, so you're 'it.'"

Jamie grinned outright. "I most certainly am."

"It"—the luckiest man alive.

"Mama, I'm tired."

Caitlyn glanced up at Maddie on Logan's lap. Her russet curls splayed on his pin-striped shirt as she lay against his broad chest in front of a fire waning as much as the people around it.

"Goodness, it's after midnight," Alli said with a yawn. She lumbered up from her wrought-iron patio chair and stretched, arms high as if reaching for the harvest moon overhead.

Before Caitlyn could clear the chaise, Blake jumped up to bundle Maddie in his arms. "I'll take her up, Mother," he said with a kiss to Maddie's nose, "if Alli puts her to bed."

"No problem there." Alli tugged Cassie up. "Come on, Cuz, you can help." She bussed her mother's cheek while Cassie and her younger cousins followed suit. "Good night, Mother."

"Good night, girls. Liddy, Patricia, if you need anything, just let Alli or me know."

"You up for a game of pool, Uncle Logan?" Blake said, Maddie now draped over his shoulder. "Rumor has it Mac's been humbled considerably these days."

Logan chuckled. "So I hear."

Jamie ambled up from his chaise, eyes following Cassie to the door before zeroing in on Blake with a mock scowl. "Just part of my game plan, McClare, to catch you unaware."

Blake grinned. "Oh? Something you learned from my cousin?"

Bram chuckled. "I'd say that's a given. Good night, all."

"That settles it." Jamie prodded Blake and Bram through the door. "You're both going down." He shot a smile over his shoulder. "Thanks, Mr. and Mrs. McClare, for a great evening."

Caitlyn flushed at the innocent implication of Jamie's words. "Good night, boys."

"At the risk of appearing to be a killjoy, I fear I must turn in as well." Father Harry rose and slapped Logan's back. "I'm not as young as I used to be, and neither are you, my friend." He yawned. "But then I suppose one of us has far more experience with burning the candle at both ends." He gave Caitlyn a short bow. "A delight to see you again, Caitlyn. Good night."

"Good night, Father Hough." Caitlyn buffed her arms, wishing she could just flee to her bedroom as well rather than asking Logan's support with the Board. She scooted forward to hold her hands to the fire, shaky at the thought of the two of them being alone.

"G'night, Harry." Logan added another log to the fire, and sparks shot into the summer sky as he squatted to stoke the flames. The fire's glow burnished his chiseled face, illuminating the dark shadow of beard that bristled his jaw like a pirate.

Caitlyn hugged her arms to her waist, eyes focused on the flames that leapt and popped rather than on Logan, who rose to drape a blanket over her shoulders. "Thank you," she whispered, the intimacy of fire furling into a sky studded with stars making her feel shy with this man she'd known more than a quarter of a century. He pulled his chair close—too close—and she gulped. At least he wasn't sharing her chaise, for which she was most thankful.

"So, Mrs. McClare . . . ," he said softly, hands clasped on parted knees. "Must be important to spend time with me under the stars past your bedtime."

She peeked up, the words stuck in her throat as she pinched the blanket close.

His husky chuckle warmed her cheeks more than the fire. "Come on, Cait," he said, "you've never been afraid of me a day in your life, so what is it? What do you want?"

She drew in a deep swallow of air, her stomach awhirl from the import of her request . . . *and* from his presence. "I . . . need your . . . support," she said quietly.

"You already have that, Cait, you know that."

Her throat shifted. "On the Board." Her voice quivered like her body beneath the blanket.

Silent for several moments, he finally sat back to assess her with hands braced behind his neck, studying her through pensive eyes. "What do you want, Cait?" he whispered.

She forged on, absently picking at the nubby edge of the blanket. "Well, you see, the Vigilance Committee . . ." She paused, avoiding his gaze. "Or I should say *I* . . . have drafted a proposal for the San Francisco Board of Supervisors regarding the Barbary Coast, but I didn't want to present it to the Vigilance Committee until I . . ." Chancing a glance, she was encouraged by the smile hovering on his lips, giving her the distinct impression he enjoyed the fact that she needed him. Emboldened, she lifted her chin. "Well, it's an important initiative, you see, and I don't want to go in blind, presenting a mere piece of paper, so I was hoping to . . ." She nervously clamped the blanket to her chin. "Gird it with some . . . clout."

"You want my vote," he said simply, effectively releasing the breath she'd been holding.

The blanket slid to her shoulders. "Oh, Logan, I realize this is highly improper, with you being an influential member of the board, but . . ." She stared at him openly, honestly, without the least bit of guile. "Cleaning up the Coast means everything to me, outside of my family, and I was just hoping . . . well, praying, really . . . that you might . . ." He was watching her with such affection that she caught her breath, suddenly aware that in his own way, this man loved her and would do anything for her and her family. The thought stunned and energized her all at the same time, and with the barest hint of a smile, she stated her plea. "Present my plan to the Board." The air left her lungs in a whoosh of relief.

"You're aware I have vested interests in the Coast?" he said slowly, eyes never straying.

She nodded, arming herself with another deep intake of air. "Yes, but phase one of this initiative primarily targets the brothels and opium dens, Logan, not the gambling halls or bars."

"Yet."

She gave a little gulp, not to be deterred by his businesslike tone. "Yes, later phases will focus on the dance and gambling halls, some of which, I'm well aware, you hold controlling interests in." She bent forward, her words as earnest as the plea in her eyes. "But the restrictions I propose will only improve your bottom line, Logan, I assure you, promoting a safer, more upstanding environment that will actually draw the upper class."

"Might I remind you it already draws the upper class, Cait?" Logan said in a matter-of-fact tone, his statement taking a turn toward dry. "At least the male component."

The insensitivity of his statement stunned. She sat straight up, fire singeing her cheeks. "I assure you no reminding is necessary, Logan—you proved that long ago."

It was Logan's turn to blush, blood crawling up his neck when he realized his mistake too late. He closed his eyes, scouring his forehead with the ball of his hand. "Sorry, Cait, that was a stupid thing to say." Heavy lids edged up, revealing both sorrow and regret. "And do."

She released a wavering breath. "My concern is for the future, not the past, which is why I need to know—will you help me?" Dropping her gaze to the fire, she awaited his answer for what seemed like eons, heart pounding. *Please, Lord, let him see the good he can do.*

"Yes."

She froze, not fully comprehending until her head lurched up in shock. "You'll do it? You'll present my proposal to the Board?"

He smiled. "It's a sound business decision, Cait, one that bodes well for our city." He paused, gaze tender. "Of course, it doesn't hurt you hold my heart in the palm of your hand."

His words barely registered, such was the excitement whirling in her brain. She rushed on, almost giddy. "And you'll help me garner votes from other members of the Board?"

The smile slid into a grin. "You're a beautiful woman—how can I say no?"

"Oh, Logan!" She lunged to give him a tight hug before pulling away with a squeeze of his hand. "I don't know how to thank you! Honestly, you're the best friend I could ever have."

"Friends, yes," he whispered, eyes dimming. "But we both know we were meant to be more."

Her mouth opened and closed. Biting the edge of her lip, she tried to ease her hand from his, but he held on tight. "Logan, I—"

"Cait, please—I don't mean right away. I understand you need more time, but I have to know . . ." His thumb feathered the palm of her hand. "I *need* to know. Do you think . . . is it possible . . . ," the chiseled jaw flickered when a knot ducked in his throat, "you could ever love me again? Because I love you, Cait, and the fact is, I always have."

She jerked her hand free and shot to her feet, taking several steps back. "Logan, I'm sorry, but I'm . . . happy with my life the way that it is . . ."

He rose slowly, his heated gaze welded to hers. "Don't you ever get lonely, Cait? Miss the touch of human affection?"

"No, of course not," she said too quickly, hands locked to her body like an emotional straitjacket. "I have my children, my niece, my friends . . ." She attempted a weak smile. "And, of course, I have you . . . a friend who just offered his help for something so dear to my heart."

He moved in, and she stepped back, closer to the fire, a scorching reminder this man had burned her once, searing her heart with scars that had yet to heal. Her voice trailed to a whisper. "A very good friend."

Logan inwardly winced, "friendship" no longer enough with a woman he craved more every day. He'd spent a lifetime knowing women—wooing them, winning them, making love to them—certainly enough to know when a woman was drawn to him, cared for him. And there was no doubt in Logan's mind Cait had feelings far deeper for him than she let on. He drew in an empowering breath and gentled his tone. "I'm asking for your help too," he whispered. He carefully caressed her arms, her shivering apparent even through the blanket. "Help me make amends to someone dear to my heart as well—" His pulse surged, both at the prospect of kissing her and the fear she'd bolt before he ever got the chance. "What about the touch of a man, Cait?" he said quietly, his voice suddenly gruff with desire. "Do you ever miss that . . . ?"

"No!" she rasped, pushing him away. The chin lashed up into battle mode, all gentleness burned away by the fire in her eyes. "How dare you ask such a thing! For the love of decency—I'm your sister-in-law and the wife of your brother."

"No, Cait—" His whisper was harsh. "You're the love of my life and my brother's widow. There's a difference, you know." He forced his temper back with a slow exhale of air. "I need you, Cait—more than as a friend." His jaw tightened. "And I think you need me . . ."

"What I *need*," she said with a thrust of her jaw, "is for you to understand that I have no desire to get involved with you or any man. That part of my life is ended, Logan—done, finished, over—so you may as well let it go, because my mind is made up."

A muscle jerked in his temple. "And your body? Has it made up its mind, Cait? There's a powerful attraction between us, and I defy you to deny it."

She heaved a weary sigh and shook her head, her shaky laugh far from convincing. "I'm sorry to break your record, Logan, with the endless hordes of women who fall under your spell, but it's best you realize here and now that I see you as nothing more than a brother-in-law . . ." She paused to draw in a deep breath and her eyes softened, as if she realized how harsh that sounded. "A brother, really, of whom I am quite fond."

"A 'brother'? Really?" He squinted in amazement, hands on his hips. He was torn between laughing out loud or losing his temper. "I never figured you for a liar, Mrs. McClare, but I guess each of us has our vice."

Even in the moonlight, he could see the blush that tainted her cheeks, indicating he had triggered her anger as thoroughly as she'd triggered his. "Yes, we do, Mr. McClare, but I can tell you most emphatically—you will never be one of mine. Good night."

"Cait . . ." He stayed her arm, his voice hoarse with regret. "I was out of line, and I apologize. Please . . . don't leave angry."

She turned, and the anger slowly seeped from her face while the breath seeped from his lungs. The edge was gone from her voice, replaced by a gentle tone that matched the kindness in her eyes. "Logan, please know you are very dear to me and an integral part of our family. But you need to understand and accept that my heart, my love, will always belong to my husband."

The words sliced through him deeper and sharper than any blade, and he deflected his hurt with an awkward slide of hands into his pockets, heart aching more than when she'd left him the first time. Because now he knew what he'd lost. He cleared his throat, wanting to make amends for angering her, for hurting her years ago, and for pushing so hard when she obviously still harbored feelings for his brother. "I understand," he whispered, then swallowed hard, his gut clenching at the idea that maybe this time he was wrong, maybe she didn't have feelings for him like he'd hoped, and maybe the only attraction that truly existed was his. To her. Head bowed, he lifted a shaky hand to his eyes to knead the bridge of his nose, suddenly aware for the first time in his life, his love for Cait was as deep, if not deeper, than his desire. He sucked in a sharp breath, wanting more than anything to show her his love in a tangible way, to give her back a piece of Liam . . . and a piece of himself.

"I have something to give you," he said quietly. Hands still in his pockets, his thumb grazed the ring on his finger, knowing full well what he was giving away. Not his heart as he'd hoped, but a piece of his heritage and the only ring he would apparently be able to put on Caitlyn McClare's hand. He could almost feel the raised gold outline of the lion and Celtic cross against black onyx, the McClare signet ring passed down from centuries past. It had belonged to his ancestors of old . . . on down to his grandfather, his father, and then Liam, who'd never taken it off till Cait gave it to Logan the day Liam was buried. His father's will delegated ownership to the McClare heir, but it had pained her to part with it, he knew, from the tender way she'd fingered it with such care. *Just as I'm doing now.* Pulling his hand from his pocket, he removed the ring, thumb gliding against the smooth onyx one last time before he held it out, determined if he couldn't love her the way he wanted, he'd love her the only way he could. "I want you to have this," he whispered. "It belongs to you."

"No . . ." She shook her head as tears pooled in her eyes. "I can't take it—it's yours."

Yes, it is. And it claimed a piece of his heart for so many reasons.

The connection to his heritage, his father, his brother . . . and to her. For almost twenty-six years it had grazed her skin when Liam had held her hand, touched the warmth of her body every night when they slept, and when she'd given it to Logan, it was as if she'd given him a piece of herself. A piece he realized he no longer had a right to. Not if she didn't care like he did. Not if she wasn't drawn as he was.

"Take it, Cait," he whispered. "You lived with it for almost twenty-six years—it belongs to you more than me." He took her hand and placed the ring in her palm, closing his fingers over hers. "And maybe—just maybe—it will give you a touch of Liam, easing your heart like I long to do."

Her hand trembled to her mouth as tears trickled down her face. "Oh, Logan . . ."

She launched into his arms, clutching him so tightly, it paralyzed him to the spot. Moisture stung and he closed his eyes, resting his head against hers, the scent of lavender invading his senses and taunting his soul. *Oh, Cait, I'd give anything to have you love me once more, want me again . . .*

She pulled away and swiped at her eyes, her lips quivering into a smile. "You must think I'm crazy, but I'm just so very grateful . . ." Peering up, she gently braced his jaw with her palm, eyes shimmering with gratitude. "I don't think I've ever loved you more than right this moment, Logan McClare. Thank you!"

His heart seized when she pressed a kiss to his cheek, and almost by accident, he turned into her touch, their lips so close he could smell the hint of hot chocolate they'd enjoyed around the fire. They froze in the same split second of time, and his pulse thudded slow and hard as he waited for her to pull away. Only she didn't, and heat scorched his body. "Cait," he whispered, barely believing her lips nearly grazed his. He waited, not willing to push for fear she would retreat, but when her eyelids flickered closed, his fate was sealed. "So help me, Cait, I love you," he rasped, quickly caressing her lips before she could retreat. The moment his mouth took hers, he was a man hopelessly lost, bewitched by her spell. She jolted in his arms as if suddenly realizing her folly, but he refused to relent, his grip at the nape of her neck strong and sure, allowing him a taste of the sweetest lips he'd ever known. A groan trapped in his throat, and he devoured her, delving deeper with a passion stoked by almost twenty-six years of denial and longing. "Cait," he whispered, voice hoarse as he nuzzled her ear, "I need you in my life."

He felt it the moment the winds shifted, pulse skyrocketing when her blanket dropped to the ground and she melded in his arms. His mouth explored with a vengeance, the frenzied beat of her heart throbbing beneath his lips as he grazed the hollow of her throat. He skimmed up to suckle the lobe of her ear, and his heart swelled with joy when a soft moan escaped her lips. Blood pounding in his veins, he wove fingers into her hair to cradle her face. "Marry me, Cait, please!"

Her eyelids fluttered open to reveal a glaze of desire so strong, his mouth descended again, dominant and possessive until her lips surrendered to his. "Marry me," he repeated, his kiss gentling to playful nips meant to coax and tease. "I need you, Cait . . . and I *want* you."

In the space of a painful heartbeat, she hurled him away, breasts heaving and eyes wild. "You're a devil, Logan McClare, always lusting after what you can't have!"

Sleet slithered through his veins. "No, Cait, it's not true—I want you because I love you."

He reached for her, and she thrust back, fury welling in her eyes. "You want me because you can't have me. And once you had me, you would just throw me away again, returning to your old habits of carousing with women all hours of the night."

"You're wrong—let me prove it, please. Marry me."

She shook her head, an auburn curl quivering against her neck. Her tone trembled with a violence that stunned. "I-don't-want-you, and I-don't-need-you, do you hear?"

His anger surged, but he tamped it down with a clamp of his jaw, his words as hard as hers. "Really, Cait? Why don't you tell that to the woman whose body just responded to mine?"

The lightning force of her slap shifted his jaw clean to the right, the sound of it like a crack of thunder. "How dare you?" she whispered, tears streaming her cheeks. "You forced yourself on me in your usual callous way, and if you ever do so again, it will be the last time you step foot in my house, is that clear?" He didn't answer, and she took a step forward, her jaw engaged once again. "I said, is-that-clear?"

Gritting his teeth, he turned away. He sucked in a harsh breath and released it again, fighting to keep his temper under control, the only control he apparently possessed with the woman before him. Well, she might hold all the cards and he might lose this hand, but he would *not* lose the game. With a heavy blast of air, he turned—and stopped—all anger fading at what he'd reduced her to. A quivering mass of tears. *God, forgive me . . .* He studied her with sorrow in his eyes. "Yes," he whispered, all of his emotion finally spent, "it's clear." She started for the door and he stopped her with a gentle hand. "Forgive me, Cait—I never meant to hurt you. Not then, not now."

She nodded stiffly and started to leave.

"Cait?" She turned at the door. He plunged his hands in his pockets, no longer a man of the world, but a little boy whose heart was on the line. "I love you, and deep down inside, I think you know that, know I would never cheat on you again." He stared, his eyes naked with the truth for the very first time. "That said, I need to know why? What else are you afraid of?"

She must have sensed his honesty because the hard plain of her face ebbed into a look of such sorrow, it plucked at his heart. Her voice was gentle and low once again, the Caitlyn he was privileged to love. "I love you as family, Logan, but I can never be 'in love' with you again."

The words stabbed. "Why?" he whispered, his voice no more than a croak.

Her bodice quivered with a burdensome sigh. "Because I don't trust you."

"Why? I swear to you, Cait—I will be faithful."

"No, Logan, you can't. A man of your habit and ilk can't be faithful without God."

"Let me prove it. I can do this."

"Maybe. But I can't. I refuse to fall in love with a man who doesn't share my faith."

He took a step forward, his eyes intense. "I believe in God, Cait."

"No, Logan, you believe in yourself first, God after. There's a difference."

His jaw sagged in disbelief. "You're attracted to me and love me, yet you turn me away because my faith isn't up to snuff?" Fury boiled in his veins, trumping his passion. He chilled her with a look so cold, he saw her shiver. "Even if it means your precious Vigilance Committee?"

The blood leeched from her face. "You wouldn't," she whispered, her words laced with shock. "Y-you agreed, and it's the decent thing to do."

He moved in, fists clenched and a nerve twitching in his cheek.

"No, Cait, the decent thing to do is to forgive the past and admit you're in love with me."

Her legs faltered before steel appeared to fuse in her spine. "That's your price, then?"

He stared, his jaw as rigid as his pride. She loved him, she wanted him, but she wouldn't have him because of God? Outrage like he'd never known singed his very soul. "It is."

She winced as if she'd been struck, pain contorting her face while she listed against the wrought-iron chaise. Firelight flickered across her beautiful features, illuminating myriad feelings that tore at his heart. Shock, fear, fury, resolve . . . and sorrow. The same sorrow he saw in himself, a man of missed opportunities. The flames spit and popped behind him, as if portending a fiery future that would ravage both him and the woman he loved.

He watched as the anger slowly siphoned from her body, softening her features, welling in her eyes, and he was reminded once again what a rare woman she was. Prone to gentleness rather than anger, giving rather than taking, others rather than self. Despite the fact he would rob her of something so dear, her eyes bore no retribution or blame, only a sadness that seemed to personify Caitlyn McClare where he was concerned.

"Then it's too high," she whispered, the trace of a tear glazing her cheek as she placed his ring on the chaise. She turned away, her voice a broken whisper that prophesied their doom. "Even for my precious Vigilance Committee."

20

"So . . . do we have a courtship?" Legs dangling over the side of the swim platform that was anchored in the middle of Logan's cattail lake, Blake chuckled and scooped water into Jamie's face. "I'm assuming since Cass didn't boot you out of her hiding place last night, you made some headway on that score?"

Soaking up Napa sun on the dock, Jamie lay flat on his stomach, head on his arms. Nothing moved but his eyelids and the curve of his lips as he peered up at Blake. "And then some." He batted at a fly that landed on the bare shoulder of his sleeveless swimsuit, then jerked his leg when it flitted to the back of his knee-length swim shorts.

Blake scooped a handful of mossy water into Jamie's face with an edge to his tone. "What's that supposed to mean, MacKenna? Did you make advances to my cousin?"

Jamie swiped at his eye with a chuckle. "Don't get your knickers in a knot, Blake, my intentions are completely honorable where Cassie's concerned." He closed his eyes, the memory of the kiss last night heating his body more than the sun. "But you know Cass—I had to do a little nudging to get her to see things my way."

"Yeah, that's what I'm worried about. I've seen your 'nudges,' Mac, and I'm not sure I want you 'nudging' my cousin."

Jamie hiked one lid. "Even into marriage?"

The fly could have landed in Blake's mouth. "No joke? You're that serious already?"

"He's been serious since he laid eyes on the woman, Blake, where've you been?" Bram said with a faint smile, flat on his back with elbows splayed behind his head while he sunned in a black and white striped swim shirt Jamie swore he stole from an ex-convict.

Blake scratched his head. "I suppose doing some 'nudging' of my own, too busy to notice." His low chuckle rumbled over the water. "Only not the respectable kind."

"Yeah, well my days of nudging other women are over—Cassie's the one I want, and I plan to propose, the sooner the better."

"Well, what d'ya know?" Blake said. "The Three Musketeers will be the Three Cousins."

Bram slid Jamie a sideways glance. "Yeah, one big happy family, but educate me first." The edge of his lip sloped up. "Does this mean you've actually changed and seen the light and not just going through the motions?"

The question caught Jamie by surprise, clearing his mind of all banter when he realized something that slowed the blood in his veins. Holy thunder, he *had* changed. Somehow between church with both Cassie and his family and debating theology with Cassie and Bram over the last month, the hard callus around his heart—the one that kept God at bay—had slowly eroded. Stripped away every time he saw the light in Cassie's eyes when her prayers were answered or the glow in her face when she sang a hymn at church. All those times she was patient and kind to Patricia when he could tell she simply wanted to hamstring her. His lips crooked. Well, she'd certainly hamstrung him, crippling him of the notion that any other woman could even come close.

And when she'd insisted on praying together for his sister every week—out loud, no less, like some crazy person—she'd rendered him completely powerless at doing anything but falling deeper in love. Had he seen the light? His smile softened. Oh yeah, and it shone bright and strong from the pale-green depths of the eyes of Cassidy McClare.

"Please say something, Mac," Blake said with a grin. "You're starting to scare me."

Jamie squinted in the sunlight, first at Bram and then up at Blake, giving in to a sheepish smile. "Well, let's just say for the first time in a long while, I'm on speaking terms with God."

"It's about time," Bram said, sitting up with a grunt. He finger-shot a dead dragonfly at Blake. "I thought you were as hopeless as this joker here."

Blake ducked, shooting back a cocky grin. "I'm not hopeless, I'm smart. A man gets religion and the next thing he knows, some woman ties him down with a rope around his neck." He flicked Jamie's head. "Like Mac here."

Jamie slapped him away. "Hey, McClare, it's not 'tied down' if it's where I want to be."

"Even so, Uncle Logan's the smart one." Blake jutted his dimpled chin. "Enjoying lots of women without the hassle of a wife, a bachelor for life and far happier for it." Arms braced to the dock, he lifted his face to the sun. "A role model if ever there was."

"Yeah, if you don't mind being lonely." Bram's tone was as dry as the weathered wood he commenced picking on at the edge of the dock.

Blake's eyes flipped open in shock. "Lonely—Uncle Logan?" He stared as if Bram had just sprouted wings. "The man has more women in his life than a convent."

"Yeah? Then why is he always at your house lately, weekends included?"

Blake blinked, the question giving him pause. "Probably because Cassie's here for the summer, and everybody knows he's a man who loves family."

"Which only underscores my point," Bram said with emphasis. "His bachelor life is lonely, hordes of women or no."

"Aw, you're batty. You missed your calling to be a priest like your parents wanted, you know that?"

Jamie gaped at Bram. "Your parents wanted you to be a priest?" His voice rose several octaves. "You never told me that. No wonder you're the saintly one whenever we go out."

"The saintly one who never has any fun," Blake pointed out.

Bram's smile took a tilt. "The saintly one who doesn't wrestle with hangovers or guilt."

"Or women." Jamie grinned.

It was Bram's turn to chuckle. "Nor will you, my friend," he said with a douse of lake water, "once that ring goes on your finger. Marriage is for keeps, you know."

Marriage is for keeps. Oh, yeah, Jamie thought, chest swelling with pride despite the murky water dribbling his cheek. Cassie, a surgery for his sister, a political career, and a house on Nob Hill for his family—definitely for keeps—and everything he needed to "keep" him happy.

"Ahoy, there!"

All three men glanced up as Patricia swam the last few strokes to the dock. Jamie jumped up to offer a hand, and she hoisted herself up with a smile. Chestnut strands of hair trailed her neck from her fluted mob hat, accentuating the creamy line of a graceful neck Jamie's lips had roamed more than once. Her navy swim dress fell just below the knees, sopping wet and clinging to a

234

shapely body he couldn't help but notice. Tearing his gaze away, he sat back down and focused on her face. The violet eyes that stared back carried a message he knew all too well. Nervous fingers toyed with the sailor tie of her swimsuit while she aimed her smile straight at him. "Hate to break up your party, but Alli's scrounging up a game of croquet. Any takers?"

Bram lumbered up. "I'm game."

"Me too," Blake said.

Jamie started to rise and Patricia implored him with her eyes, fidgeting with the tie as she wrapped it around her finger. "Jamie—do you mind if we talk? Just for a moment?"

He paused halfway to his feet, then slowly dropped back. "Sure," he said, hands loosely clasped over tented knees. This was as good a time as any to let her know about Cassie.

"See you on the mainland," Blake said and plunged into the water. "Hey, Hughes," he called over his shoulder, "five bucks says I can leave you in my wake."

"Not in this lifetime," Bram called, obviously confident his athletic prowess was superior to his cousin's. He grinned and offered Jamie and Trish a salute. "As Cassie would say, see you back at the ranch." Poised on the edge of the dock, he executed a perfect dive.

Silence prevailed while Jamie and Trish watched Bram outswim Blake. "Cassie seems to be a popular girl," she finally said, sliding down to sit on the dock. With blue stockinged legs bent like his, she hugged knees clad with sopping ruffled bloomers.

"Cassie's just unique, being from Texas and all."

"Do you like her?" she asked, voice timid and head cocked, hand shading her eyes.

"Sure, she's a great gal." Jamie picked on a loose thread from the hem of his swim shorts, uncomfortable both with the conversation and the news he had to share.

"I just wondered," she said slowly, averting her eyes, "because before Cassie, I thought that you and I . . ."

His stomach tightened at the quivering bob of her throat, making him feel like a cad.

She looked up then, gaze vulnerable as she twirled a soggy curl around her finger with a touch of hurt in her eyes. "Well, you know . . . liked each other."

He swallowed hard, wishing this wasn't so difficult. He liked Patricia, had from the start. She was beautiful, smart, and most important of all, a wealthy senator's daughter—a senator who'd made it perfectly clear he wanted Jamie in the family. He had no doubt that if Cassie hadn't happened along, he would have married her—and soon, if she had any say. He sucked in a deep breath. "I do like you, Patricia—a lot. But when Cassie arrived for the summer, I just . . ." He paused, desperate to find words that wouldn't cut. "Well, we just sorta became good friends, you know? And now . . . well, now I want to court her."

His heart twisted when tears pooled in her eyes. "Court her?" she whispered. "But what about your dreams—a surgery for your sister and your political aspirations?"

He blinked, confused by the question. "They're still there, Trish, just like before."

Avoiding his gaze, she rested her chin on her knees, eyes wandering into a faraway stare. "You've always been honest with me, Jamie, making it clear you have aspirations to rise to the top. Politically, yes, but also to provide for your family, which is something I've always admired. Especially your dream to acquire a surgery for your sister." A muscle jerked in the smooth line of her throat. "So you see—I was never foolish enough to think it was just me you wanted."

"Trish, please—"

236

She turned to face him, twinges of sadness in her face. "Do you deny it?"

He drew in a harsh breath and slowly released it again, his voice barely audible. "No."

"Thank you for being honest," she whispered, returning her gaze to the water. "You know, Jamie, it's a tight-knit group, the families of Nob Hill, and women do talk." A sigh shuddered from her lips. "Especially about a man like you."

His eyelids weighted closed with a silent groan, his words to Bram returning to haunt. *May as well fall in love with a rich girl as a poor one, right?* His anger rose to battle his guilt. And why not? The cause was just and his mother and sister were worth it.

And you? He blanched at the taunt of an inner voice.

She continued, her words as shaky as his conscience. "Of c-course, we all found it curious you only pursued wealthy girls with strong political connections, but none of us pretended we didn't know why."

"Trish . . ." His voice was a pained whisper.

"Oh, it didn't matter to me, I assure you, because my affection for you runs deep. Deep enough to help you achieve all your heart longs for with my money and influence." She paused, her eyes slowly capturing his as her voice faded to soft. "Deep enough to talk to my father about his connections with Cooper Medical for your sister's pro bono surgery."

The breath seized in his throat before it escaped once again in short, shallow breaths, his pulse pounding so loud in his ears, he thought he'd heard wrong. "W-what did you say?"

Her eyes softened. "I know how much your sister means to you, Jamie, and I know you've worked hard to procure a surgery for her someday. My father admires that and said if it means that much to the man who courts his daughter, then it means a lot to him and he wants to help."

The man who courts his daughter. Blood drained from his face so fast, his vision blurred. Hand to his eyes, he swallowed hard, tongue as parched as the brittle dock bleached by the sun.

"Daddy's excited about your ambition for politics, as am I, and if we were to . . ." He actually heard the gulp of her throat rather than saw it, but no more than his own, the hesitation in her tone clearly as awkward as he felt. "Well, you know—end up together—he said he'd want you to be his counsel and would introduce you to his friends, which he believes would put you on the fast track for the political career of your dreams."

His body jolted at the sudden touch of her hand to his foot, her voice as tentative as the shaky glide of her fingers. "I was meant to be a senator's wife, Jamie, born and bred to be all you need me to be. Which is why," she said with a definite waver in her tone, "it's so hard to understand your attraction to Cassie, a woman who can't further your dreams."

He glanced up beneath his palm, his heart in a pause. "What do you mean?"

She turned to face him then, a fragility in her eyes that confirmed just how much she cared. "A woman who's neither affluent nor a senator's daughter," she said quietly, "although I suppose you could be wealthy in love."

The heat on his face felt like third-degree burns. "What are you talking about, Trish? Cassie's a McClare and an oil heiress at that."

"A McClare, yes," she said slowly. "But an heiress whose wells have run dry."

He couldn't blink, breathe . . . "That's not true," he finally whispered, his voice a rasp.

Her lip trembled the slightest bit. "Maybe, but I'm sure I heard correctly, so maybe you should ask Cassie." Her eyes were soft with concern and an innocence he didn't quite believe. "Why do you think her fiancé broke the engagement?"

His eyes shuddered closed, shards of shock slicing through his gut. *Cassie, no, please . . .*

"Maybe I misunderstood," Patricia reasoned. "After all, I stumbled in on the tail end of a conversation between Alli and Cassie that I obviously wasn't meant to hear." She paused, her voice genuinely contrite. "I'm sorry, Jamie, but I just assumed you knew."

Sure you did. He gouged his eyes with the ball of his hand, bile rising from the bitter disappointment that roiled in his gut. Every hope, every dream, all snuffed out by a God he had actually pursued, a God who turned a deaf ear to him just like he'd done to his mother and sister.

Foul words he didn't even think he knew spewed from his lips, defiling the summer day just like God had defiled his life, and with a rage he wasn't sure he could contain, he shot up and dove into the water, ragged air pumping in his chest like fury pumped through his veins.

"Jamie, I'm sorry . . . ," Patricia called.

But not as sorry as he.

Sorry he was too poor to help his sick sister.

Sorry his plans had been foiled.

Sorry he loved a woman who may be poorer than him.

Thoughts of Cassie assailed his mind, and his lungs burned in his chest till he thought he would die. Because therein stabbed the sorriest sorry of all.

Having to say goodbye.

Caitlyn McClare's Packard pulled away from the curb as Jamie watched from the front porch of Mrs. Tucker's boardinghouse.

The aroma of fresh-baked apple pie wafted through the screen door, reminding him he'd bolted from Napa before the picnic lunch at Logan's estate. Just as well. His appetite had crashed along with his mood after Patricia destroyed his day.

Cassie was poor. At least compared to the San Francisco Mc-Clares, a fact alluded to by Mrs. McClare herself when Hadley drove them home after Jamie announced he needed to leave. "Something's come up," he'd explained, and Caitlyn had jumped on it as if she were more anxious than he to escape the weekend. *Not possible*, although her mood had certainly been as edgy as his, a fact that seemed to loosen her tongue considerably on the hour-long drive. As a skilled prosecutor, he hadn't found it difficult to glean bits of information to confirm Patricia's claim about Cassie. A question here, an observation there, and Caitlyn supplied enough threads to weave a tapestry of financial doom for the Texas McClares. *And* the daughter who was jilted when her fortune went awry. A daughter who, unlike her wealthy cousins, was now forced into the workplace where women were rare and wealthy ones almost nonexistent.

Hand on the latch, he carefully slipped through the screen door, hoping Mrs. Tucker was too busy baking to note that one of her boarders was home. Nerves strung tight, he took great pains to quietly scale the squeaky wooden stairs to the second level where his mother and sister occupied the same room across the hall from his. Threadbare throw rugs and polished, albeit scarred hardwood floors indicated a boardinghouse that was clean if not plush, in a neighborhood where dirty-faced children played in patched clothing and middle-class neighbors chatted long after dark. His lips compressed. *The Celestial City compared to the Barbary Coast.*

Striding down the hall, he tapped on his mother's door, easing it open when he heard her soft voice. He was met by a wash of warm sunshine, and his heart swelled with gratitude that his family now lived in a sunny room where crisp ruffled sheers fluttered at the window, ushering in the smell of honeysuckle and roses from Mrs. Tucker's backyard.

"Jamie," she whispered, glancing up from where she was reading in a comfy armchair in front of the window close to his sister's bed. Her face was pinched. "What are you doing here?"

He noticed the Bible in her lap, and resisted the scowl that pulled at his lips. *For all the good it will do*. His gaze flicked to where his sister lay sleeping, pale and drawn in the warm summer light, and his heart constricted. *Jess?* He carefully closed the door, ignoring his mother's question. "What's wrong?" he said, his whisper harsh as he moved to the side of her bed, stomach cramping at the dark circles under her eyes. "Why is she in bed?"

His mother rose to stand beside him, a tender arm to his waist. "She reinjured her hip," she said, the emotion in her tone as thick as the panic in his chest. "Dr. Morrissey sedated her."

"What?" He turned to stare at his mother, pulse sporadic. "When? How?"

She opened her mouth to speak, but no words came as moisture welled in her eyes.

"Mom?" Jamie gripped her and gave her a little shake, heart battering his ribs. "Tell me now—what happened to Jess?"

A hand flew to his mother's mouth as a heave escaped. "S-she . . . was . . . ," tears slipped down her cheeks when another heave broke from her throat, "attacked."

The very word froze the blood in his veins. "Attacked?" he whispered. "How?"

Jess moaned, and his mother drew him to the window, urging him to sit in her chair.

"I don't want to sit," he hissed. "Tell me what happened."

241

"I will, Jamie, but please—sit down first. This will not be easy to hear."

With abrupt strides, he retrieved a wooden chair on the other side of Jess's bed and placed it next to his mother's. She sat and he did the same, leaning forward. "Tell me," he said, eyes fused to hers.

She picked at her nails, blinking hard to obviously keep the tears at bay. "Well, you know how excited she's been since feeling better lately, taking short walks outside, pestering me to let her do more and more." His mother's eyes flicked to where Jess lay almost comatose in the bed. "Cocky almost," she said with a tearful smile, her gaze returning to Jamie's. "So when she saw the package of clothing I'd sewn for Bess, she insisted she could take it over—"

"What?" Jamie rose up in his chair, a nerve flickering in his jaw. "Is she crazy?"

"That's what I thought, and I told her no, but you know your sister when she sets her mind to something, and she swore she'd take the trolley, insisting everything would be all right." His mother swiped at her eyes. "Well, she delivered the package to Millie sure enough and had just left the building, not twenty feet away, when a man grabbed her . . ."

No, please . . . Jamie's eyelids shuddered closed while a low groan cleaved to his throat.

"Of course Jess tried to get away, but he . . . he forced her to the alley and threw her down—" His mother's voice broke on a sob.

Jamie's head jerked up. "Did he—?"

She shook her head violently, the tears streaming freely now. "No. Jess was in so much pain when she tried to wrestle away that her screams brought Millie and Julie to her aid, among others. Some kind man pulled that animal off of Jess before he could . . ."

A shiver rattled her body that matched the shudder of revulsion in his soul. "But it was too late for Jess's hip. He'd slammed her to the bricks, bruising her badly."

His mother started weeping, and Jamie handed her his handkerchief before clutching her close, his face buried in her hair while moisture pricked his own eyes. Horrendous pain wrenched in his chest at the thought of Jess—sweet, beautiful Jess—assaulted in such a manner. "Where is he?" Jamie's voice was a deadly whisper, the calm of his question belying the fury burning in his gut. *So I can kill him . . .*

"He ran off, the drunken coward, and neither Julie nor Millie knew who he was. The gentleman who rescued her was kind enough to carry Jess home, while Millie, Julie, and Bess followed." Patting his back, his mother pulled away, her gaze drifting to her daughter while a knot jerked in her throat. "That was late yesterday, and she's been in so much pain since that Dr. Morrissey doubled her laudanum." Her hand quivered to her mouth. "He says now her pain will be worse than ever . . ."

Not if I have anything to say about it. Jamie rose to move next to his sister's bed and his mother shored him up with a hand to his waist. His skin fairly crawled with fury, itching with the need to avenge, to protect, to heal . . . "I shouldn't have gone . . . ," he whispered.

The touch of his mother's hand to his shoulder caused more tears to sting, but he blinked them back. He hadn't shed a tear in front of his mother since he went to work on the docks, the youngest stevedore Boss Tandy'd ever hired. Jamie had a hunger, a desperation about him, the freighter boss said, more than any kid he'd ever seen. "Here, catch, street rat," an older boy had shouted with a sly smile, tossing a small crate of nails to Jamie, and he caught it with pride, never feeling the nail that impaled his flesh.

Moments later blood pooled and tendons throbbed, squeezing tears from his eyes that earned him nothing but scorn. He swore then no one would ever see him cry again. But he hadn't counted on his sister's agony over the years, nor had he counted on the guilt. Steeling his jaw, he bit back moisture that would never, *ever* fall and bent to brush back the damp curls around his sister's face. "Why didn't you call me?" he said, his voice strained.

His mother patted his back, tone fraught with worry. "I didn't want to ruin your weekend—you seldom have any time off, son, and I knew you'd be home tomorrow." Her voice was nasal, as if she were struggling with tears. "Before this happened, we had a lovely day, tea on the back porch and all, and she was feeling so good, better than she had in years." Her voice faltered as her fingers twitched at his waist. "She's been drifting in and out of sleep since then, which is good because the pain has been particularly . . ." He felt her fingers spasm, as if to take the place of the word she couldn't say. "Dr. Morrissey says it will take months to put this behind . . ." Her silent heave shuddered his arm. "If at all . . ."

He clenched till nails bit into his palms. "I shouldn't have gone." His whisper was harsh.

"You have a life, Jamie, you're young—of course you should've." She cupped his fist, her fingers as cold as the dread scaling his stomach. "You're a good brother," she whispered.

"I could be better," he said, his voice a hiss. His jaw ground till it ached. "I will be better," he swore, knowing full well what he needed to do. He was running out of time and patience, and if Cooper Medical wouldn't consider pro bono surgery for his sister, then that left no alternative but to pay for it. And pay for it he would—at a price that would cost him his all.

He'd marry it.

21

Caitlyn sat in her wicker love seat in the conservatory, head resting on its muted floral pillows while her arms hung limp at her sides, eyes as glazed as the steamy panes of glass overhead. Hadley had obviously misted the jungle of plants this morning and now the late-afternoon sun coaxed earthy smells of mulch and loam and flora that usually brought a sense of calm to Caitlyn, not unlike an herbal tonic.

Except for today.

She closed her eyes, and two languid tears trickled down her cheeks like the humidity on the glass, allowing the room and the woman to weep together. But the tears from the glass walls nurtured and fed the bounty of palms and ferns that thrived all around her while her own only served to bleed her soul dry. Of peace and joy and certainly hope, and for one reason alone.

Logan.

Her eyes opened as if doing so might banish his image, but all she saw was the love in his face when he'd handed her the ring, a love and gesture so potent it had weakened her at the knees. She'd seen glimmers of regret and fear and finally resignation until she'd done the unthinkable and rushed to embrace him . . .

her gratitude so strong, she'd felt compelled to give him a kiss on the cheek.

The kiss of death. For her and certainly for him, given the desire that had flamed in his eyes, the warmth she'd felt from shallow breaths as his mouth hovered so close to hers. A proximity that had paralyzed her, unable to move or breathe or think of anything but the hypnotic skim of his thumb as it grazed at her waist, the scent of lime and wood spice that disarmed like an opiate as it had so many years ago. Her heart had pulsed like that of a doe caught in the crosshairs of the hunter, powerless to escape and stricken with fear. And something even more deadly . . .

Desire.

For the first time since she'd taken Logan's engagement ring off almost twenty-six years ago, she'd *wanted* him to kiss her, to feel the throb of blood in her veins once again, the hot rush of adrenaline coursing her body—coaxing, caressing like his touch seemed to do. She should have bolted at the danger she'd seen in his eyes, fled at the leaning of her traitorous limbs, but she had not. Oh, no—she had closed her eyes and willed him to taste her lips, and he had.

Oh my . . . how he had, awakening longings she'd tried so hard to ignore the last eight months, shoving them deep as if they didn't exist. But they did. *Oh, Lord help me, they did* . . . each and every one now entangled with shame.

A violent heave crumpled her body as she sagged over the arm of the love seat to weep, trembling at the thought that one safety barrier had fallen—Logan now knew she was attracted to him—but another had been erected. She had rejected him outright and wounded his pride immeasurably, to the point of unleashing his rage. *"You're attracted to me and love me, yet you turn me away because my faith isn't up to snuff?"*

"Oh, Lord, what have I done?" she whispered. Not only had she damaged their friendship and family in the process, but the hopes of the Vigilance Committee as well. And all because of a single moment of lust—the very thing of which she accused him, further proof that Logan McClare was poison in the realm of love. She could not trust him and now, to her dishonor, she could no longer trust herself. The magnitude of what she'd done overwhelmed her, and a broken sob wrenched from her throat.

The gentle touch of a hand startled her and she jerked up to see Rosie studying her with misty eyes, concern deepening the soft age lines etched in her face. The nanny who was more like a mother sat beside her, and instantly Cait fell into her arms, swallowed up in the cocoon of her youth when Rosie had stepped in after Mama passed away. "Oh, Rosie," she whispered, voice nasal and hoarse, "I miss Liam so very much."

"Aw, darlin', sure you do." Rosie stroked her hair while her soft brogue lulled Cait's eyes closed. She paused. "But I'm thinkin' that's not what brought you home from Napa so early, now is it?"

Cait's lashes lifted over Rosie's shoulder, her pulse slowing. Rosie's vendetta against Logan was already bone deep, and Cait didn't want to add to it. She hesitated, her words shaky. "I didn't sleep well," she confessed, "and today I feel like I may be coming down with something . . ." Her eyelids lowered.

Terminal heartburn . . .

Rosie's pause was longer this time. "That skunk upset you, didn't he, Miss Cait?"

Her gravelly hiss actually prompted a near-smile to Cait's lips, proving conclusively that she'd never been able to hide her true feelings from her beloved nanny. "Yes, Rosie, the skunk did. But I provoked it." She pulled away to caress Rosie's hair, her smile breaking free at the scowl on the housekeeper's face. "Now, Rosie, you know good and well you're going to have to forgive that skunk someday, don't you?"

Rosie's face bore no humor. "Not likely when he's poised to break your heart again."

Cait's smile dissolved. "What do you mean?" she whispered, her hands falling away.

Grief welled in Rosie's eyes. "I mean he's getting to you again, isn't he?" she said softly. "Charming the socks off you just like the first time."

"No, of course not . . ." But it was no use. Cait could see in Rosie's face what she felt in her own—a numb awareness of the truth: she was falling in love with Logan McClare. Unwillingly, perhaps, but effectively all the same, and the fear she saw in Rosie's gaze mirrored that which thickened her throat, stifling her air. Hand to her eyes, she sagged into a sob while Rosie gathered her up in thin but sturdy arms, soothing her with a low croon.

"Shh . . . it's all right, Miss Cait. God won't let us down, now will he?" The tiny woman rocked her like when Cait was a child, whispering with the barest roll of a brogue while she rubbed Cait's back.

Cait nodded against Rosie's shoulders, reflecting on words she knew to be true. Her eyes drifted closed while she considered the God who held her in the palm of his hand every day of her life and every dark night as well. Peace suddenly welled like a river of grace, meandering through her life with its clarity and calm. Yes, Logan abandoned her for other women once and even Liam, unwittingly, had done the same through his death, but God never would, and the very thought infused her with the strength she needed to go on. The strength to know she need never fear betrayal or abandonment again—God would always be near. Drawing in a cleansing breath, she released all her fears in a whisper of a sigh.

Rosie held her at arm's length, the semblance of a smile curling on weathered lips. "Now that's a good girl," she said with a gentle pat of Cait's cheek. "Even a scalawag like Logan Beware can't get past the defenses of prayer, now can he?" She fished a hankie from the pocket of her apron and tenderly wiped the tears from Cait's eyes. "Because first that no-good scoundrel has to get past the Almighty, don't you know." She lifted her chin, giving Caitlyn a sassy smile that quickly slid into a battle mode. "And then, God have mercy on his sorry soul—past me."

Cassie's eyes flitted to the clock for the umpteenth time, her stomach a scurry of nerves.

"Uh . . . it's your turn, Cass. *Again*." Alli leaned in, a touch of the imp in her eyes. "Mmm . . . a little preoccupied, are we?"

Heat broiled Cassie's cheeks, making her grateful it was almost eight—the time Jamie arrived for book study. "Not at all," she said with a jut of her chin, her faint smile belying the truth. She feigned a yawn. "Just bored silly beating you at dominoes. *Again*."

Alli chuckled. "Not as interesting as *Pilgrim's Progress*, I suppose," she said with a wink, "*or* a handsome 'pilgrim' who's undoubtedly made great 'progress.'"

Face blazing like a furnace, Cassie shot a nervous glance at Aunt Cait who read a book instead of playing cribbage with Uncle Logan while he played Go Fish with Maddie and Meg. Maddie won for the third time, and her uncle swooped her up in a mock threat, spinning her till giggles bounced off the walls. Cassie's gaze flicked back to Alli, her words sharp with warning. "Will you hush, please? No one's supposed to know."

"Ha!" Alli said with a wicked grin. "Everybody knows how he feels about you—the man couldn't be more obvious." She jiggled her brows. "Nor you, dear Cuz, with that pretty blush in your face, a sure-fire indicator you prefer games of midnight to dominoes."

That did it. Cassie lunged across the table to threaten Alli with a tickle—something she knew her cousin deplored. "So help me, Allison McClare, I am going to tickle you senseless, which shouldn't be too hard since you're already ninety percent there—"

"Ahem." Hadley interrupted Alli's wild shriek, his stoic figure impeccable as always in black tails and tie, and his manner and tone as starched as his crisp white shirt. "Mr. James MacKenna to see Miss Cassidy. May I show him in, miss?"

Cassie shot up as if coil-sprung from her chair. "Yes, Hadley, please," she said, near breathless, "but in the conservatory, if you will—for our book study."

"Very good, miss—in the study. Would you care for refreshments?"

Chewing the edge of her lip, Cassie pushed in her chair and raised her voice several levels. "Lemonade would be lovely, Hadley, thank you, but in the conservatory, if you will."

"Ah, very good, miss."

The butler disappeared, and Cassie nervously patted her hair, avoiding all eyes as she hurried to retrieve a Hershey bar—Jamie's favorite—from a small chest Rosie kept filled on the coffee table. Striving for nonchalance that didn't exist, she straightened her shoulders and slowed to a leisurely stroll in a sad attempt at exiting with decorum.

Aunt Cait's voice followed. "Cass, will you ask Jamie how his sister is doing, please? I've been quite worried since Blake said she took a fall."

"Certainly, Aunt Cait," Cassie said over her shoulder. Once across the threshold, she bolted for the powder room, locking the door to assess herself in the gilded mirror, stomach twirling more than Maddie in Uncle Logan's arms. Her pale-green eyes blinked back, registering a heady mix of excitement and anticipation that made her woozy and just a wee bit scared at what lay ahead in a courtship with Jamie MacKenna. Pinching her cheeks to heighten her color, she smoothed her loose updo one more time and adjusted the lavender gossamer dress Jamie complimented once before. "Lord, help me not to faint," she muttered before making her way to the conservatory at the back of the house. She paused at the door to catch her breath, her nerves doing cartwheels at the sight of his broad back and narrow hips in a charcoal business suit while he stared out the open French doors. The pink and purple hues of dusk filtered through the glass panes overhead to bathe the room in an ethereal glow, while a briny breeze fluttered a stray curl of his ebony hair. She attempted to calm herself with a deep draw of air, infusing her senses with the tang of the harbor, the earthy scent of moss . . . and Jamie.

"How is your sister?" she whispered, suddenly shy with this man with whom she'd shared the most intimate of kisses.

He spun around, eyes caressing head to toe in a single glance that warmed both her cheeks and her belly. "S-she's . . . fine," he stuttered, oddly ill at ease for a man so prone to confidence. He closed his mouth, its compression almost imperceptible.

Almost.

Cassie took a step forward. "Are you . . . sure?" she asked, prickles of concern nettling.

His mouth twisted into a tight smile. "Sure, Cass, if one can be considered 'all right' writhing in pain day in and day out." His clipped tone stung before he turned away to knead the bridge of his nose, shoulders rising with a heavy inhale. "I'm sorry," he whispered. "I don't mean to take it out on you, truly. It's just that . . . ," he turned to face her, his trademark sparkle painfully absent, "I can't stand to see her suffer any longer," he said with a bitterness she'd not heard before. "And I need to do everything in my power to stop it."

Her heart squeezed, his pain becoming her own. "Jamie, I'm so sorry," she whispered, her approach hesitant. "Would you like to pray—"

"No!" Shock fused her to the spot at the violence of his tone. Ruddy color mottled his face as a tic pulsed in his neck, muscles taut as if to contain a temper. "No, thank you," he said in a strained voice that came off curt. "I don't need charity from anyone, especially a God with a deaf ear."

"Oh, Jamie, no—" She started toward him.

He paralyzed her with a look. "No, Cass, I don't want to hear any defense of your God."

His words snatched the air from her lungs. "He's your God too, Jamie," she whispered, voice hoarse as she moved in close, stopping mere feet away. "If only you'd give him a chance."

She flinched when he stabbed a finger in the air. "I *gave* him a chance," he hissed, "and guess what? My sister is *still* in agony." His jaw flickered as he stared, hands taut on his hips. He shook his head, gaze shifting to the carpet. "It's not going to work," he whispered.

The blood iced in her veins. "What's not?" she breathed.

He avoided her eyes while a nerve pulsed in his temple. "God . . . this . . ." His Adam's apple jerked in his throat. "Us."

The blood seeped from her brain, making her more lightheaded than the summer she'd passed out in that Texas heat wave when people and cattle were dropping like flies. "What?" Her voice was a shallow whisper, her next words barely audible. "But, why?"

Seconds passed before he looked up, and when he did grief glazed his eyes. "Because it's really quite simple, Cass," he said quietly. "I can't meet term number four."

The memory of her courtship conditions swirled in her brain, making her dizzy, and her eyelids fluttered closed as she swayed on her feet. Not the euphoric "dizzy" of Jamie's kisses. Oh no, this was a white-blinding dizzy that forced cold sweat to bead on her brow. *"Because I need to know, Jamie, . . . that if we become one as man and wife, we'll also be one in our faith."*

"I'm sorry, Cass—I know this is a shock . . ."

Shock? No, this is a total broadside. Bile crawled in her throat while fear sank to the pit of her stomach, cramping into nausea, spinning the room. *Oh, God, no, please—not again . . .*

He caught her the moment her knees buckled, sweeping her up in his arms to lay her on a white wicker couch amid myriad palms. "Cass, forgive me, please . . . ," he whispered, his voice as far away as the feel of his fingers as they tenderly buffed her arms, stroked her face. Her mind and her body seemed to be whirling, an eddy of stun and stupor and pain that threatened to dispel the contents of her stomach as thoroughly as his words had disgorged the joy in her heart.

He had befriended and bewitched her, then pursued and pleaded until he had won her heart. *"I've never wanted any woman like I want you,"* he'd said, and now that he had her, he was throwing it all away. Throwing *her* away.

Just like Mark.

Her breathing was raspy and shallow as she struggled to sit up, eyelids flickering open to face a man she never wanted to love, a man who'd badgered and broken her defenses until she was wholly his. An icy cold slithered through her body. Only she wasn't, and never would be . . .

He squatted before her, voice urgent as he massaged her hand, the same pain etched in his face that she felt in her gut. "Cassie, I wish there was some way I could tell you how sorry I am."

Sorry. He was sorry. Fury rose within like a sleeping giant, sloughing off the hurt and betrayal and sick feeling inside. She would *not* let a man do this to her again, she would not! He may have stolen her heart, but he would never, *ever* rob her of her pride.

Tears pricked, but she refused to let them fall, rising up on the couch with battle in her bones. Meeting his gaze with a steady one of her own, she slowly slipped her hand from his and rose, legs wavering, but resolve firm. "Oh, but there is, Jamie," she said quietly, her voice as cool as the relationship they now shared. "You can leave me alone and never come back."

Drawing in a deep breath, Jamie could feel the sweat at the back of his neck as he knocked on Logan's office door, dreading the need to ask his boss for a favor. Logan McClare was a self-made man at a relatively young age, parlaying a good-size inheritance into a massive fortune that wielded power on every front, be it politically, socially, or financially. The last thing Jamie wanted was to appear weak or needy in front of the one man he admired more than any other, and yet he had no choice. His sister's life was wasting away, and whatever it took, he was bent on securing a surgery that would end her pain. Whether it was asking Logan McClare to use his clout with Cooper Medical or courting Patricia Hamilton to curry the influence of her senator father, either way, Jamie would find a way. And when he did, one thing was for dead sure—it would *not* be charity. The muscles in his throat tightened as he adjusted his tie, thinking how Jess had paid for his mistake with years of pain and ridicule. Well, now it was his turn. He had no choice. His mistake, his debt. And he *would* pay for it. At any cost . . .

"Come in." The voice was all business—brusque, no-nonsense with almost an edge.

Jamie opened the door and popped his head in, grateful Logan offered a semblance of a smile despite the piles of legal briefs on his desk. "Excuse me, sir—do you have a minute?"

Logan tossed his fountain pen on the desk and leaned back, peering at Jamie over wire-rim reading glasses that made him look more like a meek scholar than one of the city's most intimidating legal and political figures. "Sure, Mac, what can I do for you?"

Venting a slow exhale, Jamie closed the door and took a seat in one of two leather arm chairs, easing back as Logan had done to convey an air of confidence he didn't quite feel.

"The appellate brief on the Dunn case was stellar work," Logan said, approval warm in his eyes. "You're a quick study, counselor."

Heat ringed Jamie's collar, both from the outright compliment and the warm glow it provided, coming from a man whose respect he desperately wanted. He nodded. "Thanks, Mr. McClare—it means all the more coming from a legal mind of your caliber, sir."

"How long have I known you, Mac?"

Jamie paused, the question taking him by surprise. "Eight years, sir, since that first day I waited on you at the Oly Club."

Logan nodded slowly, his eyes reflective. "That's right. I remember being impressed with any kid from the streets who would work three jobs to put himself through college. You were a rare kid then, Mac, and you're a rare man now, still impressing me with your drive and hard work." A half-smile flitted on his lips. "That said, don't you think it's time you call me Logan?"

Jamie blinked, his words stumbling. "Y-yes sir . . . if that's your preference."

"It is, at least after business hours, which . . . ," he squinted at an exquisite antique grandfather clock that graced his far wall, "it's well beyond. You're Blake's and Bram's good friend and mine too. *And* unless my eyes have deceived me," he said, smile shrewd, "I believe you're chummy with my Texas niece as well, at least until the last few weeks when we haven't seen hide nor hair of you at family dinners."

The heat from his collar fired all the way up his neck. "Yes, sir, Cassie and I are very good friends." He swallowed hard. "But regrettably, the Dunn case has kept me quite busy."

"Well, don't be a stranger, Mr. MacKenna," Logan said with a formality that indicated he'd made his point and was ready to move on. "You had something on your mind?"

"Yes, sir," Jamie said, spine stiff. "I think you may be aware my sister sustained a hip injury at the age of two that has hindered her life."

He nodded, concern shading eyes that studied him keenly.

"I've been saving for a surgery down the road, of course, but after a recent . . . ," Jamie faltered, a sudden flash of fury in his throat, " *fall* . . . her pain has escalated considerably, so it's more critical than ever before that I . . . escalate the process of obtaining a surgery. I'm not sure if you're aware or not, sir, but I've spent countless hours over the last six months petitioning Cooper Medical School on her behalf."

"To what end, Mr. MacKenna?"

Jamie fortified himself with a deep inhale. "To procure a medical procedure on a pro bono basis, which as you know, the college will periodically provide." So intent on stating his case, he shifted to the edge of his seat, forging on before Logan could utter a word. "You see, I've done a fair amount of research on a fairly new procedure called a hip cheilotomy introduced by a Dr. John Benjamin Murphy of Mercy Hospital in Chicago. Surprisingly, it's a relatively simple surgery to alleviate pain in damaged hip joints such as my sister's. Consequently, I've left no stone unturned in attempting to secure such a surgery for Jess."

Logan nodded. "Yes, I've heard of it. I understand they've met with good success."

"They have, sir, based on my research, which is why I've been relentless in pursuing this course of action for my sister." The walls of his throat thickened. "My sister's lived with pain all of her life, and although she's been some better recently, she had an accident over the Fourth that jarred her hip and left her bedridden much of the time." He swallowed hard, working to keep his tone calm and his emotions in check. "Of course Jess is the type of person who bears it all without a single complaint, but to be honest, sir, I don't know how much longer I can."

A muscle flickered in Logan's jaw and he nodded. "I understand. And you've exhausted all avenues, I suppose—letters of recommendation, medical contacts, political contacts?"

"Yes, sir, all dead ends except for one I'm still pursuing," Jamie said quickly, hoping Logan's curiosity would not venture into Jamie's plan to court Patricia.

"I see." Logan retrieved his pen to absently twirl it, jaw taut as he considered Jamie's problem. He finally heaved a weighty sigh and placed the pen down, fingers resting on the arms of his chair. "I do have an old fraternity brother on the funding committee for Cooper, but—" he glanced up with regret in his eyes—"unfortunately we butted heads in college over a girl and haven't spoken since. Also the surgery wait list is long and the opportunities, few, so I don't want to get your hopes up, but . . ."

With a tight nod, Jamie waited, the air fused to his lungs.

Pausing for several seconds, Logan glanced up over his specs, the barest of smiles curving on lips clamped tight. "I'll see what he can do, Jamie, but I can't guarantee anything."

Euphoria exploded in his veins, and he jumped to his feet with a grin, hand extended. "I understand, sir, and I can't thank you enough for your willingness to try."

Gray eyes capable of being as cold and tough as pewter when battling in a courtroom now glinted with a hint of affection that warmed Jamie's soul. "My pleasure, Jamie. As inseparable as you, Bram, and Blake are, I think of you as family."

More heat braised his cheeks, and he nodded. *Oh, that I were* . . . "Thank you, sir. Good night." He turned to go.

"Jamie." Logan's words halted him at the door.

"Yes, sir?"

Empathy radiated from the older man's eyes that Jamie hadn't expected from someone so skilled at guarding his emotions. "I'm sorry about your sister, son," he said quietly, "and for what it's worth, if she's a tenth the fighter her brother is, she's gonna lick this thing."

Tears threatened and Jamie nodded before quickly looking away, unable to speak for the swelling of his throat. He closed the door and leaned against it, lids closed to thwart all moisture. Swiping his eyes with the sleeve of his shirt, he returned to his office and at least thirty minutes of work before he was expected at Patricia's house for dinner, something he wasn't looking forward to. He'd much rather be home with his mother and Jess, playing dominoes or whist after one of Mrs. Tucker's meals, as was his custom of late. *Or sparring with Cassie at the McClares'* . . . A heavy malaise settled on his shoulders—also his custom of late.

He dropped in his chair to stare at the deposition before him, head in his hands. But all he saw was Cassie—so sweet and sassy, his throat ached. Steeling his jaw, he forced himself to think of Patricia instead—beautiful, smart, and the daughter of an influential man with ties to Cooper Medical. His eyes shuttered closed. Something he needed if Logan didn't come through.

"Soooo . . . you've certainly been making yourself scarce lately." Bram stood, hands in his pockets and hip cocked to the door, studying Jamie through pensive eyes that spelled trouble.

Jamie stifled a groan, gaze flicking to the clock on his desk that registered almost six-forty-five. Which meant Bram should be long gone by now, on his way to wining and dining at the Mc-Clares'. Nausea roiled in Jamie's stomach—the same sick feeling he'd had for the last two weeks. "Too much to do," he muttered, doing his best to focus on his deposition.

"Yeah, I know," Bram said, strolling in with a casual air. He ignored Jamie's obvious attempt at being too busy and plopped in a chair, brown oxfords crossed on top of Jamie's desk. "Avoiding Cassie's a full-time job."

Fingers kneading the bridge of his nose, Jamie huffed out a sigh. "Come on, Bram, I feel like garbage as it is—don't you have someplace else to be?"

Bram propped hands behind his neck, his eyes far more serious than his relaxed manner warranted. "Yeah, I do, Mac—the McClares'. Remember them?"

Jamie slapped the papers down on his desk. "Look, Hughes, I already told you—Cassie threw me out. She doesn't want to see me again, all right?"

"I got that, MacKenna," Bram said with a squint, "it's the 'why' that has me in a fog."

A tic twitched in Jamie's jaw. "It's personal," he bit out. "Just let it go."

Bram arched a brow. "You're right, it is personal, especially when it affects people I care about, and no, I won't let it go." He sat up and leaned in, feet back on the ground. "The McClares are family to both of us, and what's going on here is taking its toll—on them, on Cassie, *and* on you." With a quiet exhale, he sloped back in his chair. "Not to mention me." He probed Jamie with a questioning gaze, concern etched into every wrinkle of his brow. "You're more of a brother than a friend, Mac, and I hate to see you like this."

"I know," Jamie whispered, near depleted as he sagged back in his chair. He massaged his temple with the pads of his fingers. "Me too."

"So, what's going on? How do you go from being crazy in love with a woman one minute and then she's out of your life the next?"

Jamie winced, Bram's question a barb with deadly aim. His chest rose and fell with a heavy sigh, eyes trailing into a glazed stare. "Not without a lot of pain, I'll tell you that."

"So, why are you doing this? You were walking on air the morning after the Fourth in Napa—what happened to change your mind between then and now?"

"We're just not a good match, Bram," Jamie whispered, closing his eyes to rest his head on the back of his chair. "Friends, yes, but not anything more. I'm not the right guy for her."

"That's horse manure, Jamie, and you know it. I've never seen you happier than the last few months, falling in love with Cass." He hesitated, his voice quiet. "Falling in love with God."

Jamie's eyelids snapped up like a tightly wound shade. "Yeah? Well, there's no love lost between God and me now, Padre, so just lay off, will you?"

Hurt flickered on Bram's face, and Jamie felt like a heel. *So, what's new?* Venting with a loud exhale, he gouged his forehead with the ball of his hand. "Look, Bram, I'm sorry, but I'm worried about my sister right now, and frankly, I'd rather not discuss Cassie, if you don't mind."

Bram studied him for painful seconds before rising. "I do, but I'm not here to sling guilt."

The edge of Jamie's lip curled. "But you're so good at it, Hughes, almost no effort at all."

A sad smile lined Bram's lips. "Not good enough, apparently." He slipped his hands in his pockets. "The real reason I'm here is to extend an invitation from Mrs. McClare herself."

Blood warmed his face, Bram's "guilt" evidently not through with him just yet. "Sorry, Bram, can't tonight."

"Why? Plans with the senator's daughter?"

More heat infused Jamie's cheeks. "Maybe." He rifled through his bottom drawer for milk of magnesia, the acid in his stomach churning into high gear.

Bram exhaled, the sound depleted of all energy. "I suspected as much. So, tell me, Jamie—why would you throw over a down-to-earth woman like Cassie for a socialite like Patricia?"

"We're better suited, okay?" Jamie snapped. He upended the bottle, then capped it and tossed it back into the drawer.

"No, it's *not* okay." Bram knuckled the front of the desk, his expression tight. "Something happened between Fourth of July weekend and now, and I want to know what it is."

Jamie stared, pulse throbbing in his ears. He wanted to tell him it was none of his blasted business, but the dangerous look in Bram's eyes told him he couldn't damage their friendship that way. Bram had taught him long ago that one of the liabilities of having people who cared about you was telling them the truth because they mattered more than your pride. Muttering a rare curse, he blew out a wave of frustration and put a hand to his eyes. "I swear, Hughes, you're worse than a nagging wife." He huffed out another sigh and averted his gaze, unwilling to look his best friend in the eyes. "I can't court Cassie because she's . . . ," he gulped, realizing just how shallow it would sound, "dirt poor," he whispered, the very words making him feel like scum.

His statement was met by silence, and Jamie reluctantly lifted his gaze, his gut threatening to pull rank at the look of shock in Bram's eyes.

"What are you talking about?" Bram breathed.

Harsh air expelled from Jamie's mouth. "Cassie's father lost his fortune when his wells ran dry. She's not an heiress," he whispered. "She might even be as poor as me."

"Tell me you're joking."

Annoyance pinched his brow. "No, I'm not—I found out the day I left Napa."

"*No*," Bram said with deliberate emphasis, "tell me you're joking about turning your back on Cassie—because she's *not* rich?"

Fire engulfed him. "That's right, Hughes, something you would know nothing about because you were born with a silver spoon in your mouth, so don't judge me."

Bram rose to his full height, the tic in his hard-chiseled jaw a completely uncommon occurrence. "Judge you? I don't even want to *know* you, MacKenna."

Jamie slammed his fist on the desk, eyes burning in their sockets. "I have never lied to you, Bram. I told you from the beginning I planned to marry well, and now you act like it's some big shock to your system. Before you judge me, why don't you live in the streets awhile, share space with rats and vermin in the Barbary Coast, watch your sister rot before your eyes from some godforsaken injury, and then you come back and tell me I'm wrong."

Facial muscles sculpted tight, Bram seemed to wrestle with a scathing response, cheek pulsing. And then with a deep exhale of air, a calm settled that bespoke the godly man Jamie knew him to be. "No, Jamie, I won't tell you you're wrong," he whispered, "just misguided." He looked up, face composed, but eyes dark with concern. "You're a smart man, Mac, but when it comes to the spiritual side of life, you are a lost soul and not all that bright. Because if you knew just how much God loves you, you would know you could have your dreams and Cassie too."

Fury flushed through his body. "Yeah? And where's my sister in all of this, Hughes? Somebody's gotta save her because God sure hasn't. Only money and influence will, and Cassie being poor is just another example of God shortchanging me like he's done all of my life."

"You know what I think?" Bram said quietly. "I think it has less to do with your sister, and more with your pride. A Barbary Coast street rat, determined to prove to the world he belongs on Nob Hill instead of the gutter, a man putting himself before the people he loves."

"That's a lie," Jamie hissed.

Bram hiked a brow. "Is it? Think about it." He reached inside his suit coat and tossed an envelope on the desk. "Cassie asked me to give this to you. I think it's her way of trying to restore your friendship, although to be honest, Mac, at the moment, I'm not sure why she would even want to." He strolled for the door. "I'll tell them you can't make it tonight."

Jamie fingered the envelope, his name written in Cassie's graceful script. "Wait . . ."

Bram halted, back stiff at the door. "What?"

"Tell them I'll be there next week," he said, body bent from the nausea roiling in his gut.

Nodding, Bram walked out, leaving Jamie to stew in his guilt. He reached in his drawer for more milk of magnesia and threw back several hard swallows.

"A man putting himself before the people he loves."

Issuing a silent groan, he dropped his head in his hands. Bram's words gnawed inside his chest like the acid that ate at his stomach, and he wished more than anything he had a remedy to alleviate his pain. Because at the end of the day, he could coat his nerves with milk of magnesia. But there wasn't a whole lot he could do about shame.

22

oom. Boom. Boom. The strike of the gavel reverberated in the meeting room of City Hall to finalize the prior motion, the very sound thudding in Caitlyn's heart at the same time.

Eleven male board members presided over tables draped with the city seal, expressions ranging from intense to comatose as they studied the agendas before them. Stomach quivering at the prospect of speaking, Caitlyn's gaze flicked to where Logan sat on the board. Eyes cool, he gave her a short nod, his stone face weakening her knees at the prospect of butting heads with him now while the goals of the Vigilance Committee hung in the balance. For the briefest of moments, she almost wished she'd succumbed to his advances in Napa for the sake of this sacred cause.

And yet, not. Logan was a man used to getting his own way, but some things were simply not up for barter. Certainly not her heart, especially with a man she couldn't trust. She noted the steel glint in his eyes, recalled his cool manner the last few weeks and knew that when it came to Logan McClare, there was only one thing she *could* trust—he would fight her tooth and nail over the Barbary Coast. Just like she'd fought him tooth and nail in Napa.

"Ordinance amending the San Francisco Administrative Code

Section 10.82 approved and motion carried by the ayes." The Budget and Finance Committee supervisor glanced at the clock on the wall, then peered at the paper in his hand. "Next item on the docket, Vigilance Committee proposal presented by board president, Mrs. Caitlyn McClare."

Caitlyn slowly rose to her feet, grateful she could stand despite the wobble of tendons at the back of her knees. Murmurs skittered through the hall, an unwelcome reminder that women had no business chairing a board, much less addressing the Board of Supervisors. Two points she had debated ad nauseam with Walter and the board, to no avail.

"Now, Cait," Walter had said earlier with a reassuring look that missed the mark, "Liam still has friends on the board and as Liam's widow, so do you. Not to mention your brother-in-law, who is sure to throw his weight your way."

Caitlyn smoothed her skirt to deflect the tremble of her hands. *Not likely—a wounded ego hardly makes for a cozy endorsement.* She felt the gentle pat of Walter's hand and slid him a nervous smile, his presence a stabilizing force.

"You'll be fine," he whispered, "trust me. Just be yourself, and your honesty and sincerity will win them over."

"Mrs. McClare?" The president adjusted his glasses. "Are you ready?"

"Yes, sir." Caitlyn returned his smile, then scanned each face, stopping short of Logan, whose dour look did nothing for her confidence. "Gentlemen, thank you for allowing me to address the board this evening on a matter of utmost importance to the success and welfare of our great city. As I speak, degradation runs rampant, both in our city and in the lives of thousands of women who sell their bodies in the vilest of circumstances in the cribs and cow-yards of the Barbary Coast. Not only has this area become a

266

debilitating stain on a city destined for greatness, but a stain on the very soul of every human being caught within its tentacles of sin and corruption. Benjamin Estelle Lloyd was correct when he stated that 'the Barbary Coast is the haunt of the low and the vile of every kind. The petty thief, the house burglar, the tramp, the whoremonger, lewd women, cutthroats, and murderers,' all thriving in a cesspool of dance halls, concert saloons, gambling houses, brothels, peep shows, and opium dens."

Caitlyn rose up tall, legs weak but voice strong as she addressed the board, conviction ringing despite a tone that was humble and low. "A cesspool, gentlemen, that I'm afraid we've allowed far too long. Edmund Burke stated 'all that is necessary for the triumph of evil is that good men do nothing,' and I hope and pray each of the good men on this board will join forces with the Vigilance Committee to do something rather than nothing to protect our city."

A smattering of applause broke out, buoying her spirits as well as her shoulders. Replenishing with a deep draw of air, Caitlyn laid out the board's plan—a three-phase strategy she hoped they would consider due to gradual implementation that would give both the board and the city time to adjust. "Phase one," she began with a lift of her chin, "will focus on closing two of the biggest blights on the Coast, the Nymphia and the Marsicania brothels. As you may or may not be aware, gentlemen, the Nymphia's 450 'residents' are required to remain . . . ," Caitlyn swallowed hard, unable to prevent her tongue from stuttering over the next word, ". . . n-naked at all times in order to . . . e-entertain their c-customers, both those in close p-proximity and those who pay to watch through plentiful peepholes provided." Heat broiled her cheeks as her voice weakened to a mere rasp, the clearing of throats from several board members clear indication she was not alone in her embarrassment. "And then, of course in conjunction with the esteemed Father Terence Caraher, we hope to dismantle the Marsicania as well, which opened last month."

Despite frowns and awkward looks from the board, Caitlyn continued to present phases two and three, encompassing a time period of two to five years when all businesses in the Barbary Coast would have to comply with stringent guidelines mandated and upheld, she hoped, by the Board of Supervisors. "Gentlemen," she said in conclusion, "the Vigilance Committee has prepared a detailed brief on the plan itself, which Mr. Walter Henry will distribute to each of you at the close of this meeting. Please feel free to contact me or any of the board members with questions or concerns you might have."

Logan leaned forward, and goose bumps prickled Caitlyn's flesh at the glint of challenge in his eyes. "Radical and abrupt changes such as you propose, Mrs. McClare," he said slowly, emphatically, "often do more damage than good in an undertaking of this magnitude, polarizing many who believe the Coast provides needed tax revenue."

Silence cloaked the room with unease so palpable, Caitlyn could taste it along with the bile in her throat. Steeling both her jaw and her nerve, she met his cool gaze with a steady one of her own. "I suspect, sir," she said quietly, "that given the chance, most decent people would concur revenue obtained through debauchery is never 'needed'—nor wanted—at all."

She ignored the ruddy color that bled up Logan's neck and pressed on, desperate to deflect his disapproval. "That said, sir, I assure you most heartily that the Vigilance Committee has worked diligently to ensure this plan is neither radical nor abrupt, building in graduated time tables and sound provisions we believe will grow tax revenue rather than diminish it."

Arms on the table, Logan slanted in with a hard smile that

quickly braised her cheeks. "Excuse me, Mrs. McClare," he said, his manner far more relaxed than the look of defiance in his eyes. "I believe the appropriate word is 'restrictions' rather than provisions. Restrictions I fear may trample the civil rights of legitimate businesses in an effort to eradicate the unsavory ones." He patronized her with a paternal tilt of his head, causing her to bristle. "You understand, of course, Mrs. McClare—the danger of throwing the baby out with the bathwater?"

"Only if the 'baby' is prone to licentiousness and obscenity, Mr. McClare," she said carefully, "which is seldom the case when one is innocent, wouldn't you agree?"

The gavel hammered. "Thank you, Mrs. McClare, we'll take this under advisement," the president said with a stiff smile. He dismissed her with a cursory nod and continued with the next course of business while Caitlyn slowly slid into her seat, knees all but giving way.

"You were wonderful," Walter whispered, and Caitlyn offered a weak smile, barely hearing another word spoken until the gavel sounded moments later to dismiss the meeting.

"Can I give you a lift, Caitlyn?" Walter asked, helping her on with her wrap.

"No, thank you, Walter, Hadley is waiting outside."

He leaned to embrace her. "Well, then, good night, my dear. You had them eating out of your hand, you know," he whispered, sending a fresh rush of blood to her cheeks.

Her chuckle did not echo the confidence in his tone. "Eating certainly, Walter, but it remains to be seen whether that is out of my hand or chewing me up and spitting me out." She linked her arm with his and headed for the door, her body weak from relief that the ordeal was finally over. A smile crooked on her lips. "Either way, I fear I'll have indigestion."

His laughter boomed in the high-ceilinged corridor of City Hall as he escorted her to the front door. "Nothing a bromide can't cure," he remarked with a smile. "Good night, Caitlyn."

"Good night, Walter." Heaving a heavy sigh, Caitlyn made her way to the Packard.

"Cait!"

Her eyelids flickered closed before she pivoted at the curb, said indigestion roiling at the sight of Logan striding her way. She lifted her chin, brows arched in question. "Yes, Logan?"

He halted mere inches away, so close another step would send her tumbling from the curb. "You handled yourself well in there," he said, breathing winded as if he'd run all the way.

"Really? I didn't get that impression." She smiled. "At least not from you."

She watched a nerve pulse in his cheek, the grinding of his jaw, signs he was attempting to contain a temper she knew that he had. His smile seemed forced—like every conversation they'd had since Napa. "Come on, Cait—this isn't a sewing circle here, this is the government body for the city of San Francisco. I'll give no preferential treatment just because you're family."

She blinked up with a sad smile, fighting the pull of late whenever he was near. "Of course not. Just if I'd said yes in Napa . . ."

The plains of his face hardened. "You don't belong in politics, Cait." His whisper was harsh. "If you would just trust me, I'd fight this battle for you and win. But, no, you have to push in a time frame that isn't right, when too many on the board oppose what you're doing."

"Including you?"

He hesitated, the look in his eyes confirming her question. He huffed out a sigh and gouged his forehead with the span of his head. "Blast it, Cait, people have investments. Not just me, but almost every man in that room tonight, and a woman can't just waltz into a Board of Supervisors' meeting and expect them to see things her way."

"Even if it's the decent thing to do?" she whispered, fighting the sting of tears.

He stared at her long and hard, facial muscles sculpted tight. "Even if it's the decent thing to do," he repeated, his eyes never wavering from hers. "You're certainly proof of that."

His words stung, conjuring unwelcome memories of Napa. *"No, Cait, the decent thing to do is to forget the past and admit you're in love with me."*

"I have to go," she said too quickly, turning to the Packard as Hadley stood at the door.

Logan grasped her arm before she could get in, voice as strained as the fingers latched to her cloak. "Don't expect me to side with you on this one, Cait."

She paused, eyes trained on the dark hairs on the back of his hand. "No, Logan," she said quietly, "I would never expect that from you." Slipping into the car, she closed her eyes and rested her head on the back of the seat. *Or on anything . . . ever again.*

23

If ever a polecat there was . . . Cassie studied Jamie MacKenna through slitted eyes while he and Bram played piggyback badminton with Meg and Maddie on the back lawn. A summer breeze ruffled her hair as she sipped lemonade, her mood as sour as the drink in her hand.

Casually comfortable, both men wore buttoned waistcoats over pin-striped shirts rolled to the elbow, neckties askew from dashing about with young women astride their shoulders. Peals of laughter took flight in a cozy backyard fragrant with honeysuckle and Aunt Cait's cottage roses, while a battered shuttlecock soared with every whack of the racket. Cassie's smile thinned considerably. *Mmm . . . I'd like to swing a racket right about now, but not at a shuttle . . .*

"So . . . this is progress, right?" Alli leaned close while they watched the game from a wrought-iron settee on Aunt Cait's stone patio.

"If you call no eye contact and occasional grunts 'progress.'" Cassie scowled and popped cashews in her mouth from a candy dish, voice low as she eyed Logan and Blake embroiled in a game of chess while Aunt Cait focused on needlepoint. "At least he showed up, even if he'd rather be out there romping with Maddie than talking to me."

"I just think he's nervous and embarrassed—"

"And guilty?" Cassie added, mouth in a slope.

Alli chuckled, bumping her shoulder. "Oh, yes—very, *very* guilty. It's written all over his handsome face—the man feels like a dog after what he did to you."

"Good." Cassie pelted more cashews, grinding them into dust like she wished she could do with her *feelings* for Jamie MacKenna. *Or the polecat himself.*

"Ah-ah-ah . . . ," Alli said with a wag of her finger, "you promised you'd forgive Jamie and try to be sweet, remember?"

"Forgive? Yes. But sweet?" Her lips curled into an evil smile. "As sweet as a hive of honeybees with three-inch stingers."

"Well, I'm just grateful you decided to forgive and forget even though the pretrial courtship didn't work out." Alli fanned herself with the letter she just wrote to Roger Luepke. "After all, Jamie's like a brother, so it's strange when he's not around."

"Not as 'strange' as when he is," Cassie muttered. She lobbed a few more nuts to the back of her throat. "At least now."

"Come on Cass, look at it this way—it's better to find out now he's not the one before a courtship where you fall head over heels, right?"

Wrong. Cassie tossed more nuts, chest expanding with a quiet sigh. "I suppose."

"Cassie, Alli—we're going to play charades, girls against boys!" Maddie flew across the lawn, auburn curls bouncing as she launched into Cassie's arms.

"Are we, now?" Cassie kissed Maddie's nose, ignoring Jamie and Bram when they ambled over for lemonade. "Won't that be unfair? You know, since girls are smarter than boys?"

"Ha! Girls are 'smart,' all right," Jamie said with one of the first smiles he'd sent her way all evening. His eyes twinkled as he took a deep glug of lemonade. "Smart-aleck, that is."

"Oh, really?" Cassie hiked a brow. "Would you care to make a wager, Mr. MacKenna . . . or have you lost all your gambling money on pool and poker?" She gave him an innocent blink.

Jamie patted his pocket. "Nope, Miss McClare, I've just enough left to prove my point." A flash of white teeth confirmed the old Jamie was easing back, and a silent sigh feathered her lips. After all, she cared about the mule-brained dope even if he *had* led her on.

Maddie tugged at her mother. "Mama, Blake, Uncle Logan—we need you to play too."

Aunt Cait glanced up, obviously hesitant. "Darling, you all go ahead. It will be an unfair advantage if I play, with more ladies than gentlemen."

Logan ambled past to stretch out in a chair with a cautious smile. "Oh, come on, Cait," he said, hands braced to his neck. "Ten more of you still wouldn't be an unfair advantage."

Lips pursed, Aunt Cait pitched her needlepoint on the table and rose with a jut of her chin. "On second thought, darling, I believe there are egos to burst."

"What's an ego?" Maddie asked.

Alli grinned. "A bit like those balloons at your birthday, re-member? All full of hot air?"

Maddie's eyes went wide. "Golly—do we get to pop 'em just like Herman Hatfield did?"

Cassie chuckled with Aunt Cait as Alli provided paper and pencils. "Oh, honey, you bet."

"Goody!" Squealing, Maddie squeezed between Cassie and her mother on the settee.

"Listen up," Alli said, handing out supplies. "Write down the name of a book, play, famous person, or song and toss it into this bowl." She wrote her own, then collected the others. "Uncle Logan will time each turn, but ladies first. And Cass gets to pop the first balloon . . ." She winked at the men. "Uh . . . I mean the first draw."

Eyes closed, Cassie plucked a paper from the bowl. With a throaty chuckle, she splayed a hand to her chest, her smile smug. "Oh my, this really is too easy." She cupped a hand to her ear, eyes in a squint. "Wait—did you hear that? I believe I heard something pop."

"That would be your grand delusions, Cowgirl," Jamie said with a lazy drawl.

"I don't know, sounded more like an overinflated ego to me." Alli grinned.

"A particularly large one, if I'm not mistaken," Cassie replied, wadding her paper up and lobbing it onto the table. "Okay, Uncle Logan, start timing—now!" Chin up, Cassie posed like Napoleon, tips of her fingers tucked inside the pearl buttons of her blouse.

"Famous person," Alli shouted.

Cassie tapped her own nose and held up a finger, patting four more to her arm.

"One word, four syllables." Aunt Cait leaned in, competitive juices obviously flowing.

Raising a single finger to indicate first syllable, Cassie pointed to herself.

"Cassie!" Maddie shot up from the settee, arms in the air.

With another skim of her nose, Cassie faced her palms to each other, slowly closing the space between.

"Shorter version of Cassie—Cass?" Alli said with a hopeful slope of brows.

Cassie patted her nose, then casually hiked a thumb at Jamie with an angelic bat of eyes.

"Casanova!" Alli launched in the air with a squeal.

Jamie's lips took a wry twist as laughter erupted. "Very funny, Cowgirl."

Sucking air through clenched teeth, Logan shook his head. "Uh-oh, ten seconds—we've got our work cut out for us, boys. You're up, Bram—make us proud."

The laughter and levity were high and the competition as fierce as the fun while the lead bounced back and forth like the shuttle over the net. The pink haze of dusk lent a warm glow on the final round when Aunt Cait redeemed the win with a record-breaking nine-second pantomime, cheeks flushed as pink as the sky. "Goodness, humiliated by *Pride and Prejudice*," she said sweetly, sending a rare smirk Uncle Logan's way. "Imagine that."

Jamie rose with a wide stretch of arms. "As painful as it is to leave you gentlemen at the gloating and mercy of these ladies, I fear I have tasks to which I must attend."

Cassie fought her disappointment with a saucy tip of her head. "Nursing your pride?"

The side of his mouth crooked. "No, ma'am, if I wanted to do that, I'd challenge you to pinochle because it would be my extreme pleasure to take you down a few pegs, Miss McClare."

"Good luck with that," Blake said. "Cass is as good at pinochle as she is at poker."

"So I hear." Jamie quirked a smile. "A rain check, perhaps?"

"Certainly, but do make it on a payday, Mr. MacKenna," she said with a flutter of lashes.

Alli straightened Jamie's tie with a pout. "Come on, Jamie, do you really have to go?"

Jamie tweaked a loose lock of Alli's hair. "Sorry, Al, but I promised Jess I'd be home early. We're finishing up a chess game, and she's anxious to take me down." His gaze flitted to Cassie with a swerve of a smile. "A desire I evoke in a number of women, it seems."

"How is Jess doing?" Caitlyn's tone softened at the mention of Jamie's sister.

Cassie noted the sudden strain in his jaw. "Her fall over the Fourth took a toll, I'm afraid, but she's slowly recovering, although not quick enough to suit me."

Aunt Cait rose to give him a hug. "We'll continue to keep Jess in our prayers, and you, as well." She kissed his cheek. "Give your family our love, and please tell them I'm hoping they can join us for the holidays this year, so please try to coax them, will you? You're like family, James MacKenna, and that goes for your mother and sister as well, is that clear?"

"Yes, ma'am," Jamie said quietly. His cheeks colored as he cleared his throat, the invitation clearly uncomfortable. "I'll certainly extend your invitation, Mrs. McClare, as always, but since Jess's fall, it seems Mom sticks closer to home more than ever before, so I can't promise they'll come." He quickly squatted to give Maddie a tight squeeze, then rose and drew in a breath, flashing a stiff smile. "Well, good night, everyone."

Alli poked Cass with her elbow as goodbyes followed Jamie to the door.

"I'm going, I'm going . . . ," Cassie muttered, catching up in the foyer. "Jamie?"

He turned, and she couldn't help but notice the hesitation in his eyes.

She halted several feet away, absently picking at a sliver on nails chewed to oblivion the last two weeks. "I . . . wanted to . . ." She cleared her throat. "No, I *needed* . . . to tell you something."

Inhaling deeply, she winced when she yanked the hangnail clean off, down to the nub. The pain from her nail coincided with that in her heart over the polite distance in his eyes. She looked down, noting the blood on her finger. "I . . . owe you an apology—"

"Cass, no—"

Her head shot up. "Yes, Jamie, I do. You've every right to court whomever you please."

Lips firm, he averted his gaze, eyes fixed on the floral pattern of Aunt Cait's foyer rug.

"True," she continued, exhale shaky, "you shouldn't have led me on, especially in Napa."

His eyes met hers, and the sorrow she saw plucked at her heart. "Cass, forgive me—I was wrong."

"Yes, you were, but so was I." Emotion bobbed in her throat as she stared at the man who'd inched his way into her heart. Opting to follow Alli's advice to make amends, she blew out a halting breath, determined to be Jamie's friend if nothing else. "Over the last few months, I've touted faith in God and forgiveness until you were blue in the face, and then when I have the opportunity to show it firsthand, what do I do? I let my hurt and disappointment embitter me to the point that I throw you out on your ear." She clutched her arms to her waist, chin elevated to keep it from trembling. "My only defense is I was so mad I wanted to spit in your eye, brand you with a red-hot poker, hang you from the highest—"

He raised a palm. "I get the general idea, Cowgirl." He slipped his hands in his pockets, a grin tugging his lips. "So I guess I should be grateful you only threw me out?"

She smirked, the tangle of nerves in her chest slowly unraveling. "You have no idea, Pretty Boy. Mark has a permanent bruise the shape of my boot."

His smile faded. "I deserve that and more," he said quietly.

"Yes, you do, but to show you I live the faith I tried to drill into that hard head of yours, I've chosen to forgo on the bodily harm." Melancholy crept into her heart . . . as well as her smile. "Because the truth is, Jamie, I value your friendship." She extended her hand. "So . . . friends?"

He stared, his words soft and low. "That didn't work out too well the last time, Cass."

"Oh, trust me—this time it will." She hiked a thumb to the ceiling. "And I have boots and a lasso to prove it."

He lowered his head and chuckled, finally peering beneath dark lashes. His smile was wistful. "You're one in a million, you know that?"

"As a matter of fact, I do," she said with a sassy hike of her brow, thrusting her hand.

He moved in to clasp it, and the quiver in her stomach raced clear down to her toes.

"Good—friends it is, then," she said with as much nonchalance as she could possibly muster given the heat creeping into her cheeks. With one firm shake, she eased her grip from his. "Good night, Jamie, and just for the record?" She flicked a loose strand of hair over her shoulder. "I hope Jess grinds you into dust."

He laughed. "No worries there. When it comes to chess, my sister makes me look like an amateur." Affection warmed his tone. "Kind of like you with poker and pool."

"And pinochle," she said with a cocky tilt of her head, "*if* you're man enough to try."

"Next time," he said softly, then glanced at his watch. "I better go, but before I do, there's something I need to tell you as well—as friends."

"Yes?"

He drew in a slow breath and instantly she felt like she was wearing a corset made of steel. "It's about Blake's birthday dinner at Cliff House next week," he said weakly.

"I do hope you're coming." Her forehead creased. "Blake would be upset if you didn't, and goodness, I'd hate to think you wouldn't because of what happened between us."

"Yes, I'm coming . . . ," he said, his voice more somber than usual, "it's just that . . ." He looked up then with a sobriety that stuttered her pulse. "I won't be alone."

She blinked, his statement drifting in her brain like an autumn leaf that had yet to light, but when it did, she was certain it unleashed a burst of scarlet in her face. She opened her mouth to speak, but the words seemed to be fused to her tongue.

"Blake wants Liddy there," he said quickly, as if to dispel the awkwardness of the moment, "and Liddy's father insists Patricia come along, so I offered to escort her." His pause was painful. "You see, Cass . . ." A muscle jerked in his throat indicating this was as uncomfortable for him as it was for her. *But not quite.* "Before you, Patricia and I were . . ."

"Courting . . . ?" It was a whisper that barely cleared her lips, the sound frail and hesitant.

His eyes softened despite the barest hint of a flinch. "Not officially," he whispered, "but there were . . . expectations . . ."

Expectations. Yes, she understood them well. "Of course." She forced a bright smile she hoped wouldn't crack on her face. "So you've decided to resume seeing her again . . . to pursue c . . ." It wouldn't come . . . *couldn't* come for the hurt clogging her throat.

". . . c-courtship, yes," he said slowly, as if he, too, had trouble saying the word.

And yet he did.

Never had she missed the ranch more than right at that moment—the warmth of Mama's comfort, the security of Daddy's arms, telling her she mattered to them if not to the men in her life. Tears welled beneath her lids, and she fought them off, desperate for the shield of anger she'd felt before. But it had left when she'd given Jamie over to God, forgiven him and accepted only friendship. Suddenly she was defenseless from the hurt that paralyzed her to the spot. "I . . . need to get back," she whispered, blinking hard to ward off the moisture that would betray her.

He took a step forward, her name a rasp of regret. "Cass . . ."

It didn't matter his voice sounded as broken as hers or that the faintest sheen of wetness glimmered in his own eyes. All that mattered was getting away before her pride was nothing but a puddle of tears lapping at her feet. "I . . . whist . . . I . . . need to play whist," she muttered and took several steps back, whirling to head back outside. Only her feet didn't carry her to the terrace where her family waited and laughed. No, she found herself hurrying to the staircase, the click of her heels dying on the carpet as she fled up the steps. "Good night, Jamie," she called, unwilling to glance back for the tears streaming her cheeks.

"Cass, wait—"

But she didn't. She was done waiting. For men like Mark and Jamie. For love to heal her heart. For happiness to find her in the arms of a man. Blinded by tears, she stumbled to her room and closed the door with a painful heave. Memories of Mark and Jamie bombarded—their charm, their kisses, their relentless pursuit—and she vowed she'd never fall prey again.

Anger swelled as she marched to her pitcher and basin to repair the damage Jamie had done. She splashed cold water on her face, wishing she could repair her heart as easily, but it would take time. Time and prayer, she decided, but by God, she would do it. Fingers quivering, she patted her skin dry, mouth pinched with resolve. She was through with pretty boys who stole her kisses and then her heart. From now on, she'd wait on God and God alone for one virtuous man, faithful and true. A purebred who would run the race—for her heart and the faith that would bind them together. She powdered her face, a glint of steel in eyes glazed by tears she would *no longer* allow . . . at least to the world.

She sniffed. *Or* to a pretty-boy stallion . . . who was clearly nothing more than a coyote in disguise.

24

Assessing her tearstained face in the mirror, Cassie gouged a final hairpin in, wishing she could rip them all out and just go to bed. Heaving a deflated sigh, she stared at her pitiful reflection, not even blinking an eye at the knock on her door.

"Cass?"

"It's open," she said, tone lifeless and nasal.

"What are you—" Alli stopped mid-sentence when Cassie turned, red-rimmed eyes apparently giving her dead away. "Aw, Cass," she whispered, closing the door before she hurried over to wrap her in a tight hug. "What did that little brat do now?"

Cassie sniffed and plopped on the edge of her bed. "What pretty-boy brats like him do so well, Al—he broke my heart. *Again.*"

Alli sat and looped an arm to her waist. "But I thought you agreed to forgive and forget and just be friends?"

A grunt rolled from Cassie's lips. "Oh, I did, but I didn't expect him to make it so blamed easy." She sniffed. "Or maybe I should say 'hard.'"

"What do you mean?" Alli asked, appearing ready to take Jamie on with a square of her shoulders.

Cassie's gaze wandered into a vacant stare, shoulders slumped. "He's courting Patricia."

"What?" Alli's back went stiff as a rod. "But he hasn't looked twice at her since you came to stay, and then there were all those advances he made to you . . ."

"Which he apologized for," Cassie said, voice wavering into a sigh.

It was Alli's turn to grunt. "Humph—too little, too late, if you ask me." She shook Cassie's arm. "I refuse to believe he cares more for Patricia than for you. Why, the man couldn't keep his eyes off of you, let alone his hands."

Cassie turned, lip in a quiver. "Do you think that's it, Al? That he lost interest when I gave in to his kiss—the night we played midnight? You know, suddenly I was no longer a challenge?"

"Horsefeathers," Alli said, tone indignant. "Why, Liddy said she's caught him with Trish in the past . . ." Her voice trailed off at the sudden tears in Cassie's eyes. She squeezed her in a fierce embrace. "Oh, Cass, I'm sorry, but knowing Trish like I do, I doubt that's the reason." She gently brushed hair from Cassie's face. "I don't know why this happened, but I do know Jamie cares for you."

A hiccup broke from Cassie's mouth. "Sure he does—as a friend."

Alli sat straight up, the gape of her mouth curving into trouble. "Maybe—maybe not."

Cassie's eyes narrowed. "Oh, no . . . I don't like that look in your eye."

"Great balls of fire, I'll bet that's one way we can flush out his true feelings."

Cassie moaned. "Come on, Al, his true feelings are obvious—he has no interest in me other than as a friend, and I've accepted that." She sniffed, eyes trailing into a pitiful stare. "Daddy always says 'every trail has a few puddles,' but dash it all, Al, I'm tired of getting wet."

"Well, then, let's send a little storm Jamie's way, shall we?"

Cassie glanced up, shaking her head. "Oh, no—"

Alli stared her down. "Look, you may've accepted it, but I refuse to allow you to sit there at Blake's party pretending everything's hunky-dory while Jamie fawns over another woman."

"But what am I supposed to do?" Cassie said with a groan.

"Maybe a little fawning of your own?"

"Excuse me?"

A devious chuckle rumbled in Alli's throat as she hopped to her feet. She grabbed Cassie's hand and tugged her to the door. "Blake can invite whomever he likes." Alli winked. "Especially if they happen to be eligible bachelors."

Cassie balked, heels skidding across the polished wood floor. "Oh, no you don't," she said with panic in her chest. "I am through with men for the summer and maybe forever."

Alli folded her arms. "All right, Cass, if you want to be the only one without an escort while Jamie dances the night away with Trish . . ."

"I won't be the only one—you'll be there." Cassie crossed her arms right back."

"*With* an escort," Alli emphasized. "Blake's been hounding me to meet a friend of his, so I think this party is the perfect place, don't you?"

"You wouldn't." Cassie felt the blood drain from her face.

Alli leaned in. "You bet I would, to force you to stand up to Jamie MacKenna? Unless, of course," she said, brow angled high, "you won't mind the gloat in Trish's eyes?"

That did it. The blood returned to Cassie's cheeks in force. "But only for Blake's party, right?" she asked, her nervousness giving way with a chew of her lip.

"Absolutely," Alli said, "unless *you* want it to be more . . ."

Cassie nodded, swallowing hard. "You'll ask Blake for me?"

"In a heartbeat."

"It has to be somebody Blake trusts, of course—nice, kind, and a perfect gentleman." Cassie found another hangnail to punish.

"Keep in mind this is Blake here, but we'll do our best." Alli opened Cassie's door.

"And, Al?" Cass stood there, thumb in her teeth.

"Yes, Cass?" Alli's gaze was tender.

"Can you make sure he's prettier than MacKenna?"

Alli grinned, hooking Cassie's waist to usher her down the hall. "For crying out loud, Cass, give me a little credit, will you?" Her smile slid into a smirk. "That's a given."

"Are you crazy? Harper's a womanizer from the word go!" Jamie ignored the curious glances at the entrance of The Cliff House Dining Room, channeling all his frustration over a bad day at work into upbraiding his best friend, birthday or no. Hands stiff on his hips, he stared at Blake like he'd just arranged for Cassie to go out with an axe murderer. Music and conversation filtered from the palatial dining room where endless rounds of linen-clad tables circled a dance floor filled with beautiful people. Bejeweled matrons of society glittered and glowed like the candlelight sconces throughout the pillared room, creating a fairy-tale setting enjoyed by the darlings of Nob Hill.

Blake grinned. "So are you, Mac, but I let you come around, don't I?"

"This isn't funny, McClare—Cassie's too innocent for the likes of that . . . that . . ."

"Pretty Boy?" Blake patted Jamie's cheek. "Come on, she handled you, didn't she?"

"This is different—I'm your best friend. I care about your family."

Blake's smile went flat. "Yeah? Tell that to Cassie—I watched her mope around the house for two weeks, remember?"

Heat scalded Jamie's neck. "I already told you—I'm not religious enough to suit her."

Blake chuckled. "You're not religious at all, which is one of the reasons I like you, although I wish you'd rub off on Bram instead of the other way around." He cuffed Jamie's shoulder. "Come on, MacKenna—lighten up. Brad Harper's not religious either, so he doesn't stand a chance with Cass. Besides, I keep telling you—she handled you, she can handle him."

Jamie's jaw ground into a mulish press, remembering with painful clarity how he'd practically seduced Cassie during a game of midnight. *No, Blake, she can't . . .*

"Uh-oh, don't look now, but the senator's daughter is heading this way."

Jamie groaned, gouging the bridge of his nose with the ball of his hand. *Great. First a trying case consumes my whole day and now a trying woman wants to consume my whole night.*

"Here you are," Patricia said, her long, dark hair swept up in a graceful pompadour that allowed for a single curl trailing her shoulder. She flipped it back, violet eyes a perfect match for a shapely dress that turned every male head in the room, reminding Jamie once again how lucky he was. His lips clamped in a tight line. Too bad he needed reminding, although he'd certainly felt that way once—before Cass. She slipped her arm in his and gave him a dazzling smile. "I believe you owe me a number of dances, Mr. MacKenna."

Jamie forced a smile. "I believe I do, Miss Hamilton, an oversight I hope to correct." He led her to the dance floor and took her in his arms, easing into the heady whirl of a waltz. She chatted away while he listened with half an ear, his mind on his trying day at work until Cassie caught his eye a few feet away. She didn't possess the beauty of the woman he held, but his heart thudded all the same over powdered freckles she tried so hard to hide and the sparkle in green eyes now focused on another man. The lilt of her laughter cinched his jaw, her off-the-shoulder gown fluttering in the breeze as Harper spun her in his arms. In natural reflex, Jamie's eyes roved the length of her, cream-colored chiffon flowing down a body that had haunted too many of his dreams.

"Jamie?"

His gaze jerked to Patricia, and fire broiled the back of his neck. "Yes?"

"You seem . . . distracted," she said, a flicker of hurt in her eyes.

The fire combusted in his cheeks. "A little, I suppose." He worked hard to focus only on her, hoping to assuage her concern with an apology and a little-boy smile. "Forgive me? I'm afraid my mind keeps straying to a particularly difficult case at work."

With a blink of violet eyes, Patricia glanced over her shoulder in Cassie's direction, returning her gaze to his with a tilt of her head. Concern was etched into every pore of her beautiful face. "Or maybe a particular person?" she said, a hint of a tremor in her tone.

The music ended and Jamie drew in a deep breath. "Cassie and I are only friends, Trish," he said quietly, leading her back to the table. He sat beside her and downed the last of his water.

"But only because she's poor . . ." Her voice trailed off, barely a whisper.

The sheen in her eyes pierced, and he took her hands in his. "Trish," he said softly, "you and I—we're good together. We like each other a lot, we have fun and most importantly, we have a mutually beneficial relationship that's totally honest. You want to marry an up-and-coming lawyer with political aspirations? I need your father's influence to secure a surgery for my sister and help achieve my political goals." His heart constricted at the vulnerable look in her eyes. "I have feelings for you, you know that, and they will grow, trust me."

Her bodice quivered as she drew in a shaky breath. "But will your feelings for Cassie go away?" she whispered, and the fear in her voice tore at his gut. She was in love with him, and he knew it even though he'd done everything in his power to take it slow when they'd first met, playing the field and seeing others in addition to her. But for some reason she'd fallen hard, determined to stake her claim. Maybe because her father seemed bent on him as well, a rags-to-riches politician who admired Jamie's fire and spunk in climbing out of the sewers of the Barbary Coast. He'd made it abundantly clear he welcomed Jamie as a prospective son-in-law as much as Patricia wanted him as a husband, and Jamie knew the coffers were lined with gold if he courted his daughter. Including a house on Nob Hill and society approval as never before, not to mention government connections Jamie could only dream about. And most importantly, the political clout and bank account to provide a surgery for his sister. Everything he'd ever wanted.

Until Cassie.

Yes, Cassie had changed the flow of his heart, but he couldn't allow her to change its course. A course he'd decided on six months prior when he'd suspected Patricia was the one. Would his feelings for Cassie go away? He didn't know, but he *did* know what Trish needed to hear. He pressed a gentle kiss to her nose. "I'm sure of it—in time."

"Trish, care to join me in the ladies' room?" Liddy hurried over, face flushed from dancing with Blake.

Jamie glanced up at Patricia's sister and smiled, giving Trish's hand a light squeeze. "Go—I'll step out for some fresh air, and we'll dance after, all right?"

She nodded and rose to her feet, bending to bestow a peck to his cheek.

His heart felt like lead as he watched her and Liddy depart and exhaling a heavy breath, he rose and headed in the opposite direction of the crowded veranda. He preferred the near seclusion of the observation tower several stories above and quickly scaled the numerous flights of steps that deterred most patrons. Anxious to clear his mind with fresh sea air and views of waves crashing the rocky shore, he stepped out into the briny air. And stopped. His heart thudded at the sight of Cass and Harper at the far end, chatting as they both leaned over the stone wall.

Harper's shoulder grazing Cassie's triggered a spark of anger, and striding over, Jamie thumped him on the back. "Sorry to disturb, old boy, but Blake's looking for you."

Harper glanced over his shoulder. "What for?" he asked, irritation evident in his tone.

"Didn't ask." Jamie smiled. "But I'll be happy to stay with Cass while you go find out."

"No, thanks." Harper cupped a hand to Cassie's waist. "We were just heading down."

"Actually, Brad," Jamie said easily, his smile and manner casual,

"I need to talk to Cass about something if you don't mind, so I'll escort her back shortly if it's all right with her."

Harper glanced at Cassie and she nodded. "It's fine, Brad, really."

"All right," Brad said with a light squeeze of her hand. "I'll see you downstairs."

The moment he was out of earshot, Cassie turned to Jamie with a fold of arms. "So . . . something tells me you just sent Brad on a wild goose chase, MacKenna. Mind telling me why?"

The cool sea air ruffled Cassie's hair and dress, but did nothing to cool Jamie's temper. Searing her with a scowl, he butted a hip to the wall, his words far more clipped than intended. "You have no business up here with a man like him, Cass—Harper has a reputation."

"Really?" She tilted her head, eyes in a squint. "An odd declaration from a man whose reputation would make most men look like a monk."

His jaw began to grind. "I thought you didn't like pretty boys, Miss McClare."

"No," she said with a lift of her chin. "I don't *trust* pretty boys. You cured me of that."

He slammed a palm to the wall, hand stinging as much as his pride. "Blast it, Cass, what are you trying to do to me?"

"I have no idea what you're talking about."

He jerked an arm towards the door. "Harper drooling all over you tonight, you coming up here alone with him?" He leaned in with a tic in his jaw. "I've never seen you play the flirt before, and it's not becoming."

Her chin lashed up. "No? Well, I trust your opinion about as much as I trust you. And I don't know why you're so all-fired worried. Worry about Patricia—she's your concern, not me." She pushed past. "Excuse me."

He grabbed her wrist. "Don't you dare walk away from me," he hissed.

She whirled around, flinging his hand off. "Why, Jamie? Isn't that what you did to me?"

The raw truth of her words hit dead-center, unleashing a guilt he'd tried so hard to ignore. The lie to himself that she would understand because they were good friends. And that, as good friends, she'd wish him well with Patricia and not be hurt. His stomach cramped at the wounded look in her eyes and with a brutal ache in his chest, he wrenched her close, burying his face in her hair. "God help me, Cass, I did, and it was the hardest thing I've ever done . . ."

"No!" She jerked free, sparks of the old Cassie glinting in her eyes. She brandished a dangerous finger right beneath his nose. "Don't you dare touch me—you don't have the right. I will not be beguiled again, do you hear? You're a smooth talker, Jamie MacKenna, and I've accepted our friendship for the sake of the family, but that friendship no longer entitles you to the closeness we once shared. We are friends who border on mere acquaintances and nothing more."

He knew it was anger speaking, but her words still slashed like the icy wind at the back of his neck, chilling him to the bone. Throat convulsing, he stared, voice low. "Nothing more? We both know that's a lie," he whispered hoarsely. "We are dear friends who started to fall in love before we found out it wouldn't work, that's all." He moved in, eyes fused to hers. "I can't just turn that off, Cassie—you're important to me, and I don't want to lose your friendship."

She stepped away, arms clutched to her waist. Green fire snapped in eyes that were now guarded. "Don't worry, MacKenna, it's not my friendship you've lost—it's my trust."

He flinched, remembering how long it had taken him to establish that very trust. He swallowed hard. "I suppose I deserve that, but in my defense, *you* set the terms." Feeling awkward, he shoved his hands in his pockets with a shrug of his shoulders, hoping to defuse her temper with a soft tone. "I'm just the poor slob who couldn't meet them."

Some of the anger faded from her eyes as her chin thrust up. "You could have told me before you took advantage in Napa."

He huffed out a sigh and pinched the bridge of his nose, eyes closed. "I didn't realize it at the time, I swear."

Her grunt confirmed her disbelief. "Oh, really? Just when did this great revelation occur? When you fell out of bed on your head the next day and realized I wasn't worth the trouble?"

His head snapped up, the heat in his eyes going head-to-head with hers. "You're worth the trouble, Miss McClare, make no mistake, or I wouldn't have attempted to follow your inane rules in the first place." He vented with a noisy breath while he fixed his gaze on the floor, unwilling for her to see the guilt in his eyes. His voice was harsh. "It occurred when I went home and saw my sister in pain after some blood-sucking lowlife attacked her." He looked up when her gasp drew his gaze, desperate to salvage their friendship. "I'm sorry, Cass, but I realized then I couldn't trust some God who'd allow that to happen."

She blinked. "Oh, Jamie, I . . . I didn't know." A pause. "He didn't—"

He shook his head. "No, the slime only had time to slam her to the ground, but he damaged her hip even more." He hung his head. "She's been in severe pain ever since."

"I am so sorry," she whispered.

He sucked in a deep breath, a sliver of guilt gnawing over the half-truth. "Me, too, Cass, because you mean the world to me, truly, but the truth is I can't give you what you want."

She nodded slowly, buffing her arms. His heart wrenched when wounded eyes peeked up. "And that's the only reason?"

The innocence of her question gouged at his heart, and he hated himself for the man he'd become. "Yes, that's the only reason," he said, the lie almost making him wince. He lifted her chin with his finger, desperate to lighten the mood with a poor attempt at a smile. "No question—term number four is a back-breaker, and I can't accept it any more than you can accept me without it." He rubbed her arms. "Unless, of course, you're willing to overrule it?" He held his breath while he awaited the answer he needed to hear—even if it wasn't the one he wanted—and when she shook her head, his silent exhale slowly seeped out. "Well then, Miss McClare, I suppose there's only one issue yet to discuss." He feathered the stray curls back from the side of her face. "Harper's not the right man for you, Cass—promise you'll be careful."

Her lip quirked, but the sheen in her eyes remained. "Like I tried with you?"

Chest constricting, he fished his handkerchief from his pocket to blot at her tears, wishing more than anything things could be different, that poverty didn't stand in the way of his dream for Jess, for his family, and for himself. "Yes, like you tried with me," he said, his regret as raw as the sudden bite of the wind. He pressed a soft kiss to her brow, desperate to repress the desire she provoked in order to maintain the friendship they both needed to have. Releasing a weighty sigh, he rested his forehead against hers. "It won't be easy, Cass, but trust me, we can do this—love each other as good friends who want only the best for the other."

"I suppose." She pulled back, her manner suddenly serious. "But trust?" She shivered. "I'll be honest, Jamie—my heart's still pretty bruised, and we lost a lot of ground." She relinquished a weary sigh. "It's going to take time."

"I know." He cocooned her in his coat. A bittersweet relief flooded as he closed his eyes, grateful they could still be friends. "But look at it this way," he said with a note of levity, desperate to chase the gloom away. "I'm far more trustworthy as a friend than a—and I quote—'pretty-boy polecat' you're looking to court, right?"

He felt her body expand against his as she huffed out a noisy sigh. "One can only hope."

A smile tipped his lips at the trace of humor in her tone. He pressed a gentle kiss to her hair. "Well, trust me, I am. Just ask Blake or Bram."

"Excuse me—Jamie?"

His head lunged up, blood chilling at the sight of Patricia a few feet away. "Mr. McClare is rounding everyone up for a toast and dessert in fifteen minutes," she said quietly, her face as expressionless as the chiseled stone columns sheltering the open deck.

Rooted to the spot, he felt Cassie shiver and immediately stripped off his coat to drape it over her shoulders.

"No, Jamie," she said, pushing it away. "I'll be fine. Go with Patricia—I'll follow soon."

"It's getting chilly, Cass. You can't stay up here alone."

She nodded toward several couples here and there on the deck. "I'm not alone, and I just need a few minutes by myself, really. I won't be long, I promise."

"Then you'll take my coat." His tone was stern as he slipped his jacket over her shoulders again, then bent to envelop her in a tight hug. "I care about you, Cass," he whispered in her ear, "and your friendship is one of the most precious things in my life. Never forget that, please."

———

Oh, that I could . . . She pulled away, offering a shaky smile. "Please tell Brad and Uncle Logan I'll be along soon—in time for the toast, okay?"

"Certainly." Patricia's smile, though stiff, bore none of her usual disdain as she looped her arm through Jamie's. "Ready, Jamie?"

"Yes." His gaze flicked to Cassie. "Not too long, all right?"

She nodded and watched them leave, heartsick that friendship was the only thing she would ever have with Jamie MacKenna. She turned back toward the sea and crossed her arms on the stone wall, resting her head on top while she closed her eyes to ward off more tears. As crushed as she was, she couldn't blame Jamie alone. The terms had been hers, not his. She'd known better than falling in love with a man who didn't share her faith, and yet she'd compromised her convictions under the guise of bringing him closer to God. And in the end, it'd been Jamie himself who had done the right thing—stepped aside to honor her wishes.

She brushed the wetness from her eyes, face to the sky. "All right, Lord, if this is the way it must be, then I pray to be the friend Jamie needs—and the caliber of friend he's been to me. I'll need grace, Lord, and please—*please*—purge my heart of this longing for more." With a sniff, she retrieved his handkerchief to dab at her eyes. Expelling a formidable sigh, she turned, body jolting at the sight of Patricia a few feet away. Feeling awkward, she started for the door. "I was just on my way . . . ," she said quickly, not interested in conversation with Jamie's date.

Patricia's touch iced her to the spot, as chilling as her tone. "Don't think I don't know what you're trying to do."

Cassie turned. "Pardon me?"

Patricia's smile was as cool as the night. "That cow-town innocence may work on Jamie, Miss McClare, but it won't work on me." She took a step closer, but Cassie refused to budge. "Jamie and I are going to be married, so it's no use wasting your time trying to lure him back."

Anger surged. "How dare you! We are friends and nothing more."

Her gaze flicked down and up with disdain. "Yes, I know. But Jamie has a bright political future, and as the woman who will be his wife, I'd rather you not be 'friends' at all."

His wife. The words may as well have been the back of Patricia's hand—the effect was the same, sending Cassie's heart reeling. She fought the spark of tears with a thrust of her chin. "You can't stop us from being friends, Patricia."

"Oh, but I can, Miss McClare," she said with cool deliberation. "All it takes is the truth."

"The 'truth' as you call it, Miss Hamilton, is that Jamie and I care about each other a great deal. We have a friendship based on respect, honesty, and deep affection, and I doubt a ring on your finger will ever change that."

Patricia smiled, an action that prickled Cassie's skin more than the biting bluster of the wind. "Yes, I do believe Jamie respects you a great deal, and there's no doubt his affection for you runs deep . . ." She paused, a sliver of pity in her eyes. "But I'm afraid his honesty where you're concerned, Miss McClare, leaves something to be desired."

"I'm leaving," Cassie whispered, attempting to pass.

Patricia's hand cinched her arm like a vice, fingers dug into Jamie's coat like her claws were dug into the man. "Why? Afraid of the truth?"

Cassie paused, keeping her temper at bay. "No, not as much as you, apparently."

"That's where you're wrong, Miss McClare," she said with a sympathetic smile. "You see, I know the truth, but I love Jamie anyway. I'm not sure you could say the same."

Goose bumps skimmed Cassie's body despite the warmth of Jamie's coat.

"Yes, I know Jamie considered courting you," Patricia said, "but I also know why he isn't."

The air clotted in Cassie's lungs, as thick as the pity in Patricia's tone. "It's an issue of sharing the same faith, Miss Hamilton, but I fail to see what business that is of yours."

"The same faith, yes," she said smoothly, as if their conversation were no more than exchanging niceties over tea, "and the fact you don't have the most important thing Jamie MacKenna needs and the one thing he wants more than love."

Cassie clenched her fists at her sides, afraid she'd be tempted to smack the smirk off the woman's face. "And what's that, Miss Hamilton, your favors?"

"No, Miss McClare," she said quietly, her tone actually humble. "My money."

Ice slithered through Cassie's veins, freezing the words to her tongue.

"Oh, I was worried you had him," she continued, fidgeting with the cashmere shawl she wore over her lavender dress, "until I discovered your family is broke. When Jamie realized that, I'm afraid there was no decision to be made."

Cassie's lips parted to speak, but the words slowed to a crawl, escaping as a hoarse crack. "I don't believe you."

"No? And when exactly did his affections cool?" she asked, one perfectly manicured brow angled high. "I'll wager it was after Napa, when I told him you were as poor as he."

Cassie's eyes weighted closed while the breath whooshed from her lungs. The deck beneath her feet began to spin, and she grasped for the stone wall, legs buckling. *God, please—no . . .*

"You see, Miss McClare," she whispered, voice softening with empathy that hadn't been there before. "I *knew* Jamie McKenna was courting me for my money, but I'll wager you didn't."

No, I didn't . . . Cassie turned away as hot tears sprang to her eyes, Jamie's deception battering her heart as thoroughly as the waves battered the rocks below. Fists clenched on the wall, she squeezed her eyes shut as if to silence the drum of her pulse in her ears, the sound of shallow heaves from her throat . . . the echo of lies bludgeoning her mind. *"And that's the only reason?"* she'd asked. *"Yes, that's the only reason,"* he'd answered, and the awful weight of that untruth doubled her over, effectively wrenching a sob from her throat.

"Jamie is nothing if not ambitious . . ." Alli's words returned to haunt with brutal clarity, and suddenly Cassie understood Jamie's drive to win her over despite her unwillingness to play at his game. She was a McClare, after all, one of the wealthiest political families in California and he'd obviously pegged her from the start as a woman vulnerable to his charm. Nausea curdled her stomach at the fool she'd been, not once, but twice. Mark had broken her heart, yes, but Jamie had broken her trust and her spirit, wounding her soul so completely, she was loathe to ever see him again. She pressed a shaky hand to her mouth and in one heart-wrenching heave, slumped over the wall, head in her hands as sobs wracked her body.

Cassie flinched at someone's touch. "I . . . never meant to hurt you like this, Cassie, truly," Patricia said, "but I thought you needed to know." Her voice suddenly wavered, fear threading her tone to reveal vulnerability for the very first time. "You see, I love him, and before you arrived . . . well, he cared about me too, as well as my money." Patricia gave her an awkward pat before removing her hand. "Do you . . . do you understand?"

Cassie remained silent, her head hanging limp and body depleted. Yes, she understood. Patricia and Jamie were a matched pair—selfish and manipulative to the core.

"Well, I . . . I need to get back." Patricia paused. "Are you . . . coming?"

She didn't answer until she heard the rustle of Patricia's dress when she turned away. "Wait." Cassie spun around, flinging Jamie's coat off her shoulders. She balled it up and threw it at Patricia, the shock on the woman's face blurring from the tears in Cassie's eyes. "Here, take his coat and take him too—you deserve each other."

Patricia smoothed out the jacket and carefully draped it over her arm, her face a mask except for the faintest shadow of regret in her eyes. "I'm sorry it had to come to this, Cassie, and I hope someday you'll find it in your heart to forgive us." With a stiff smile, she gave a short nod and made her way to the door, leaving Cassie to agonize alone.

Over a man she loved who betrayed her, a friend she trusted who deceived her, and a future deprived of them both. Tears slipped from her eyes and she pushed them away with a hard swipe, her anger surging like the waves on the shore. Forgive them? Maybe. But it would take time. And distance. She bowed her head as grief fisted her heart.

Oh, yes . . . miles and miles of distance.

25

Closing her book, Caitlyn glanced at the clock on her nightstand and sighed, her concern for Cassie foremost on her mind.

"Cassie isn't feeling well," Alli had informed her at the Cliff House, insisting she and their escorts would see her home. And, indeed, her niece had appeared as pale as her champagne-colored dress when she'd kissed her goodbye. But it had been the hollow look of grief in her eyes that set Caitlyn so on edge, she'd asked Logan to take her home early. When she'd peeked in Cassie's room, the poor thing had been sound asleep and her forehead cool, and yet Caitlyn couldn't shake the uneasy feeling that prevailed. She could sense it—something was wrong. Reaching for her robe, she slipped from her bed and put it on, tying the sash with a firm tug. The grandfather clock in the parlour chimed the midnight hour as she hurried down the hall, its deep bongs eerily foreboding while they echoed through the house like a portent of gloom. Reluctant to enter without knocking, she put her ear to Cassie's door, ready to give a gentle tap. Her body stilled at the sound of muffled weeping. *Oh, Cassie!*

"Cassie?" Silence. A reedy breath escaped her lips as she tried again, unwilling to let her niece be alone if something was wrong.

She waited, wondering if she'd only imagined it. Inhaling, she turned the knob and poked her head in the door. "Cass . . . are you awake?"

No answer.

Silently crossing the room, Cait bent over Cassie's sleeping form to place a hand to her forehead, grateful it was still cool. She released a shaky sigh. Thank goodness—obviously her imagination was working overtime. Relieved, she caressed a gentle hand to her niece's cheek and stopped, her fingers suddenly wet to the touch. She straightened to stare at the sleeping girl and noted the sheen of moisture on her face in the moonlight. *Oh, Cass . . .*

Whether asleep or not, she was tempted to leave and close the door, but only because she knew it was what Cassie wanted, to be left alone, to fend for herself in this sudden malaise she'd found herself in. And yet, Cait could not. Not when her own heart had been wounded by the hurt she'd seen in her niece's eyes. "Alone" might be the coping mechanism for Cassidy McClare, but not while Caitlyn drew air. Padding to the door, she leaned to shut it with a quiet click of the lock and waited, suspecting her niece was still awake.

A muffled sob broke from the shadows, and Caitlyn's heart broke in her chest, propelling her forward with tears in her eyes. "Oh, Cassie, I will not allow people I love to cry alone. Not when prayer can heal an aching heart."

Cassie jolted up, face slick with tears and her voice nasal from weeping. "Aunt Cait . . . ?"

Caitlyn eased down on the edge of the bed, and with a quiver of her lip, Cassie launched into her arms with a sob that wracked both of their bodies.

Head bent to hers, Caitlyn soothed with a gentle massage of her back. "It's okay, darling, you just go ahead and get it all out."

She stroked her hair, eyes closed and heart heavy, until the last sob trailed into a shuddering heave, leaving Cassie limp in her arms. Tugging a handkerchief from her pocket, Caitlyn wiped the tears from her niece's eyes before handing it over. Her gaze was tender as she watched Cassie blow her nose. "Oh, darling, what's wrong?"

With a sorrowful sniff, Cassie inched back against the headboard, shoulders slumped and voice congested. She stared at the handkerchief in her hands, gaze lapsing into a soulless stare. "I did it again, Aunt Cait," she whispered, "fell in love with a man who broke my heart."

Cait's stomach lurched. "What? But who—" She sucked in a sharp draw of air, Jamie's absence at family dinners of late suddenly making more sense. Exhaling slowly, she laid a hand to Cassie's leg. "You mean Jamie? Goodness, Cass, I knew he was interested in you, of course, but I thought you just opted to be friends."

A harsh laugh tripped from Cassie's lips. "Oh no, Aunt Cait, a man like Jamie MacKenna wouldn't settle for 'just friends.' No, he pushes and prods and pretty boy's his way into a girl's heart whether she likes it or not, until the chase is over, and then he's gone."

"What?" Caitlyn's body went cold. "What do you mean?"

Cassie peered at her aunt, eyes narrowed enough to convey her anger. "I mean Jamie pursued me since the night I arrived, making advances that I deflected at every turn. I insisted on friendship, but no . . . the man was so desperate to win me over, he proposed courtship."

Caitlyn stared, mouth agape. *Good heavens!*

"But I remembered what you said about God's best, about saving myself for a man who loves God as much as I do, and Jamie's faith was minimal at best, if he even believes at all."

"No . . ." Caitlyn's voice was a shocked whisper.

"So I put him off again, which only challenged him more." She sniffed and blew her nose while some of the anger ebbed away. "But he was winning me over, Aunt Cait, with his attention, his charm, his persistence. So much so that I . . ." A heave shivered her chest. "Well, I agreed to give him a chance to court me if he drew closer to God . . ."

Caitlyn blinked, the pieces of the puzzle taking shape. "Which is why he started attending church with us on Sundays and then book study with you on Thursday nights," she whispered.

Cassie nodded, blotting her face. "Yes, along with the stipulation he make no more advances until we were officially courting. But then in Napa, he . . . ," her throat shifted as she stared at the handkerchief in her hands, her voice wavering, "kissed me to coerce me into courtship, and when he did, I knew . . . knew that I loved him and wanted to say yes."

Caitlyn caught her breath. "And now he's courting Patricia?" She cupped Cassie's face, the hurt in her eyes a mirror reflection of her niece's. "But why?"

Why, indeed. Cassie's eyes weighted closed, her aunt's question piercing her heart. *Because money's more important to Jamie,* she wanted to say, but knew she could not. As much as Jamie had wounded and betrayed her, she would not do the same to someone she loved. And although every nerve in her body railed and raged against it, love him she did, even still. Albeit a love so steeped in hurt and anger that there was no way she could stay. She opened her eyes to see the worry in her aunt's face and determined she would not burden her further with what Jamie had done. She had no desire to damage her family's opinion of a man they loved and counted as their own, and if Alli hadn't badgered her tonight, she wouldn't have told her either. As it was, she had to beg Alli not to scratch Jamie's eyes out—something she herself was inclined to do at the moment. Heaving a weary sigh, she stared at Aunt Cait through eyes blurred with tears. "Why? Because he said he couldn't have faith in a God who would his allow his sister to be in such pain."

"Oh, Cass . . ." Aunt Cait swallowed her in a hug.

She sniffed, tone wobbly as she leaned into her aunt's embrace. "Why do we have to fall in love with men who are no good for us?" she whispered.

Her aunt paused a long while, and Cassie suspected she was thinking of Uncle Logan. A wispy sigh feathered her face as Aunt Cait stroked her hair, her voice soft and low. "Why, darling? Because you see, as crazy as this sounds, men like Jamie and your Uncle Logan are . . . ," she paused to cup Cassie's face in her hands, the barest trace of a tease on her face, "chocolate layer cake." Her smile turned sad. "And sometimes, my love, one has a weakness for sweets."

Cassie sat up, a crimp in her brow. "What do you mean, Aunt Cait?"

She smiled and tugged Cassie back, settling in once again. "I mean sometimes we want what we shouldn't have." She paused, her gaze wandering into a faraway stare while the faintest of smiles tipped on her lips. "I remember the first time your Uncle Liam took me to our favorite restaurant—oh, how my mouth watered when I saw the dessert tray that night. There, under a crystal dome, sat the most beautiful piece of cake that I just *had* to have—my favorite, of course, white cake with seven layers of chocolate buttercream icing. Oh my, how your uncle laughed when I closed my eyes for that very first taste, promptly spitting it into my napkin when I discovered it was dark chocolate."

She shivered, and Cassie couldn't help but smile. "Good heavens, how I despise dark chocolate, so your Uncle Liam was kind enough to trade desserts." A soft chuckle drifted from her lips as she shook her head. "Do you know that I ordered that *same* piece of layer cake at least four times throughout the course of our marriage? I was so enticed by how it looked, I was convinced it would taste different each time." Her chest rose and fell with a wispy sigh. "Of course it never did, but oh, how it would make your uncle laugh." Her smile turned melancholy. "He claimed I was bedazzled by sweets, and of course he was right. Goodness, how I would moan and groan when Mother or Rosie threatened no dessert until I ate my vegetables, especially broccoli, which I detested almost as much as dark chocolate. Once when Rosie made one of my favorites—vanilla bean cheesecake—I made up my mind that this one night I would eat dessert first. So while Mother napped and Rosie ran errands, I helped myself to half a cheesecake."

"Oh, Aunt Cait, no!"

She chuckled. "Yes, I'm afraid I did, not only earning the biggest bellyache I'd ever had, mind you, but ruining me for cheesecake ever again." She tucked a strand of Cassie's hair over her ear, offering a smile tinged with sadness. "You see, Cassie, when I met your Uncle Logan, his pull over me was a lot like that seven-layer cake—I just had to have him. No matter that he had a reputation my parents didn't trust or that he didn't seem to have a heart for God, all I knew is that he was oh, so sweet and his kisses tasted oh, so wonderful. It wasn't until I married Liam that I realized Logan was a dessert that enticed, while Liam was a main course with substance that would nurture and help me grow strong. A man of faith who drew his sustenance and strength from a God who is the Bread of Life, whose very Word sustains us and grows us into the women we are meant to be."

Her aunt shifted to look into her eyes, the affection in her gaze as warm as the gentle hand that now kneaded Cassie's arm. "Why do we fall in love with men who aren't good for us? Perhaps because God wants us to know that without him, a relationship will not grow or sustain like he wants it to and may, in fact, make us sick. That without him, we will never fully be satisfied or enriched in anything we do, especially our relationships. Which means, Cassie," she said with a tender touch of her face, "as wonderful as Jamie is, without God, he's not the man for you, and God is likely allowing this heartache to spare you a bellyache down the road."

Cassie drew in a deep breath and released it in a shuddering sigh. "I know," she whispered, aware that God had, indeed, spared her from a man she obviously could never trust. But that didn't stem the pain at the moment. Only time and distance could do that. "Aunt Cait?"

"Yes, darling?" Aunt Cait skimmed a hand over Cassie's hair.

"I . . . don't think I can face him again . . ." Tears welled.

Aunt Cait stared, finally consenting with a nod. "You want to go home . . ."

Cassie nodded, the motion unleashing a trail of moisture down her cheeks. "Just until next summer, when you'll be readying the school to open in the fall." She pushed her tears away, chin jutting enough to let Aunt Cait know Jamie would not deter her from her dream. "Nothing will stop me from being here for you then—nothing!"

It was Aunt Cait's turn to nod, her sigh mournful to Cassie's ears. "When?"

"Tomorrow . . . before Jamie even knows I'm gone." She swallowed hard, her eyes pleading with Aunt Cait's. "I . . . don't want to leave, Aunt Cait, truly, but I just can't face him right now." A heave rose in her throat, but she fought it off with anger, infusing a hint of humor to temper her tone. "Or so help me, God—I will seven-layer the man."

Aunt Cait half chuckled, half sobbed as she gathered Cassie in her arms with a groan. "Oh, we are going to miss you, Cassidy McClare." She pulled away to study her face as if memorizing every detail. "And you mark my words, darling, by this time next summer?" A melancholy sigh drifted while her smile belied the sadness in her eyes. "You may well have a fondness for broccoli that will put layer cake to shame."

"I don't understand, Mama, why does Cassie have to leave?" Maddie asked.

Cassie tucked her toiletries into her luggage and glanced up with a tender smile. "I miss my family, darling, just like you missed your mama when she left early from Napa, remember?"

Tears pooled in the little girl's eyes. "But we're your family too."

Cassie's heart buckled. "I know, Maddie, and I love you all very much, but my visit is almost over anyway and Mama and Daddy need me, so it's time to go home."

"But you talked about getting a teaching job here," Meg reminded with a glaze in her eyes that matched her little sister's. "Why did you change your mind?"

Cassie glanced at Alli, who sat against the headboard, her tight-lipped smile infusing Cassie with the strength she needed to see this through. She'd sworn Al to secrecy regarding what Jamie had done, of course, but she deeply regretted Alli's loss of respect for him, now as flat as her own. She closed her suitcase with a firm click that sounded all too final. Yep, squashed just like her heart, as thoroughly as a june bug beneath the hooves of a twelve-legged mule. Releasing a withering sigh, she chanced a peek in Meg's direction. "Yes, I was considering a teaching job here, Meg, but I could tell from Mama's last letter she needed me at the reservation, so I've decided to teach there till your mama and sister open their school next year."

"It won't be the same here without you." Aunt Cait's usual bolstering smile was as shaky as Cassie's. "Heaven knows Jamie'll be impossible to live with, winning at pinochle and pool."

Cassie's smile dimmed. Impossible to live with. *Ah, yes . . . the very reason I can no longer stay.*

"Will you come back?" Maddie's eyes were hopeful.

"Of course she'll be back, shortcake," Alli said. "Maybe at Christmas, right, Cass?"

"Absolutely," Cassie said with a grateful smile. She angled a stern brow at her youngest cousin. "And, I fully expect you to best Blake in checkers by the time I return, is that clear?"

Maddie giggled. All at once her rosebud smile wilted. "I'm gonna miss you, Cassie."

"Oh, me too, sweetheart." Cassie scooped her up in a hug, kissing the top of her head.

"I hope you packed that nasty rope," Alli said, a touch of the imp in her smile. "Heaven knows what Rosie would do with it."

"Hog-tie your Uncle Logan, no doubt," Aunt Cait said with a droll smile. "Which come to think of it, might not be a bad thing." She glanced at the clock on Cassie's nightstand and rose. "Time to get Cassie to the station. I'm surprised your uncle isn't clamoring downstairs, as prompt as he likes to be."

"I can't believe Uncle Logan's taking off work just to drive me to the station." Cassie hefted her bag with a grunt. "He's way too busy for that."

Aunt Cait retrieved Cassie's hatbox. "Well, it's Logan's firm and the man can do what he wants." Her lips twisted. "And usually does." She paused to sear Cassie with a mock glare. "Put that suitcase down this instant, young lady—Hadley will carry it down, you hear?"

"Yes, ma'am." Cassie drew in a deep breath and dropped her bag, giving the room a quick scan. "Well, that's it, I suppose. Ready?" She linked arms with Aunt Cait to head downstairs, wishing she didn't have to run away from those she loved to heal a heart twice broken.

"All set?" Uncle Logan stood in the foyer, fedora in hand and face so somber, it prompted more tears in Cassie's eyes. He and Aunt Cait were certainly an unconventional family, but family nonetheless, and Cassie ached at the prospect of leaving. All at once Uncle Logan swallowed her up in his arms, and her heart ached at the hoarseness in his voice. "You tell your parents I want you all here for Christmas, understood? My gift, no argument."

She nodded against his chest, the scent of lime shaving soap and the barest trace of wood spice tugging her heart. Oh, how she would miss them all!

"Humph . . . you gonna hog her like you hog the best chair in the parlour?" Rosie darted down the hall from the direction of the kitchen to shove a cylinder tin against Logan's chest. She yanked Cassie from his grasp to crush her in a strong hug that was nothing short of remarkable given the housekeeper's petite form. She pulled away to cup both of Cassie's cheeks, a squint of a warning in blue eyes as firm as the woman's backbone. "Now, so help me, lass, if you care a whit about this big lug uncle of yours, you and your family will be here for Christmas or I will make his life so miserable, he'll hightail it to Texas himself."

"Miserable?" Logan grunted. "Don't you mean 'more' miserable?"

Rosie patted Cassie's cheeks as she sent Logan a scowl. "You haven't seen miserable," she muttered, "except in the mirror." She snatched the tin and handed it to Cassie. "Here—your favorites—snickerdoodles for the train. For you, not him, you hear?"

"Oh, Rosie, I'm going to miss you so much," Cassie said with a fond embrace. She leaned close to the old woman's ear. "And Uncle Logan really is wonderful, you know."

"Humph—matter of opinion. Gotta get back to the kitchen—don't want to burn the roast." She turned to hurry down the hall, tossing a thin smile over her shoulder. "Rump roast," she said, searing Logan with a look. "Because somebody invited *him* to dinner."

"Come on, Cass," Uncle Logan muttered, "before I ruffle the feathers of a cranky old bird." He opened the door. "And I'm not talking Miss B."

Hadley arrived with Cassie's suitcases in hand and affection in eyes that belied his usual stoic manner. "You will be sorely missed, Miss Cassidy."

"Thank you, Hadley, and the feeling is more than mutual, I assure you." Cassie gave the butler a tight squeeze, leaning close to his ear. "Don't let Rosie bully you, you hear?"

The makings of a grin inched across his lips. "No, Miss, I shan't."

"Hadley!" Rosie poked her head out the kitchen door. "I need you to snap the peas, lickety split."

The butler clicked his heels. "Yes, miss, tap the bees—honey coming right up."

"Peas!" Rosie screamed.

"Very good, miss," Hadley said loudly enough for Rosie to hear. He gave Cassie a wink.

Uncle Logan braced Cassie's shoulders. "It's time to go," he whispered, nudging her to the door. She leaned into him all the way down the steep marble steps lined with boxwoods to the cobblestone street where his black Mercedes Double Phaeton glimmered in the August sun. The others followed as Hadley and Logan placed her things in the backseat.

Aunt Cait tugged her into her arms. "Oh, Cassie, how I wish this had turned out differently, darling. My heart breaks for you . . . and for all of us."

Wetness pricked Cassie's eyes, and she was grateful no one but Al knew of Jamie's true motives in turning her away. As far as Aunt Cait, Uncle Logan, and Meg knew, she cared for Jamie so deeply that friendship was too painful an option to stay. She pulled back, attempting a grin she hoped would deflect the grief in her eyes. "Well, like Daddy always says, 'keep all skunks, bankers, and lawyers at a distance'—and I reckon this way, I'm doing two of the three."

"Ready?" Uncle Logan helped Cassie into the front seat while the others crowded around.

"Bye, Cassie—we love you!" Maddie's little fingers pinched tight on Uncle Logan's car, and it was all Cassie could do to keep from bawling.

She stroked her cheek. "Love you, too, shortcake," she whispered.

Alli hefted Maddie up in her arms, blinking the gloss from her eyes. "So help me, Cass, the next time I see MacKenna, I have a good mind to slap him alongside the head for being so blamed stupid. I swear, the boy's so slow, he couldn't catch a cold."

"Just give me the word, Cass, and I'll dock his pay." Uncle Logan rounded the car, the humor in his tone at odds with the sobriety in his eyes.

Aunt Cait's chuckle seemed forced. "Well, as difficult as it may be, I suppose it's best if we all try to forgive and forget. Come Christmas, Cassie will be back and it'll all be behind us."

Cassie sighed while Uncle Logan started the car, the rumble

of the engine drowning out all farewells. *One can only hope*, she thought as the automobile veered away from the curb, the family she loved slowly fading from view. "Forgive and forget," Aunt Cait had said. The sea breeze cooled the tears on her face while Jamie's memory lingered in her mind. Forgive? She swallowed hard, painful emotion clogging her throat. Most certainly. But forget? Uncle Logan gave her hand a gentle squeeze and more moisture pooled in her eyes.

Oh, not for a long, long while.

So this is what it feels like . . . a child leaving the nest. Caitlyn stared blankly out the open French doors of her study, gaze fixed on the cobblestone street where Cassie said goodbye not twenty-four hours ago. Last night the house felt like a tomb—no cousins giggling or whispering secrets, no laughter from games of whist, no playful gibes between Rosie and Logan. A sad smile edged her lips. Even Miss B. seemed blue, her raucous squawks notice-ably absent.

Caitlyn sighed and wandered aimlessly into the foyer where the early-morning light peeked through the glass of the lead-crystal front door. The noisy clatter of pots and pans in the kitchen confirmed Rosie's grumpy mood as she prepared for another day as somber as the house in Cassie's absence. Caitlyn paused with a hand to her eyes, heart heavy over the grief of her niece's departure, certainly, but also the painful circumstances that precipitated it. Few things weighted a heart more than loving someone you could never have, and all at once Jamie's image merged into Logan's. Perhaps that was part of the reason she was taking Cassie's de-parture so hard—her niece and she shared a common bond that had knit them close—loving two men who didn't share their faith and were now estranged from them both. Thank goodness Cassie would have the strength of distance to help ease her pain. *Unlike me*, Caitlyn realized, the polite chill of Napa between Logan and her growing cooler all the time. Which was exactly why she'd sent her resignation to Walter a few days ago—clearly her feud with Logan made her an albatross around the committee's neck, especially in light of their proposal being denied.

The front door opened and Hadley stepped through with a newspaper under his arm, distinguished as always in his crisp white shirt with black tails despite the sprig of juniper in his hair. A smile played at the corners of Caitlyn's mouth as she stared at her beloved butler, his craggy face especially handsome with the absence of his new glasses. "The paperboy missed again?" she asked loudly enough for him to hear, plucking the juniper from his silver hair.

"I'm afraid so, miss," Hadley said with his usual calm, a smile shadowing lips that never voiced a complaint. "I do believe the young ruffian relishes the thought of me rifling through the brush each morning. But I don't mind. Rather like a trek through the jungle, if you will."

She stood on tiptoe to graze an affectionate kiss to the old butler's cheek. "Perhaps because you've misplaced your glasses again, Mr. Hadley?"

His eyes actually sparkled. "At times I find life to be more of an adventure without them, miss," he said with an imp of a smile, "especially where Mrs. O'Brien is concerned."

Caitlyn chuckled. "I do believe there's a scamp beneath that regal pose, dear Hadley."

He smiled. "Well, with Mrs. O'Brien, miss, one finds his pleasure wherever he can."

The doorbell rang, and she startled, glancing at the beveled glass door where the image of a man shone through along with the sunlight. She heard Rosie's shouts for Hadley to answer the door and patted his arm. "I'll get it, Hadley," she said with a grin, "and I'll leave Rosie to you."

"Very good, miss," he said with a click of his heels, but she noted humor in his eyes.

Peering through the thick glass, she sighed, grateful for something to do other than lament a niece who was more like a daughter. She opened the door to the disgruntled look of her dear friend, Walter Henry, and instantly unease churned over the resignation she'd tendered. "Walter," she said with more enthusiasm than she felt, "what a pleasant surprise."

His lips flattened into a wry smile. "Come on, Cait, we both know my visit is neither a surprise nor pleasant, judging from the pallor of your face." He removed his hat and nodded toward the foyer, sparse head gleaming with silver. "You plan to invite me in or do you want to duke it out here in the street?"

The blood that drained from her face upon Walter's arrival now whooshed back, heating her temper along with her cheeks. She opened the door wide, motioning for him to enter, but her knuckle-white grip on the crystal knob was a key indicator he wouldn't get far.

He marched past and turned mid-foyer, the pinch of his hat in gnarled fingers as taut as the clench of his jaw. "Resignation denied," he snapped, one bushy white brow jagging low. "Never figured you for a quitter, Cait."

Her anger seeped out on a weary sigh as she carefully shut the door. "I'm a liability, Walter," she said quietly, "and the Vigilance Committee will achieve far more if I'm out of the way." She reached to take his hat. "Would you like some lemonade to cool off?"

He snatched his bowler away. "The only thing that will cool me off, Mrs. McClare, is your retraction. And you're wrong—we'll achieve far more with you presiding over this board."

Her lips curved into a gentle smile, her affection for this friend as deep as if he were the doting father he always appeared to be. "Dear Walter," she said with a look of tenderness that eased the furl in his brow, "if I had misgivings about accepting the position before, I certainly have them now when my very presence has jeopardized the committee's most critical vote, and this after tireless months of work to even bring it before the Board. I just think it's best if—"

"It passed." The glint of anger became a twinkle as a smile crooked his weathered lips.

She blinked, her mouth still open from the statement he had so effectively halted. Shallow breaths wisped forth. "Pardon me?" He knew as well as she that the resolution had been defeated six to five after the meeting, including Logan's negative vote. "I don't understand," she whispered, barely able to speak. "The vote was taken—we lost."

The twinkle in his eye turned mischievous. "The preliminary vote, yes, Mrs. McClare, but the final vote debated behind closed doors?" He winked. "We won six to five."

"S-someone c-changed his v-vote?" Her mind scrambled to envision the faces of each and every board member. She recalled Logan's granite scowl while she'd taken the floor, and knew this would only deepen the divide of any civility they shared. "Who would do that?" she whispered, too stunned to be fully impacted by the victory they'd won.

Walter raised up on rolled heels as a satisfied smirk curled the edge of his lips. "Why don't you ask your brother-in-law?"

She blinked. "Excuse me?"

He grinned. "The deciding vote was his, Cait, although no one is supposed to know that."

With an audible gasp, she listed against the glass door, utterly speechless.

Walter's low chuckle prompted a blush to her cheeks. "You and I both know, Caitlyn, there's only one reason why a man with a vested interest in keeping the Coast as is would change his mind." He winked. "And she's standing before me right now." He grasped her hand to graze a soft kiss to her fingers. The warmth of his laughter tickled her skin. "So you see, Mrs. McClare, if you are a liability, it's to the opposition, my dear, not us."

"I . . . I c–can't believe that." Her voice was a rasp caught in her throat, the shock of Logan's actions effectively stealing her wind. And then in a rush of giddy air, laughter rolled from her lips in a little-girl giggle that brought a wide grin to her friend's face.

"Believe it, Cait—as you know, the closed-door vote is supposed to be secret, but I have it on good authority as to the board member who changed his mind." He lifted her gaping jaw with a gentle finger. "But you didn't hear it from me, understand?" The tenderness in his eyes was matched by his look of paternal pride. "There's only one person alive who could have changed Logan McClare's mind on that vote, male or female, and we need that person's influence on this board." He gave her chin an affectionate tap. "We need you, Cait."

"But—"

Head cocked, he held up a hand, the stiff bent of his mouth evidence he wouldn't take no for an answer. "No 'buts,' young lady. I expected at least a year's commitment from you, not a mere month, and besides, your position on this board can only assist in your plans to open a school for the poor in the Barbary Coast, can it not?"

The breath caught in her throat. The Hand of Hope School—her dream to bring hope to an area so badly in need—could certainly be served by her influence on this board. The moment Walter uttered the words, Caitlyn knew he was right. She drew in a calming breath and squeezed his hand. "You're a wily one, Walter Henry," she said with a tilt of a smile. "I may have the board chair, but it's a certain gentleman who garners the influence."

"Ah, yes, my dear, but when it comes to Logan McClare?" He leaned close with a sparkle in his eyes. "I'm not the one who has his ear, now, am I?"

Caitlyn shook her head, giving Walter a scold of a smile. The realization of what Logan had done suddenly spread through her chest like embers aglow that seeped all the way up to her cheeks, warming her blood. *No, Walter, not his ear.* Her stomach did a little flip. *Nor his heart . . .*

26

*T*hank you, God!" Replacing the telephone receiver, Jamie shot up from his desk with a shout before realizing God had nothing to do with it whatsoever. Nope, the credit for this was entirely Jamie's.

Regrettably, Logan hadn't been able to garner any influence, but Senator Hamilton was as good as his word and now Jess was on the docket of pro bono surgeries to be voted on next week. Adrenaline pumped through Jamie's veins as he glanced at the clock on his desk, grateful it was only six and Bram would still be here, no doubt preparing to assist Logan in court tomorrow. Jamie reached into his bottom drawer for two glasses and a bottle of his precious Dr Pepper, the last of a case Logan had given him for Christmas last year from the Dublin Dr Pepper Bottling Company in Waco, Texas. He usually reserved it strictly for special occasions, but this was clearly one. He needed to celebrate, and no one knew better than Bram the obstacles he'd overcome—most of which his friend approved, some he didn't. He thought of Bram's anger over his courting Patricia and hoped this news would soften his stance.

"Toss that witness list aside for the moment, buddy boy, we have serious celebration at hand." Jamie kicked Bram's door closed with the heel of his shoe and carried the Dr Pepper and glasses into his best friend's office, clunking both down with an ear-to-ear grin. "Jess is on the docket," he said, not even a bit embarrassed by the sheen of moisture that sprang to his eyes.

A grin that mirrored Jamie's inch for inch eased across Bram's lips despite the look of fatigue on his face. "No kidding?" He took the quarter glass of Dr Pepper Jamie poured and held it aloft like it was aged whiskey, clinking it with Jamie's. "That's great news, Mac," he said, belting his drink back as his friend did too. "So, who gets the credit—Logan, you, or the senator?"

Jamie dropped into the chair and poured a second round for them both with a laugh that sounded more like a grunt. "I think it's safe to say I had absolutely no clout in this whatsoever, counselor. The credit goes to the senator who not only legislated funding for Cooper Medical in the past, but just so happens to be golfing buddies with several key members of the board."

Bram let loose a low whistle. "I knew Hamilton had political influence, but I didn't know he had social pull too."

"Yep." Jamie crossed his legs on Bram's desk, swirling the dark liquid in his glass. "Which is why Patricia was my first choice right out the gate." He took a deep draw of his soda pop. "I'm just lucky she's smart and beautiful too."

"Yeah . . . lucky."

Jamie glanced up at Bram's sour tone, eyes in a squint. "How many times do I have to tell you—I had no choice."

A heavy exhale vented from Bram's lips. "Yeah, well, neither did Cassie, I guess."

Jamie's lips thinned along with his eyes. "What's that supposed to mean?"

Bram paused, watching him closely. "It means she's gone, Jamie."

The Dr Pepper curdled in his stomach the exact moment the air left his lungs, Bram's guarded look not boding well for this conversation. "What do you mean 'gone'?"

A sigh escaped Bram's lips. "I mean gone, Mac—left, called it quits, hightailed it home, you know—*vamoose* in Texas vernacular."

The soda turned to sludge in his system, obstructing his windpipe. *Cassie? Gone?* "Why?" It came out as a croak.

Bram studied him over the rim of his glass. A mix of sympathy and frustration shone in sky-blue eyes that darkened to the same stormy gray of San Francisco Bay during a squall. "Well, Blake said she went home to help her mother teach at a reservation school, but judging from the look in Alli's eyes when I played tennis with her over the weekend? I'd say it's something more."

Jamie tossed a hefty swig down his throat, the pop burning as much as his conscience. "What do you mean 'more'?" he whispered, gaze focused on the bottle on Bram's desk.

"Well, let's put it this way, Mac. When I asked why Cass left so suddenly without saying goodbye to you or to me, Al muttered something I obviously wasn't supposed to hear, but I managed to catch the tail end . . ."

Jamie peered up, the knot in his chest getting tighter all the time. "Which was . . . ?"

Sympathy radiated from his best friend's eyes. "Sounded an awful lot like. . . 'pretty-boy fortune hunters.'"

All blood drained from Jamie's face.

The edge of Bram's lip crooked. "Right before she unleashed the most wicked swing I've ever seen. Could have peeled the flannel from the ball."

Jamie's eyelids lumbered closed as a silent groan rose in his throat, heart constricting at the thought of Cassie ever finding out why he'd chosen Patricia over her. He put a hand to his eyes, his breathing shallow. "How could she possibly know? You're the only one I've ever told the whole truth to. I only told Cassie part of it, that I couldn't meet her demands of faith in God and nothing more, which was certainly true, especially after God socked me in the gut with the news that her family was poor." He gouged a hand through his hair, stomach wrenching at the prospect of causing Cassie such pain. He glanced up, the same panic he felt in his gut bleeding into his voice. "We were fine at Blake's party, I swear. She was resigned to just being friends—she told me so. So what on earth happened between now and then?"

Bram shook his head, setting his drink back on his desk. "I don't know, but if it's true, I can't imagine the damage it did, first getting jilted by a fortune hunter in Texas, then by you . . ."

The reality of Bram's words sliced through him, and he slammed his drink down and angled in, eyes itching hot and fists clenched on the desk. "I am not some callous fortune hunter!" he shouted, the very word making him feel dirty. "I'm just a man taking care of my family because God won't, and blast it, Bram—I have every right to court whomever I please."

Expelling a weary sigh, Bram leaned against the leather head-rest while his hands draped over the arms of the chair, eyes wary. "Yes, you do, Jamie, but the truth is, if money and influence are your governing motives, well, I'm afraid you have a difficult defense, counselor, convincing anyone the title doesn't fit." He paused, voice fading to soft. "Especially Cassie."

Jamie stared while ragged breaths pumped from his lungs, the truth exposing him in his mind's eye for the very first time, forcing him to see himself through Cassie's eyes instead of his own. Branding him for what he truly was—a man who used his charm and looks to prey on wealthy women, no matter the rationale. His heart cramped in his chest. He'd always told himself the end justified the means, that he was only taking care of his family the best way he knew how. Trying to convince himself—and Bram—that if he planned to marry anyway, he may as well marry rich. But Bram had warned him once he would fall in love with whom God chose, not him, and sometimes a fortune didn't come with it. A painful truth Jamie learned all too well.

He sagged back in his chair, eyes wandering into a glazed stare. He'd convinced himself as long as Cassie was a part of his life, as long as they remained friends, he could do this, sell his soul to the highest bidder. But suddenly her absence and the pain he'd caused left a gaping hole, not only stripping away his pride, but his joy and hope as well. "She must hate me," he whispered, the glow over the potential surgery as stone cold as Cassie's feelings for him.

"I doubt it," Bram said quietly. "She's hurting, certainly, but she cares about you and she cares about God, which means she'll do what he asks her to do—she'll forgive you."

Jamie put his head in his hands, despair sucking the life from his soul as surely as it sucked the air from his lungs. "But can I forgive myself? I wounded her, broke her trust . . ."

"Yes, you did, Mac, but keep in mind her trust isn't in you anymore—it's in God—where it belongs." His chair squealed, and Jamie looked up, almost desperate enough to listen to his best friend's prattle about God for once, anything to alleviate this suffocating feeling. Bram bent forward, arms folded on his desk and eyes intense. "Because Cassie knows no matter the pain or situation, God'll see her through . . . just like he'll do for you, Jamie, if you'd let him."

"And how would he do that, Bram?" His voice was hollow, echoing the hopelessness he felt inside. "He hasn't been there before, what makes you think he'd be there now?"

Bram's eyes softened. "He's been there, Jamie, you just never acknowledged it before, but think about it. You're a kid from the Barbary Coast, poised to become one of the best lawyers in the city and a legislator down the road." Bram hesitated. "Do you really think you did that all by yourself?"

Jamie blinked, fully aware of the near-impossible task he'd accomplished. It was unheard of for a boy from the slums to ever finish school, much less graduate Stanford Law with honors. His eyes weighted closed and suddenly he remembered all the breaks that had come his way—the men on the docks taking a liking to him, his aunt sending his mother funds after his father died, jobs that had been so plentiful when he needed to earn money, not to mention the doctor's discounts for Jess's medicine. Realization pricked like a pinpoint of light through a dark, damp fog of despair. Could it be true? Did God actually care about him? About his mother and Jess?

As if sensing Jamie's train of thought, Bram slanted in, the fervor in his tone matching that in his eyes. "If God has taken care of you all these years without your consent, Mac," he said quietly, "just imagine what he could do if you let go and gave him free rein . . ."

Jamie's eyes flicked up. "Free rein . . . ," he whispered, wishing more than anything he could do just that, shift the burden of worry off his own shoulders onto those of some invisible Being, to be finally set free from the guilt that gnawed at him day in and day out. To trust someone other than himself. He shook his head. "Trust me, Bram, there's nothing I'd rather do than turn this mess I've made of my life over to God or anybody, but there's too much at stake."

"Yeah, there is, Mac—your happiness, Cassie's, and your family's. Right now, you're barely one for three. Do you really want to trust the people you love to that kind of record?"

Jamie kneaded his temple with the ball of his hand, frustration roiling in his gut. "No, but you don't understand—I don't have a choice. Believe me, I'd give anything to be courting Cassie instead of Patricia, you know that, but I need the senator's influence."

"And his money?"

Pretty-boy fortune hunter. Jamie winced, hand to his head. He paused, taking too long to answer. "I thought so, but now I'd give anything just to have Jess well and Cassie by my side."

"Anything?"

Jamie seared him with a look, vehemence in his tone taking him by surprise. "*Anything.*"

The faintest glimmer of a smile played on Bram's lips. "How 'bout that stubborn pride, then, MacKenna? Laying it down to let God have his way? After all, faith can move mountains, you know—be they granite . . . ," the smile edged into a grin, "or pig-headed pride."

As if in a trance, Jamie lapsed into a cold stare, jaw shifting the barest amount while Bram's statement rolled around in his head. He finally looked up. "What if God's way doesn't include a surgery for Jess?" he whispered, the tension in his neck seeping into his tone, clipping his words. "And she has to live in pain the rest of her life?"

"Tell me, Mac—do you love your sister?" Bram asked quietly.

"What kind of stupid question is that, Hughes—I'd give my life for my sister." A scowl tainted Jamie's lips. "Blast it, I *am* giving my life for my sister!"

Bram sighed and leaned back in his chair. "Then, it's no different with God. He loves you and he loves Jess—so much that he gave his life for you both. If you want the very best for your sister, Mac, then do it his way, not yours. And 'his way' says to 'commit your way unto him, trust him, and he shall bring it to pass.'"

Jamie shook his head. "You have no idea how much I wish I could believe that, Bram, but I've come too far in helping my sister. I can't risk throwing it all away now because I wish things were different—I can't do that to Jess."

"And what about Cass?" Bram whispered, her very name twisting Jamie's gut.

He closed his eyes, seeing her face, missing her so much, it was a physical ache. The pinprick of hope flickered briefly and then faded to black, sealing Jamie's decision. "Jess's health has to come before anything I want, even my love for Cassie." He downed the rest of his pop. "That's just the way it's gotta be."

"For now," Bram said softly. "I know you don't understand this, but God's Word says not to lean unto your own understanding. Tells us to acknowledge him in all our ways, and he will direct our paths." He slid his empty glass across the desk. "That's how I plan to pray for you, my friend, that you'll relinquish control and let God lead the way to your future and Jess's." He paused, a measure to his words. "And I'm asking you to do the same. Will you?"

Jamie peered up with a half smile. "Me? Pray?"

Bram grinned. "Yeah—you. I get real sick of hauling your sorry life out of the pits all by myself, you know that?"

A chuckle escaped Jamie's lips, easing the tension in his jaw. "Yeah, I do." Collecting the bottle and glasses, he rose to his feet, not sure if the warmth he felt was from the Dr Pepper or the comfort of words from a man he trusted. "And I will," he said on his way to the door. He raised the bottle in a mock toast. "Because it sure in the blazes can't hurt."

27

*S*oooo, young lady . . ." Virginia McClare doled out a Texas-size piece of peach cobbler for her daughter in the cozy, candlelit dining room where Cassie had eaten many a holiday meal. Her mother topped it with a scoop of homemade ice cream, then sailed it across the polished oak table now graced with a crystal vase of Mama's yellow tea roses. "You've filled us in on everyone in San Francisco except for that nice young man you always talked about in your letters." She looked up with a smile. "Jamie, was it?"

Coffee pooled in Cassie's mouth. Oh drat, why had she written so much about Jamie in her letters to her parents? *Um . . . because I was falling in love with the mangy, flea-infested mongrel?* She swallowed her coffee in a thick gulp while she reached for the cobbler, scrambling for an answer that would satisfy a woman who could read her daughter's mind like the front page of the *Humble Gazette*. It was bad enough the low-down, mealy-mouth weasel of a womanizer invaded her thoughts on a daily basis, but the last thing she wanted was to ruin her welcome-home dinner with talk of a skunk named Jamie MacKenna. *Talk about indigestion!*

"I was sure I detected a spark of interest on your part, darling," she continued, cutting cobbler for herself, "which is why I was

327

surprised you wanted to come home." Her mother eased into her seat to partake of dessert, assessing Cassie with an innocent stare that was anything but. Knowing her mother, she wanted details, and Cassie would have killed for a peach pit to choke on, anything to keep from talking about Jamie. "So, why the rush to come home, Cass?"

Why the rush? *Because another yellow-bellied, dirt-sucking snake of a man slithered into my life to steal my heart, that's why.* "Goodness, Mother, I swear even Rosie can't touch your cobbler, and peach no less—my very favorite."

Shoving his empty plate away, Quinn McClare folded burly arms on the table, his penetrating gaze more deadly than her mother's. As handsome as his brother in a laid-back flannel kind of way, her father was every bit as shrewd as Uncle Logan, parlaying barren farmland into one of the biggest cattle spreads in East Texas before debt and disease took its toll. And, like his political brother, an influential force in Humble government. That is, until his oil investments veered south, bleeding his assets—and his reputation—as dry as a Texas drought. Green eyes darker than her own studied her with an unflappable air of calm that typified her daddy, grounding her with the stability to come clean with the two people she loved most.

He cleared his throat and reached for a toothpick. "Sidestepping the question isn't going to fly in this neck of the woods, Sweet Pea. Both your mama and I can sense you're not right, so you may as well spit it out, 'cause none of us are getting up from this table till you do. Something happened in San Francisco to steal the roses from your cheeks, darlin', and we aim to know what it is." His jaw set while the toothpick rolled around the corner of his mouth. "Now . . . just who is this Jamie character and what's your relationship with him?"

A groan escaped on the wave of a blustery sigh. She dropped her fork on the cobbler and pushed her plate aside, sagging back in her chair. She'd forgotten how prying two parents who loved her could be. "Jamie is Blake's best friend and a lawyer in Uncle Logan's firm and practically family, so we became friends."

"Just friends?" The furrow in his brow was so like Uncle Logan's that Cassie's heart cramped in her chest, suddenly homesick for San Francisco.

"At first," she whispered, avoiding his eyes while she toyed with the handle of her fork.

Her mother leaned in, eyes tender but smile wary. "You're in love with him, aren't you?"

She should have expected it—her parents' keen intuition when it came to her happiness, but still the question shook her to the core, water filling her eyes like a flash flood. With a shaky nod, tears spilled down her cheeks and instantly they both shot from their chairs, Daddy tugging her up in his arms while Mama hovered close with a gentle hand to her back. "I . . . n-never int-tended t-to, but h-he p-poured on the charm and I . . . I . . ."

Her voice broke on a sob, and Daddy cradled her shoulder to usher her into the next room with its hewn wood beams and simple oak furniture while her golden retriever Gus trotted behind. Tucked between her parents, Cassie sagged back on a rough-sawn wood couch Daddy had built and Mama upholstered in hues so earthy and vibrant, like the hill country of Texas. With liquid brown eyes as sorrowful as Cassie's own, Gus plopped down in front of her, sinking against her with a comfort as warm as the two people beside her. "What happened, Cass?" Daddy whispered with a stroke of her hair, and suddenly Cassie knew she'd done the right thing in packing her bags to head home. Pulling away with a sniff, she took the handkerchief he offered and blew her nose while Mama soothed with a steady caress of her back.

"I didn't like him at first because he reminded me so much of Mark—too good-looking for his own good and more charm and blarney than a Dublin peddler convention." She drew in a wobbly breath and released it again, dabbing her eyes with the cloth. "But he wouldn't take no for an answer, you see, and kept pressing to court me."

"Did you say yes?" Mama asked, tucking several flyaway hairs behind Cassie's ear.

"No, he has no faith in God, Mama, and Aunt Cait warned me about that."

Daddy squeezed her waist. "Good girl. Aunt Cait's a wise woman in matters like this."

Giving a nasal sniff, Cassie looked up. "I know, she told me—with Uncle Logan."

"She told you that?" Mama said, eyes wide as she bent forward.

Cassie nodded. "We became very close, Mama—Aunt Cait's a lot like you, you know."

"So what happened with this boy, Cass?" Quinn McClare was apparently in no mood to dally when it came to the welfare of his daughter.

A sigh withered on Cassie's lips. "He said he would do anything to court me, Daddy, so I told him the only way I would even consider courtship was if his faith in God matched mine. I made a deal that if he was willing to remain friends while he went to church with me and discussed *Pilgrim's Progress* once a week, I might reconsider."

"And?" Mama shifted to face her.

"He did and so I did." A heave bubbled in Cassie's throat and she blew her nose, her voice trailing off into a weak sob. "And then he said he only wanted to be friends . . ."

"Aw, Pumpkin." Daddy swallowed her up in a bear hug that smelled of pine and leather and hay. "Why would that scalawag say something like that after tracking you like a coyote?"

"B-because of God, he said. Claims we don't think the same way and he wouldn't meet my expectations."

"The boy has a point, darling," Mama said quietly.

"B-but that wasn't the real reason, Mama," Cassie said with a quiver in her throat. "I found out from the girl he's courting now that it was because she's rich and I'm not."

"What?" Quinn McClare sat straight up, fire in his eyes that could have singed his brows. "The polecat's already courting somebody new *and* he's a fortune hunter? Does Logan know?"

"No, Daddy, and I don't want him to, please. Alli is the only one I told, and all I want to do is forget that I ever met Jamie MacKenna."

"Well, you can bet your sweet bloomers we'll certainly see to that—"

"Boss?"

Quinn McClare glanced up to where his foreman John Redstone stood with another man in the door, hats in their hands. He waved the men in. "Come on in, Red."

Red ambled in, affection etched into every wrinkle of his craggy face. "Well, I'll be bound and gagged! Miss Cassidy, you sure are a sight for sore eyes—welcome home." He strode across the room to give her a hug that lifted her clear off her feet. "It's just plumb dull around here without you, sweetheart, so I sure hope you're here to stay."

"Uncle Red!" Swiping at her eyes, Cassie squeezed the big man who'd fawned over her since she was paw-high to a prairie dog. "I missed you too, and yes, I'm home for good."

"Good to hear." He set her down and waved the other gentleman forward, more lines crinkling at the edges of his eyes. "Sorry to interrupt your homecoming, Cass, but the Boss Man's been hankering to meet this here feller for a long time." Red hooked an arm to the shoulder of a man dressed in a pin-striped shirt and tie that would have been fashionable if the sleeves weren't rolled up and his tan muscled arms splotched with mud. "Boss, Mrs. McClare, Cass—Mr. Zane Carter—the man who's going to help us turn those dry wells into rivers of oil."

The gentleman extended a hand to Cassie's father, pumping it with a flash of white teeth that instantly put Cassie on edge. Matching her father's six-foot-two height and then some, the man reminded her of Mark in a more rugged, natural sort of way. Coal black hair neatly combed back explained a shadow of beard on his angular jaw, and khaki trousers displayed smudges of dirt matching those on his arms, indicating a man who didn't mind hard work. "It's a pleasure to meet you, Mr. McClare," he said, tone conveying respect. "Captain Lucas speaks highly of you."

"Not as highly as he speaks of you," her father said with a deep chuckle. "Says you're the son he never had and the answer to my prayers. Thank you for agreeing to bring the new drill bit and oversee the drilling in what so far has been a very disappointing venture. We're certainly hoping you can change that." Quinn looped an arm to Cassie's waist. "Mr. Carter—this is my wife Virginia McClare and our daughter Cassidy."

"Call me Zane, please," the man said with a quick smile to both her mother and her. "I hope so too, sir. I spent the afternoon at the drilling site and there's no question the cable tool you've been using is ill-equipped. It can't handle the tricky sands of the salt dome, which is the problem Captain Lucas had at Spindletop. The new drill bit is expensive, to be sure, but I have every confidence it'll be the best money you ever spent. Between it and the solution Captain Lucas's partner Mr. Hamill came up with to pump mud down the hole instead of water, I expect to see a gusher that could give Spindletop a run for its money." The grin flashed again, revealing dimples that put Cassie on guard. "And we all know what happened there."

"Yes, sir, we do," Quinn said with a deep chuckle. "My friend Captain Lucas went from near bankruptcy like me to an oil gusher the likes of which the world has never seen."

Cassie eyes spanned wide. "Daddy, do you mean . . ." She swallowed a swell of hope in her throat. "The Bar J might not go to auction after all? That things may turn around?"

Quinn McClare cupped his daughter's face in hands rough from an honest man's work and a tireless spirit. "We didn't want to get your hopes up, Cass, till we were sure we had the funds to implement our plan, but now that you're home, you need to know—I believe this young man is the answer to our prayers." His lip crooked. "Along with your Uncle Logan, of course."

"Uncle Logan?" Cassie's gaze flicked to her parents, noting the exchange of a smile.

Hip cocked, her father folded thick arms. "Yes, young lady. Apparently *someone* leaked we were on our last legs down here," he said with a jag of his brow.

She bit her lip. "I know I wasn't supposed to say anything, Daddy, but I was so worried and you know Uncle Logan . . ."

"Yes, I know Uncle Logan—the talent to drill deeper than any newfangled bit this young man has to offer. When you spilled the Texas beans, darlin', my brother went behind my back after I turned down his offer of a loan. Made an investment in Spindletop contingent upon aid given to Bar J to staunch the red ink. Which," Quinn said with a nod at Zane, "is why Mr. Carter is here. He was the chief engineer at Spindletop after countless dry wells." Her father slapped Zane on the back. "Welcome aboard, young man. Care for some coffee and peach cobbler?"

Zane's smile eased into regret. "I wish I could, Mr. McClare, but I was so anxious to check out the drill site, I left my bags at the station. I really should check into my hotel and clean up."

"Hotel?" Her father cuffed the man's shoulder. "Nonsense. I insist you stay on the ranch, young man. My wife and daughter will be happy to ready a guest room for you upstairs."

Shock replaced the smile on the man's face—*and* Cassie's. "I really couldn't impose, Mr. McClare, after all I could be here for the next few months or longer."

"And I'll be in your debt even longer than that, young man, if you're a tenth the miracle worker Lucas says. You retrieve your bags and hightail it back. Your room will be waiting."

Zane shook her father's hand. "Thank you, sir, that's very kind. Well, I best be going, but rest assured I intend to focus my efforts on seeing that your days of dry wells are over." He nodded to her mother and her, gaze lighting on Cassie with a veiled smile of interest. Her jaw tightened when she returned his smile with a stiff one of her own. *Oh, no, mister, get that pretty-boy gleam right out of your eye. Daddy's days of dry wells may be over, but if you're looking to dig anything but oil, yours are just beginning.*

"What a nice young man," her mother whispered when Daddy walked them to the door.

Cassie raised a hand. "Don't even start, Mama. In order for me to look twice at another pretty boy like that, he'll have to grow a wart and develop a slight-to-moderate case of lazy eye."

Her mother's laughter warmed her spirits. "No he won't, Cass," she said with a gentle pat. "God'll send a man who'll turn both your head and your heart without a cross-eyed stare."

"By thunder, gotta feeling we're fixin' to turn a corner here." Her father strode into the parlour with a broad smile. "Ginny, tell Teresa we'll be able to hire more help soon."

"Oh, Quinn, I hope you're right." Her mother hurried to give him a hug. "Even so, I've enjoyed helping Teresa in the kitchen again." She cupped his face, eyes glowing with love, and Cassie wondered if she'd ever feel that way. "It takes me back to when we were first married."

"*You* take me back to when we were first married," he said with a brush of his lips to hers. "So," he said with a wink in Cassie's direction, "hope you've been practicing your billiard skills in San Francisco, Sweet Pea, because suddenly I'm feeling mighty lucky."

"Lucky, eh?" Cassie said with a chuckle, smile fading when thoughts of Jamie flashed in her mind. "Well, I hope your luck is better than mine," she said with a cumbersome sigh. She followed her father to the knotty-pine game table he'd built for her, now sitting in front of the hearth. Her lips swagged to the left. *And Mr. Zane Carter's.*

28

Jamie studied the chessboard with a keen eye in the cozy parlour of Mrs. Tucker's boardinghouse, wishing just once he could trounce his sister at chess. "I'm afraid the wrong MacKenna went to law school," he muttered, his fraternal side proud his sister was such a prodigy at "the thinking man's game." His competitive side? A wee bit testy at getting beat by a girl. His thoughts leapfrogged to Cassie, and his sour mood ebbed into the aching malaise that had engulfed him since he'd learned she'd gone home. Biting back a scowl, he moved his pawn, well aware when it came to strategy, Jess had him right where she wanted him.

Just like Patricia and her father.

Eyes dancing from the shimmer of the gas chandelier overhead, his sister eased her queen up to capture his pawn. "Checkmate!" she said with a glow that indicated she'd had a rare good day, made even better by a win over her brother.

Jamie relented with a smile, the little-girl grin on his sister's face more than enough to chase his shadows away. "I'll tell you what, Jess, you're going to cause quite a stir in college."

The light in his sister's unusual ochre eyes dimmed imperceptibly, although her smile never faltered. "*If* I go to college, dear brother . . . ," she said, commencing to reset the board.

"Oh, you're going all right." Jamie's voice lowered as he glanced at several gentlemen boarders who were preoccupied with newspapers while his mother chatted with Mrs. Tucker over needlepoint. "We've been planning this far too long, and your pro bono surgery is just the first step." Excitement edged his voice as his gaze connected with hers. "Which, as I mentioned before," he said with a flicker of a smile, "will be voted on next week."

"But they may not vote in our favor," Jess said, nibbling at the edge of her lip.

"Not to worry, Peanut." He winked. "I have a strong suspicion they will."

A wispy sigh floated from her lips. "Even so—a college education is expensive, especially for a mere woman." Her pert chin dimpled in a dubious frown, voice dipping low to mimic Dr. Edward Clark in his widely respected *Sex and Education* treatise: "'A girl could study and learn, but she could not do all this and retain uninjured health, and a future secure from neuralgia, uterine disease, hysteria, and other derangements of the nervous system.'"

"Balderdash," Jamie growled under his breath. "I'll wager you could show Dr. Clark the error of his ways in one game of chess."

She gave him a patient smile that made her look older than sixteen despite the youthfulness of pale cheeks framed by lustrous black curls. "Dr. Clark's ill-spoken words may be fallacy, James MacKenna, but the expense of a college education is not."

Jamie repositioned his chess pieces with a grunt. "You let me worry about that."

Her frail hand lighted upon his with a tender gaze. "That's just it, Jammy," she whispered, resorting to his childhood nickname as he had with her. "I don't want you to worry."

"A little late for that now," he grumbled in jest. "Where was your concern when you so handily stripped your brother of his male pride only moments ago?"

"Oh, pish-posh." Her soft chuckles warmed his heart. "You let me win and you know it."

"I beg your pardon," Jamie said with a true note of indignation. "I'll have you know that James MacKenna does not throw a game for anyone, even a precocious baby sister."

"Really and truly?" She clasped her hands, eyes a twinkle like a child at Christmas.

"Really and truly." His gaze softened. "I would never lie to you, Jess."

Her lips curved into the most beautiful smile. "I know." She paused long enough for tears to well in her eyes. "Which compels me to ask something to which I need an honest answer."

"Yes?" He slanted in, arms crossed on the table, pinning her with a mock serious gaze.

"Why are you so sad?" she whispered.

His skin chilled, puckers popping at the bridge of his nose. "Sad? What kind of harebrained question is that? You just obliterated me in chess, you little dickens."

"No, not that," she said softly. "You're not as happy as you used to be and lately you never . . . ," she hesitated, teeth grazing her lip, "mention your friend Cassie anymore."

His heart thudded to a dead stop as he stared, the mere mention of Cassie's name siphoning the blood from his face. "She's gone back to Texas," he whispered, rising to his feet as casually as possible given the boulder in his gut. "Give me a chance to redeem my pride, kiddo—how 'bout a game of Persian Rummy instead?" Avoiding her eyes, he carefully lifted the chessboard to an ornate wood buffet and replaced it with a deck of cards from the top drawer.

"Why?" Jess asked with an innocence that stabbed. Just like the stab of Alli's loaded response when he'd finally gotten the nerve to pose the same question to her the week after Cassie had left.

"To heal from the damage you've done."

The damage he'd done. To a woman he cared about. His eyes faltered closed for a split second as realization throbbed. *No, to a woman I love ...*

"Jamie?"

He blinked up at his sister, suddenly too depleted to hide the ache that he felt. "Because I hurt her," he said, the admission all but stealing the air from his lungs. He proceeded to shuffle the cards, desperate to fight the awful malaise that always settled whenever he heard her name, saw her face in his mind's eye, remembered the awful decision he'd made.

"How?"

His palms stilled on the stack of cards. "I decided to court Patricia instead of her."

"And that hurt her because she cares about you?"

He nodded dumbly, finally shaking off his stupor to shuffle the cards one final time.

Jess paused, the truth dawning in her eyes. "Oh, Jamie ... and you truly care about her, don't you?" The words were uttered in awe.

"A great deal," he said quietly, dealing thirteen cards to them both.

"Then why are you courting Patricia?"

He glanced up, wincing at the childlike simplicity of such a question. "It's complicated, Jess, but suffice it to say that Patricia is better suited for me."

Jess's pause was longer this time, her voice a strained whisper. "And me?"

His fingers froze on the card he'd just flipped face up on the discard pile. "What?"

Her chin rose the slightest degree, a motion he'd noted well the rare times he'd led in a game of chess. "How much influence has Patricia's father wielded on my behalf, Jamie?"

He strove for nonchalance, studying his cards while a neck muscle twittered. "Some."

"Because you're courting his daughter?"

"Partially," he muttered, eyes still averted. "Your draw, Jess."

"No."

His gaze flicked up. "You don't want to play rummy?"

She blinked against a fresh sheen of moisture that pooled in her eyes. "No. I won't let you sacrifice your life for mine."

Ice glazed in his veins. "What are you talking about?"

Her chin quivered despite the firm press of lips. "I won't have the surgery, it's as simple as that, even if they vote on it. Not if it means you courting a woman you don't even love."

His jaw went slack. "You can't be serious—"

"Do you love her?" She angled in, fingers pinched on the table. "This Patricia?"

Heat singed the back of his neck. "I'm courting her, aren't I?"

"That's not an answer. And you said you would never lie to me, Jamie." Her chin jutted higher as the moisture in her eyes glinted into anger, giving her the force of a woman rather than a little girl. She enunciated each word, voice climbing in volume. "Do-you-love-her?"

He slapped his cards on the table, gaze darting to where his mother paused in her conversation to send a cursory glance their way. "No," he emphasized, "but I will."

"Do you love Cassie?"

Blood gorged his cheeks. "That's none of your business, Jess."

She banged a fist on the table, displaying a temper he seldom saw in his shy and gentle sister. "It is if I'm the reason you're opting for a marriage without love."

He gripped her hand, eyes locked on hers with an intensity that fairly shimmered the air between them. "Don't do this, Jess," he whispered harshly. "I need this surgery as much as you. Don't fight me when I'm giving you my all."

His heart cramped when a tear dribbled down her cheek, and her words quivered as much as her lip. "It's not your 'all' I want, Jamie," she said gently. "It's God's."

A heave ricocheted in his chest as he dropped her hand. *God. Always God.* First his mother and sister, then Bram and Cassie. "The Hound of Heaven," as the tortured poet Francis Thompson proclaimed, an apt description for a God in relentless pursuit of a soul. *His.* A tic pulsed in his jaw. "How can you say that, Jess? What has God ever done for you?" he hissed.

"Oh, Jamie . . ." Her voice was a broken whisper underscored by the wetness that pooled in her eyes. "Don't you know?" She grasped his hand and lifted it to her lips for the softest of kisses. "He's given me you."

He stared while her childlike gaze of adoration blurred before him, and in a violent rush of love, he lurched up from the table and knelt by her side, clutching her tightly. "I love you, Jess. Don't you know I would sell my soul to make you well?"

Her wobbly chuckle tickled his skin while he buried his head in her hair. "Your soul?" She kissed the side of his neck. "May I have that in writing, counselor?"

"Etched in stone," he vowed.

Pulling away, she placed a frail hand to his jaw, the glow in her eyes nearly ethereal. "Good, because that's exactly what I need you to do, brother dear—sell your soul." She patted his cheek. "But to God, Jamie MacKenna, not to Patricia . . ."

His pulse jerked to a halt. "Jess, no, please—"

"Oh, yes, Jammy, because you have no choice. Either you break it off with Patricia before the vote, or I will not agree to the surgery at all, and Mama will back me up."

Jaw gaping, he rose to his feet. "Tell me you're joking," he said, his voice strangled. "If I break it off with Patricia, there will be no surgery. All my time, work, research—all for nothing."

The light in her eyes seemed to intensify rather than dim. "Not for nothing, Jamie—in preparation for a miracle." She reached for his hand. "And not just in my hip."

He shook his head and backed away. "I can't, Jess. This is too important for blind faith."

The smile on her lips softened to tender. "It's only 'blind' to those who don't believe, Jamie, but once we lay our will down for God's, it's amazing just how much we can suddenly see. Some say 'seeing is believing,' but faith says 'believing is seeing.'" She tilted her head. "Will you do that for me? Will you merge your faith with Mama's and mine?"

Shame scalded the back of his neck. "I can't," he whispered. "I have no faith."

She started to rise and he lunged to anchor her, heart stopping at her grimace of pain. It quickly vanished when he cradled her close, her voice as pure and childlike as the girl he held in his arms. "'If ye have faith as a grain of mustard seed, ye shall say unto this mountain, remove hence to yonder place; and it shall remove; and nothing shall be impossible unto you.'" She glanced up with a smile so full of love, it thickened the walls of his throat. "Promise me, Jammy, you'll lay your will down for God's so he can bring us the miracle we all so desperately need."

Pulse staggering, he stared at his sister, his breathing shallow. Lay his will down for God's? Pry his fingers apart and let go, just like that? Trust a God he'd never trusted at all, just on a whim? His eyelids weighted closed. No, not on a whim. On a request from the sister he loved, the mother he cherished, and the friend he respected. The sting of tears burned in his nose when Cassie's image came to mind. *And the woman I want.*

His breath caught at the twine of Jess's fingers in his. "Let go, Jamie, and let God be God," she whispered, the trace of an imp in her smile. "He does it so much better than you."

Let God be God. He closed his eyes and in the whoosh of an exhale, he felt his will crack, a fissure of hope no bigger than a thread in a smothering shroud of disbelief. Relinquishing a weary sigh, he finally nodded, Bram's words echoing in his mind. *"Faith can move mountains, you know—be they granite . . . or pigheaded pride."*

His mouth quirked despite tears burning his lids. Pride he had plenty of, but faith? He drew in a shaky breath and released it, fluttering her ebony ringlets as he pressed a kiss to his sister's head. "Okay, Jess," he said, finally willing to let go—not the precious sister he cherished in his arms—but the pride that separated him from her God. Delicate arms quickly swallowed him whole.

Her God, yes. His heart skipped a fractured beat. And now, apparently—his.

Stifling a yawn, Caitlyn glanced at the crystal clock on the parlour mantel, wishing Blake had never challenged his uncle to a game of chess. Good grief, it was almost eleven and Maddie, Meg, and Alli had gone up to bed long ago. *Which is where I should be.* Caitlyn vented with a silent sigh. But Logan was finally here for dinner after a week out of town and she needed to speak to him tonight—alone—to thank him for what he'd done. Since Walter had given her the good news last week, she hadn't been able to sleep a wink, too excited about the victory. Her pulse sped up. *And* too overwhelmed by Logan's change of heart. Why had he done it—sacrificed his pride and his profits?

"I love you, Cait, and the fact is, I always have."

Her fingers quivered as she turned a page in her book, well aware his actions on her behalf did indeed seem to be a confirmation of his declaration at Napa, something that scared her to no end. But . . . not as much as losing his friendship. Since then, his visits had decreased and his manner toward her had become guarded and polite, focusing more on the children than on her. As reluctant as she was to admit it, she missed his tease and attention and longed to restore the close friendship they'd shared. *But please, Lord, don't let him press for more . . .*

"Checkmate!" A wide grin split Blake's face as he extended a hand across the table, his jubilant tone an indication of how seldom he bested his uncle. "Good game, Uncle Logan—I don't know if you're slipping or I'm getting better, but I'll take the win any way I can."

Pushing away from the table, Logan rose and shook Blake's hand, his low chuckle belying the tired slope of his shoulders. "Maybe a little bit of both, Blake, although I wouldn't count on it becoming a habit. Once the Barrows case is over, I'll be getting more sleep."

Blake stretched and glanced Caitlyn's way, surprise registering on his face. "Speaking of sleep, Mother, what are you still doing up? Lately you usually turn in when Maddie does."

Heat braised her cheeks as she delivered a smile with a casual turn of the page. "Yes, well it seems Miss Austen is one of the few who can capture my attention well beyond bedtime."

"And one of the few who could have me asleep in five minutes," Blake said with a chuckle. He nudged his chair in before striding to give her a hug. "Good night, Mother." On his way to the door, he gave his uncle a salute. "Good night, Uncle Logan. See you in the morning."

"Good night, Blake," Caitlyn called, gaze venturing to Logan while he slipped his jacket on. She rose, hands sweating as she smoothed the lines of her teal silk dress. "You heading out as well, I suppose?" she said and then blushed when she realized how stupid that sounded.

A faint smile shadowed his lips. "Unless you've a hankering to trounce me in chess too?"

"No, not chess . . ." She clutched arms to her waist, offering a bright smile to deflect the burn in her cheeks. "But I would appreciate a few words with you, if you can spare the time?"

He paused, the smile playing on his lips while piercing gray eyes took her measure with a narrow gaze. "I can spare all the time you need, Cait. After all, I'm just going home . . . not carousing with women all hours of the night."

The jab referencing her hurtful statement in Napa blazed her cheeks hot. "I should have never said that, Logan," she said quietly, eyes fixed on the floor. "I apologize—that was unkind."

"But true at one time, Cait, so apology accepted *and* totally understood." He strolled over to the divan by her chair and sat, hands loosely clasped. "So, what's on your mind?"

Eyes still averted, she eased down to perch on the edge of her chair, arms crossed tight as if she were cold. "Walter came by last week to tell me the good news, that our proposal passed."

"Yes, I know," he said with a scowl. "Apparently you have friends in high places—congratulations."

Her gaze rose to meet his. "Yes, one very good friend in particular," she whispered.

He stared, his face a mask except for a slight twitch in his cheek. "So it would seem." He stood and tugged on the sleeves of his coat, one of the rare times he appeared ill at ease. "It's late, Cait—is that all you wanted to say?"

"No," she whispered, rising to face him head-on. "I wanted to thank you, not only for giving me great joy, but for being the one person whose friendship I cherish above all others."

His eyes softened despite the press of his mouth. "Don't thank me, I had nothing to—"

She halted him with a gentle hand to his arm. "You had everything to do with it, Logan, so don't deny it." Her arm quivered as she touched tentative fingers to his cheek, the bristle of his late-day beard tickling her palm. "Thank you for your support—I will never forget it."

His body stilled before he cupped her fingers against his face, eyes suddenly tender. "I'd do anything for you, Cait," he whispered. "Don't you know that?"

A smile trembled on her lips. "No, actually I didn't . . . not until this." She slowly tugged her hand free and stepped back, exhaling a shuddery breath.

He folded his arms with a gruff clear of his throat. "Well, don't think this will become a habit, Madame President, because it won't."

"I understand," she said softly. She nervously buffed the side of her arms, almost shy as she avoided his eyes. "But I was hoping that maybe . . . well, you know, maybe we could let bygones be bygones and return to . . . ," a knot dipped in her throat as she peeked up, her vulnerability wavering her words, "being good friends again because the truth is I've . . . ," she swallowed hard, "well, I've . . . missed you, Logan."

He paused, his voice husky and low. "I've been right here, Cait," he said quietly.

She drew in a stabilizing breath, heart stuttering at the intensity in his eyes. "I . . . know, but . . . it wasn't the same. In Napa I said things, you said things, and it ruined what we had, made it stiff and formal and I . . ." Her gaze lifted, begging him to understand. "I miss our friendship."

He studied her for several moments, the burn of his gaze sputtering her pulse. "I miss our friendship too," he said softly, "and more." He extended a hand. "But it's a start, so why not?"

Oh, Logan, I can think of a dozen reasons. A sigh trembled from her lips as she placed her hand in his, the warmth of his touch traveling clear to her cheeks. "Friends forever, then," she whispered, giving a firm shake to dispel the trepidation she felt. She tried to pull away.

He held on, gaze fused to hers. "Friends forever, Cait, yes." Her stomach fluttered at the graze of his thumb to her palm. "For now . . ." Lifting her hand to his mouth, he skimmed her knuckles with his lips. "Good night, Mrs. McClare." He gave a short bow, then turned and strode from the room, her eyes fixed on his broad back until he disappeared from view.

She heard the click of the front door, and with a shaky whoosh of air, she sank to the edge of her seat, her breathing as ragged as her nerves. Head bent, she put a hand to her eyes.

For now.

Her insides quivered at the memory of his lips on her skin, the caress of his thumb to her palm, and she knew Logan McClare was waging a battle she wasn't sure she could win. But the question that shivered her mind, her body even more than his touch was one single thought.

Did she even want to?

29

"Nothing short of a miracle." Jean MacKenna's whisper held a note of awe as she gently tucked a raven strand of hair behind her daughter's ear while Jess lay sleeping in a hospital room as dark as her future was bright.

Jamie couldn't agree more. Forbidden tears swelled as he stood next to his mother, but he didn't even care, arm firmly latched to her waist with a staggering sense of gratitude. Medicinal smells that normally turned a stomach—the sharp odor of carbolic acid and pungent smell of linseed oil—filled both the room and their nostrils with the blessed scent of hope. Hope that the sister and daughter they loved would no longer limp or suffer with pain, but would enjoy a life full of promise and laughter and joy.

Jamie absently caressed Jess's fingers, too overcome to utter a single word lest water stream from his eyes. His little sister had been right. "Let go, Jamie, and let God be God," she'd whispered that day, conveying to him in her humble and sweet way a lesson many had tried to teach him before: "He does it so much better than you."

Emotion jerked in his throat. *That he does, Jess, that he does.* For the first time in his life, he had laid down his will for God's, an act of love and sacrifice at the bequest of his sister, and the result had stunned him to the core. Despite breaking his courtship with Patricia and her tearful threats, the board had voted to approve Jess's pro bono surgery. And as if that were not enough, his sister now resided in a private room on the coveted fourth floor of Lane Hospital following a surgery that the doctors proclaimed a resounding success. Jamie blinked, desperate to stave off the wetness that begged to fall. By all practical means, the vote should have failed, but God intervened, not only softening Patricia and Senator Hamilton's hearts, but Jamie's as well. *God, forgive me*, he thought, head bent to his mother's, *for turning my back on you all of these years, for being so blind, so stubborn* ... His lids weighted closed as Cassie came to mind, and his heart wrenched in his chest. *And so very, very stupid.*

He opened his eyes at his mother's touch. "I think I'll slip out to get us both a coffee."

"I'll go," he whispered, pressing a kiss to her hair.

"No, you need to be here if the doctor comes." She lifted on tiptoe to kiss his cheek, the sheen of wetness in her gaze threatening his own. "I love you, son, with every breath in me."

Clutching her tightly, he squeezed his eyes shut. "Me too, Mom, more than I can say."

She patted the scruff of his jaw, eyes brimming with pride. "You've more than said it, son, in your ceaseless devotion to your sister and me. Sit and get some rest. I'll be back soon."

He nodded and sank into the chair next to his sister's bed. Hand on her arm, he lay his head back and closed his eyes, overwhelmed by the goodness of God. In his pride and anger, he'd struggled all of his life to take care of his mother and sister when help had always been just a prayer away. He'd scaled mountain after mountain, when all it would have taken was a tiny seed of faith. His mouth tipped even as moisture stung beneath his lids.

The smallest of seeds, and yet enough to level mountains of pride and set his sister free.

And me.

Free! His eyelids popped open as the realization fully developed in his mind. *Free . . . to follow Cassie!* He jolted up in the chair, heart stumbling over the fact that the woman he loved hated him and with good reason. His breathing accelerated as hope sprung in his chest. But God wouldn't bring him this far to leave him high and dry. Would he?

Hope stalling, his gaze lighted on his sister, her chest rising and falling with a calm and steady rhythm so like her faith—peaceful, hopeful—and he suddenly knew God would not forsake him. At the thought, his body relaxed, the barest of smiles lining his lips as he rested his head on the chair, exhaustion and an unfamiliar peace luring him to doze . . .

"Our girl still sleeping?" Startled awake, he glanced up to see his mother enter the room, steam billowing from two cups of coffee she held in her hands.

Jamie jumped up to relieve her of his. "Like a baby. Dr. Morrissey said the more sleep, the better." He nodded at the chair. "Sit, Mom, you look as tired as Jess."

A soft chuckle parted from her lips, but it couldn't hide the sag of her shoulders when she dropped in the chair. "Thanks, Jamie—I'm quite certain we could all sleep for days after this. I'll tell you, I've never prayed so much in my life, and that's saying something."

Perching on the sill, he sipped his coffee, lips in a slant. "Me neither, and that's saying something too." He grazed the warmth of the cup. "But I plan to remedy that from now on."

She paused over the rim of hers, surprise flickering across her features. "Seriously?" Her wide gaze glistened with affection.

"Oh, Jamie, do you have any idea how long I've prayed for that?" Mischief laced her tone. "So dragging you to church all these years wasn't for naught?"

He laughed, peering up with a sheepish look. "No, it wasn't, although Jess gets the credit for pushing my back to the wall."

"How so?" His mother took a taste of coffee, head cocked in question.

His sigh was weary as he stared into the black liquid of his cup, mind wandering to how he'd escaped a future as bitter and dark. Since he'd begun courting Patricia, a gloom had descended, whisperings that he wouldn't be happy with a woman who wanted control of his heart or a father-in-law who wanted control of his life. But he'd convinced himself seeing Jess happy and whole would make *him* happy and whole, and that Cassie's friendship would fill in the gaps. But he hadn't counted on Cassie leaving and he hadn't counted on Jess sensing how miserable he was. He glanced up, heart aching that now he wouldn't be able to give his family all he had hoped. "She refused to have the surgery if it was contingent upon my courting Patricia."

"What?" Cup paused at her lips, her hands slowly drifted to her lap where she cradled the coffee. "What does that mean?"

He exhaled heavily. "It means I was courting Patricia to secure her father's help in swaying the vote for Jess's surgery."

"Oh, Jamie, no . . ." His mother rose to sit beside him, setting her coffee aside. "But I thought you liked Patricia . . ."

"I do, but not enough to marry her, and Jess called me on it." His smile tipped. "Told me to let go and let God, which I did, but it's kind of ironic." He placed his cup on the sill to scrub his face with his hands. "All I wanted was to save Jess's life, and here she ends up saving mine."

"Well, for the love of all that is decent and good, James

MacKenna, at least I have a daughter with common sense even if my son does not." Bracing his shoulder, she pressed a gentle kiss to his cheek, then clucked her tongue. "Hard head, soft heart," she whispered.

"I'll say. Patricia was furious. Said her father would never lend his support on the vote, which is why this surgery is such a miracle because apparently he did."

His mother hugged him, then pulled away, sympathy softening her tone. "I'm sorry it didn't work out, Jamie, but God will bring the perfect woman for you, you'll see."

He peered up, giving his mother a sideways glance. "Mom?"

She turned to look at him, cup halfway to her lips. "Yes?"

A slow smile traveled his face at thoughts of Cassie. "He already has."

His mother blinked. "But I thought you said you broke it off with Patricia?"

He grinned. "I did, but I'm not talking about Patricia, I'm talking about Blake's cousin." His chest expanded with hope. "I'm in love with Cassidy McClare, Mom, and I want to marry her." He exhaled slowly, offering a sheepish smile. "That is, if she doesn't spit in my eye first."

The mug slipped from his mother's hand and clunked to the floor, spilling coffee down her brown gabardine skirt, but she didn't seem to notice.

Jamie snatched a cloth napkin from Jess's lunch tray to mop up the floor, grateful the ruckus didn't awaken his sister. Blotting his mother's skirt, he glanced up, concern creasing his brow. "Are you all right?" She didn't answer, and he rose to grip her hand, which was as cold as the needles of ice suddenly prickling his skin. "Mom, tell me what's wrong—are you ill?"

She shook her head, lips parted as if to speak words that would not come, and he felt his own fingers go cold. She began to shake and tears welled as she searched his face, her eyes issuing a silent plea. "Jamie, no, please . . . not the McClares."

His blood chilled. "What are you saying, Mom? Cassidy Mc-Clare is the love of my life."

"No, son," she whispered, her voice a rasp as tears trailed her cheeks. "Cassidy McClare is your cousin."

Jamie rammed a finger to the elevator button, the groan and grind of gears and pulleys rivaling the taut strain of his nerves and the angst in his gut. His eyes burned in their sockets while anger burned in his chest, the searing jolt of his mother's revelation paralyzing him to all rational thinking. Chest heaving, his lungs pumped harsh air like a bellows igniting a blaze of hate.

Logan McClare was his father.

Fury swelled anew as rage coursed through his veins. A father who had not only abandoned him and his mother, but had denied him the rights of a son. A man he had admired and revered, now no more than a coward who turned his back on his own. The thought of Logan touching his mother made him sick, bile rising at what she'd endured at the hands of a wealthy law student who promised her the moon and gave her a child instead. Fifteen-year-old Jean Kerr, barely making a living as a dance-hall girl on the Barbary Coast, had fallen hard for a man with a silver spoon in his mouth that matched a silver tongue. Desperately in love, she'd succumbed to the deadly charms of a social aristocrat with whom she had a six-month affair. But Logan had broken it off, anxious to avoid scandal on the eve of his engagement to socialite Caitlyn Stewart, only to discover Jean Kerr was pregnant with a child Logan conveniently denied. To ensure her silence, he offered a monthly stipend that ended when his mother married Brian MacKenna, the man she'd allowed him to believe was his father. Jamie's jaw ground till it ached.

Better a sorry sot than a lily-livered liar.

The doors of the elevator squealed open, and Jamie shoved past several well-dressed gentlemen, bumping the shoulder of one, but too enraged to utter a pardon. Fists clenched, he strode toward a frosted glass door emblazoned with gold lettering. McClare, Rupert and Byington—yesterday a future he'd aspired to, today a past he'd avenge. Flinging the door wide, he ignored the saucer stare of the receptionist to storm down the hall, gaze fixed on Logan McClare's door, closed as always to distractions he didn't want.

Like his illegitimate son.

"Mr. MacKenna, please—wait! Mr. McClare asked not to be disturbed . . ." Miss Peabody's voice trailed him down the hall, alarm evident in the crack of her voice, but he paid no mind. Every nerve in his body itched for revenge, to extract a pound of flesh and give the devil his due. Oh, he'd "disturb" him all right—with a hard-knuckled fist and some well-placed guilt.

He hurled the polished cherrywood door open with a loud crack to the wall, fresh hate gurgling in his stomach at the sight of the man who had used his mother and cast her aside.

"What the—" Pen in hand, Logan peered over wire-rim reading glasses with a scowl.

Miss Peabody's babbling echoed behind. "I'm sorry, Mr. McClare, I tried to stop—"

Jamie slammed the door in her face, his muscles quivering with rage.

Logan took off his glasses, lips ground in a tight line. "Something on your mind, Jamie?"

"Yeah, *Mr. McClare*, there is." He strolled forward, a tic pulsing in his jaw. He singed him with a look. "How about you, *sir*, anything on your mind . . . *or* maybe your conscience?"

Eyes narrowing, Logan tossed his pen on the desk and sat back, arms braced casually on the chair. "Look, son, I don't have time to play games . . ."

Jamie stepped forward, fists knotted at his sides. "Don't you dare call me 'son,'" he hissed, "you haven't earned the right. And no time for games? You sure had plenty twenty-five years ago, didn't you?"

All blood drained from Logan's face, his skin as pale as the papers stacked on his desk.

"What, cat got your tongue, Pop?" The razor edge of Jamie's tone sliced through Logan's typical calm, bloodying his face with a ruddy shade of shock.

With ragged breaths, Logan carefully rose like a man twice his age, the truth of Jamie's outburst apparently sapping his energy. Head bowed, he steadied himself with a palm to his desk, broad shoulders slumped as if in a stupor. His face finally lifted to meet Jamie's, regarding him with a sorrowful gaze he'd seldom seen in a man he'd all but idolized. "Jamie, I—"

Jamie leaned in, eyes on fire. "You gonna say you're sorry you took advantage of my mother, is that it? Sorry she tossed a glitch into your perfect life with an unwanted brat?"

"No, it wasn't like that—" His voice, hoarse with repentance, cracked as he quickly made his way around the desk.

"No? Well how was it, Mr. McClare? Just exactly what makes a man turn his back on his own flesh and blood?"

"Give me a chance to explain—"

Logan reached for his arm, but Jamie slung it away, bile eating away at his words like acid. "Give you a chance? You mean like you gave my mother and me?"

"For pity's sake, Jamie, I was nineteen years old," he said, gouging blunt fingers through perfectly groomed hair. "A kid sowing wild oats and too stupid to count the cost. And then I met someone else . . ." A spasm jerked in his throat. "When your mother told me she was pregnant, I was scared, desperate, and to be honest, not even sure you were mine."

A curse hissed from Jamie's lips as he lunged, fist flying.

Logan deflected the blow with surprising skill, shoving Jamie back. "But I supported her anyway," he shouted, his breath coming out harsh and hot. Shoulders square, he steeled his jaw while fire sparked in his eyes and for the first time ever, Jamie saw the resemblance as if in a mirror. He had his mother's hazel eyes, certainly, rather than Logan's gray, and thick black hair to Logan's brown, but in the height, the build, and the jaw, he was a McClare through and through, evident in the temper that now pulsed in both of their cheeks. "I sent money every single month, I swear, even though I didn't believe you were mine. Even though you looked nothing like me when you were born." He paused, the only sound the thick wheeze of his breath as his chest rose and fell. His gaze wandered into an aimless stare as if he were somewhere far away. Or wanted to be. "In my mind's eye," he whispered, "I always denied it, unwilling to believe it was true. But when I saw you again . . ." He slowly looked up, a rare sheen of moisture coating his eyes as his voice trailed off. "I knew you were mine. And as God is my witness, Jamie, I vowed to do everything in my power to give you all you deserved."

"Except your name." Jamie spit the words like venom.

Sorrow welled in Logan's eyes despite the lift of his jaw. "It's too late for your mother and me, Jamie, but it's not too late for us. To become father and son, in heart if not in name."

Jamie's lip curled in contempt. "No thanks, Pop, I don't want anything you have to offer—not your sorry apology, not a relationship, and not this job."

Logan moved in, a command in his tone. "Don't be a fool and throw this all away—"

"Sorry, Pop, guess it just comes naturally." He glared. "You know, like father, like son?"

"We're blood," Logan rasped. He clutched Jamie's arm, the press of his jaw as tight as his grip. "You have to know, I would do anything for you."

"No, Mr. McClare," Jamie said, voice deadly. "You're a liar. You wouldn't do anything for me—you wouldn't marry my mother." He thrust Logan back, causing him to stumble. "That's from me, Pop," he said, then landed a blow to Logan's gut. "And that's for my mother."

And without the slightest bit of remorse, he turned on his heel and strode to the door, slamming it closed on both his father and his future. Because this was the man who'd stolen everything from him—his name, his inheritance, and now the only woman he ever really loved.

His cousin.

30

"So . . . are you going?" Cassie's friend, White Deer, seemed to wait with baited breath as she sat on Cassie's bed, arms circling her knees while bare toes peeked beneath the hem of her buckskin dress. Gus lay beside her curled up in a sleepy ball.

"Of course she's going," Morning Dove said in a clipped tone that suggested White Deer had husks between her ears instead of brains from a morning of making cornhusk dolls at the reservation school. She played with the long, wispy curls of a doll she'd made for her sister, pink lips crooked in a dry smile as she sprawled across Cassie's colorful quilt. "The Bluebonnet Ball is the social event of the season and Cassie needs to show up on the arm of a beau." Her dark eyes thinned into a gloat. "Because Mark Chancellor needs to feel the pain."

Pulling a chambray shirt and fresh pair of jeans from her bureau drawer, Cassie smiled over her shoulder, grateful for her two best friends. "Not unless I can wear blue jeans," she quipped. Clothes bundled in hand, she hurried over to White Deer and turned, desperate to shed the serviceable gray silk dress her mother insisted she wear to the school. "Because heaven knows I'm not putting a corset on for another man for a long time to come. Will you unhook these infernal buttons and please set me free?" She sighed while White Deer went to work. "Although I must admit, I'm sorely tempted just to see the look on Mark's face now that Father is close to striking oil again."

"He's been asking about you all over town, you know," White Deer said coyly.

"Not to mention he broke it off with snooty Olivia Balzer once he heard you were back." Morning Dove's dark brows dipped low in a face of deep bronze. "It'd serve him right to see the likes of Zane Carter fawning over you. Especially since every woman in town seems to be fawning over the eligible engineer who," she said with a sly wink, "sleeps right down the hall."

"Stop!" Cassie tugged her dress over her head, cheeks flaming from Morning Dove's remark. She hurried to hang it and her petticoat up before donning the chambray shirt, quickly buttoning it over her chemise. "Zane Carter is a respectable and honorable man whose keen mind and wealth of drilling knowledge is literally saving my father's life."

"And his daughter's?" White Deer tilted her head, brown eyes sparkling.

"Absolutely not." Cassie slipped a bare foot into one leg of her boy's jeans and then the other, making quick work of the button fly as she thought of the man who made it perfectly clear he wanted to know her better. "Look, I already told Mr. Carter, my parents, and now I'm telling both of you—*again*. I have no desire to tangle with another man anytime soon." She tucked her shirt in, then wove a leather belt through the loops before plopping on the bed to tug her boots on with a grunt. "When it comes to hunting for romance, I am completely and unequivocally off-season." She stood up and slapped hands to her hips. "Understood?"

White Deer gently pulled her back to the bed. "You're not still hurting over that low-down skunk from Frisco, are you, Cass?" she said quietly, kneading Cassie's arm.

Moisture stung at the mention of the polecat Cassie longed to forget. But two and a half months and a schedule chock-full of teaching, family, and friends hadn't put a dent in the ache inside whenever she thought of Jamie. Not to mention the longing to see her cousins and aunt and uncle again. Head bowed, she swiped her eyes with the back of her hand, tired of the malaise that always resettled whenever she received a letter from Al. Her cousin generally avoided all reference to Jamie except for mention of his sister's successful operation several weeks ago, which brought a sad smile to her lips. Although his faith had been tentative during their friendship, they'd prayed many a night for this very outcome, and for that Cassie was grateful. Heaving a sigh, she squeezed White Deer's hand. "A little bit," Cassie fibbed, unwilling to burden her friends with the true depth of her sorrow. "But I'll get over it like I got over Mark."

"Zane Carter might be the answer, you know." Morning Dove squatted before Cassie.

Cassie's smile crooked. "Tried that last time, remember? Didn't work out so well."

"But Zane is different, you said so yourself," White Deer reminded.

A wispy breath drifted from Cassie's lips. "I know."

But he's not Jamie.

White Deer bumped shoulders with Cassie. "So, if I were you, Cassidy McClare, I'd reconsider. If nothing else, for the sheer joy of stomping on Mr. Chancellor's toes and spitting in his eye." She leaned forward with a dance of her brows. "Now come on, wouldn't that be fun?"

Cassie peeked up, a faint semblance of a smile edging her lips.

"Maybe," she said with a teasing pout. "But if I had my druthers, I'd much rather spit in Jamie MacKenna's eye."

"Well, look at it this way—you can practice on Mark at the ball so you'll be ready for Jamie come Christmas, right?" Morning Dove's grin was wicked.

Christmas. Cassie's humor faded at the thought. That's right, they would be in San Francisco for Christmas. *With him.* Her hands went clammy. *Her. Jamie. And another round of heartbreak.*

Her lips compressed in a grim smile. *Great balls of fire, not if I can help it.* She narrowed her eyes. And this time she'd pack the cattle prod just to make sure.

Jamie held his breath while Jess took tentative steps with the crutches, the chew of her lip indicating she was focusing hard. Almost immediately, a grin worked its way across her face, clogging the air in Jamie's throat. "So, how does it feel?" he asked, voice raspy with hope.

She glanced up with a joyous smile that brought tears to his eyes. "Like I could win a two-mile race against my big brother on the heels of winning at chess."

His laughter echoed off the walls of the small hospital room as he studied her, hands parked low on his hips. "A wee bit cocky for someone who just spent the last two weeks in bed."

She wrinkled her nose and hobbled back to sit, plopping down. "Sorry—bad habit I got from my brother." A noisy sigh parted from her lips as she smiled, her eyes tired but happy. "Are we ready to go? Mom promised warm apple pie as soon as I came home."

Glancing at his watch, Jamie leaned to give her a peck on the cheek, rubbing her back with the palm of his hand. "Almost, kiddo.

I have a few papers to sign, then I'll be back pronto with a wheel-chair and a nurse to give you a proper send-off." He tugged on a springy black curl before heading for the door. "Don't move—I don't want you overdoing it before we go, okay?"

She gave him a firm salute. "Yes, sir, but I hope you won't be this bossy at home."

He grinned over his shoulder. "Worse, 'cause you're gonna have two of us breathing down your neck, make no mistake." Hands in his pockets, he strolled toward the nurses' station with a grin on his lips, guilt-free for the first time since Jess had been two. His heart swelled with gratitude. "Thank you, God," he whispered, "for healing my sister."

"Ready, Mr. MacKenna?" A pretty brunette flashed a smile that Jamie easily matched.

"You bet, as soon as I sign the release and give my thanks to your boss." He nodded to an office where several nurses were laughing. "Is Nurse Stadler here?"

"I'm afraid she was called away on an emergency, but she left a release for you to sign and said if you have any questions, to call her personally." She handed him the papers and pen.

Two orderlies wheeled a gurney followed by a troop of med-ics and nurses, and Jamie shook his head. "I'll tell you what, you people run a tight ship here, and I plan to personally commend Nurse Stadler and her staff to the Board of Directors." He scrawled his name across the bottom of the first sheet, then tackled the others with a broad smile, nodding at several doctors who walked by. "All I have to say is Senator Hamilton must wield a lot of power for a pro bono patient to receive such care and attention and a private room to boot."

"Pro bono?" A wrinkle pinched the bridge of her nose. "I'm not sure I understand."

Jamie glanced up, pen poised mid-scrawl. "You know, the unanimous vote earlier this month on the docket of surgeries Cooper Medical performs at no cost?"

She blinked. "Well, I may be new on the floor, Mr. MacKenna, but I do know your sister wasn't on the pro bono docket. Goodness, pro bono patients share a ward on the second floor, not a private room and around-the-clock attention on the fourth." She leaned forward, lowering her voice as if she had a secret to share. "No, siree," she said with a knowing smile, "I'd say you're a definite VIP. Now if you'll just wait right here, I'll get the care instructions Mrs. Stadler left and call an orderly to transport your sister downstairs." She turned to go.

"Wait." Jamie stopped her with a hand to her arm. "Jess's surgery wasn't free?"

Color flooded her cheeks. "Of course, but not because it was on the pro bono docket."

Jamie whistled, shocked over what Patricia and her father had obviously done. He exhaled loudly, shaking his head. "Holy thunder, Senator Hamilton sure carries some weight."

"Well, I don't know about Senator Hamilton, but I'd say you definitely do." She lowered her voice. "Don't say I told you, but rumor has it you're responsible for a brand-new wing."

His heart stalled in his chest. "What? What are you talking about?"

Her eyes sparkled as she nodded. "Yes, sir, the largest donation Cooper Medical and Lane Hospital have ever received."

The air thickened in his throat, making it hard for him to breathe. "I don't understand," he whispered, his words hoarse. "From Senator Hamilton?"

She glanced both ways down the hall before cupping a hand to her mouth. "No, sir, but you didn't hear it from me." Leaning close, she gave him a wink. "The name was McClare . . . Logan McClare."

"May I cut in?"

No! Cassie's lips clamped down on the word she wanted to spit in Mark Chancellor's face as he gave a slight bow, nearly a head taller than every other man dancing at the Bluebonnet Ball. He was dressed in a stylish gray sack suit that deepened the blue of his eyes. His gaze flitted from her to her partner. She hadn't wanted to come to the ball in the first place, but her parents had badgered until she'd accepted Zane's invitation, not to mention White Deer and Morning Dove insisting she needed to give Mark some of his own. But at this particular moment, she didn't want to give Mark Chancellor anything except distance. Staring hard at Zane Carter, she forced a tight smile she hoped would convey her thoughts loud and clear. *No, no, no!*

Zane offered Mark a stiff nod and to Cassie's horror, turned her over to the man who had ripped her heart out and stomped on it for good measure. The sound of "Ain't Dat a Shame" drifted through the crowded ballroom of Humble's most prestigious hotel, and Cassie couldn't agree more as Mark whirled her away. *So much for mind reading . . .*

"Tell me, Cass," Mark whispered, his voice husky as the scent of Bay Rum stirred sour memories. "Were you always this beautiful, or is it just absence making the heart grow fonder?"

Cassie pursed a smile. "Nope, pretty sure you can rule out the absence theory."

He chuckled, blue eyes sparkling. "Nobody bottom-lines it like Cassidy McClare." He spun her around, eyes suddenly serious. "I've missed you, Cass—I was a fool to let you go."

Her smile was painfully polite. "Well, at least we agree on something."

The impossibly blue eyes went into hypnotic mode, a shuttered gaze that had always tumbled her stomach. "Trust me—I won't make that mistake again."

Sealing her eyelids, she held her breath and waited for the flutter sensation he always evoked. *One second . . . two seconds . . . three seconds . . . nothing!* The air whooshed from her lungs in blatant relief. Her lashes flipped up with a patient smile. "I know, and neither will I."

His smile never faltered as he nodded to an arched opening at the far end of the room that led to a garden she knew all too well. "How 'bout some fresh air? We need to talk—about us."

She released a weary sigh. "Mark, we have nothing to say to each other, and if memory serves, there is no 'us.' Now, if you'll excuse me—" Turning on her heel, she left him—and his sagging jaw—on the ballroom floor, the feeling of payback surprisingly flat. She threaded her way through the crowd to the ladies' room, stopping short at the sound of a voice.

"Cassie?"

She turned. Zane ambled forward with a grim smile. "I owe you an apology, it seems. I would have never turned you over to that dandy had I known. Your parents just informed me Mark was the man who broke your heart." His gaze was gentle. "Will you forgive me?"

She stared, his words suddenly registering. *The man who broke my heart.* Water welled in her eyes. *No, you're mistaken—he's still in San Francisco.* She gave him a wobbly smile. "Of course I forgive you, Zane, and I was bound to run into him sooner or later, so no apology needed."

He shifted as if her sudden blur of tears made him uncomfortable.

"Cass, if you'd like to go home, I'd be happy to take you." His tender smile confirmed he'd like nothing more. "If being here gives you bad memories, I say we hightail it to the ranch to make new ones, maybe with a game of pinochle?" His eyes twinkled. "You know, just to see if I can actually win?"

She chuckled, dispelling her melancholy somewhat. "I'd like that, Zane."

He twined his fingers in hers, and his look didn't bode well for a woman not high on romance. "I'll tell your parents we're leaving, then meet you in the lobby." He squeezed her hand. "I care for you, Cass, and I'd like to help chase your heartbreak away . . . if you'll let me."

If I'd let him. She released a quiet sigh, assessing Zane Carter through wary eyes. He was a good man who was helping her father reclaim his fortune, and she knew her parents liked him. His faith in God was strong, and deep down, she sensed she could trust him. With a smile and a quiet nod, she turned to enter the ladies' room, thoughts of Christmas foremost on her mind. The question wasn't trusting Zane Carter to help her get past the heartbreak of Jamie. Her heart fisted. No, the question was—could she trust herself?

31

Swallowing a knot the size of the brass door knob under his hand, Jamie stared for several moments at the frosted pane of McClare, Rupert and Byington, then opened the door. The ever-pleasant Miss Peabody looked up, and he stifled a grin when the whites of her eyes expanded. Offering a sheepish smile, he greeted her in the same cheerful tone he had for the last five months, hoping it would disarm her enough not to throw him out on his ear. Heat ringed his high-necked collar. Which is exactly what he deserved after his deplorable behavior two weeks ago. Hat in hand, he squared his shoulders. "Good afternoon, Miss Peabody, I trust you're well?"

The swift rise to her feet was comical, her face nearly the color of her crisp, white shirtwaist while she stuttered a response. "Mr. M-MacKenna—Mr. M-McClare's not in—"

Covering his embarrassment with an awkward smile, he glanced at his watch, then fiddled with the brim of his Homburg while he kept a polite distance. "If it's not a problem, Miss Peabody, I'd like to wait." Her pause was decidedly suspicious, and more heat inched up the back of his neck. "To apologize, of course."

There was an almost audible release of air from her lips before a smile finally broke through. "Certainly, Mr. MacKenna, I expect him any moment, and you're welcome to wait."

"Thank you," he said with a slow exhale, "I appreciate that." He paused. "If Mr. Hughes is in and it's all right with you, I'd like to pop in to say hello."

Her face eased into a genuine smile. "By all means. Mr. Hughes will be delighted to see you." She paused, a hint of pink toasting her cheeks. "It's not the same without you, you know."

The tension in his neck and shoulders relaxed. He grinned. "Better, I presume?"

Her chuckle warmed his spirits. "Only when the steam is coming from the teapot in the back room, sir, instead of your head."

He cleared his throat, suddenly too warm in his charcoal gray suit. "Yes, well, about my outburst, Miss Peabody, I . . . well, I'm sorry for barging in and treating you so poorly—it was rude, and I apologize."

"Apology accepted, Mr. MacKenna, as I imagine it will be with Mr. McClare as well." Her kind tone diminished the strain in his face. "I'll let you know when he's returned."

Jamie flashed a grateful smile. "Thank you. I'll be in Bram's office, no doubt disrupting his nap." He breathed in a deep swallow of air while her laughter followed down the hall, grateful most of the partners' doors were closed and Blake was on the phone. Easing Bram's cracked door open, he cocked a hip to the doorjamb and folded his arms. A wry smile tipped at Bram stretched in his chair with eyes closed and arms crossed, legs propped on his desk. Jamie cleared his throat. "And Miss Peabody thought I was joking about disrupting your nap."

Bram jerked in the chair before giving him a lazy grin. "Go ahead—begrudge me the only sleep I've had in twenty-four hours."

Chuckling, Jamie closed the door and strolled in, plopping in a chair before tossing his hat on the desk. He hiked his legs up like Bram, arms braced to his neck. "The Miller case?"

"Yeah, the family feud that will not die." He squinted at Jamie, smile waning. "Everything okay with Jess? Logan said you took time off to spend at the hospital."

Jamie paused, eyes in a squint. "You mean he didn't tell you?"

"Tell me what?" Concern wedged at the bridge of Bram's nose.

A shudder of air drifted from Jamie's lips as he studied his best friend, wondering why Logan hadn't told him Jamie was gone. Had Logan assumed he'd be back, tail between his legs? He sucked in a heavy dose of air to quell the irritation that rose and released it, gaze fused to Bram's. "I quit . . . the day of Jess's surgery."

"What?" Bram shot up in his chair, feet back on the ground. "Why?"

Jamie ground the upper socket of his eye with the pad of his thumb, feeling a headache coming on. "I found out something about Logan that made me blow."

Bram stared at him, jaw distended. "So you quit your job? Just like that? That's just plain stupid, Mac. Sure, Logan's no choir boy, but that's no reason—"

"He's my father, Bram." Although spoken quietly, the words hung heavy in the air like the slack of Bram's mouth, his facial muscles frozen in shock. Their meaning pierced Jamie's heart anew, and he lowered his feet to sit on the edge of the chair, shoulders slumped. He put his head in his hands while a strange mix of fury and pride roiled in his gut.

"You can't be serious . . ." Bram's strangled whisper broke the silence. The chair squealed as he sagged back, as if Jamie's statement had siphoned the energy from his body along with the blood in his face. "But how? And how in the devil did you find out?"

Jamie dropped back with a heavy exhale, fingers limp over the edge of the chair. "After Jess's surgery," he said, his voice lifeless, "I was so euphoric over what God had done, providing Jess with a pro bono surgery despite my breakup with Patricia, that I just knew he was giving me a second chance with Cassie." He grunted, eyes lumbering into a lost stare. "Or at least that's what I thought." He looked up while a nerve twittered his jaw. "Until my mother informed me of a minor detail she failed to mention over the twenty-five years of my life." He mauled his face with his hands before dropping them on the arm of the chair. "Seems she fell in love with a law student who frequented the dance hall where she worked when she was fifteen, a real smooth talker. A rich boy who had no problem taking, but wanted no part of giving back to the illegitimate son he sired." His voice calcified. "To think that all these years he watched me work three jobs just to get through law school, watched my mother and sister and me struggle to put food on the table." Jamie peered up, his tone edged with disgust. "Stood by and *watched* while I flirted and kissed and fell in love with my own cousin."

Bram's face went pale, accentuating the dark stubble on his jaw. "Holy thunder—consanguinity," he muttered, the term for blood relationship with common ancestry as shocking as the word "incest" for first cousins forbidden to marry. "Sweet saints, Mac, that never even occurred to me."

Jamie's gut wrenched at the mere mention of the horrific word, his blood chilling over the scandal of relatives marrying. He closed his eyes and laid his head back, throat swelling with regret that he craved a woman he would never be able to have. His mouth pressed into a grim line. And all because Logan's blood flowed in his veins. Forbidden fruit—the taboo of such a union, the medical risks involved, the illegality in various states. Pain slashed in his chest. Not to mention it was forbidden by the Church. He fisted his fingers on the arm of the chair, his anger at Logan resurging. "When I found out, I lost my temper, something I haven't done in years. Confronted Logan with a fist before I quit and walked out the door." He deflated with a sigh. "But that was before I found out he was responsible for Jess's surgery."

"What?" Bram's gaping ramped up. "I thought Patricia's father influenced the vote?"

Jamie's smile felt sculpted in stone. "He did—but *against* us, evidently. When I broke it off with Patricia, the senator was so angry, he threatened to kill the vote, so I was certain he would. Then I got the call that the surgery had been scheduled and just assumed he'd changed his mind. But when I probed, I learned the senator was true to his word—Jess was declined."

"Then how—?"

Jamie peered up, tone tinged with the same shock he saw on Bram's face. "Logan donated a wing to the hospital. Apparently I wasn't supposed to find out, but I pried it out of some new nurse on the floor. It seems his 'anonymous' donation was contingent upon Jess receiving the surgery and hospital care for the rest of her life, along with my mother and me."

Bram's low whistle pierced the air. "Holy blazes, Mac, that's gotta go a long way in tempering your anger." He shook his head, slack-jawed at Jamie's revelation. "Man alive! You—Logan's son—talk about a high-voltage jolt."

"Yeah, we're talking spontaneous combustion," Jamie said with an edge to his voice. "And trust me—I would have never darkened his door again except for what he did for Jess. Which is why I'm here today—to apologize."

"And ask for your job back?" Bram studied him with a hopeful eye.

"No, I don't think so. I appreciate what he's done for Jess, but he's never lifted a finger for me when I needed him most—as a dirty-faced kid living in the sewer of the Barbary Coast. He didn't want any part of me growing up, and now I don't want any part of him."

"You'll have to forgive him sooner or later," Bram said, "for your sake as well as his."

Jamie pinched the bridge of his nose. "I know, but it's going to take a while, I'm afraid. The man denied me as his son and then abandoned my mother and me to the streets, never lifting a finger until now. And I'm sorry, Bram, but that's just a hard thing to forgive."

With a fold of his arms, Bram leaned back in his chair, a fist to his mouth as his eyes narrowed in thought. "You know, Mac, I wouldn't be so all-fired sure of that," he said slowly, face in a scrunch as if trying to remember something he'd long forgotten. His gaze connected with Jamie's as realization dawned in his eyes. "I never thought about it before, but if you remember, it was Logan who introduced you to Blake and me at the Oly Club, wasn't it?" A smile eased across Bram's lips. "And if memory serves, he also encouraged Blake and me to take you under our wing at Stanford, said we should show you the ropes, if you will."

Jamie stared, the meaning of Bram's words crystallizing in his brain. He suddenly thought of the coveted three-year merit scholarship to Stanford he'd been awarded, established to assist needy and worthy students. The air thickened in his throat as his pulse accelerated. Was it possible Logan had used his influence there like he had at Cooper Medical?

"Mr. MacKenna?" Miss Peabody knocked on the door.

"Come in, Miss Peabody," Bram called.

She peeked in with a tentative smile. "Mr. McClare is in and will see you now."

Jamie released a heavy breath as he rose to his feet. "Thank you—I'm on my way." He paused to shoot Bram a wary glance. "This is just between you and me, Bram, all right? You're always harping about prayer, Padre," he said with a dry smile. "Now would be a good time."

"Count on it," his friend said, and Jamie's heart stalled. No, he suddenly realized, not just his friend—his *cousin*. Jamie swallowed hard, the affection in Bram's gaze infusing him with the strength he needed to face his father again.

My father. Battling the sting of moisture, Jamie made his way to Logan's office, a jumble of anger and gratitude warring in his mind. *Please—give me the grace I need to forgive.*

Hesitating at Logan's door, he studied the man who stared out the window, head on the back of his chair while his arms lay motionless on its sides. The same man who'd gone out of his way to be kind to him at the Oly Club, left exorbitant tips, and suggested he contact a friend at the Blue Moon for a job. Emotion obstructed Jamie's throat, stifling his air. The very man who'd treated him like a son since the moment he'd met him and the only man alive he'd ever revered like a father. His heart thudded as he stepped through the door. "Thank you for seeing me, sir."

Logan spun around, looking years older than Jamie remembered, just in two weeks. Clearing his throat, he leaned forward and steepled his hands, elbows stiff on his desk. "You're always welcome here, Jamie, you know that." He nodded toward the chair. "Come in, sit down."

Avoiding Logan's gaze, Jamie obliged, closing the door before moving forward to sit, rigid in the chair just like his father.

"Bram tells me the surgery was a success," Logan said, breaking the silence. "I'm glad."

Jamie looked up, meeting his eyes, seeing himself in Logan's face in ways he'd never noticed before. "Yes, sir, it was—thank you."

Logan nodded, ruddy color braising his cheeks as he shifted in the chair. "Well, I care about you and your family, Jamie, so naturally I'd ask."

"No, sir," Jamie said with a firm press of his jaw. "I meant 'thank you' for what you did to secure the surgery for my sister."

Paralysis claimed Logan's features for the briefest of moments before he lowered his gaze, a muscle twitching in his cheek. "That was not for public knowledge."

"No, sir, it wasn't, but it was knowledge I needed to know nonetheless." He hesitated, drawing in a bolstering breath. "In order to forgive you," he said quietly.

His father's gaze met his, and the glossy-eyed connection caused the pressure of tears to sting in Jamie's nostrils. Logan cleared his throat, his voice hoarse. "I love you, son, have from the moment I realized you were mine, on the docks of Meigg's Wharf."

Jamie's rib cage closed in. "On . . . the wharf? When I was . . . twelve?"

Logan nodded with a glaze of moisture that matched his son's. "Hadn't seen you since you were born, and like I told you before, you looked nothing like me, so I didn't believe you were mine." His eyes clouded, trailing into a fog. "Then one day your mother contacted me after your father died. Begged me to come, just once, she said, because one look would tell me all I needed to know." Logan swiped at his eyes with the sleeve of his coat. "She was right, of course. I saw this scrappy, little kid who looked like I'd spit him out of my mouth, and in my heart

I knew." He looked up, his gaze locking with Jamie's. "Knew you were mine."

"Then why—"

"Why didn't I claim you? Marry your mother?" A harsh laugh erupted. "Because I was selfish, Jamie. I was a thirty-one-year-old bachelor who liked my freedom and had no inclination whatsoever to settle down with a woman or a kid. Especially a woman like your mother who didn't want the influence of someone like me in her son's life. Oh, I made a sad attempt at doing the right thing, I suppose, but neither of us felt anything for the other and your mother saw right through me." He grunted. "Told me flat out she only wanted one thing from me and that was for you to have a chance at an education, a chance to have the things that she couldn't give you."

"So the scholarship was *your* doing," Jamie whispered, "not mine."

The muscles in Logan's face tightened as he leaned forward, fingers gripped on the edge of his desk. "Understand one thing, Jamie. My money and influence opened doors for you, no question, but it was your drive and intelligence that marked you as a cut above every other candidate vying for that scholarship. Yes, I paved the way, but you earned it, make no mistake." Logan eased back in his chair, the sheen returning to his eyes once again. "And as God is my witness, I have never been prouder of anything or anyone more in my life."

Emotion thickened in Jamie's throat, but he warded it off with a press of his jaw. "A man approached me on the docks when I was sixteen, told me to come to the Oly Club and he'd give me a job." He peered up, waiting for Logan's response. "That was your doing as well?"

Logan exhaled and nodded, pinching the bridge of his nose as

Jamie was prone to do. "Please understand—I didn't want to just throw money at you, Jamie, like so many of the snot-nosed elite. You weren't the kind of kid who would take to charity anyway, so I worked to find ways around it. The job at the Oly enabled me to introduce you to Blake and Bram, which in turn allowed me to spend time with you as well." He paused, as if gauging Jamie's reaction. "And, then, of course, I'm part owner of several establishments on the Barbary Coast."

Jamie's mouth dropped open. "The Blue Moon," he whispered, almost to himself. He shook his head. "I always wondered why Duffy never batted an eye over my schedule, making allowances for me he wouldn't do for anyone else."

"In the beginning, yes, but it wasn't long before he recognized your work ethic and unquestioned honesty, saw the caliber of man that you are. And I swear to this very day, Duffy thanks me every time I see him." Logan drew in a deep breath. "The truth is, Jamie, you made the difference in your life, not me. All the money and influence in the world wouldn't have made you the man you are today. You did that on your own, son." He smiled. "You and your mother."

Jamie nodded, unable to speak for the spasm in his jaw.

Body rigid, Logan leaned in. "Come back to the firm, Jamie," he whispered, "not just because I need your legal skill, but because I need you—here—by my side."

Muscles convulsed in Jamie's throat. "As your son?" he asked, voice gruff.

Seconds ticked by while Logan stared, every tendon in his face as taut as his tone. "If that's what you want."

"And what do *you* want?" Jamie spit out, a flash of fury igniting his temper. "To go on as before, I suppose, doing what you do best—living a lie?"

Logan dispelled a slow exhale, his face a mask despite a flicker of pain in his eyes. "I deserved that, but no—I have my reasons for keeping silent about our relationship, but I will defer to you on this one, Jamie, you have my word."

Twenty-five years of frustration and anger boiled over, spilling from his lips with such vehemence that Logan winced. "Your word?" Jamie said with a sneer. "And why do I feel that's as flimsy as your reasons for keeping silent?"

The gray of Logan's eyes glinted like polished steel, his temper going head-to-head with his son's. "You may not respect me as your father, son, but you *will* respect me as your employer—is that clear?"

Jamie shot to his feet. "You're not my employer, Mr. McClare, any more than you're my father." He stormed for the door.

"Jamie!"

He froze, the authority in Logan's voice stopping him cold. "The McClare men are known for their tempers, but I've learned to master mine. I thought you had, too, but maybe not."

Hand on the knob, Jamie ground his jaw so tight, he thought it might crack. He pivoted slowly, searing his father with a look that burned the walls of his eyes. "I had, but that was before I learned I was abandoned and betrayed by my father."

A low chuckle rumbled from Logan's chest as he canted back in his chair. "No question, the melodrama hales from the Kerrs. Sit down, Jamie, and let's discuss this man to man."

Heat blasted Jamie's cheeks. The walls shook as he slammed the door hard, returning to his seat with fire in his eyes.

"Now," Logan said with a jag of his brow, "every lawyer worth his salt knows the basic tenet of justice is both sides must be heard. That said, it would behoove you, counselor, to hear me out." He rose and paced to the window, hands clasped behind as he stared into the street below, voice calm as if addressing a jury. "My reasons for keeping quiet are not as you suppose."

He turned, eyeing Jamie with the same air of confidence he utilized in a courtroom, the barest wedge of sympathy in dark brows tented high. "First of all, it was your mother's idea, not mine, to keep my paternity a secret. Granted, I was more than willing to go along in the beginning because as I said before, I was—and still am in many ways—a selfish man. But your mother made it perfectly clear she was worried that too much of my influence would insure you'd end up like me as a—and I quote—" a smile squirmed as he stared at the floor, hands clasped to his back, "'a godless man about town who drinks like a fish and takes advantage of women.'" He peered up beneath shuttered eyes that held a hint of a twinkle. "Since you're a man who goes to church with his mother and sister, seldom drinks, and has a mildly dangerous reputation with women that in no way can compete with his father's, I'd say your mother exercised wisdom."

Logan paused and drew in a loaded breath that he slowly expelled. The twinkle in his eye suddenly diminished, replaced with concern. "One of the reasons I didn't fight her on this was the obvious—had I claimed you as my son, your mother's privacy would have been impaired and her reputation ruined if it were known that Brian MacKenna's son was, in fact, not only illegitimate, but not his son at all."

Jamie's eyes lumbered closed at the truth of Logan's words, something he had never considered with all the anger seething inside.

"So, you see, Jamie, I didn't make this decision lightly, I assure you, and to be honest, I now have a reason of my own as to why I prefer to keep this between us—at least for the immediate future."

Opening his eyes, Jamie studied the man whose blood he

shared. "Because I would be a burden?" he said calmly, issuing a thin smile.

"Hardly." With a fold of his arms, Logan perched on the edge of the sill, regarding Jamie through narrow eyes. "I'm one of the richest men in the city if not the state. The truth is my so-called notorious bachelorhood has lost its appeal and family, quite frankly, has become the only thing that really matters to me anymore." The edge of his lip lifted in the barest of smiles. "Trust me, claiming you as my son would be a joy, not a burden."

"What, then?" Jamie asked, his curiosity piqued.

Logan rose and returned to his chair, slanting back to rest both his head and his arms. His chest rose and fell with a deep breath before he pierced Jamie with a starkly honest look devoid of all humor. "I'm in love with a woman I hope to marry, and to be truthful, she simply wouldn't understand. I plan to tell her someday, of course, but I honestly believe if she knew now, it would ruin any chance I may have."

Jamie blinked, totally caught off-guard by Logan's candor. In love with a woman? Logan McClare? His mind scrambled for who it might be, suddenly realizing he knew very little about Logan's social life. As far as Blake, he, or Bram knew, the man spent most of his time at the McClares' with his family . . . Jamie's heart skidded to a stop. No, it couldn't be. His mouth dropped as he stared, never suspecting the rumors might be true. Alli always insisted her Uncle Logan had feelings for her mother that went well beyond fraternal, but Jamie, Bram, and Blake never believed it, figuring it was just Logan's way with all women, including Caitlyn McClare. But staring at the blatant humility he saw in Logan's eyes, Jamie knew Alli was right. He slowly shook his head, lips curving into a faint smile. "You may have to give up poker, sir."

He smiled, relieving the tension in his face. "Among other things, but don't think I wouldn't consider it in a heartbeat." His eyes sobered. "But the decision is yours, Jamie. I'll do whatever you want."

Jamie nodded. "I appreciate that, sir, but I think you're right. A revelation of this nature would only hurt the people we love."

"I agree—at least for the time being. But it's important to me that I be a part of your life, son, as much as possible within the context of secrecy. Which means I'm asking you to come back to the firm." He paused to draw in a deep breath. "Will you?"

Peering up, Jamie studied his father, the realization of what he shared with this man eradicating all anger for the first time, replaced instead by a sense of awe and longing. He gave a slow nod, not trusting himself to speak.

Logan's exhale carried across the desk as he bent forward, the intensity in his eyes deepened by the respect and affection Jamie saw. "Good. Because bottom line is, son, you're my flesh and blood and I love you. And I hope you know I would do anything to make you happy."

Jamie thought of Cassie, and a sad smile lined his lips as he rose. "Thanks, Mr. McClare." His voice sounded barren of hope and so very far away—just like his dreams of Cassie. "Trust me, sir—I wish that you could."

"Jamie, it's Logan, not Mr. McClare, and all you have to do is ask. Money is no object."

Absently fingering the stiff felt of his hat, Jamie released a weighty sigh, fraught with regret and longing for a woman he couldn't have. "I'm afraid money won't fix this, sir, as much as I wish it could." He glanced up, painfully aware Logan may well realize his dream of a union with Mrs. McClare, but Jamie would never realize his with her niece. "I'm in love with Cassie—my cousin," he said with a somber face, "and not even you are powerful enough to change that."

Logan blinked before a slow, languid smile spread across his face like the sun rising on a new day, his low chuckles reverberating like thunder before they rose to fill the room.

"You think this is funny?" Jamie asked, his frustration bristling all over again.

"A little." Logan raised a palm to stall while his body shook with laughter. "It would appear we have yet another reason to keep our relationship under the hat." He rose and circled his desk, irritating Jamie further with his all-too-casual air. "As a man who's in love with his cousin, I suppose there is something you should know." Smiling, he gave Jamie's shoulders a solid grip before tapping his son's face. "There's not a drop of McClare blood in her veins," he said with a crook of his mouth. "Because my brother didn't just marry Cassie's mother, mind you. . ." His smile eased into a grin. "But a beautiful widow with an equally beautiful little girl."

32

hristmas with family. Cassie sighed. Was there anything better? Her tongue swiped at the whipped cream on her eggnog as she reveled in the excited chatter of cousins and family and people she loved. The warmth of the fire crackled and spit in the McClares' cozy parlour while the heady scent of pine and wood smoke mingled with nutmeg and cinnamon from snickerdoodles still warm from the oven.

"Awk, Blake cheats, Blake cheats!"

A grin tipped Cassie's lips as Alli leaned over Miss B.'s cage, schooling the parrot in yet another insult to make the family laugh, cheered on by Bram while Blake bested him in chess. Across the way, her parents' laughter rose as brothers and sisters-in-law caught up with Bram's parents on old times and the latest news, not the least of which was the miraculous revival of an oil field no longer defunct. With grins of anticipation, Meg and Maddie shook brightly wrapped presents that circled a glittering tinsel tree while Cassie snuggled deeper into the love seat, stockinged feet tucked beneath. Another wispy sigh feathered her lips. The perfect Christmas.

Almost.

With a gulp of eggnog, Cassie glanced at a mantel embellished with holly-berry greenery and scarlet stockings, feeling her holiday euphoria melt away with every tick of the clock. The eggnog roiled in her stomach as the minute hand inched toward eight. Rosie had cooked a feast for the senses and Christmas toasts had been made. Tradition followed with a reading of the Christmas story from the family Bible before games ensued. The night would be filled with feasting and fun until midnight when each would open a gift of their choosing. No question it had been a glorious day and was on its way to an even better night, *but* . . . Cassie nipped at her lip. If so, why were her hands sweating and the eggnog suddenly a lump in her throat?

One reason and one reason only. Pretty Boy Jamie MacKenna.

She drowned a groan with another rich slide of her drink, grateful Jamie had begged off dinner to celebrate Christmas Eve with his mother and sister. If only Uncle Logan hadn't insisted he come later for games, it would have been the perfect evening. Cassie's lips pursed in a flat line. Correction—the "perfect evening" would be not caring at all, which if Zane Carter got his way, would be the case come spring. Or at least Cassie hoped.

The night of the Bluebonnet Ball, Zane had asked to court her, and she'd told him she needed more time, but now she wasn't so sure. Over four months had passed since she'd seen Jamie and yet her heart ached as if it were merely yesterday. She was tired of pining for a man who had deceived and betrayed her, a man with no faith in God. She could never trust him again, and suddenly the notion of courting Zane held great appeal as a buffer for her heart. Upending her eggnog, she placed the glass on the table and rose, brushing her lavender chiffon dress. Okay, it was settled—as of this very moment, she was courting Zane Carter.

"Hey, Cass!" Alli waved her over to Miss B.'s cage with a wicked smile. "Let's teach Miss B. something nasty to say about Jamie." She waggled her brows, and Cassie laughed as she strolled over. Rubbing her hands together, Alli grinned, her tone thick with conspiracy. "How 'bout 'Jamie's a polecat,'" she asked with a sparkle in her eyes.

Cassie's lips twisted. "I prefer something from the rodent family, if you don't mind."

"Oooo—how 'bout 'weasel'?" Alli poked a finger into the cage to get Miss B.'s notice.

"Not actually a rodent, but it does work," Cassie said with a chuckle. She put a finger to her chin in thought, her smile as devious as Al's. "'Rat' has a rather nice ring, don't you think?"

"Oh, you're right, and probably easier for Miss B. to say too." Alli glanced up with a tilt of her head, smile dimming enough for Cassie to notice. "You're okay, right?" she asked softly.

"Sure," Cassie said, hooking an arm to her cousin's waist. She kissed her cheek and gave her a misty smile. "I love you, Al, you know that? I think I missed you more than anybody."

Alli rolled her eyes. "Oh, stop! Now I'll have to teach Miss B. to say 'Cass lies through her teeth.'"

Cassie pinched her. "It's true, you little brat, although I don't know why because you give me so much grief."

"But not as much as the 'rat,' right?" She turned to the parrot. "Okay, Miss B.—try this on for size. 'Jamie's a rat. Jamie's a rat. Jamie's a rat . . .'"

Arm to Al's waist, Cassie rested her head to her cousin's while Al worked with Miss B., her grin softening into a smile as she thought of the "rat." She supposed she owed the "rat" a note of thanks for teaching her something it had taken a lifetime to learn—that people may reject you, but God never would. When she'd gone home to Texas, Jamie's rejection had been raw, inflicting a pain deeper than anything she'd ever known. Yes, returning to face a town and a fiancé who had rejected her on the heels of

Jamie's betrayal had nearly leveled her, but it also brought her to her knees before God. That's when she'd finally learned that it was God's approval she needed, not man's, God's love that would set her free, not Jamie's. She released a wispy sigh. Aunt Cait's layer-cake analogy in a nutshell—that without her faith in God, she would never fully be satisfied or enriched in anything she did, especially in relationships.

"Awk, Jamie's a rat, Jamie's a rat . . ."

Cassie laughed, delighted with the antics of Miss B. and the fact God had brought good from the pain the "rat" had caused. It made it a lot easier not to fall apart when she finally saw him again, and certainly easier to forgive him. Her lips quirked. Although she wasn't about to let *him* know that anytime soon. A little groveling never hurt anybody, especially a pretty-boy polecat way too sure of himself. She inhaled deeply and squared her shoulders. *Bring the pretty boy on, God. I'll hog-tie him tighter than the presents under the tree.*

"Mr. James MacKenna," Hadley said with great ceremony, and Cassie's arm dropped from Alli's waist like a sack of potatoes from a three-story barn. She swallowed hard, knees buckling while the eggnog frothed and swirled inside worse than whitecaps on the bay.

"Thanks, Hadley." Jamie strode into the parlour with a broad grin, toting a box brimming with presents. "Merry Christmas, all," he said while return greetings sailed through the air.

"Jamie!" Maddie flew across the room, tackling him with a squeal as he put his presents under the tree. "We're going to play the white elephant game—wanna play?"

"Sure, squirt." He scooped her up to deposit a kiss to her nose. "Got something special for you, kiddo," he said, grinning when she wobbled like a drunken sailor after he set her back down.

"Oooo . . . did you bring something for me too?" Alli moseyed over to give Jamie a hug. She ruffled his thick dark hair until a stray curl toppled.

He slapped Alli's hand with a mock scowl. "Nope, Blake said he got you a lump of coal, so I figured you're all set."

"What are you doing buying presents for everyone, son?" Logan said with a firm cuff of Jamie's shoulder. "Heaven knows I don't pay you that well."

"He's buttering the boss up, aren't you, Mac?" Blake called. "To look better than me?"

Bram laughed and moved his pawn. "As if that's hard to do, and then there's the extra bonus that *he* doesn't cheat."

"Awk, Blake cheats, Blake cheats!"

Jamie chuckled and turned, his body going completely still when his eyes found Cassie. His grin softened into a smile as his gaze traveled from her face down the ruffled bodice of her form-fitting dress to her hem and back up as naturally as the dimples that deepened his cheeks. "Well, well," he said in a husky voice that tingled her skin, "welcome back, Cowgirl—I've missed you." He disarmed her with a smile. "Especially when I have a cue in my hand."

She delivered a saucy smile, desperate to deflect the heat in her cheeks. "Me too. After all, nothing says 'happy holidays' like hog-tying a city boy."

He grinned, and her heart took a tumble. "Is that so?" He eased into that lazy drawl reserved just for her. "I'd be pleased to oblige, ma'am, but I don't like takin' advantage of a lady."

Batting her lashes, she gave him a smile as sweet as Texas tea. "I do declare, Mr. MacKenna—that's a little bit like saying a skunk doesn't like stripes, isn't it?"

"Or a rat doesn't like cheese," Alli said loud enough to cue in Miss B.

"Awk, Jamie's a rat . . . Jamie's a rat . . ."

"Your reputation precedes you, MacKenna," Bram said with a grin.

"And it's worse than mine, thank heavens," Blake said with a chuckle.

Alli's grin was diabolical. She nodded at Cass. "Great to have her back, isn't it, Mac?"

He recovered with a smile that put a hiccup in Cassie's pulse. "Only if she left her cattle prod at home." He winked, then ambled over to say hello to Aunt Cait and Bram's parents.

Alli leaned close. "He's been practicing at pool, you know," she whispered, bumping Cassie's shoulder with her own. "'To whittle the Texas McClare down to size,' or so he says."

"Ha—as if he could!" Cassie scowled, annoyed at how Jamie laughed with her parents, no doubt charming them with his pretty-boy looks. "I'll beat him with both hands tied behind my back."

Alli chuckled. "Wouldn't advise it. Our boy's been known to take advantage."

"I hope he does." Cassie watched him through narrow eyes, her smile taking a hard slant. "I brought my cattle prod *and* my spurs."

"Come on, Cass, be nice. Besides, he's not seeing Patricia anymore, so he's free as a bird . . ."

"A vulture, no doubt, looking for his next wealthy victim since Patricia threw him over." Cassie bit her tongue, disappointed at herself for holding a grudge. She sighed. "I'm sorry, Al. I didn't realize I was still angry until the rat crawled through that door." Another sigh quivered her bodice. "I thought I'd forgiven him and gotten it out of my system."

Alli anchored gentle palms on her cousin's shoulder. "Come on, Cass, face it—he's still in your system *and* in your heart. And just for the record, he ended it with Patricia, not the other way around, I'll have you know. Yes, he made a mistake, but he rectified it, so why not give him another chance?" She gave Cassie a sympathetic smile. "I did, and you should too." Her tone was gentle. "He still cares for you, you know, and Bram said he was really upset when you left."

Upset? Cassie sniffed. *Try crying into your pillow every night for a solid two months.* Her resolve hardened. "Sorry, Al, I refuse to put myself through that again—*ever*." She smoothed her skirt and pasted on a smile. "It's Christmas, so I'll be nice, yes, but nothing more. My heart can't take it." Her chin nudged up. "Besides, I've already decided to court Zane, so I'm completely unavailable."

Alli folded her arms. "Oh, really? Since when—the moment Jamie walked through that door?" She shook her head. "Come on, Cass, it's not like you to back down."

Cassie pursed her lips. "No, but it is like me to protect myself from further hurt, and that's all I'm doing. The last thing I want is to get involved with Jamie MacKenna again."

Alli hiked a brow. "The last thing your heart wants? Or your head?"

"Doesn't matter." Cassie adjusted the ruffles of her bodice with shaky hands. "My head's in charge here, not my heart, and there's nothing Jamie MacKenna can do to sway either."

A slow grin spread across her cousin's face. "Wanna bet?"

Ignoring the question, Cassie looped an arm through Alli's, leading her to where Bram and Blake just finished their game. "Come on, it's time to play white elephant—"

"Cassidy!"

Her head snapped up when her father waved her over to where he, Uncle Logan, and Jamie stood while her mother chatted with Aunt Cait and the Hughes. She swallowed a groan.

"Let the games begin." Alli squeezed her shoulder and gave her a wink. "If you're not back in two minutes, we'll start without you."

"Oh, I'll be back," Cassie said through gritted teeth. Turning, she swallowed a knot and took her time on the approach, her smile stiff and her legs dragging as if wading through quicksand in a cast-iron hoop.

"Yes, Daddy?" She warmed at the twinkle in his eyes while avoiding Jamie's gaze altogether.

Thumbs latched to the pockets of his dress trousers, Quinn McClare nodded at Jamie. "This young whelp here tells me he can beat you two games out of three at pool—is that true?"

Cassie's jaw dropped. Her eyes flicked to Jamie, his smug look thinning her gaze along with her smile. She mustered an air of innocence with a flutter of lashes. "Why, yes, Daddy, it is," she said sweetly. She tilted her head. "If I'm bound and gagged or completely passed out."

Male laughter erupted as Logan slapped Jamie on the back. "Sounds like a challenge to me, Mac, what do you think?"

"It does, indeed, sir," he said with a slow grin. "And I'm particularly intrigued by the bound-and-gagged option." He bowed at the waist, extending his hand. "Shall we, Miss McClare?"

Her pulse sputtered. Circle a pool table with Jamie MacKenna? She'd rather be hind-quartered. "I wouldn't dream of humiliating you again, Mr. MacKenna," she said with a sweaty palm to her chest. She took a quick step back. "Now, if you'll just excuse me—"

"Whoa, hold on there, young lady." Her father hooked her shoulders. "The Texas McClares have a reputation at stake here, and I don't think I like this young pup challenging it, do you?"

She pinched her father's waist, a signal that this was one challenge she had no desire to take on. "But, Daddy, you always say not to kick a dog when it's down." The wide-eyed look she gave her father issued a plea before it narrowed on Jamie. "I already embarrassed the poor mongrel once last summer, so I really think we should just let sleeping *pups* lie."

Uncle Logan fished his wallet from his pocket and pulled out a twenty-dollar bill. "Sorry, Quinn—my money's on Jamie."

"Uncle Logan!" Cassie gaped, heat swarming her neck. "You would betray your own flesh and blood?"

"Never," he said with a firm clasp of Jamie's shoulder before giving Cassie a wink. "I just think you need a little incentive to rise to the occasion, Cass."

Quinn patted his vest. "You're on. Got the funds to match it right here . . ."

"Daaaadddy!" Cassie dragged out his name through a clenched smile. "I do *not* want to—"

"Wait a minute—you aren't scared, are you, Miss McClare?" Jamie dared her with that same mischievous grin that had always wreaked havoc with her pulse.

Scared? Of a pretty-boy polecat? Humph—only in matters of the heart. In pool? Her lips gummed in a tight line. She'd squash him like a stinkbug. "You're on, Mr. MacKenna, but let's make this fast—I've got a game of white elephant to play." Whirling on her heel, she marched to the door and up the staircase while Jamie, her father, and Uncle Logan moseyed behind.

Ignoring their banter, she made a beeline for the billiards room, grateful she wouldn't be alone with a skunk who had trouble keeping his paws to himself. She snatched her favorite cue, well aware her agitated state would only hurt her game. "Easy does it," she muttered, fortifying with a deep draw of air that calmed her somewhat. Jamie reached past for a cue of his own, and the brush of his arm sent heat zinging, causing her to bobble on her feet.

So much for calm . . .

"Sorry." He steadied her with a brace of her arms from behind, his breath so close, it grazed her ear with dangerous warmth. "It would appear, Miss McClare," he whispered, "that I have a habit of sweeping you off your feet."

She jerked free and spun around. "I assure you, Mr. MacKenna, the only sweeping tonight will be your pride up off the floor."

"We'll begin with the traditional coin toss," Uncle Logan said from across the room, dipping into his pocket to retrieve a coin. "Verified by both my brother and me—agreed?"

Jamie glanced at her father. "Sir, if I may, I'd like to make my own wager."

Lips pursed, Cassie crossed her arms. *Typical pretty boy—cocky to the core.*

"All right, son—shoot," her father said, slapping his money on top of Logan's at the edge of the table. He folded brawny arms over his thick chest.

Jamie's eyes flicked from her father's face to hers. "If it's all the same, sir, I'd rather keep my wager private till I win."

Till you win?? Cassie rolled her eyes. *Good, then I won't have to hear it at all.*

"That all right with you, Cass?" Her father jagged a brow in her direction.

"Perfect," she said with a bright smile, "and I'll do the same." She carefully chalked her cue. *Which means the rat won't speak to me unless spoken to—ever again.*

Uncle Logan glanced up, coin positioned on the side of his fist. "All right, Cass, ladies first—call your toss."

"Heads," Cassie said, breath suspended as the coin twirled high in a loop-the-loop.

Snatching it midair, Uncle Logan quickly slapped a palm on top, gaze flicking from Jamie to her before he took a peek. His face revealed nothing as he exchanged looks with her father. "Tails—Jamie has the break." Logan pocketed the coin, brows arched in sympathy. "Sorry, Cass."

She bit back a groan and nodded, her smile as wooden as the cue in her hand. *No matter*, she thought with a hike of her chin. *The next break will be mine when I win.* She watched as Jamie ambled over to chalk his cue while Uncle Logan and her father dragged two stools from the bar.

Racking the balls, Jamie rolled the cluster several times until satisfied and then shed his coat, tossing it over a chair before rolling up his sleeves.

She slacked a hip and blew some stray curls out of her face. "I wouldn't get too comfortable, Mr. MacKenna—this isn't going to take long."

He bent over the table and positioned his cue, peering up beneath thick lashes. "I know," he said with a half smile that made the butterflies in her stomach dizzy. Refocusing on the ball, he slid the cue through his fingers like a caress, taking his sweet time. He finally made his move with an explosion of ivory that smoothly pocketed five of the fifteen.

"Whoo-ee!" Logan slid off his stool to pound Jamie on the back. "That was the finest piece of shooting I've ever seen anywhere, Mac, pool hall or Oly." He pulled out another twenty and plopped it over Quinn's. "Double or nothing on my boy, Jamie MacKenna."

"Uncle Logan!" Cassie stood slack-jawed, barely able to believe her own uncle was siding with the enemy.

He strolled over and tucked an arm to her waist. "Aw, come on, Cass, even you have to admit that was the finest shot you've ever seen. After all, we have to give the boy his due."

Oh, I'll give him his due, all right—where's that cattle prod . . . ?

Tossing another bill on top of his brother's, Quinn hooked thumbs in his buckled belt, eyeing Jamie with an air of grudging respect. "Hate to admit it, son, but that shot took the starch out of my little girl's chances. Where'd you learn to shoot like that?"

Jamie fairly glowed, the back of his neck tingeing a faint pink. "Johnny Kling at the Oly Club, sir." His gaze flitted to Cassie with a sheepish smile. "Your daughter made mincemeat of me last time we played, so I decided it wouldn't happen again." He winked before turning back to her father. "I have my pride, you know. So when Johnny was in for a tournament recently, he was kind enough to work with me for a solid week."

Drop-jaw was here to stay, apparently, as Cassie stared open-mouthed, one hand plunked on her hip. "Johnny Kling? *Johnny Kling?* Why, you're nothing but a low-down, flea-bitten cheat, Jamie MacKenna."

"Uh-uh, young lady," her father said with a slant of his brow, "watch your tongue there. With the best of teachers, most pool players couldn't make that shot in a lifetime, much less after a week. Besides, I'm no Johnny Kling, but down Texas way I wield a pretty mean cue, and you've had the benefit of my tutelage since you were knee-high to a billiard ball."

Jamie shot a grin, preening like a tom turkey the day after Thanksgiving. Cassie clamped down on the insult that burned on the tip of her tongue while her eyes narrowed into slits. "Yes, sir."

"All right, Mr. MacKenna, may as well finish her off so we can move to the next game."

"Daddy!" Cassie was appalled.

He winked. "Sorry, Sweet Pea, but I've been looking for a man who could take you on for a long time now, and I think we just may have found him, wouldn't you say, Lo?"

Logan chuckled, tweaking the lobe of Cassie's ear before

returning to his vantage point on the stool. "Sure looks like it to me, but Cass has a stubborn streak as wide and long as the Rio Grande, so let's not count her out just yet."

"Thank you, Uncle Logan," Cassie said. A crimp popped in her brow. "I think."

Cue in hand, Jamie bent low and squinted. "The six, far right pocket." A clash of balls sent two more swishing into the baskets. And then, with all the grace and charm of a pool hustler, Jamie finished her off with a neat sink of the eight.

Uncle Logan's whoops effectively drowned out the groan that rasped from Cassie's lips. "Stellar game, Mac," he said with a back-pounding that rattled Jamie's broad shoulders, the annoying grin on the hustler's face enough to cause her supper to rise. "Set 'em up, Quinn, so my boy here can put your girl out of her misery."

Cassie ground out a smile, jaw ready to pop. *When polecats fly*, she thought with a tic in her cheek. He may have won the next break, but nobody's that lucky twice. She held her breath as Jamie's muscular body curved low over the table, those hazel eyes fixed on the rack of balls with hypnotic focus. Full lips parted, he gently teased and coaxed the cue to do his bidding. Cassie's lips pinched. *Just like he does with women, the weasel.*

Crack!

The blood froze in her brain. *No—it wasn't possible!*

"Holy thunder!" Logan sprung from the stool to swallow Jamie in a bear hug that literally lifted him off his feet. "That's the first time I've ever seen the eight buried on a break to steal the game. Tarnation, son, I have a mind to fire you outright so you can hustle pool for a living."

"Mighty fine shootin' there, young man," Quinn said with a firm shake of Jamie's hand. He moseyed over to drape an arm over Cassie's shoulder, sliding her close with a peck on her cheek. "Sorry, Cass."

"Me, too, Daddy," she whispered, head to his chest. "Sorry I lost your money."

He pulled away to chuck her chin with his thumb, eyes almost misty. "I didn't lose, darlin'—I'm the proud papa of the best daughter this side of the Pecos. Besides," he whispered, planting a kiss to her hair, "gotta feeling this may just end up a win."

Cassie blinked. *Excuse me?*

He squeezed her shoulder and moved to the door. "Come on, Lo, let these two young people settle their losses. Suddenly I have a powerful appetite for Rosie's red velvet cake."

Cassie watched her father and uncle leave, her spirits sinking lower than that traitorous eight ball. *End up a win?* For Jamie, maybe. But her? She whirled around to replace her cue in the wooden rack, fingers lingering because she didn't want to turn around and face the smug look on his face. The one that said she'd lost again—first her heart to a pretty boy, then her pride to a pool hustler. She bowed her head, fingers fused to the cue on the wall as if it were a lifeline. And she needed one badly—her heart was racing and her stomach quivering at the thought of being alone with the polecat. Of facing the fact she was in love with a man she couldn't trust, a man whose faith in God didn't exist. She closed her eyes, the thought evoking a sudden sting of tears. Which meant as a couple, *they* couldn't exist—ever.

"Cass." It was a whisper over her shoulder, warm and soft, and she spun around so quickly, she tottered against the wall.

He anchored her with a gentle hand, and the look in his eyes held not a hint of gloat. "We need to talk," he said quietly, twining his fingers with hers while he drew her to the sofa.

"About the terms of my loss, I suppose?" Tone brittle, she dragged her heels all the way.

"Yes." He tugged her down on the seat, then turned to face

her, their knees almost touching while his hold locked onto hers. That blasted scent of clove and spice from his shaving soap filled her senses, triggering her pulse along with the slow graze of his thumb. She tried to ease her hand from his, but he held fast, so she opted to close her eyes instead, refusing to look at him.

"Cass, look at me—please."

She shook her head. "No. I don't want to."

His low chuckle filled the air before he skimmed her jaw with the pad of his thumb. "Please? I'd like to apologize, and I'd rather you watch because it doesn't happen all that often."

The edges of her pout tilted up the barest degree as she snuck a peek, her stomach somersaulting at his close proximity. "All right—I'm listening."

"Thank you." His smile was tender. "Now, before we get to the terms of my win, let me say that you were right when you called me a 'yellow-bellied snake of a womanizer' the first time I kissed you in this very room—"

"I knew it!" She attempted to twist free, arms flailing to no avail when his grip tightened all the more. "You're every bit the flea-bitten skunk I knew you were, Jamie MacKenna—"

"Yes, I *was*," he emphasized strongly, his gaze probing hers. He loosened his grip when she stopped thrashing. "But I'm not that man anymore, Cass, I promise."

"Ha! You promised a lot of things, Pretty Boy, with your kisses and your charm, but all I had to show for it was a heart stomped on by a low-down polecat who claimed to be my friend."

"I *am* your friend," he said, his calm demeanor dissipating somewhat. He drew in a deep breath while his thumb circled her palm. "But now I want more."

She jerked free and shot to her feet, slapping her hands to her hips. "Ohhhhh, no you don't, City Boy. I may be a country girl, but I'm not some dumb cluck born in a chicken coop. I'm not about to agree to court you a second time, you snake-bellied boll weevil!"

He slowly rose, towering over her by an entire foot while he mirrored her pose to a T, hands slung low on his hips and eyes snapping. "That's real good, Cowgirl, because trust me—the last thing I want to do is to court a girl like you."

Stunned by his barb, she blinked hard to fight the tears and raised her hand, ready to haul off and smack him silly.

He clasped her wrist midair, taunting her with that exasperating grin. "Nope, I want to flat-out marry you, Cassidy McClare," he breathed, eyes intense as he gently tugged her close. The heat in his eyes did funny things to her stomach, sealing the air—and her words. "The sooner, the better," he whispered, his voice warm in her ear.

She tried to blink but couldn't, every muscle paralyzed.

"I love you, Cass," he said, pulling back to trace his fingers along the curve of her face. "I think I have from that first night in this very room, when you called me a conniving womanizer and pesky hornet." His gaze dropped to her mouth, and all at once, his smile faded along with his voice, lowering to a husky whisper. "I need you in my life, Cass . . ." Her stomach dipped when he leaned in.

She shook off her stupor before his lips could take hers. "Whoa, you hold it right there, City Boy!" Slamming two palms to his chest, she shoved him back, heart stuttering at what the polecat was trying to do. "That's mighty convenient, you yellow-belly fortune-hunter, just as my daddy's wells are pumping again."

"What?" Jamie stared, the blood leeching from his face. "Wait, Cass, no . . ."

She jerked away, arms folded tight. "And don't act like you didn't know, you wolf in sheep's clothing."

Slacking a leg, he braced hands low on his hips, jaw like rock except for the pulse of a single nerve. "No, I'm not going to 'act' like I don't know," he said, mimicking her, "because I do, but the fact is I broke it off with Patricia long before I found out about your father's wells, so you can just hang that gun up along with those Texas spurs you're so anxious to dig in my hide."

Her jaw shot up, frustration crawling at the way her anger was on the thaw. Great balls of fire, she couldn't afford to be hoodwinked by another no-good louse who was lower than a snake belly in a wagon rut, no matter how weak in the knees—*or* head—he made her! "Ha! And I'm supposed to believe you?"

He let loose with a heavy blast of air, smile flat. "No, I don't expect you to believe me, because frankly I wouldn't believe me either. But I am asking you to believe Bram and Alli or even your uncle, because they'll all confirm it's true."

She felt the barest waver of her jaw and locked her arms closer. "Even so, Jamie MacKenna, I'm not sure I can ever trust you again or . . . or . . . even want to."

Her breath caught at the barest curve of his smile when he slowly reeled her into his arms. "Oh, you want to, Cass," he whispered, "'cause you're as crazy over me as I am 'bout you, so don't try to deny it." His gaze dropped to her lips and her stomach looped when he leaned in.

She quickly ducked, avoiding his kiss with hands splayed hard to his chest. "Even so, Jamie, I'm sorry, truly, but nothing's changed." Twisting free, she stepped back to clutch her sides once again. "You say you love me, but you chose Patricia because my father was poor, and if that wasn't enough, you turned your back on God as well as me."

With a noisy exhale, he dropped his head to knead the bridge of his nose. "You're right, I did choose Patricia, but not because I didn't love you." He plunged his hands in his pockets, pausing before he spoke. "You knew my sister was crippled, Cass, but what you didn't know was . . . I was to blame." He closed his eyes then, while a nerve vibrated his cheek, his voice a low monotone threaded with pain as he slowly divulged all that Alli had confided to her in this very room so many months ago. From Jamie's intense desire to provide a surgery for his sister to his unwavering resolve to marry well, the truth spilled from his lips in a raspy confession rife with shame and regret.

Exhaling hard, he twined his fingers with hers and tugged her to sit down next to him, finally shifting to face her while he held her hands in his. "I was stupid, Cass, and I'm asking you to forgive me. When Patricia told me your father lost his money that day in Napa, I panicked, thinking my dreams for Jess, the desire of my heart to see her well, would never come to pass unless *I* could bring it about." He shook his head. "Ironically, it was Jess herself who convinced me that there's only one way the desires of our heart can ever be met. She flat-out refused the surgery unless I trusted God to bring it to pass—not Patricia or her father." He sighed. "So I did, and she was right. God did it."

Cass swallowed hard and placed her hand over his. "Alli wrote me about the surgery, and I'm happy for you and your family, Jamie, truly."

He glanced up, a faint smile on his lips. "But not 'happy' with me."

Her cheeks warmed as she removed her hand. "No, not at the time."

He cupped a palm to her face with a rare humility in his eyes. "I was wrong, Cass, about so many things. About God, about you, and about me, thinking my happiness and that of my family depended on me. Jess convinced me otherwise, and I thank God, because if she hadn't, I would have married the wrong woman and never had the faith to know just how much God loves me." A muscle jerked in his throat. "Nor the faith to know just how much I need him." He caressed her with his eyes. "And you."

Cassie's breath hitched along with her pulse. "Faith?" she whispered, barely able to believe she'd heard correctly. "Y-you have f-faith?"

He grinned. "As solid as the wood in my head."

"Oh, Jamie . . ." Her hands flew to her mouth, as if poised in prayer, and then she lunged into his arms so hard, it jolted him back.

His chuckle tickled her ear. "I was hoping that would be your response, Sugar Pie, which brings me to the terms of our bet tonight—the one that you lost, if you remember."

She swallowed hard, not sure what the man had in mind. "Yes?"

His dimples deepened. "You lost, Miss McClare, which means I won, and God willing, it'll be the biggest win of my life." Reaching into his pocket, he pulled something out and slowly slipped to his knees. She gasped when he placed a ring on the tip of her finger, a question in his gaze before he slid it all the way on. "I'm in love with you, Cass," he said softly, "and it may have been you who took a tumble that day at the train, but I was the one who fell hard. So in the dead-center words of a Texas Mc-Clare, Cowgirl, I've been a horse's hindquarter, and I'm hoping you'll forgive me and say yes to hog-tying us together for the rest of our lives."

"Oh, Jamie!" Moisture welled while she gently touched the ring, a watercolor blur of green and gold, as he carefully eased it all the way on. Blinking hard, her breath caught when the most beautiful ring in the world came into focus—a delicate band with a square emerald circled by tiny diamonds. She looked closer and blinked. "Goodness, I can't believe it," she whispered. "My nana had a ring just like this."

"I know," he said quietly.

"You know?" Cassie teetered on the edge of the couch, face in a squint as she brushed at the wetness now glazing her cheek. "But how could you possibly know?"

"Uh, Cass, maybe you better sit back." He tugged her farther into the couch, buffing her arms while he paused, a trace of trepidation edging his tone. "It *is* your grandmother's ring."

She blinked, whirling to face him. "But I don't understand—how did you get it? It belongs to Blake."

"Blake?"

Her face screwed in a frown. "Yes, of course—Nana's first and only grandson—Uncle Logan is supposed to give it to him when he takes a wife."

Jamie skimmed a finger along the inside of his collar, color seeping up his throat. "Yeah, well about that . . ."

She shot to her feet, hands back on her hips. "Jamie MacKenna, if you won this ring from Blake in a bet—"

He jumped up and gripped her arms. "No, Cass, I swear—the ring belongs to me."

She folded her arms and stepped back, toe tapping. "Now how in the name of Sam Houston can my grandmother's ring belong to you, and where in the world did you get it?"

With a grit of his teeth, he shook his head. "This isn't going to be easy . . ."

Her eyes narrowed. "So help me, MacKenna, if you don't spit it out right now . . ."

He hesitated, finally exhaling a noisy breath. "All right, I will."

His chest expanded with the apparent need for more air before he released it again. "My father gave it to me."

She folded her arms with a tilt of her head. "Your father," she said, tone as flat as her lips. She angled a brow. "Brian MacKenna?"

"No," he said carefully, head bent but eyes fixed as if anticipating her response. "My real father—Logan McClare."

Paralysis struck, his words welding her to the spot and petrifying everything in her body—lashes, limbs, brain, breath—right on down to the pulse at the hollow of her throat.

He chuckled, drawing her close to tuck her into his arms. "I'm afraid my reaction was a bit more vocal."

She lurched away, palm quivering against his chest. "But how? When?"

Massaging her arms, he told her the whole impossible tale, finishing with his and Logan's vow to keep the silence for the time being, except for Bram and her. Even her parents weren't to know until the time was right, although they'd already given Jamie their consent at a private meeting arranged by Logan.

Cassie couldn't have been more stunned if she'd been bucked from a horse. "Good grief, my parents knew you were going to propose? But Daddy threatened to brand you!"

His smile was close to a grimace as he drew air through clenched teeth, finger tugging at the inside of his collar. "Yeah, I know, but I explained everything just like I did to you, and then Logan vouched for me as well." The strain in his face eased into a grin. "And when I told them that I flat-out couldn't live without you anymore, Cowgirl, they pretty much just up and handed you over."

She fought the squirm of her lips. "Oh, they did, did they?" Her chin notched up as her brows arched in a tease. "And just who else knows about this conspiracy, City Boy?"

He gave her a sheepish smile. "Pretty much everyone, Sugar Pie, including Miss B."

She angled a brow. "Awfully sure of yourself, were you?"

His eyelids shuttered halfway as he slowly leaned in to nuzzle her ear. "Well, I knew if I could get this close, Cowgirl, I was pretty much home free . . ."

She batted him away. "Jamie MacKenna, you are nothing but a pretty-boy womaniz—"

He silenced her with a kiss that could have curled her boots. Easing her back against the sofa, he explored her mouth with his own, eliciting a groan that made the man chuckle. "We sure have some chemistry, Cuz, if I say so myself."

She jerked from his arms. "Oh, sweet sanctity of family—we're cousins!" she whispered, body limp from the shock.

Jamie lifted her open jaw, caressing her lips with the pad of his thumb. "In name only, Cass, not blood." He brushed a curl from her face while he exhaled a heavy sigh. "Why didn't you ever tell me you were adopted?"

She blinked. "I . . . don't suppose I ever really thought much about it. Daddy's always been there for Mama and me since I was a baby, so I tend to think of him as my real father."

"Well, never in all my born days have I been happier to hear someone was adopted, let me tell you, Cassidy McClare." Gaze flitting to her lips, he swallowed hard and rose, extending his hand with an off-center smile. "Uh . . . maybe we better join the others before I'm tempted to take advantage of that ring on your hand."

He led her to the door and stopped, one palm on the knob while the other slowly nudged her to the wall. He traced the shape of her face with tender fingers. "I love you, Cassidy McClare," he whispered, "and you need to know the pretty-boy womanizer is dead and gone. From now on, I'm on the straight and narrow, doing things *his* way—safe and proper." His eyes strayed to her lips while a muscle dipped in his throat. "But I think it's only fair to warn you, Cowgirl—I don't cotton to a long engagement." With a sweet catch of her breath, he caressed her mouth with his own, palm cradling her jaw while he took his time with a slow, deliberate kiss. He finally pulled away, his breathing ragged and his eyes as glazed as hers. A grin inched its way across his lips as he deposited a kiss to the tip of her nose. "Kind of gives a whole new meaning to the term 'kissing cousins,' doesn't it?" he whispered, mouth trailing her jaw to suckle her ear.

Her eyes drifted closed, his touch all but melting the bones in her body. "Oh, sweet Texas tea," she whispered, sigh shaky and stomach awhirl. "It most certainly does."

Acknowledgments

First and foremost, to my reader friends all over the world who have blessed me with their precious friendships—when I count my blessings as a writer, *you* are right at the top.

To Julie Gilmore Graves and Rachel Fallin—not only winners of my newsletter contest to have a character named after them in this book, but two of the sweetest reader friends I've ever had the privilege to meet. You guys ROCK!

To the truly remarkable people at Revell with whom I am privileged to work—you guys deserve an award for putting up with this CDQ (caffeinated drama queen)! Extra hugs to Michele Misiak for her cheerleading and patience, to Cheryl Van Andel for her creativity and patience, to Barb Barnes for her good humor and patience (and for keeping me honest), and to Donna Hausler and Claudia Marsh, two sweet friends who can warm my day with a single email. You guys are amazing and just like family . . . *without* the danger of actually being related.

To my agent Natasha Kern and my editor Lonnie Hull Dupont—two of the most amazing women I have ever met, who have brought the best out of me as a writer, both with laughter and with tears. I treasure your friendship and am in awe of your wisdom.

To the Seekers—my lifeline in the world of writing—what a gift from God you are in my life!

To my prayer partners extraordinaire and very best friends—Joy Bollinger, Karen Chancellor and Pat Stiehr—this ship would sink without your prayers and friendship to keep me afloat.

In loving memory of my precious Aunt Julie—I cannot tell you how many times in a week I miss your sweet smile. And to my simply amazing mother-in-law Leona Lessman, whom I love to pieces—if there was a Miss Mother-in-Law pageant, you would win hands down!

To my sisters, Dee Dee, Mary, Pat, Rosie, Susie, Ellie, and Katie, and to my sisters-in-law, Diana, Mary, and Lisa—I humbly retract the first line of my debut book *A Passion Most Pure*—sisters (and sisters-in-law) are *not* overrated but so very necessary to the joy and fun of family.

To my daughter Amy, son Matt, daughter-in-law Katie, and truly gorgeous grandbaby Aurora Grace—my love for you all grows deeper and deeper with every breath I take.

And finally to the love of my life, Keith Lessman—I never, *ever* get past the awe of you in my life. Twenty-four/seven, babe, and it only gets better and better.

Julie Lessman is an award-winning author whose tagline of "Passion with a Purpose" underscores her intense passion for both God and romance. American Christian Fiction Writers 2009 Debut Author of the Year and winner of 14 RWA awards, Julie Lessman was voted #1 Romance Author of the year in *Family Fiction* magazine's 2012 and 2011 Readers Choice Awards, as well as #1 Historical Fiction Author, #3 Author, #4 Novel, #3 Series and *Booklist*'s 2010 Top 10 Inspirational Fiction. Julie resides in Missouri with her husband, daughter, son, daughter-in-law, and granddaughter. You can contact her through her website at www.julielessman.com, where you can also read excerpts from each of her books.

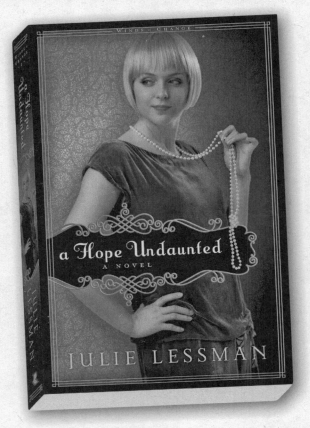

The delightful story of Kate O'Connor, a smart and sassy woman
who has her goals laid out for the future—including the perfect
husband and career. Will she follow her plans or her heart?

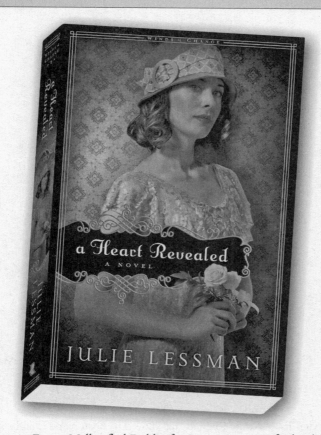

Ten years ago, Emma Malloy fled Dublin for Boston, running for her life. Her emotional wounds have finally faded, and her life is now full of purpose and free from the pain of her past. But when she falls for her friend Charity's handsome and charming brother, Sean O'Connor, fear and shame threaten to destroy her. Could Sean and Emma ever have a future together?

Revell
a division of Baker Publishing Group
www.RevellBooks.com

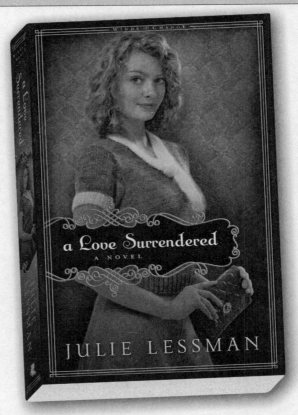

Orphaned in Iowa, Annie Kennedy has moved to Boston and is embracing the city life, with a new name and a wide-open future. When she gets involved with a fast crowd at Ocean Pier—one that includes the handsome Steven O'Connor—she is pulled deeper and deeper into a world of rule breakers and mischief makers. She finds herself drawn to Steven and the whole O'Connor family. But a secret Annie is keeping has the power to destroy her best-laid plans.

 Revell
a division of Baker Publishing Group
www.RevellBooks.com

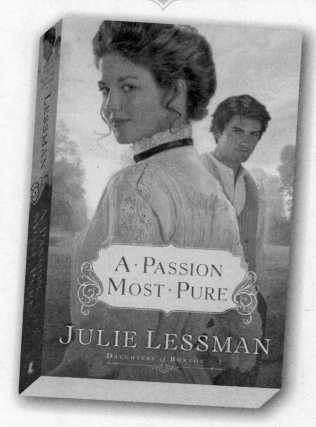

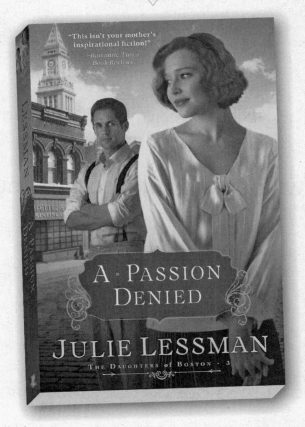